PAPALA SKIES

PAPALA SKIES

Stephen Geez

Fresh Ink Group
Roanoke

PAPALA SKIES

Fresh Ink Group
An Imprint of:
The Fresh Ink Group, LLC
PO Box 525
Roanoke, TX 76262
Email: info@FreshInkGroup.com
www.FreshInkGroup.com

Edition 1.0	2002
Edition 2.0	2012
Edition 2.1	2016

Book design by Ann E. Stewart

Cover design by Stephen Geez

Cover by Janet Shelby & Stephen Geez / Fresh Ink Group

Cataloging-in-Publication Recommendations: General Fiction; Multi-cultural (Fiction); Coming of Age (Fiction); Thriller (Fiction); Paranormal Romance (Fiction); Scuba Adventure (Fiction); Pacific Mythology (Fiction); Volcanoes (Fiction); Hawaii (Fiction); Big Island (Fiction); Hilo (Fiction); Chicago (Fiction)

Library of Congress Control Number: 2011933987

ISBN-13: 978-1-936442-07-2

For Todd C. Tessin

Be where you must

Strive for where you belong

Acknowledgements

Thanks to the following brahs and nā wahine:

Team Leader: Ann E. Stewart, Managing Director,
The Fresh Ink Group, LLC

Production Team: Janet Shelby, Tom Stockbridge

Content Team: Lucas Cale, Beem Weeks, Mark Allen North

Support Team: Kent D. Casey, Todd Tessin, Marcha Fox,
Vicky Riner, Marshall Shearer MD, Mary Watson, Susan Stewart, Jean Buchanan, Lendia Buchanan, Dillard Greenwell

Member Team: All of *you* who subscribe to the newsetter updates, free stories, and more at
www.FreshInkGroup.com. It keeps us going when you buy books and spread the good word.

Nā Lewa Papala

Papala Skies

Rochelle at 13

Squeezing her eyes shut, Rochelle tried to picture her mother, to make real again the reassuring smile that reminds a loving daughter she belongs, but a single image slammed into her, wrenching her loose: the undeniable truth of a broken and lifeless body, smears of darkening blood, a battered and broken face, every trace of belonging drained from her mom's lifeless eyes.

Pressing her footied feet against the gnarly plank floor, she hugged the wadded bed sheet and dared to peer about the room. Fading glimmers from a gas lantern confirmed her banishment to this desolate hovel halfway around the world. Muffled murmurs through crude slat walls hinted at ritual incantations, those primitive boys somehow content to dwell in this forsaken place.

She felt for the pulse at her throat, and she wondered how the girl from school could endure the gradual end of too many pills, yet somehow keep clinging to the illusion that trifling hurts can possibly ever matter in the fullness of a lifetime. That pathetic girl had given purpose to her own passing, the implication of blame, a determination to leave others to wonder with guilt and regret. Rochelle simply had no choice, no way to live, for she understood that even halfway around the world no place exists where she could ever stop being the girl who killed her own mother.

The lantern flickered and winked out, the onrush of darkness barely stanched by a pale curtain of moonlight washing the stone window-sill. An insect chirruped through the screen while intermittent breaths of warm breeze swirled about the room. She tried not to cry, but her eyes blurred, her face all tears and snot. The urgency of what must come tugged at her tummy, yet she persisted in dread, now trembling and afraid. Only an instant of violence might bring relief—a deep slash, a measured plunge into the void.

And even as she lay back and felt herself falling, Rochelle cried as a child needing to be held, a teen now accepting that she had lost the only one she ever counted on to hold her.

"Haole-girl," summoned a voice in the night. "Howww-leee gir-ull."

"Rochelle," whispered the other one, young Mikalu, both boys now standing right outside the door. "You okay in there?"

She buried her face in the damp sheet, determined to keep quiet, to feign sleep.

"Haole-girl!" Pocomea called louder, this time rousing grumbles from his sleeping grandfather, the old Hawaiian who'd agreed to let Rochelle live here while her own father flew to Chicago and dismantled the only life she'd ever known.

"You be okay," Mika soothed, summoning all the reassurance a twelve-year-old could muster.

She tried to ignore them, pushing the sheet away as she turned to gaze out the window. Tropical fronds and bloom-drenched foliage stirred in the night's wan light, dancing to the rhythmic hum of trade winds gusting up through this isolated valley along the coast of a remote island.

Poco called her again. "You come, Haole-girl. You come say *mahalo*."

"That is meaning *thank you*," Mika explained, his mouth right up to the door jamb.

"You come call your *makuahine*," Poco insisted, "—your mama."

"Go—go away," she said, her voice breaking.

"Please," Mika begged. "It is *good* you come with us. We say *mahalo* for *my* mama, too, and for Poco's poppy."

"My mother's dead!" she shouted, curling into a ball as those relentless swells of grief rose up to pull her over the edge.

"But now she looks for you," Poco insisted. "She must come to Coulée Makai to watch over you. Moon is full now, the best time. You burn *papala* with us; show her where to find you."

"This is true, Rochelle," Mika promised. "I never lie to you. Please come. Please?"

She wanted to believe them, but ancient legends and ridiculous superstitions grant no absolution. Still, these two immature boys were trying to help, their simple faith challenging her to prove them wrong.

She found them waiting expectantly in the hallway, both barefoot, clad in shorts and tank tops. Pocomea studied her with dark and penetrating eyes peering from pudgy folds of bronze skin, absently scratching his thatch of ink-black hair. A full head taller than Rochelle, with a budding sumotori's enormous bulk, the oversized eleven-year-old native Hawaiian turned and headed toward the door.

"I bring flashlight for you," Mika offered earnestly, the skinny boy's sapphire eyes sparkling beneath a shaggy mop of frizzy blond hair.

"*Haole* eyes, they see okay in moonlight, brah," Poco called back, lumbering out to the screened *lanai*.

"You change clothes?" Mika suggested, his tan cheeks blushing furiously as he averted his eyes from her brief nightgown and fuzzy footies.

Rochelle hesitated, then sighed and stepped back into the room, firmly closing the door. She quickly donned walking shorts, then ankle-protecting bobbysocks and tennis shoes. Slipping from her nightie, she reached for the new petite brassière that only weeks before had made her feel so grown up; but she hesitated, then stuffed it back into her suitcase before pulling on a simple t-shirt.

Finding Mika still waiting patiently, she followed him out to where Poco stood clutching sprigs of berry- and blossom-laden vines, a bundle of wooden spears hoisted to his shoulder. Mika retrieved a rolled sleeping mat—"*lau hala*," he explained—and they stepped outside to an eerie scene awash in the translucent glow of full moon.

They started down the main walkway, but veered onto an ascending path overlooking the lagoon. Rochelle paused to study the tableau, entranced by how the shimmering panorama seemed to float in open space against a backdrop of star-sequined sky. Stretching to her right, a meandering stream stitched a zigzag seam up the velvety carpet of valley floor, a series of waterfalls rising toward the pleats of Volcano Kilauea before disappearing under a veil of highlands mist. The stream's run-off spread wide where it spilled onto the horseshoe beach, glistening like molten glass as it riffled across obsidian sands before washing into the secluded cove. Moonlight reflected off intermittent breakers crashing through the narrow inlet a quarter-mile to her left, casting shadows across sheer faces of towering cliffs to reveal a cortège of sad expressions watching from amid the rocks, all waiting expectantly for Rochelle to pass. The scene whispered with patrolling crabs tracing lines in the powdery lava sand.

"Rochelle?" Mika said, shattering her reverie.

She looked up to see him waiting several yards along the trail, his brow furrowed with concern. Poco had gone ahead, a phantom floating up among the rocky crags toward the cliffs.

"I can't go up there!" she gasped, the young teen who thought she wanted to die now suddenly very afraid.

"It is okay," he assured softly, coming back to her. "It is easy path. I stay close, not let you fall. We go across to low part, stay there and watch *papala*. I promise."

A breeze fluttered fitfully, then faded to nothingness, the humid air weighing heavily. She touched her face with both hands, then lightly stroked her long raven tresses, trying to make herself real again. The wind returned just as quickly, rushing up through the valley. She felt trapped in a colossal arena, surrounded by the bleacher-seat slopes of a living mountain, the only escapes an open slot toward certain death in the sea's pummeling waves, or a lonesome road cut deeply through the lava bedrock of a distant rise.

"Will you try? For me?" Mika whispered, standing beside her now, fidgeting nervously, maybe afraid to touch her.

She gazed past him toward the escarpment, searching for clinging vines to grab in case she slipped; and she wondered if plummeting would feel like the dream, or if she could capture an instant of serenity in that moment of floating free before slamming to the jagged rocks.

Would she, at the last moment, think of some reason to live after all?

She grew dizzy, reached out to steady herself, and felt Mikalu take her hand, twining his fingers firmly around hers. They climbed slowly at first, her hesitations eventually yielding to a tentative confidence buoyed more with each conquered section of narrow ledge.

They found the bundle of spears on an outcropping over the mouth of the cove, maybe thirty or forty feet above the ocean's waves. Poco appeared some distance up the slope behind them, ceremoniously laying the branchy vines of berries and blossoms on a higher ledge. They watched as he worked his way with surprising agility down the tortuous trail to rejoin them.

Realizing Mika still held her hand, she slipped free and crept toward the precipice, peering down at moonlit swells of frothy water surging along the rocks and up into the lagoon. She tried to imagine how it would feel simply to step out and disappear into the void. Suddenly terrified, she backed away, understanding she could never be so brave, grudgingly admiring the determination of that girl from school who'd chosen the slow escape of pills.

Rochelle flinched, startled by the sound of Poco chanting something unintelligible. Mika spread the *lau hala* mat and unrolled the bundle of spears, then tested the flame of a disposable lighter. She sat on the mat beside the curiously confident blond-haired boy, wondering what to expect.

"The *papala* strips," Mika explained quietly, gesturing toward the spears, "they are soaked with palmetto oil, just as Pocomea's ancestors practiced.

They sailed them on the winds while people watched from canoes, celebrating holidays, saying *mahalo* to the gods, and to *nā lapu*, the spirits who come here. *Lapu* spirits, they are like my mama, who die during my birth; and like Poco's poppy—his father—who drown when fishing boat sinks; and now like your mama, who is lost and needing help to find you here."

"Do you really believe this stuff?" she whispered back.

Looking hurt, then sad, Mika admitted, "Sometimes no, but Poco, he is my best friend, and *he* believe very much. I do miss Mama, so even if she cannot come here, I am showing her my love all d'same."

Poco stepped to the edge, calling toward the sky.

"What's he doing?"

"He sing *mele*, chant of d'fathers; then he light *papala* to show them where we wait."

Pocomea lifted a spear and set fire to the tip, then hurled it out over the lagoon, calling out, "Pocokai! Pocokai!" Remarkably light, the narrow strip of wood rode the trade winds and danced high into the sky, leaving a stardust trail glittering like fireworks. He repeated the ritual a half-dozen more times, then turned to Mika, who stood and joined him.

The smaller boy shouted, "Martina!" as he sailed his own spear into the winds, repeating the summons and flinging several more.

Rochelle found herself entranced by the magical effect, hypnotized by sashaying embers reflecting in the water as each spear faded to glowing wisps finally doused in the rippling lagoon. She decided there'd be no harm in pretending, if only for one night, that her mother's spirit really could come here and forgive the foolish girl trapped in this place that exists only in some other world.

Eyes brimming with sudden tears, she felt Mika helping her up and showing her how to hold the *papala*. Realizing he'd led her to the edge, she held tightly to his arm, turning from the chasm and lifting her face to the sky. She caught the briefest glimpse of movement atop the ridge, the faint silhouette of a stooped and bedraggled old woman, an apparition holding the berries and blossoms Poco had offered in tribute. Rochelle tried to speak, but no words would come. She pointed, but tears blurred her vision, and she barely heard Poco gasp and breathe a single reverent word:

"Pele."

The pounding surf roared anew, crashing waves filling her head and drowning out anything else he might have said.

She rubbed her eyes and looked again, but the woman had disappeared.

"Are you ready?" Mika urged, apparently unaware of the fleeting vision. She nodded, fishing a tissue out to wipe her face.

"Call out your mama's name when you throw the *papala*," he advised, lighting the tip of her spear.

She shouted, "Gina!" as loud as she could, then hurled the flaming projectile flatly into the sea.

Mika showed her how to keep the tip up and push it into the wind, so she tried again, sailing the sputtering stick straight into the water. Frustrated and angry about failing her mother even with a silly ritual, she snatched more spears and screamed, "Gina!" again and again, flinging one after another as fast as he could light them, yet failing every time.

"Please slow down, Rochelle," Mika implored. He placed a reassuring hand on her trembling arm.

But he didn't understand. He didn't realize that if her mother could come here, she could also rescue Rochelle and take her home.

She gazed into the lagoon's rippling waters and imagined herself back in Chicago, peering curiously into Shedd Aquarium's giant tank, great schools of iridescent fish swirling around a playground tropical reef, mercurial communities welcoming a mother and daughter to their spectacular realm; and she noted the cliffs rearing their mighty heads, monstrous dinosaur skeletons watching a young girl roam the Field Museum's great halls, guided by her mother's encouraging hand; and she cast her eyes to the sky, the sparkling dome of Adler Planetarium transporting her beyond the horizon, her mother whispering of summer nights watching the stars from a cushion of soft meadow grass in the beloved French countryside; and she listened for the Chicago Symphony Orchestra performing a matinée children's concert, trade winds strumming chords in the branches of swaying trees, a rousing melody echoing from the clifftop balcony, her own pulse a backbeat while ocean waves cymbal-crashed along the rocky mezzanine.

Rochelle closed her eyes and savored the warm breeze caressing her face, her mother's gentle breath kissing her good-night, and she remembered Mika's reassuring touch. She opened her eyes, and this time discovered a new spark of hope flaring at the end of her *papala* spear, so she took a chance, gathered her strength, and dared again to call out, "Gina!" while heaving the fiery invitation with all her might . . .

And watched helplessly as it faltered and dropped into unsympathetic waters.

Only one *papala* remained, and she understood that it would fail her, that it would finally prove she had lost more than just her mother. She must accept that Gina would never come back to her, that she would never find her way home.

She lifted the last spear, resigned to showing Mikalu and Pocomea that neither ancient rituals nor superstitious chants could ever summon a lost spirit, but she trembled too much to hold it firmly. Giving up, she lowered herself to the ground and cried.

"Please, Rochelle," Mika whispered, his voice quavering. "It is okay; we go now."

She shook her head, gasping for breath, desperately trying to summon the courage to tumble forward, to feel for an instant the helpless terror she'd inflicted on her own beloved mom.

She felt Mika pulling gently at the *papala* still clutched in her hand, but she held tightly, suddenly furious with herself. She leapt to her feet, stood poised like a goddess destined to pierce the heavens, paused only long enough for him to light the tip, then called out, "Mommy!" and hurled the *papala* with all her might.

The flaming spear lifted high into the sky, caught the winds, and twirled and looped and danced higher and higher, spraying sparkles this way and that, moving slowly up beyond the cove as if searching the entire valley for something or someone who might, just possibly, someday be found.

She watched the last embers fade into misty moonlit sky, then noticed Mika's eyes glistening, too, and Poco staring raptly up at the ridge behind them. She followed his gaze for another glimpse of the old woman, and this time the hazy vision looked back before shimmering into the shadows and disappearing.

Poco chanted a few words without turning, then pronounced, "Your mama, she will find you here."

Rochelle nodded solemnly, holding her breath.

After a moment, Mika broke the spell, insisting, "We go now." He quickly rolled the mat and hoisted it over his shoulder.

Rochelle wiped her nose and accepted the blond boy's hand, following him down the trail, those faces in the cliffs watching as if they knew some never-spoken truth.

She looked back to where Pocomea stood at the precipice, enshrouded in swirling mist, his arms stretched toward the sky—

Swaying unsteadily, entranced—

Leaning forward—

"*Poco!*" she cried.
Without warning, he stepped out . . .
And disappeared into the void.

NĀ HOʻOLOLI ANA

BACKTRACKS

Rochelle at 21

Rochelle gasped and grabbed the seat-back, startled from her reverie as the train burst from a gloomy tunnel. Horizontal shafts of evening sunlight flooded the car and cleansed its passengers. She settled back and closed her eyes again, breathing deeply, her pulse the urgent backbeat of iron wheels.

She tried to recapture the fantasy, transporting herself again from Boston's MBTA to her imaginary seat aboard the *Train à Grande Vitesse*, France's TGV high-speed bullet line. Pressed into soft cushions, she rocketed southward from Paris while a montage of hazy landscapes beckoned from the window, images punctuated by living postcards of Tours and Portiers, Angoulême and Bordeaux.

As the train slowed, she felt her heart's beat quicken, anticipating her first tentative steps across the platform, a friendly gendarme guiding her toward the local track, a private seat in the very last car, a window view. She would press her face to the glass and savor every moment, wending along the banks of River Garonne, rolling to a jerky stop at the village of La Réole where she would hurry down to the street and pause to breathe the fragrant potpourri of her mother's childhood home. Already she could distinguish musty livestock odors stampeding through a delicate bouquet of springtime vineyard blossoms, and she drank hearty drafts of spiritous fragrances wafting from the local distilleries, while still more insistent aromas urged her to sample warm marmalade and chilled compote dolloped sinfully on butter-slathered French rolls cooling at this very moment on flour-dusted hearths.

A stooped old man would greet her, cocking his head as he studied her curiously, maybe discerning something familiar, an instant of serendipitous purpose passing between them.

"I am Rochelle," she would say to him, her confidence rising, "—Rochelle DuFortier."

His eyes would sparkle with recognition, his face stretching into a smile of reassurance.

"My mother once brought me here when I was very young. This is where she grew up. Perhaps you knew her—Gina Naroux?"

He would nod, then graciously hand her into his weather-worn horse-drawn longue, tinkling a tiny bell to herald Rochelle's return. As they rolled into the town square, young and old alike would pause to gather round, elders celebrating an old friend, children welcoming her anew. Everybody would laugh as she struggled to draw upon four college semesters of unmastered French, but they would help her with the words, imbuing their every gesture and touch with meaning and affection.

"We have missed you, child," they would say, each following the other with more questions and remarks:

"You have been away for much too long."

"Such a pretty little girl, now a beautiful young woman!"

"Your mother was in my school class; we were the best of friends."

"How is Gina Naroux? I've not heard from her in so long."

Then a mysterious yet somehow familiar old woman appeared somewhere just beyond the fringes of the growing throng. Everybody fell quiet as she whispered the challenge: *"Qu'est arrivé à votre mère?* Rochelle—whatever happened to your mother? *Qu'est arrivé?"*

And Rochelle felt that long-familiar pull from her own guilt, an instant of childhood mistake now tearing her loose from yet another world. She watched helplessly as the unforgiving townsfolk turned their backs one by one and led their children away, condemning her to stand alone and afraid with no place left to go.

"Rochelle!" summoned a voice in the wind. "Hey, Rochelle!"

"College girl!" called the younger one.

She opened her eyes and saw her boyfriend, Galway, waving from behind the wheel of his Uncle Hammond's Cadillac. His horny-toad teenage brother unleashed a piercing whistle, climbing halfway out the passenger window to flail his arms.

Framingham, the sign on the platform reminded her, Massachusetts.

"You okay?" shouted Galway.

Realizing she'd clutched her purse and overnight bag to her chest, she slung them over her shoulder and hurried down the ramp. Shunting hornball Todd to the back seat, she climbed up front and accepted Galway's enthusiastic kiss and furtive grope, a stolen moment before submitting to the disapproving scrutiny of his stout old Uncle Hammond and meddlesome Aunt Keefie.

"How come you space out like that?" Todd demanded, leaning over the seat for a not-so-subtle glance down her blouse.

Galway shoved him back. "Shut up, dick-face." Pulling out for the two-minute drive, he admitted, "You do look nice, Ro."

She glanced self-consciously at her outfit. He'd urged her to wear a dress, but she'd chosen an elegant pantsuit with a French-cut jacket. "As do you," she said, reaching to adjust his collar. Galway sported his Ivy League ensemble, button-down blue with the quintessential tan blazer stretched over a torso sculpted by years of relentless weight training.

"What'cha got in here?" demanded the fifteen-year-old, reaching for her bag.

"I'm gonna thump you one," Galway threatened.

Rochelle ignored him, asking Galway, "Have they said anything else about the trip?"

He shrugged, so Todd answered, "They argued about it all afternoon—"

Galway tried to backhand him, a near miss owing to the wiry teen's well-practiced dodge.

"Argued about what?" They'd dreamed of this post-graduation summer sojourn since their first date after meeting as lab partners in Structural Thermodynamics 410. Now, two weeks before both would earn engineering degrees from MIT, Rochelle feared yet another obstacle to escaping New England and the constant interference from Galway's adoptive family.

"You know *them*," Galway downplayed, "always needin' to have an opinion about everything."

Todd started to say something, but Galway glared mortal threats at the rearview mirror as he pulled up to Hammond's immaculate English Tudor. The toad apparently decided to keep quiet.

Rochelle hesitated as she stepped through the front door, glancing upward, half-expecting to spy whatever hidden device pelts Galway with secret magic rays that somehow transform him into an acquiescent family drone every time he enters. Her substantial education in the field of physics offered no explanation for this mind-altering power, for how Hammond's or Keefie's mere proximity, or their simple gestures like a raised eyebrow or cleared throat, could turn Galway into one of *them*. Young Todd, who also inexplicably referred to his adoptive guardians as "aunt" and "uncle," had somehow nurtured some resistance to their spell, the frequently disobedient child always in trouble for failing to think before he speaks.

As everybody gathered in the formal living room, Galway steered Rochelle to a chair directly across from the inquisitors, then fled to the side, away from the line of fire. Only Todd proved brave enough to sit close to the object of attention.

Keefie sat up straight and rigid, her legs pinched together, while Hammond unbuttoned his cardigan and sat back, stabbing the air with an unlit pipe as he opened the proceedings with a direct query to Rochelle: "With graduation looming large in your future, what exactly are your plans?"

She could almost hear the doors dead-bolting, window bars grating into place, a pressure chamber sealing, burners whooshing to full flame. She would endure this for Galway.

"Well, I lose my apartment right after graduation, so I'll put my things in storage while we summer in France. The people who rent my house in Chicago should be out by mid-August, which'll leave us a couple of weeks to move and settle in before Galway starts his job."

"Living together in sin," Keefie spat, but Hammond reached over and gripped her arm, a short leash on the old bird.

"And what about *your* job plans?" he continued, friendly cop to his Gestapo wife.

"My father just brokered several deals for projects in Pacific-Rim countries, so he'll look into getting me freelance consulting jobs with his clients. That way I can travel and see new places, but still work from home, at least for a while."

"What's this thing about wheelchairs?"

"A small medical-supply outfit is interested in having me help develop some new products."

"For little or no pay, I understand," Keefie cut in, proving she'd pumped Galway for more information than she purported to know.

Galway blurted, "She might get stock in the company, an investment out of it." He'd helped her with the words, saving her from struggling to draw upon a scant two semesters of unmastered Keefie-speak.

"That wouldn't be much help to a young married couple," Keefie challenged, earning Hammond's hand on her arm again.

"We've not made any plans for marriage," Rochelle shot back, making Todd squirm and shake his head just enough to urge her in another direction. "At least not yet," she said, angry that she felt compelled to watch her words. "I'm offering to share the *very* nice, mortgage-free home my grandfather left me. That's bringing a lot to a growing relationship."

"That's all well and fine," Hammond said, "a matter to consider in good time. After all, your level of commitment—each of you, I mean—well, it's easy to 'shack up,' as they say; but making sacrifices for each other—well, that's when the proof's in the pudding, when you test your mettle over the long-term."

"What kind of sacrifices?" she asked with a sigh, settling back into her seat.

"The position I arranged for Galway at our Chicago subsidiary was entry-level, the best I could find near where you wanted to live; I mean, using all my best contacts—"

Keefie cut him off. "There's a much better job available in Tulsa."

Hammond picked it up. "He'd be on a research team, some kind of polymer for next-generation bearings, starting at twice the salary."

"A chance to move up quickly."

"Stock options after five years."

"Galway could stay with my brother in Sapulpa, and you could rent an apartment where my cousins live."

Tulsa? Oklahoma? Wow.

Oklahoma?

Well, at least she could still travel, maybe help develop new wheelchairs and pursue chances to work with her father. But stock options, what a scary concept. That would trap them in Tulsa for half a decade, then even longer while Galway performed the trained-seal act for an occasional fish tossed from the corporate coffers. She'd hoped to spend no more than a couple of years in Chicago, add savings to her trust fund, explore the world a bit, then move on—preferably with Galway, a young couple who could afford to follow their hearts.

Hammond watched her consider his words, Keefie's stone face resolute, Galway fidgeting with his buttons. If she could take Galway to Chicago, she'd have a chance to loosen his family's grip; but mired in the meddlesome scrutiny of Keefie's kin in Tulsa, he would never leave.

Todd clenched his mouth and stared right at her, a challenge. He wanted her to flee, to get up and go while she could, this she could sense, and she appreciated the honesty this awkward teen feared to speak aloud.

She stood up before she could stop herself. The panel rose to its collective feet, moving closer, surrounding her now. She began to feel the pull, a rapid downward spiral. She wanted to reach out to Galway, but she dared not, afraid to discover that he would offer nothing substantial to grasp.

Keefie said something.

"What?"

"I'm afraid," Hammond repeated, "the trip to France would have to be postponed."

"I don't understand."

"The job—" Keefie said, growing exasperated. "Galway's job in Tulsa begins in two weeks."

"They can't hold it any longer," Hammond said.

"But I—"

Hammond smiled. "But there's good news for *you*, too—a position with the same facility, one that may allow you to travel."

"Which seems to be your highest priority," Keefie sniped.

"With a good salary," Hammond added, ignoring her.

"Security for a young couple," Keefie supplied, the old buzzard stuck singing her one-note song.

"What job?"

Hammond explained, "In personnel—evaluating the qualifications of applicants. If you're good, some years down the line, by pushing the right buttons—making a name for yourself, so to speak—you might very well be chosen for traveling to university campuses, a person who recruits graduating seniors."

Keefie softened her tone, a change of tune, cautioning, "Now, you'd have to start right away, but this is a wonderful opportunity—for both of you—and my cousins already found you a place to stay."

Todd blurted, "Don't you think they'd rather live together?"

Keefie whirled on him. "You hush," she snarled, glaring mortal threats.

Rochelle looked to Galway, but he glanced away. "What about our trip?" she asked him.

Todd mumbled, "He's not *ever* going to France."

"Shut up, dick-face!"

"You watch your mouth, young man."

Hammond put his hands up. "Let's all calm down."

Rochelle stepped closer to Galway, insisting he look at her. Todd moved beside her, almost protectively. "How long," she asked, "before we have to decide?"

Galway shrugged, so Todd answered. "He already accepted the job."

Smack! Galway backhanded the teen across the face, sending him sprawling.

"Galway!" Rochelle gasped, stepping back.

Todd scrambled to his knees and held his face, crimson oozing between his fingers, humiliation swimming in his eyes.

"You see?!" Hammond demanded of him.

"You'll soil the carpet!" Keefie screeched, snatching tissues from the table and shoving them at him.

Galway stood there, fists clenched, chest heaving.

Rochelle stared at Todd, wanting to help him up, her own eyes blurring now. The young teen pressed tissues to his bloody face, wincing as he rose shakily to his feet. He looked right at her, a warning without words.

Galway reached toward her—

She panicked, grabbed for her purse and knocked over a lamp.

"You clumsy—!" Keefie yelled.

Galway's eyes blazed with fury.

Rochelle stammered, "I—I'm sorry." Then she turned and fled for the door.

"Rochelle!" Galway called.

"Let her go," she heard Keefie say as she rushed into darkening night. She raced down the street, chasing wisps of fog that squirmed under the harsh scrutiny of street lights.

Nobody followed.

Winded, she bounded up to the platform in time to catch the last train to Boston. She dropped into a seat and fished a towelette from her purse, wiping her face. Realizing she'd left her overnight bag behind, she glanced back toward Hammond's neighborhood and noticed the black Cadillac pulling into the station, but the train lurched forward, then picked up speed and left Framingham fading into the mist. She settled back and closed her eyes, urgently transporting herself to the French countryside. The stooped old man frantically tinkled his weather-worn longue's bell, heralding her return, while townsfolk gathered round to welcome her home.

"She's fine!" she would announce this time to the gathering crowd. "Gina Naroux sends her love!"

But the old lady appeared again, hovering just beyond the throng, another question on her mind; and Rochelle knew what she wanted to ask, could hear the words before they crossed any lips: *But what of your boyfriend, child? You didn't bring him to share your new life in La Réole? What happened to Galway?*

She opened her eyes just as the train plunged into a gloomy tunnel, fluorescent lights strobing intermittent reflections of Rochelle's face in the window, postcard fantasies fading amid the uncertainty of a sidetrack through uncharted realms. Galway would drive to Cambridge, she knew; then he would rush to her apartment and make promises away from Keefie's secret magic rays, begging her to move with him to Tulsa, to surrender control of her own destiny, to submit to the governing council of his grotesquely structured clan.

Each time the train paused at a station, she fought the urge to bolt, to leave her belongings and never return . . . but the doors would close, the cars gaining speed, her pulse syncopating the urgent backbeat of iron wheels.

Where's Galway? she heard the old woman thinking, a challenge best issued in stark silence.

And Rochelle suddenly found herself stepping through the open doors, now standing on the underground platform, alone in the crowd, watching the train head toward Harvard Square without her. She hurried up to the city, then walked quickly in the direction of her favorite spot—Cambridge Street to Longfellow Bridge—where she often lingered to collect her thoughts while staring into the canoe-riffled depths of the Charles.

She paused halfway across, taking a deep breath and gazing upriver. Mist rose from the water, spinning the young college senior into a living cocoon, insulating her from yet another world that left her feeling trapped, even as the lights of Boston flickered and faded into impressions from the past.

What happened to Galway? the old woman wondered again, the village where she belonged now farther away, her unspoken thoughts echoing from a distance.

"There you are!" Galway shouted, hurrying to Rochelle's side. He set her overnight bag on the pavement. "I knew it. You always come here to space out."

She tried to watch the water, but rising tendrils of fog obscured her view, the river dropping farther and farther beyond her reach.

"What the hell did you run out for?" Galway demanded. "I mean, you should at least hear them out."

She wondered how it would feel to climb up on the rail, simply to step out with no hesitation, no remorse . . .

Galway said something, his words drifting in and out of the masking mist.

The old woman's persistence reverberated from halfway round the world: *You left Galway behind?*

She could still hear him talking, words on the breeze, explanations, justifications, placations, demands . . . "Uncle Hammond went to a lot of trouble to get me that job."

"Did you ask him to?"

"C'mon, Ro, it's time to grow up and settle down."

"I'm not *ready* to settle yet, Galway. Look, I'm sure Tulsa is a great city, but I can't commit to a single place right this minute, not without seeing more of what's out there, not until we have a chance to discover where we *both* belong."

"Taking the job is a no-brainer, Ro," he insisted, the irony lost in his single-minded persistence.

"I understand the temptation to grab a sure thing, but you lied to me. You let me think we made our plans together, even while you were changing them behind my back. How can you expect me to trade my world for yours if I don't believe you'd be willing to do the same for me?"

"I thought you'd give up all this nonsense and get more serious when it came time to graduate. You're not going to find someone willing to just drop everything and go wherever *you* want, not unless it at least comes with a solid career boost. Trust me on this."

She closed her eyes and sensed the presence of that intrusive old woman. *You didn't bring Galway?*

"Not this time," Rochelle whispered, maybe loud enough for Galway to hear.

Ah, the old crone thought, her eyes suddenly appearing before Rochelle, points of clarity twinkling mischievously in the mist. *But you always come alone. You've never brought Galway.*

"But I . . . But . . ." She sighed, finally whispering, "I haven't, have I?"

See? You've known all along.

She opened her eyes and saw Galway walking away.

He paused to look back. "You'll make yourself miserable, Ro," he shouted, "always thinking there's someplace better."

She wanted to call out, to hurl *papala* into the sky, to show him how to find the real Rochelle, not the woman Keefie expected him to marry, not the obedient child Hammond wanted to control, not the little girl whose mother would've held her back from the precipice and helped her understand.

But no words would come.

And that old woman never existed.

Rochelle looked at Galway one last time, watching him turn away . . . And disappear into the void.

Ka Leoʻole o e Uwē Ana, Nā Pili Kahikō

Silent Cries, Ancient Ties

Rochelle at 13

"Rochelle! He's okay!" Mikalu shouted, trying to calm her. "Poco's okay! You come see!" he insisted, taking her by the hand.

"But the rocks, and those big waves—" She tried to resist the waves, felt them pulling her out, lifting her up.

Mikalu led her quickly along the moonlit lava-rock trail. "He not *pupule*—not crazy. First time he jump, he bring me much *pilikia*—much worry—but now he go all d'time, never cause trouble. He know d'ocean, know she bring him home." He gripped her arm firmly, handing her down onto a lower path. The shadowy faces in the cliffs watched curiously.

"You ever do that?"

"Not me—too chicken. Look!" he said, pointing. "See?"

A dark shape floated in through the mouth of the lagoon, its wake a series of moonglow ripples, a great ebony swan lifted and propelled forward by successive crests rolling in from the Pacific. It raised its arms into a circle, bringing both hands together.

"Diver's *okay* sign," Mika said.

"It's Poco!" she exclaimed, more relieved than angry he'd worried her. "How could he possibly get past all those rocks?"

"He catch undertow, ride it way out; then d'next wave bring him back, and he ride over top of reef, into lagoon. Sometimes he swim home, or maybe act lazy and float, let d'ocean be his friend." He paused, turning to smile at her, his eyes swimming with reflections of full-moon water. "He make show, want to impress Haole-girl, prove Coulée Makai take care of us." He led her down toward the obsidian beach, lingering for a moment while she removed her shoes and socks to cross through the riffling stream. They waited beside several man-sized lava pillars jutting from the sand, watching as Poco found his footing and walked their way.

"Papaii—Poco's grandfather—he used to ride d'ocean same way. He teach Poco and me, but I chicken 'cause oldest Taoke boy die that way."

"Jumping off that same cliff?"

"Yah, long time ago, before Poco got born."

"What's Taoke mean?"

"Taoke name of his 'ohana—his family—like you say *DuFortier*. 'Ohana Taoke all live in d'next valley." He gestured toward the ridge separating them from a plantation she'd passed while riding into Coulée Makai with her father. "Papaii, he promise boy he teach him, but Taoke not wait. Papaii run up there, try stop him, but he too late; waves break d'boy against rocks. Papaii jump in, but d'ocean take boy way out, never bring him back."

Poco joined them, his clothes dripping, patches of jet-black hair jutting up as it began to dry. "Taoke boy not respect d'ocean," he pronounced. "Same go his whole 'ohana. Just like they hurt Taoke Valley, kill animals, make one big *kuleana*."

Mika translated, "*Kuleana* means one big grow-farm."

His anger rising, Poco growled, "Now Taoke boys come hurt reef. Taoke *'aumakua* not stay here anymore. Taoke find new *'aumakua* in Hilo," he spat, turning toward his grandfather's primitive house on the rise, gesturing for them to follow.

As they walked, Mika explained, "Each 'ohana—each Hawaiian family—has spirit protector they call *'aumakua*, one who provides for them."

Surprised, Rochelle asked, "He's saying theirs lives in the island's biggest city?"

"No, no," Mika answered. "Poco, he mean they let rich man from Hilo be *like* Taoke protector, man who pay big money for making whole valley one *kalo* farm." He hesitated, then added, "Poco not say nice thing."

Stopping so Rochelle could don her shoes, they all sat on a long flat rock cornering the beach. She asked Poco, "Do *you* have a Hawaiian 'ohana name?"

"Yes, mine say Wai-Nuikai—that mean between d'valley and d'sea—same name of grandfather. I am called Pocomea Wai-Nuikai."

"Is there a spirit—an *'aumakua*—for 'Ohana Wai-Nuikai?"

"Oh yah," Poco answered. "Tonight, she watch me catch one *big* wave." He grinned, then let his eyes drift toward the mouth of the lagoon, momentarily lost in thought.

Mika leaned closer and said, "She knows Poco live here. Big wave, little wave—no matter. She all d'time bring him home."

They remained there for a while, gazing across the rippling water, the moon rising high in the sky. Rochelle avoided asking more questions, not wanting to encourage those silly superstitions. She tried not to think about her mother, but the very effort kept conjuring that image that left her reeling, an elevator-drop feeling of floating for an instant before the plunge. The shadowy faces in the cliffs scowled their disapproval. The ocean mistress sensed a young girl's guilt, her waves whispering for Rochelle to trust her, luring the intruder just as she once summoned the Taoke boy, this time condemning the lone progeny of 'Ohana DuFortier to a cruel and violent death by dashing her brittle bones against the rocks, then washing her lifeless body out to sea, never again letting Rochelle go home.

Mika eased even closer to her. She sensed his concern, how he sort of watched her without looking right at her. She knew he'd regard her very differently if he ever learned the awful truth, and she wondered what her father would do when he discovered the lie in her grief-veiled silence.

Two halos of light appeared on the far surface of the lagoon, like submerged fireflies swimming toward the ocean. "What's that?" she breathed, pointing.

"Oh no," Mika whispered.

Poco leapt to his feet. "Taoke boys! Come for stealing black coral! Rape d'reef that ocean builds for her own babies to live!"

"They already dive," Mika said. "They use tanks—too deep for catching them."

"I go make surprise when they come out," Poco snarled, leaping up and stomping away before Mika's shout could stop him. He left a telltale trail in the sand, footstep gouges filling with water.

"This not good," Mika said. "You go back," he urged Rochelle, glancing up toward Papaii's house. "I go help Poco. He get all *pupule* when they break coral—make fight, might get hurt," he added urgently, a brief glance appealing for understanding before he turned to trot the direction Poco had run.

"Wait!" she called, chasing after him, too curious to be shunted aside, too worried to leave them on their own. She splashed across the stream, ruining her expensive shoes, then tripped over a lava rock, nearly falling before Mika turned and caught her. He grabbed her hand and pulled her along.

"These are boys—he's chasing?" she asked, panting for breath as they climbed up onto the rocky trail, Poco already nearly to the interlopers' entry point.

"Wipu 'bout sixteen now, some mean Taoke, he is. Younger brother Pubo only two years older than me, same school. He not so bad 'cept when he's with Wipu by and by; then he act like one big show-off tough man."

A high-pitched scream pierced the air.

"Hurry!" Mika urged, rushing her past a jagged outcropping. They spotted the silhouette of Poco holding a small, squirming child up in the air, its frantic cries echoing from the cliffs.

"Is okay! Is okay!" Poco urged over the din, setting him down. "I not hurt you. Poco not hurt little *keiki*. You okay. You okay."

A tiny native boy with shaggy dark hair, no more than kindergarten age, stood there clad only in tattered shorts, wailing at the top of his lungs, tears streaming his cheeks.

"That be little Taoke boy," Mika pronounced, surprise in his voice.

"Please be okay," Poco pleaded. "They not hear you from d'water, but you be okay."

"I am Mikalu," the gentle twelve-year-old greeted the boy, careful not to approach too close. "We not hurt you," he added, but the hysterical child seemed not to notice him.

Rochelle knelt down and smiled reassuringly, saddened to see the fear in those big dark eyes.

Still terrified, the little *keiki* put his hands on his head, then squeezed his eyes closed and rocked back and forth, squalling and wailing a garbled, "Da-bu, da-bu, da-bu, daaa-buuuu" over and over.

"Please not cry," Poco begged him, his own voice breaking with emotion and sounding very much like the eleven-year-old trapped in a man-sized body. He sat on the ground, proof he posed no threat. The *keiki* turned to watch him, still crying, but with the "da-bu, da-bu" losing its desperate edge.

"What's *your* name?" Mikalu asked, still completely ignored. He moved slightly closer, surprising the boy, who backed away a few steps and inadvertently moved within arm's reach of Poco. Out of the boy's line of sight, Rochelle impulsively picked up a large rock and bashed it against the ground. Poco and Mika both flinched, but the *keiki* didn't react, crying quietly as he watched the two bigger boys.

"He can't hear," she breathed, walking up directly behind him and banging several more rocks. "He's deaf."

Poco and Mika looked at her, recognition dawning all at once. Poco waved to get the boy's attention, then pointed at his own ears and tapped his mouth. The boy touched his ears and shook his head, quietly moaning, "Da-bu, da-bu, da-bu."

"He not can talk, not talk story at all," Mikalu said sadly, gesturing for Rochelle to sit on the ground beside him, more reassurance for a scared *keiki* whose sobs finally faded to whimpers.

Poco's glistening eyes welled until a single tear crept down each of his pudgy bronze cheeks, moonlit streaks of unabashed empathy from an over-sized child who'd long since also faced the truth that he would always be different from other boys. Very slowly, Poco reached up and wiped his own cheeks; then he gingerly reached out and wiped tears from the little *keiki's* face. He patted the boy's shoulder, gently stroked his hair, then patted his own chest.

The boy watched curiously, his whimpers giving way to runny-nosed sniffles; then he gestured some hand signs nobody understood, adding, "Da-bu. Da-bu . . ." He stepped forward, hands outstretched, and touched each of Poco's cheeks.

And they both smiled.

Poco hesitated, then reached out to gather him in.

"Pocomea!" shouted someone from the shore. Two big teens dropped oversized mesh sacks and shed scuba gear as they bounded up toward them. "Stay back, or I break you face!"

Poco scrambled to his feet, shouting, "You one big tough guy, eh? I feed your face to Pele!"

The younger Taoke rushed in and scooped up his little brother, holding him protectively. "You *never* try hurt Dabu!"

"I not hurt Taoke *keiki*," Poco protested. "But you stop d'rip-off of black coral, or I make sure you never come up for air."

Wipu snarled back, "You try, and I make you *'ai lepo!'*"

"Nobody come eat dirt!" Mika shouted, anger clearly outgrowing his fear.

"Who *da kine?*" interrupted Pubo, staring at Rochelle.

"Yeah," Wipu added, "who *da haole wahine?*" He stepped toward her, a malevolent grin leering from his bronze face.

Mika stepped in front of her, grabbing a grapefruit-sized lava rock and crouching defensively. Poco grabbed Wipu's arm and yanked him back. Wipu whirled on him, snatching a jagged-edged scuba knife from the sheath on his calf. He waved the glinting blade right in Poco's unflinching face.

Dabu suddenly burst into tears again, watching his big brother threaten Poco, wailing, "Da-bu, da-bu, da-bu!"

Wipu glared at Poco.

Poco tried to glare back, but his eyes drifted to the little boy, his bravado melting to profound sadness.

"Da-bu! Da-bu!" squalled the *Taoke keiki*, now growing hysterical again.

Wipu stepped back, released his breath, then hurried down to gather the scuba gear and sacks of black coral, his muscular body hoisting it over his shoulders with little effort.

Poco started toward Pubo and the boy, almost as if not thinking. Pubo whirled and hurried away, picking his way along the path. Wipu pushed past everybody to follow him.

Poco watched the little *keiki* pass into the shadows. Then he lowered his head, rubbing his eyes and turning his face away, visibly wincing as the cliff walls echoed the sobs of a distraught little boy. After a moment, Poco suddenly rushed off in the same direction.

Mika grabbed Rochelle's hand and hurried her along, trying to keep up with him, finally pausing when they reached the roadway cut through the ridge separating them from Taoke Valley. He sighed, pointing up at the sight of Pocomea climbing the steep rocky slope.

"I can't go up there," Rochelle breathed, her heart still racing from the confrontation.

Mika shook his head. "He not want us following him." Still, he waited and watched, maybe to be sure Poco made it okay, until the big eleven-year-old finally reached the peak where he sat forlornly, staring off into the Taoke *kuleana*.

Dabu's faint cries echoed from the distance, finally drowned by the crash of ocean waves breaking into the lagoon.

Mika seemed momentarily self-conscious about still holding Rochelle's hand, but she made no move to slip free, so he twined his fingers in hers and quietly led her back down and across the beach toward Papaii's ancient home.

Rochelle caught herself yawning as they paused on the walkway to look back. The image took her breath away, the full moon framing a tiny silhouette of Pocomea perched atop the far ridge. "Is he coming back?" she whispered.

Mika shook his head. "He too sad; he stay all night."

"Over that boy, that *keiki*?"

Mika nodded, then took a long breath and sighed. "Poco not want Dabu being scared of him."

"Poco's just a big little boy."

Mika nodded again. "He not so—not so tough, though. Now you see what *really* make him so big. He got one big heart."

*   *   *

"Daddy? Is that you?"

The bright light obscured his face, that incessant whistle drowning out his reply. Wisps of insistent breeze fluttered her hair, calling for attention, distracting, interfering.

She lay very still, clinging gingerly to fleeting impressions of the fading dream, determined to recapture it before dawning awareness could sever the tenuous connection. That whistling persisted, but she dared not risk seeking its source, for to open her eyes would thrust her into the waking world and shatter this fragile invocation of her father's return.

"Daddy?"

There he stood, just beyond reach.

"I'm sorry," she whispered, her voice drowned by the distant roar of a great snarling beast. She tried to recapture the past, but her mother had already died, and nothing would ever bring her back.

"Daddy?" she called timidly. "Please, take me home."

I am sorry, Rochelle, he said, *but you are only thirteen, too young to live on your own, and much as I want to, I just cannot move back there now.*

"But why?"

My office is in Hilo, my clients overseas.

"Then why did you leave us behind?"

Your mother refused to give up that house, afraid of something I never understood. It broke my heart, but I needed you to stay in Chicago, to look out for her.

"I—I can live with *you* now."

He shook his head, but his face disappeared in blinding light. *I wish there was a way, but I travel too much—weeks, even months at a time. Papaii can take care of you.*

"But I would travel *with* you!"

You have to finish school, Rochelle. Maybe someday after college you could work with me, but for now . . .

"Please don't leave me here! Let me go back, and I'll board in the residence hall, then come visit you during vacations." She imagined fleeting impressions of places familiar and safe, so she willed herself to stand before majestic Rinerson Dormitory; then she marched inside with confidence and strolled the stately oak-trimmed corridors, now crossing a threshold and discovering her very own room where friends had gathered to play music and giggle about cute boys they'd spied playing soccer behind Mardalay Hall; and she would ride the bus downtown all by herself, window-shopping for treasures along Michigan Avenue, pausing to gaze at the frenzied pulse of a vibrant city, her heart racing to the cacophony of life living itself to the fullest; and the sun would kiss her hair as it rose high in the planetarium sky, harbor yachts bobbing a *Yo ho, hello, Ro!* while Oceanarium dolphins danced for joy and resounding cheers roared welcome from the storied grandstands of regal old Soldier Field . . .

But Rochelle, her father said, *you can never go back to Chicago . . .*

"Why not?"

Everybody there knows what you did.

And the Soldier Field crowd fell quiet, a million scowling faces all staring at the guilty girl suddenly thrust midfield into the blinding light.

"Mom?" she called, reaching out, her legs again refusing to move.

The beast snarled, joined by another, then several more. The crowd roared. The referee whistled. Monsters howled from the tunnel.

"But I'm still trapped in Coulée Makai!" she cried out.

And the voices faded to a lone whistle, the faces dissolving to stone as towering cliffs reared up to frown with pouty-lipped ledges, a ribbon stream stitching the frayed field of green, waterfall concessions dispensing billowy clouds of frothy mist.

Curious birds circled high in the sky.

Skittering crabs diagrammed shimmering obsidian sand.

A familiar but indistinct form watched from his lonesome station atop the distant ridge.

A palpable shadow fell across Rochelle.

She looked back toward the blinding sun and found the face of her father. "Send me home," she pleaded.

The form atop the ridge waited sadly, a gentle soul praying that Rochelle be given one more chance.

"Please?"

Her father regarded her for a moment, then bowed his head and wept with grief, his wife lost, his daughter beyond help. He turned his back and walked toward the isolated road, the only escape, the only way home.

She willed herself to follow, but the opening disappeared. She tried to focus on the lone figure atop the ridge. He extended his arm, so she climbed, scrabbling for handholds, the ground beneath her falling away.

She slipped.

"Rochelle!" cried the boy, stretching as far as he could reach.

She grabbed for some vines, but they tore loose, and she tumbled, then burst through and seized the waking world, refusing to let go.

She gasped for breath, her legs wrapped tightly in the damp bedsheet, face buried in the pillow. Her father would come today, and she would convince him to take her back to Chicago, no matter what. She would imagine this and perfect every detail, Papaii wishing her *Aloha*, Pocomea presenting a good-luck *lei*, the air-conditioned car's soft cushions caressing her while she pressed her face to the glass for one last passing postcard view, her father driving as she embarked on the long journey home.

She would look back at that lone figure atop the ridge, say good-bye forever, and never come back to this godforsaken place.

She rolled over and opened her eyes, the primitive room washed by blinding sunlight streaming through the window.

Wisps of insistent breeze strummed the screen and fluttered her hair.

The beastly roar of crashing Pacific waves echoed from the cliffs.

Whistling incessantly, a tiny red bird refereed impatiently from his perch on the sill.

*   *   *

Gross and grimy, her mouth like cotton, Rochelle crawled from the bed, pausing to stretch sore muscles and stiff joints.

She searched her bag for something casual to wear, dismayed to find only nice outfits inappropriate for this uncultured dystopia, then reluctantly donned the wadded walking shorts and smudged t-shirt from last night, an episode that now seemed like just another of her many fitful dreams. Brushing her long raven hair, she studied herself in the streaked mirror, eyes glassy and tired, skin pallid and blemished, a face revealing more than she dared to admit.

She glanced toward the door, moved closer, reached for the knob, then hesitated.

She stepped back and stood very still, trying to will herself to calm, hoping the rising panic would quickly subside. Sunlight painted the walls, exotic patterns dancing in time with tropical fronds swaying just outside the window. The fragrance of floral bouquets swirled about the room as that raucous bird strutted back and forth along the sill, his whistling diatribe a lecture reminding Rochelle about her predicament.

She wished she'd insisted on staying with the Madisons. Best-friend Mindy and her mom had rushed over to console the bewildered, grief-stricken teen, the scene a pandemonium of flashing lights and police cars and ambulances, a draped gurney parading behind cordons of yellow tape, gaping bystanders gathering to whisper and point. Mrs. Madison talked quietly with the officer who seemed to be in charge, then led Rochelle inside and helped her pack the suitcase before taking her to their house and calling her father. Mrs. M rebuffed two more policemen who stopped by to question the victim's stunned daughter; then she took Rochelle straight to O'Hare and put her on a two-leg flight to Hilo. Her father met her at the terminal, holding her for a long time while she tried very hard not to cry in public; then they stopped by the office to pick up his beautiful business manager, Lalani, finally driving straight to this isolated valley where her son, Pocomea, and the oversized boy's skinny blond friend lived with grandfather Papaii.

Rochelle had sat right here in this primitive bedroom last night while creeping darkness curtained the window, her father drying her tears and promising she would be safe in Coulée Makai.

"I must drive back now," he explained, "so I can be at my office before daybreak. There will be phone calls, arrangements to make—it is much later back east, you know. I plan to come see you again before I leave for Chicago, probably tomorrow afternoon."

She'd rather have stayed with him last night, but he insisted this would be best. Unpracticed in the art of surviving a devastating loss, she trusted his judgment, but secretly she feared he just couldn't admit that the authorities had already told him the awful truth, that for now he'd rather conceal his anger.

Everybody there knows what you did.

Maybe the police had told Mrs. Madison, too, and that's why she sent Rochelle away so soon, probably vowing never again to allow such a dangerous child to associate with her own daughter. Maybe her father had stranded her in this isolated outpost, not to punish, but to protect her, to hide her far from the police and prying reporters, here in this refuge with no phones and no TV flashing live-on-the-scene updates about the unfolding story.

She began trembling, uncertainty and fear crawling up her legs, danger churning her belly, fear squeezing the air from her lungs.

This room *did* somehow feel safer, at least for now, but she could never hide here for long, certainly not long enough for people to forget.

Her tummy ached. She needed to find a toilet.

Eventually, Lalani would discover what Rochelle had done, if she didn't already know. Then Papaii and Pocomea would turn against her, too. Even Mikalu, only twelve but so much the attentive gentleman, an earnest boy trying very hard to be Rochelle's friend . . . he may well have learned this morning while she slept fitfully, dreaming of—what? Something about her father? Yes, Mika would probably avoid her now, climbing the ridge to watch from a safe distance.

Her belly shuddered, urgency compelling her to venture beyond the sanctuary of these four walls. She listened at the door, the bird finally pausing his harangue, the house reassuringly quiet. She quietly turned the knob, eased the door open a crack, and peered out.

Mikalu dozed peacefully on the hallway floor beside neatly folded towels and a large pitcher. He stirred slightly, rubbing his nose, then reached down to scratch between his legs. He opened his eyes mid-scratch, gasping as he saw her, then scrambled to his feet, blushing furiously.

"Rochelle! Um, *aloha!*"

She tried to suppress her smile, but failed miserably, embarrassing him all the more. "Sorry to wake you."

He allowed his own sheepish grin, asking, "You like wash up? I bring you water." He hesitated, then eased past her into the room, setting everything beside an antique-looking wash basin. "I make breakfast ready," he offered, hurrying back to the hallway. "Is ten minutes okay?"

"Um, sure," she agreed reluctantly, picturing a vat of the goopy glop that droopy-breasted native women concoct for Discovery Channel cameras. "Oh, where's the bathroom?"

He gestured toward the back door. "Follow path up; then go right, find good place under *lobelia* flowers."

She hurried up the incline, mortified at the notion of squatting under a bush. To her surprise, she found a vined-over outhouse draped with pink blossoms, a wide little structure hunkered down into the crevice between two jutting points of lava-rock, a real toilet seat and roll of bathroom tissue, breezy openings around the top, surprisingly odor-free.

She washed up in her room, then joined Papaii on the screened *lanai*. The small and frail-looking elderly Hawaiian nodded and smiled from his worn wicker chair at the head of the table, gesturing for her to sit. Mika carried out a mélange of sliced fruits, some familiar, others strange and, well, highly suspect. Puffy breads in a basket, whipped butter, granola cereal, pitchers of thick green juice and milk, plus a centerpiece vase of colorful flowers completed the surprisingly civilized-looking buffet.

"No problem?" Mika asked, arranging everybody's place settings before taking his own seat.

"Um, yeah. How do you, you know, take baths here? In the lagoon?"

"No, not ocean water," he said, passing her the cereal. "We take bath *or* shower. I show you—" His cheeks flushed again with sudden embarrassment. "Show you *where*, I mean. I take you there."

"I might be leaving today, when my father gets back, so I'd like to freshen up."

Mika cast his eyes down sadly, staring at his lap until Papaii interrupted to chant something unintelligible, his leathery, gnarled hands raised high into the air. The old man smiled again, then passed the platter, urging her to sample the slimy red fruit.

"Where's Poco?" she wondered.

Mika poured her some of the green juice, answering, "He sleep now, just come home, one big tired boy."

She poured some milk into another glass, then took a tentative sip, surprised that her fillings hurt from the cold. "Where does this come from?"

"Poco's mama—you know Lalani—well, she bring all *da kine* groceries each week."

"But it's so cold."

"We have place things not spoil, work real good. I show you, give you one big look-see round Coulée Makai," Mika offered hopefully.

"Where does Lalani live?"

"She stay Hilo-side, ever since Poco's poppy die. *'Ohana* needs money, so she work in Hilo, go college all d'same time. Now she got good job with your father, stay with him, both in d'same house."

What?! She tried to feign indifference, angry she didn't know, jealous of the woman who commanded so much of her father's time and attention. Her parents may have lived apart, but they were still married, and in that Rochelle had always found a small measure of hope.

The same bird that woke her—or one just like it—perched on a branch just outside the screen, chattering at Papaii. The old man flashed it a mischievous smile, then chattered back, a perfect and surprisingly robust imitation.

"*Amakihi*," Mika explained. "Honeycreeper bird. Coulée Makai home for all *da kine* honeycreepers."

Papaii spoke up, eyes twinkling, his voice a ribbon of smooth, sweet taffy. "*Amakihi* bird come see me all d'morn, leave me present of one feather, remind us not to pick all d'flowers so his *'ohana* have plenty to eat." All these Hawaiian words and the boys' jumbled patois had proven challenging enough without also trying to learn birdese.

She summoned enough courage to taste the green beverage, amazed by the explosion of icy sweet nectar, an eclectic amalgam of flavors, some familiar, some new. "Wow," she said to Mika's barely suppressed delight. "So who else lives here?—in the valley, I mean."

"Only us," Mika said, "Poco and Papaii and me."

Looking very serious, the old man explained, "My ancestor, Napanea, he come find Makai, bring *'ohana* to stay, nine fathers past."

"Nine generations ago," Mika supplied.

"Napanea take new name: Napanea Wai-Nuikai," he sing-songed. "His title make him *konohiki*."

"He one big ol' Hawaiian *chief*," Mika added proudly.

"He honor *nā lapu*—the spirits—here in Makai, so his king grant him this land. *'Ohana* Wai-Nuikai live here all d'time since."

Mika filled in, "We learn this in school. In eighteen-forty-eight, King Kamehameha d'third give each chief one valley with water and plenty trees for building canoes and making fire. Government go pass law, make all *kine* legal deeds, call it d'Great Mahele when chiefs register with Board of Land Commissioners." He scampered inside, returning with a small map of the big island.

She followed his finger along the southeastern shoreline as he pointed out Hawai'i Volcanoes National Park, a sprawling area stretching inland to Kilauea, then to the island's heart where Mauna Loa loomed.

"We stay here," he pronounced, pointing at a coastal stream adjacent to the park's southern border.

"Makai," the old man breathed reverently, spreading his arms to encompass all four directions.

"*Makai* mean *to the sea*," Mika translated. "*Coulée* d'word from French settlers who visit five fathers past, meaning *valley*."

"Valley to the sea," she said, liking the sound of it.

Mika squared his shoulders and sat back looking very pleased. The old man nodded knowingly, then gazed at the bird, which fell quiet and watched everybody curiously. "No such thing as money back then," Papaii mused. "Chiefs make trade." He sighed, looking back at Rochelle. "Chiefs gone now, must have dollars."

"Yah," Mika agreed, "must get job now, buy groceries, pay taxes. Lalani, she work hard, and your father help lots. He one good *kāne* man, your father. One big heart."

"Yah, Ramo Doo-forty-yay," the old man agreed, pronouncing her father's name carefully, "—he one good *kāne*." A flickering shadow of sadness passed over his face. "He help my Tapakiki," he added, his sonorous, glassy voice cracking slightly. He gazed beyond the bird, lost for a moment.

"His wife, Poco's grandmother," Mika said, setting his spoon down, placing his hands in his lap. "She catch bad Alzheimer's. Your father, he find one good doctor-place where she stay now, make government pay until she get better."

Rochelle closed her eyes and listened to the whispering wind. Daddy had tried to help Mom, too . . .

"Must honor Coulée Makai," the old man intoned. "*Nā lapu* not want valley harmed."

Mika picked up his spoon again, pausing to explain, "Same rich man who pay *'Ohana* Taoke, he try take over this valley, want to make *kuleana* here, too—grow *kalo*, sell fish from lagoon. Your father help Lalani pay tax so Papaii not lose Coulée Makai, keep always for *'Ohana* Wai-Nuikai."

The old man stood gingerly, then limped around the table, favoring one leg. He surprised Rochelle with a gentle, lingering kiss atop her head. Mikalu got one, too, and blushed for a moment, his eyes darting toward Rochelle as he reached up affectionately to squeeze the old man's hand. "I go watch Pocomea sleep," Papaii said, "—see he okay." He ruffled Mika's hair with a "heh heh heh," then shuffled into the old stone-and-plank house.

"He all d'time worry 'bout us," Mika whispered, gazing after the old man, a hint that deep feelings of protective loyalty flowed both ways. A longing twinge in Rochelle's heart reminded her she understood how this simple, honest boy must feel.

After they finished eating, Rochelle helped Mika carry the leftovers inside. She stacked the dishes while he put lids on the milk and juice.

Bringing the cold drinks, they followed a path along the northern ridge, up toward the valley highlands. Only when he pointed did she notice the half-dozen ancient stone buildings overgrown with flowery vines, nature blending them back into the landscape from which they'd sprung.

"*Konohiki*," Mika explained. "Chiefs live in this place long time ago. Napanea, he live there." He gestured to the small, partially collapsed structure at the far end. "*Nā* Wai-Nuikai, they see one good view up here, that's for sure."

She turned and studied the scene below, trade winds stirring her hair. The arena waited quietly for the next event. Those cliffs looked different, too, jagged and plain, the faces gone, blind masks of indifference. A mosaic of coral reefs rippled just below the water's surface, a jigsaw fresco fringing the deep blue pool, a submerged parapet sealing the mouth, crashing white-caps the only invaders allowed to breach the private cove. She noticed the footbridge crossing the narrowest stretch of valley stream, its path intersect-ing the crude dead-end road cut into the far ridge, the only way out a brief portal receding before her very eyes.

"Why are *you* here?" she whispered, glancing up to see him waiting ex-pectantly, maybe looking concerned, certainly patient.

He reached for her hand, and she let him take it, following him along the path where delicate finches buzzed with excitement, a profusion of blue but-terflies exploding into a fluttery swarm, iridescent long-tailed dragonflies keeping a wary eye as they darted here and there for better views.

"My father, he not able to care for me, one little *keiki* whose mama die. He must work, go get job on ship and leave me with Lalani, send money. Back then, she still live here, take care of *nā keiki*—many children—like what is called *day-care*. Other little ones, they go home each night, but I all d'time stay here. Then she have own baby—one big *keiki* name Pocomea."

"You've lived here pretty much all your life?" she asked, distracted by the idea of her father waving good-bye from that distant slot in the ridge, leaving her here forever.

"Yah."

"You grew up with Poco, like brothers."

"Except I no real Hawai'i boy, born San Diego, all yellow hair." He shook his head as if trying to ward off an affliction. "Some *nā keiki*, they call me *haole*, but I not really."

"How often do you see your father?" she asked, following him up several step-like terraces where a small spring cascaded into the valley below. The water gushed from what appeared to be a small boarded-over cave just big enough for a child to crawl into. He opened the trapdoor and pulled out a jug of milk, handing her the dripping largesse. It felt ice-cold. She watched him replace it and add the two pitchers from breakfast; then she reached inside and felt the cool air, tingles of crystalline clouds billowing into her warm face.

Mika reached behind the door and retrieved a small *lei* of crimson and fuchsia flowers, awkwardly presenting it to her. "For you," he said. "*Aloha.*"

"You made this?"

He shrugged, then showed her how to wear it as a crown, several thorns woven into her hair to hold it in place. "I bring this to show you one very pretty girl," he said, handing her a small mirror from behind the door. The *lei* blazed in sun-drenched glory, her raven hair shimmering in shades ranging from obsidian to deep blue; but she still appeared somewhat pale and tired, indelible shame reflected in her eyes . . . yet the *lei* seemed somehow to be transforming her, its simple beauty a distraction, the moment a fleeting opportunity for Rochelle to try on a new version of herself.

Mika closed the door, then stood and looked across the valley, lost in thought.

She followed his gaze, feeling awkward about prying after he didn't answer the first time, but she needed to know. "Mika? Do you ever see your father?"

He took a deep breath, then lowered his head to stare at his dusty bare feet. "When I little, he come lots, every time boat stop in Hilo. Not so much later. I twelve now," he said, a catch in his voice, finally looking up to reveal glistening eyes. "He come until I was ten, but not ever since, not for last two years."

Mine left when I was ten, too, she thought, *but now I'm thirteen, and he's coming today*. She pictured her father arriving, taking her with him, and that made it seem real, something she could believe.

"He will come," Mika said, but she couldn't be sure if he meant his father, or if he'd read her mind.

"They both will," she said, maybe not loud enough for him to hear.

He led her farther along the ridge, pausing to indicate spectacular botanical displays, a tour vastly more mesmerizing than her many short walks through the university gardens back home. He pointed out large copses of crimson-bloomed *'ohi'a lehua* trees lording over supplicant six-foot ferns; blossom- and berry-laden vines of *ohelo* reaching out to explore their world, the same stems Poco had offered Fire Goddess Pele last night; *pū hala* trees lifting their can-can skirts to pose on spindly legs, pineapple-like curlers in their hair, the same fronds Mika and Poco had woven into *lau hala* sleeping mats; the sacred *maile* plant, its almond-shaped leaves hosting a mid-morning brunch for a Hawaiian Happy-face Spider, the pale yellow arachnid offering a wide red-lipped grin. Mika knew them all, the frizzy-blond San Diego boy swelling with pride as he showed her the myriad wonders right here at their fingertips. They admired wildflowers like the hanging pink tendrils of *lobelia*, picked *'akala* raspberries to squish between their teeth, invited a flash of yellow-and-gray to perch briefly on Mika's finger—a rare *palila* bird, he said. They faced down the menacing scowl of a fierce Lava Wolf Spider—from a safe distance; and when they reached the top of the rise, Mika pointed northward. Rochelle gasped when she saw it . . .

Kilauea!

She'd never seen a volcano before—not in person, anyway. Its domed peak rose in the distance, a patchwork of black and gray tracks streaking across the horizon, billows of rising yellow mist framed by cerulean sky, tourist helicopters buzzing about for thrill-of-a-lifetime views. It looked desolate, prehistoric, like some giant dinosaur that could rear its head to snatch a dragonfly chopper from the sky. Mika pointed eastward toward the lower flanks, a massive vent spewing gasses and sparks, a trail of lava extending beyond the horizon, great clouds of sparkling white steam dancing where creeping inferno kissed the sea.

She watched Mika lay a sprig of *ohelo* for Pele. Suddenly hot and dizzy, she felt vertigo from standing up so high, even more cut off from the world she knew, trapped beyond reach, scared of indifferent forces constantly re-making the world.

She followed him back down the tortuous trail, the now-familiar route more difficult to descend than she'd remembered it. Picking up the main path, they headed farther up the valley. Entering the cool canopy of rainforest, she heard a faint liquid roar, felt an invigorating mist on her face, and gasped again when she saw the picturesque waterfall. Several ribbons of sparkling stream splayed over a rock-ledge awning before showering into a pristine pool surrounded by lush flowers and ferns. A stairway of flat rocks descended into the deeper water off to the left, while a natural shale walkway led to the open sandy area ringing the shallows along the right. From its hiding place under the brush, Mika pulled a sealed plastic tub revealing towels, wash cloths, brushes, and bio-degradable organic shampoo.

"Bath or shower!" he pronounced, beaming. "I go down d'trail, wait for you."

No way would she undress out here in the open, wade into this leach-infested snake-and-piranha breeding ground, stand under those teetering rocks, let the bugs swarm over her sensitive flesh . . . "Aren't there poisonous things and stuff?"

Mika explained, "Hawai'i very safe, very tame. Islands rise up from d'ocean not very long ago, so all d'plants and animals come from mainlands, float in water, carry on wind, ride with birds—or come with man. No predators, no reason to grow poison, no need for ways to hurt. That's why people who come here must protect them."

"I never thought of that. Like Galapagos, all the native species would be newcomers, then ultimately evolve into the only true natives."

"Just like when Poco's fathers came from Polynesia. I come later, from California, so Taoke boys call me *haole*, but I live here now, too." He grinned, adding, "No poison or thorns on me, neither!"

"Don't you feel trapped here?" she wondered, watching a hint of rainbow shimmering in the waterfall mist.

"*Trapped?*"

"I mean, there's nothing to do, and your education can't be very demanding."

He looked injured by that, indignantly retorting, "We take bus to *excellent* school in Punalu'u. I good student, straight A's."

"But you talk like—" She stopped herself too late.

"I speak well when I need to," he blurted defensively. "Around you, I thought, no matter."

"I'm sorry," she said. "Really, I—" She shook her head, frustrated by her growing propensity to make stupid mistakes.

"It's okay," he said quietly, and he seemed to mean it.

A telltale *thwap! thwap! thwap!* cut through the strum of falling water. They hurried up out of the trees to watch from an outcropping along the ridge. A giant helicopter stenciled with the moniker *'Cano Airtours* passed overhead, some kind of bulldozer on cables dangling below.

"Taoke bring another Bobcat," Mikalu said sadly. "They kill more trees, spread *kuleana* farther up Taoke Valley."

She watched the chopper cross the ridge until something else moving in the distance caught her eye. A car threaded through the open slot, driving into Coulée Makai! "My father!" she shouted.

She turned and rushed down the path, breaking into a run, Mika hurrying to keep up.

Two figures emerged from the car, definitely her father, and Lalani, too. Poco appeared from below, trotting surprisingly fast as he crossed the beach, splashing through the riffling stream to greet them.

All reached the house at the same time, Papaii coming out to bow graciously and chant something solemn before breaking into a wide grin. Rochelle hesitated, embarrassed for her father to find her unbathed and dressed so shabbily, but then she rushed into his arms, trying very much not to cry again, whispering in his ear: "Please, Daddy, take me with you."

He held her at arm's length, an odd but reassuring expression gracing his face, and he nodded vaguely, maybe agreeing, maybe just acknowledging that he'd heard.

Lalani held her next, the beautiful Hawaiian stroking Rochelle's hair, whispering, "You'll be okay, child. I promise." Her eyes sparkled like glazed almonds, her face a tender bronze-tinted blossom, and Rochelle wanted to believe her, knowing somehow she could trust her. Poco beamed, Mika hovering awkwardly to the side.

"If you want to board at school," her father finally said, "a room is available in the dormitory." Her heart pounded. "But we must hurry to catch the plane. I need to buy you a ticket."

"Yes!" she practically shouted. "Yes," she said again quieter, feeling as though she'd acted rudely toward her hosts.

Poco grimaced. "Haole-girl leave so soon?"

"I'm sorry," Rochelle said, "but I must."

"Hurry and get your things," her father urged.

She caught a glimpse of panic on Mika's face as she turned and raced inside. She changed into a nice skirt and blouse, doffing the *lei* and quickly brushing her hair. With no easy way to pack Mikalu's handmade gift, she left the wreath of crimson and fuchsia flowers in the ancient wash basin, then opened the door to find Poco waiting to carry her bag.

Back outside, Papaii chanted something, then waved his arms and kissed her atop the head. "You come back," he said quietly, not asking her, but simply stating it like a known fact.

Lalani hugged her again. "I will remain here while your father is gone," she said, "—a chance to chase my boys while I can still catch them. You are always welcome back, Rochelle, and you must remember we love you."

"Thank you," she said, meaning it more than she expected. "Where's Mika?" she asked Poco, glancing around, her ubiquitous blond squire nowhere to be seen.

"We must go," her father insisted, starting down the path toward the footbridge. She followed, Poco carrying her bag.

"Mikalu, he get all weepy eyes," Poco said. She glanced up to see he wasn't joking, his dimpled face sincere. "He not like for people to see him like that, always go hide. Don't like big kids calling him one little cry-baby."

"But why would he—?" she started to ask, feeling a twinge of something unfamiliar, seeing Mika differently, somehow, than she had before.

"He all sad that Haole-girl is leaving. Me, too," Poco added.

She paused on the footbridge, glancing around the valley, searching for where he might be hiding. The lagoon shined brightly, a rippling mirror image of the sky. Her father walked ahead, but Poco stopped to wait with her.

"I've only been here a day," she said, anxious to depart, but suddenly feeling like this wasn't such a bad place for a short visit after all.

"I never expect you stay," Poco said, a knowing look in his eyes. "Poco not all *pupule*; I can see by your face."

She'd not hidden her disdain; that was true. "It's nothing against you or your family," she tried to explain.

"I know."

"And I *do* like Mikalu."

"I know. I do, too. Mika, he is my friend."

"Please, don't let him think I don't."

"He not *pupule*, neither."

"Rochelle!" called her father.

"I wish I could tell him bye."

Poco sighed, gazing up into the valley. "Mikalu, he know that, but weepy eyes just too hard for him, like when tough boys make him big trouble. He always in some *kine* hurry to get big, but I know he never be tough guy." He leaned close, wrinkling his nose, whispering as if sharing a secret. "He all d'time forget, but he already one big boy inside. He got one big heart."

"Rochelle!" shouted her father.

They hurried after him, catching up just as he reached the car.

"Thanks, Poco," her father told the gentle Hawaiian. "Look after your mother and grandfather. I shall return this weekend."

Poco placed the bag in the trunk, then waved at Rochelle. She hesitated at the door, then turned and quickly kissed his cheek, making him blush. "Thank you, and tell Mika I'll miss him."

He nodded, then watched as she climbed in and closed the door. She felt a blast of cold air when the engine roared to life. Poco turned and strolled back down toward the beach.

Her father produced a cellphone. "I best reserve your ticket while we drive," he said, reaching in back for his briefcase, "—if you are still sure you want to go."

Everybody there knows what you did.

"Should I, Daddy?" she asked quietly.

He opened the briefcase and retrieved his plane ticket, then studied her carefully. "It's up to you, sweetheart."

"I mean— Well—" Finally, she blurted it out, her lip quivering. "Does everybody know it was my fault?"

He looked surprised, concerned, calculating, lost for a moment. Finally, his voice quietly insistent, he told her, "You must never say that, Rochelle. Never."

"But it's true."

"It is not. The police are investigating an accident. That is all it was—an accident. Do you understand me?"

He was looking right into her soul, waiting, firm, non-negotiable.

And she knew. She knew he'd discovered the awful truth, but that he'd taken care of everything, covered it up, let the lie in her silence stand unchallenged by those who would condemn a mere girl. He would protect her, the real story a secret they would always share but never admit. "An accident?"

"Not your fault," he pressed. "*Nobody's* fault."

"An accident," she said, trying it on, testing the fit.

"Do you still want to go?"

"I can't stay here," she said. She'd lost too much of her world already, now facing an uncertain future. She had to go back, pick up the pieces, find her place, and move on with her life. Nothing would ever be the same, so much of what she took for granted proving only temporary, fleeting, unpredictable, unreliable. She had her friends, her school, the planetarium and Shedd Aquarium and Michigan Avenue . . .

"I want to go home," she said.

He nodded, set the briefcase in back, then put the car in gear and pulled away, heading out through Taoke Valley.

The helicopter lowered to her right, pausing to hover over a group of bronze-skinned men swarming a small dozer.

She pulled the seatbelt around herself and felt something unusual. A sprig of blossom- and berry-laden *ohelo* had been carefully twined to the strap . . . a good-bye offering from a new friend too embarrassed to show how much she'd broken his heart.

Closing her eyes, she wished she'd found a way to pack the delicate *lei* of crimson and fuchsia flowers, a heartfelt reminder from the yellow-haired San Diego boy who offered her the mirror of his tender affections.

As they drove away, she looked back one last time, her face pressed against the glass as she gazed toward the open slot.

A montage of postcard images bid her farewell, scenes of lush tropical foliage waving gently in the prevailing ocean breeze, the unshackled dragon-fly helicopter flitting into the swirling highlands mist, acrobatic *amakihi* birds air-dancing against a backdrop of cerulean sky as whispering clouds embellished the legend of one *haole* girl's very brief visit and hasty departure . . .

And the lone figure left behind, a big-hearted yellow-hair boy watching her forlornly from his station atop the towering sad-faced ridge.

Nā Nanaina

Aspects

Rochelle at 21

Lonesome in the madding crowd . . .

Rochelle strolled purposefully toward campus, a singular strand weaving through countless strangers all cross-stitching her path in a frenzy to hurry from one place to another. Except for the time she squandered dating Galway, she had kept mostly to herself these past three-plus years, enrolling year-round in back-to-back semesters, focusing steadfastly on her studies, achieving high honors in two concentrations while amassing a mechanical-applications research record to rival the ten-year résumé of any accomplished science bachelor already toiling in the private sector. Now she planned to move on after next week's commencement, satisfied to exchange polite well-wishes with a few casual friends, determined to leave Cambridge with no obligations.

Skirting the campus crowd, she made her way to the bridge and crossed, hurrying past her favorite spot without even glancing at the rowing-shell-lacerated waters of the Charles. The streets of downtown Boston proved nearly as crowded as campus, but she liked the vibrancy of big cosmopolitan cities, the indifference of busy urbanites busily carving their own niches into a busy world. Mere students still needed to find their own places, wasting their time seeking reassurance from unsure peers, chasing possible connections. She appreciated the tall buildings, too, pressure valves bleeding excess humanity ever higher into the sky, always offering room for one more, a place for Rochelle in case she ever took a notion to stay.

She found the faux French café spilling from the lobby of a squat office complex, taking a seat just as her father hurried in earlier than expected. He looked handsome as usual, tall and fit, a brush of silver at his temples and highlighting the corners of his mustache, his tailored gray Doix-dusarté suit luminescent.

"Ah, Rochelle!" he greeted her. "Still transforming your mother's beauty, I see, with the angelic face of my little girl." She stood and folded herself into his embrace, cherishing that instant when nothing matters but the love between a daughter and her doting father.

"You're early," she said as they took their seats.

"My deal, it is not going so well," he said, "so the principals have agreed to regroup in one hour." He glanced away, appearing weary for an instant, his trademark confidence maybe somehow flagging. "I hope our differences resolve quickly, for I simply *must* be on a plane by tonight." Quickly changing the subject, he asked, "So how go your examinations?"

"I took the last one this morning," she pronounced, a concept still hard to believe. "I'm sure I aced it."

"Ah, yes. You inevitably do," he praised her, fatherly approval brightening his eyes. "Present my Rochelle with a challenge, and she will triumph always."

"Just like my father," she teased.

He sighed, then slowly shook his head and began to speak, only to be interrupted by the waiter. Deciding against lunch, he ordered a double gin while urging Rochelle to eat, but she insisted a soda would suffice. "No, sweet-heart," he continued. "Making problems disappear, this I sometimes cannot do, and today I bring you unfortunate news." He took a deep breath, his face shadowed by regret. "I cannot attend your graduation."

She tried to hide her disappointment, all the while knowing she could never fool him. Countless times she'd imagined sitting in the auditorium, then rising with her class and turning to see his proud smile, but now she'd have to stand alone. "I'm sure you would, if there were any way," she said.

Without offering to explain, he shifted the subject. "It is important right now that we also consider your financial status. You and Galway, do you still plan to visit that village where your mother—?"

She shook her head, cutting him off. "We broke up."

"Oh," he said, apparently not surprised. "I am sorry," he added, not pressing her for explanation, either.

"I still want to go."

He winced noticeably, unconvinced. "By yourself?"

"I'm old enough—" she began, suddenly embarrassed to claim adult-status privilege.

"No, what I mean is, Would you not prefer to save such a trip for when, you know—"

"I still have time to decide," she admitted, backing away from the subject.

"Were you still expecting to divest some of your grandfather's trust after graduation?" Before she could answer, he continued, "I intended to liquidate your shares in the Singapore project this week, but the partnership contract requires ninety-percent occupancy before we list it. Unfortunately, the fire put us six to eight months behind, so if you or I want to sell our shares now, the other partners would be entitled to first-refusal rights—at the original investment rate. Unless we wait, we will lose our substantial gains. I had planned instead to lend you whatever you need from my own personal funds, but now—" He swirled his drink almost nervously, as if unsure how to finish his thought. "Now unexpected circumstances prevent me from, uh . . ." He trailed off, something unfamiliar haunting his eyes.

"Daddy, you're not going bankrupt are you?" she joked before realizing it might really be true.

He shook his head. "No, my portfolio, it is performing quite well. I just cannot offer you any substantial sums at the moment."

"I could probably cover the airfare, but not all of my lodging and other expenses. I have to refund my tenants' deposit, and their final month's rent was pre-paid, so I have no income."

"You could put the house on the market," he pointed out, an old idea floated with some regularity over the years. "It should fetch well above a million by now."

"No," she said quickly. "No matter where I travel, I want that to be my Chicago home, the place I can always come back to."

"What about employment with the wheelchair company?"

"That wouldn't pay very much. I'm supposed to meet with Miss Dixon this afternoon, but I'm really not very interested. Maybe I could come along on some of your jobs this summer," she suggested hopefully, fishing.

"Oh, that simply will not be possible—not yet." Then, as if feeling guilty for not explaining, he finally admitted, "I need to curtail my work schedule for a while, which will cause me to lose many of my most important clients."

"Daddy, what's wrong?" she insisted, suddenly afraid.

He drained his glass, then glanced away and seemed lost in thought, maybe trying to find the words, maybe seeking a tactful way to shut her out. "It is Lalani," he said finally, turning back to search her eyes for understanding. "That is why I need all my available cash, too—at least several hundred-thousand dollars."

"Oh no! What's wrong?"

"She prefers for Papaii and the boys not to find out," he cautioned.

"You know I can keep a secret."

He considered this for a moment, then let his shoulders slump. "She is in Sydney, where we shall live for a time. Expenses will be very high, especially the cost of, um, treatments—"

"She's sick?" Rochelle gasped, her heart pounding, tightness rising in her chest.

"The clinic there ranks among the best in the world, with cutting-edge research, an encouraging success rate—"

"For what?! For treating what?"

"It is rare, with a long name I always pronounce wrong, but she has a bone-marrow disease, a leukemia. She has cancer, Rochelle."

"Oh, Daddy," she whispered, reaching for his hand, her eyes welling, that damnable sunlight way too bright.

He squeezed her fingers, aging before her very eyes, those silver highlights in his hair now graying with worry. His calculating eyes reflected improbable odds.

"I'm sorry," she whispered.

He lowered his head, closed his eyes, maybe imagined how things could be. Then he looked up, his face steeled with determination. "We will beat it," he said.

"Yes. Yes, we will."

"I simply cannot let her die."

*   *   *

It just didn't matter anymore.

Too late to cancel the meeting, Rochelle reluctantly approached the hotel, dreading this last chance to explore the feasibility of a rewarding career in the exciting and fast-paced wheelchair industry—now the least of her priorities. Despite promising to consider postponing her trip, she'd left the café more determined than ever; she would graduate in less than a week, then depart immediately for France, admittedly embarking on a different kind of sojourn than she'd envisioned, traveling alone, the frugal way, rail pass, hostels, bistros . . . but still spending time in La Réole, discovering the people who knew and loved her mother, maybe even earning a chance to sleep for a night in young Gina Naroux's childhood room.

She strolled through the ornate lobby and stepped into a gilded elevator. She would sit politely through Miss Dixon's pitch, feign weighing her offer against several better, then beg off making a decision for a day or two, phoning later with painstakingly considered regrets.

"I am delighted you came!" Miss Dixon greeted, ushering the young prospect into a beautifully appointed suite. Two monitors showing graphics for a chart-and-graph presentation stood on a low table. "I like your ensemble," she complimented.

Rochelle thanked her, noticing she appeared much older than expected, at least sixty, if not seventy, her face lined with quiet dignity, her coiffure a back-sweep of light chestnut streaked with highlights of silver and—with the balcony sunlight catching it just right—even a hint of spun gold. An exquisite brooch of pearl and jade adorned her burgundy jacket. "Join me in a delightful chardonnay?" She gestured toward the carafe beside a tray of canapés on a low table.

Rochelle accepted graciously, sitting stiffly beside her on the sofa, already watching for the earliest chance to bow out tactfully. She agreed when her hostess gushed about the lovely cities gracing both sides of the Charles, then endorsed their shared hometown of Chicago as the premiere center of commerce and culture in the U.S.

Eventually Miss Dixon started clicking through the graphics and narrating about opportunities in the medical-prosthesis and related health-care industries. Rochelle found her attention flagging, phrases and words drifting in and out of her sphere of awareness.

". . . small company positioned for expansion . . ."

". . . challenges for an enthusiastic young engineer . . ."

". . . personal satisfaction from helping so many . . ."

Catching herself fading, Rochelle started with a jerk, suddenly standing without intending to. "I'm sorry," she interrupted, feeling foolish and tactless.

Miss Dixon studied her for a moment, then sighed and let her shoulders slump, clicking the monitors to black, failure in her eyes. "You've accepted another offer?"

"No—oh, definitely not. No. It's just that, well, I still plan to travel abroad first, to see France." She stopped, trying not to appear sheepish.

"I hear it's quite lovely there," Miss Dixon admitted, watching Rochelle carefully. "I'm curious—what is it about France that draws you?"

Rochelle sat again, her hopes for a graceful exit dashed. She wanted to protect her privacy, but she owed this earnest lady some sort of explanation, and for some reason she very much *needed* to explain. "I want to see La Ré-ole," she admitted, actually explaining nothing.

"I've not heard of it. Is it a region, or perhaps a town?"

"It's where my mother grew up—for thirteen years, anyway. Then her widowed mother married again, and they moved to Chicago. My mother took me to see La Réole when I was seven, but I don't really remember much. She told me so many stories about her childhood that I feel as if I know the place, and I've always been curious about, well, what it was like, I guess—why it made her so happy."

"Will she accompany you?"

"No." She shook her head. "No, she's—she's gone now."

"Oh. I'm sorry."

"When I was thirteen," Rochelle added, her gaze drifting toward the sun-drenched balcony.

Miss Dixon's breath caught. Rochelle looked closer and noticed her eyes had softened, her face resonating with sadness. "And your father?"

"I still have him—I mean . . ." She didn't know what she meant, unless to say simply that he still lived, still kept in touch, still hovered at the periphery of her life. "He's an international attorney, so he's away most of the time. He brokers deals, even owns a few properties himself. I own parts of some, too, with my trust . . ." She told herself to stop talking, confused as to why she persisted in divulging so much.

"He's helping to ensure you a prosperous future," she said, her voice warm and reassuring. "He loves you."

Rochelle studied the older woman, deciding she deserved to know the truth. "I hope to work with him someday—not right away, but when the time is right."

Miss Dixon nodded knowingly. "Is this why you chose engineering?"

"Well, I've always been fascinated by how things work, imagining how they can work better, or be more affordable, or safer."

"My grandniece harbors a similar infatuation, but she's a *numbers* maven," she offered, smiling a bit, lightening the mood. "Mauterre is her name. She's only thirteen now, but with that computer of hers, she can reduce just about anything in the world to a series of digits. She can divide two elephants by a loaf of bread, then factor in the square root of soiled stockings and tell you the price of tea in Shanghai."

Rochelle couldn't help but return the smile.

"Please," Miss Dixon continued, "I'll promise no more charts if I can show you one thing." She hurried to the bedroom, returning with a framed photograph, an adorable young teenage girl with long brunette hair, her smooth olive skin and dark eyes suggesting a lineage spiced with flavors of the Mediterranean. She appeared quiet and studious, introspective yet inquisitive, maybe with a hint of sadness, definitely very serious, possibly lonesome . . .

"She's very pretty."

Miss Dixon studied the photo, her eyes glowing in the late-afternoon light. "Mauterre lives with me now," she said quietly. "It was my brother, her grandfather, who started the company. When he passed away two years ago, he left it to my nephew, Armand, who had just taken his engineering degree. He started some new product designs, but then—" She held the photo close to her heart, glancing off toward the balcony. "When he and his wife traveled to visit her friend in Oujda, their plane crashed, and both were killed."

Rochelle felt that inexorable, long-familiar pull again, a sense of spiraling out of control, but she resisted it, focusing instead on graduation, on settling into her cushioned seat aboard the *Train à Grande Vitesse*, a series of landscapes beckoning from the window, Tours and Portiers and the banks of the River Garonne. "I'm sorry," she whispered.

"The company is Mauterre's now, and I'm charged with preserving it, with assuring her a secure future." She studied Rochelle, tilting her head to see the younger woman's eyes, looking beyond the engineering graduate, a rare glimpse of private feelings through a careless rend in the protective cloak. She must have seen the same train, surely the picture postcards of French countryside . . . "And I'm failing her."

"Oh my," Rochelle said rather inappropriately, unsure what else to add.

"I'm trying to recruit you to join a declining company," she confessed. "You're the last of my twelve interviews here, my last chance after eleven rejections."

"But I'm just graduating."

"With a very impressive record from one of the finest institutions in the world."

"What about people with more experience?"

"I did hire a gentleman with an extensive résumé in Chicago, letting him work on one of Armand's drawings for wheelchairs that lift people to reach items on high shelves. In the meantime, we lost two major sales accounts because our product is outdated. Well, after six months, our highly recommended engineer went to work for a competitor in Florida, a company now showing prototypes of designs very similar to ours. We're running out of time, Rochelle. Mauterre analyzed the company books and said we'd be bankrupt in a year, so I hired an expensive business consultant who spent two months telling me the same thing my grandniece figured out in one afternoon. The manager tried to solicit investors, but since we have no new products ready for launch, they all expect controlling interest for the smallest infusions of cash. They also want to show Armand's drawings, supposedly to evaluate their feasibility, but I can't take that risk anymore. I need somebody who can refine the designs and maybe even develop more new ideas, but it has to be someone I can trust."

"Caution is important," Rochelle agreed. "My father once explained his work as representing conniving clients in deals with dishonest speculators."

Miss Dixon smiled at that, then appeared serious again. "I've investigated your record," she admitted, steering the subject back to possible employment. "You spent your summers taking classes and doing grant research instead of working internships, which means you have no corporate allegiances yet, from what I've seen. It also suggests—and I know I'm out of place here—that short-term financial gain is not your highest priority, that you can afford to accept somewhat, shall we say, austere compensation for a time, which would help us preserve our limited funds for building prototypes, for retooling and for retraining our sixty-eight employees. You'll need to live nearby until you learn our operation, but then you can move anywhere while you develop the new models. If it helps, I'll make my home available so you can curtail expenses until then; it's a lovely townhouse, just Mauterre and me, plenty of room." She paused, shook her head, maybe regretting having strayed so far from her business presentation. Finally, she looked into Rochelle's eyes, very softly summing up her dilemma: "I have to protect Mauterre."

"She's very lucky to have you," Rochelle said quietly.

She shrugged and held up her hands. "But I am an old woman, Rochelle, one who thought she never needed family to be happy, one who now cherishes the only family she has. I feel afraid sometimes, wondering if I'll be around long enough to help my little girl grow into the kind of strong, independent woman you've become."

"You *will* be there for her," Rochelle promised, not sure why those words came to her, yet believing them deeply, the alternative unimaginable.

Miss Dixon's eyes glistened, and she laughed, running fingers through her chestnut-and-silver hair. "Ah, the eternal optimism of youth." She chuckled again, then reached down and lightly touched the pearl-and-jade brooch, falling quiet. When she looked up, she'd grown serious again, but her face had softened with resignation. She knew Rochelle would decline the job, for surely she could see through the young woman's crumbling façade. "What would *you* do, Rochelle? The business manager suggested I sell the assets, then invest in bonds or CDs, but Mauterre doesn't want our loyal employees to lose their jobs. I don't know, Rochelle. Tell me, is *loyalty* really so important?"

Rochelle nodded, sure of herself.

Miss Dixon spread her hands again. "We could sell it whole, but then it would fold into another company, lose its name. Mauterre wants to preserve her family's legacy, to honor her grandfather by keeping his dream alive, and her father by seeing his designs help others. Tell me, Rochelle, is *family* really so important?"

"Yes," she blurted. Then softer, "Yes, it is."

Miss Dixon nodded, pleased with the answer; then she seemed to think it over for a moment. "It's been recommended we move manufacturing south where costs are lower, but Mauterre wants to stay in Chicago, to be with her friends, to explore the city her foreign-born mother grew to love so very much. Sometimes I think I understand; other times I'm not so sure. Was your mother happy to leave her hometown behind, this La Réole?"

She shook her head.

"I wonder, should I take a young girl who's already lost so much, and spirit her away from the only home she's ever known?"

She froze, her eyes locked on Miss Dixon's, the room dissolving into an airplane-window panorama of hazy sky.

"Tell me, Rochelle, can a *place* really be so important?"

*   *   *

Reluctant to return home, yet weary from walking the streets, Rochelle climbed the twisting stairwell and trudged the long hallway.

She pushed the door wide, then hesitated, searching the gloom of her sparsely furnished apartment, mesmerized by window-cast streetlamp projections painting misshapen quadrangles across the barren walls and mottled ceiling. The building's sounds pulsed down the corridor and surged through the open doorway, a muffled cacophony of TVs and stereos and creaking floorboards and slamming doors echoing from one room to another. She stepped inside and closed the door, relieved by the dead-bolt sense of blessed isolation. The screen on her master comm-system manager flashed reminders that she had been ignoring her cellphone voicemails, a promise of friendly voices to scatter the silence and fill the void, but she dreaded touching the icon, loath to endure another round of Galway pleas. It blinked until she finally relented.

Beep! "Rochelle? It's me. Listen, I think we should get together, talk this over, anywhere but here. I'm sick of Keefie harping about what I should do. Please call me."

Beep! "It's me again. Look, I know I messed up. I should've talked to you first. We can still work something out, some kind of compromise. Call me, okay?"

Beep! "C'mon, Rochelle, you said you loved me. Well, love is supposed to overcome all obstacles. We both need to make sacrifices. Listen, I'll be tied up a while, but leave a message, and I'll call you back."

She deleted all the messages, stared at the screen for a moment, then wandered to the bathroom, squinting against a revealing flood of fluorescence. Standing before the medicine cabinet, she blinked at the reflection of a woman who appeared older than Rochelle had ever felt—*with a stain on her collar!* The unsightly blemish was growing in magnitude before her very eyes. Had that been there at lunch?—or during the interview, even as Miss Dixon complimented her outfit? Horrified, she tugged off the duplicitous jacket and flung it into the tub, surprised by such uncharacteristic disdain for a mere garment.

Something looked wrong about her blouse, too. She'd carefully matched it to project the right image: self-assured independent woman, competitive corporate applicant, graduating apprentice engineer, Ramo DuFortier's successful daughter, and—and . . . but the look no longer fit. She pulled at the collar, jerked loose the buttons, and dropped the wadded fabric to the tile floor, liberated by this deliverance from a succession of uncomfortable roles. She pushed down her slacks, kicked them into a corner, then unclasped her brassière, recalling those awkward flat-chested years of covering her boyish bosom with hopeful swatches of cloth.

I can't wait to see you all grown up, her mother once teased when Rochelle finally got her wish, only to complain of tenderness in her burgeoning breasts, a young teen already learning to dread the new monthly discomfort throbbing in her tummy.

She slipped free of the constricting brassière, her supple breasts bouncing lightly as if confirming her mother had been right, that Rochelle would finally be satisfied with the impatiently expected result.

Yes, nearly everything had changed. Even her hair appeared more luxurious, the garden where colorful butterfly barrettes once reigned now ceded to the anticipated caress of a man's gentle hand; and now subtle but unmistakable age lines mapped future wrinkles along the contours of her face.

Only her eyes remained unchanged, long familiar hazelnut flecks floating in pools of swirling toffee, keepers of the secrets Rochelle sometimes feared others might discover if allowed to gaze too deep. She dared to look there now, searching for acknowledgment that no matter how much the world had shifted, regardless of how she might change, some small recognizable fragment of Rochelle DuFortier would always dwell in this place where, whenever she felt lost, she could always count on finding herself.

I can't wait to see you all grown up . . .

She covered her breasts, adjusting her arms to mimic the plunging neckline of an elegant evening gown, and she wished her mother could see her now, could approve of the little girl who'd come into her own, could have one last chance to share her mastery of understated make-up and exquisite hair styles, of complementing accessories and alluring perfumes . . .

She lowered her arms, still considering her eyes, unable or unwilling to look away, a woman with a child's view.

Still trapped by one layer too many, she slipped from her panties, allowing the delicate assemblage of silk and lace to fall to the tiles. Wisps of cool air probed her soft curls, the faintest hint of feminine scent swirling evocatively in search of a companion aroma; and she breathed deeply as feather-strokes of anticipation invited her to play; and she understood how much this depth of yearning could never be satisfied by a simple touch, an admission that for Rochelle to accept all that a man may offer she must give all that a woman holds close and protected.

She crossed her arms to hide her breasts, banishing grown-up notions of intimacy that sheer solitude left her no means to fulfill, searching her eyes for glimmers of the young teenage Rochelle, but she'd forfeited the innocence of that little girl, and now all she could recall was the image that had unsettled her in Miss Dixon's hotel suite . . . the face of another young teenage girl, a numbers-obsessed orphan incessantly ciphering the equation that might set her world right.

Rochelle suddenly felt very cold, exposed and vulnerable, shivering now, growing inexplicably afraid.

She flicked off the offending light and broke the spell, then hurried to her bed, crawling under the duvet, pulling the sheets close and tucking them tightly, trembling furiously.

How dare that Miss Dixon trick her into feeling guilty for not helping another who's suffered what only Rochelle could truly comprehend. Never in her wildest dreams could she consider assuming that kind of responsibility, nor would she pretend to the resourcefulness needed to accept Miss Dixon's challenge. People always expected too much from Rochelle DuFortier, and too often she let them down.

She would call Miss Dixon in the morning, feign having weighed her offer against several better, then convey her painstakingly considered regrets. She would attend graduation commencement without her father, standing alone while all around her families laughed and hugged and posed for photos. Then she would be free to leave Cambridge forever, to venture out and discover all the world may offer . . . her first destination, steerage-class if necessary: France.

R-r-r-r-r-ring!

She burrowed under the covers, her heart pounding.

R-r-r-r-r-ring!

Click. "Rochelle? It's me again. Listen, I've already made a commitment to that job, but if you'll go with me, I promise only one year—that's all, just one year—then if you want to go somewhere else, we'll consider it." He paused to listen, maybe hoping she'd pick up. "I know you're there," he said quietly. He waited a moment. "Okay," he said, resigned. "Call me at home."

Beep!

All at once, the future faded beyond her immediate grasp, and she imagined Galway standing there in the gloomy shadows beside her bed, a devoted young man now heartbroken and sincere in his promise, and she felt so very lonesome she could hardly conceive waking to another morning by herself. She rustled the duvet, and it seemed as if he eased in to snuggle under the covers, gently putting his arms around her, caressing her face, stroking her hair, moving his hand toward her breasts, a familiar yet comfortable routine.

Surely Tulsa must be a wonderful place, an exciting opportunity to explore another region and sample the local culture.

She shifted forward as his fingers moved lower, his big and powerful hand navigating her navel with a playful tickle, and she rippled with tingly sensations when he paused momentarily at the first hint of raven curls.

She could buy a pair of chic hand-tooled cow-gal boots, next adding a tailored suede jacket with embroidery and fringe. That would coax Galway's appreciative smile, especially if she posed for him in a ten-gallon hat and the kinkiest little set of plastic spurs she could find on the internet.

She felt the liquid cascade of his hand moving lower, fingertips igniting dormant passions, searing ripples radiating as he gently probed. She teased him as always, feigning surprise, drawing him closer to cradle his insistent stiffness where flesh pressed against burning flesh.

He signaled his usual urgency, and she knew to let his simple manipulations carry her up the steepest slopes, every movement a pressing collision, a touch here, another there, the searing flow sweeping them higher as they joined in a summit dance, sacrificing their bodies to the all-consuming eruption . . .

R-r-r-r-r-ring!

She arched her back, her fingers ablaze with the fury, breasts heaving with every gasp, skin burning under the winter's duvet—

R-r-r-r-r-ring!

Click. "Listen, Rochelle," Galway ground out through the tiny speaker.

"No, Galway!" she shouted, knowing he could not hear.

"I don't like this game you're playing," he snarled.

She pulled her hand free and cupped her throbbing fingers against her bosom.

"And I'm sick of this bullshit," he continued louder. She heard another voice say something, Galway whirling from the receiver to shout, "Shut up!" The other voice shouted, "Tell her about—" as the phone dropped, then Galway's muffled, "Dick-face!" as something toppled and a door slammed. Rochelle envisioned young Todd sprawled and bleeding on the floor. "Anyway," he continued, picking up the phone, his breaths rapid and deep, the panting of sexual climax, the exertion of bench-pressing an extra five pounds, the exhaustion of pummeling a skinny little brother, all facets of Galway's compensations for Keefie's emasculating chokehold, a pathetic little boy hiding behind the gym-buffed body of a man not so strong after all. "If you want to be a bitch about this, fine. You're not gonna make a fool out of me." *Slam!*

Beep!

And the apartment echoed with the emptiness of Rochelle's night.

She pulled the covers tighter, rolled over and buried her face in the pillow, grateful that Todd had risen to her defense this one last time, that he'd risked himself to force Galway's hand. The next time Galway called, she would pick up the phone, and she would tell him that her only regret is not being around to see the day when Todd is finally big enough to beat his obnoxious brother's ass.

R-r-r-r-r-ring!

She scrabbled for the phone, snatched the handset from its cradle, and practically shouted, "Listen, you!"

"Rochelle?" Not Galway, but a familiar tenor whose every word sang the melody of leaves rustling in exotic trees. "Is that you?"

"Um, yeah. Mikalu?"

"Yah," he said quietly. "I'm sorry I bother you. I know you're busy, make big plans to graduate and go on long trip, but Poco's gone all *pupule*, and he say you *must* come."

"Why? What's wrong?"

"He too big now, have trouble fitting inside, needs you to come help. He doesn't want anybody else knowing about d'lava tube."

She jumped up, stood naked in darkness, the swirling cool air making her shiver. "Oh no. What's wrong? Why the lava tube?"

"It's Papaii," Mika said, his voice breaking.

"What happened?"

"Papaii, he fall, break his head, leave us to join *nā lapu*, die very fast."

"Oh no," Rochelle whispered, her eyes stinging, the room spinning, her problems suddenly very small.

"Rochelle?"

"I'm here, Mika."

"You come now, okay?"

Nā aikane lāua

Close friends

Rochelle at 14, spring break

Descending toward Hilo, young Rochelle fastened her seatbelt and closed her eyes, imagining her father waiting anxiously in the terminal, that handsome smile as he called her name, his arms wide for a true *aloha* welcome.

They would drive straight to Okiya Gardens for a long-overdue 14th birthday dinner, doffing their shoes and kneeling on *tatami* mats to sample exotic Japanese cuisine amid the splendor of flickering paper lanterns. Later, he'd take her home and help her unpack in her very own room, and they'd relax on the terrace, sorting through travel brochures to plan a year's activities squeezed into one precious week: wearing silly hats while cruising the raucous beach parties at Keaukaha Strip; taking the plunge to water-dance with playful dolphins at Waikola Village; strolling the trails of Pepe 'okeo as tour-guide hummingbirds hurry ahead to point out clusters of delicate orchids; perusing the galleries at Holualoa Village for gifts of carved *koa* or woven *lau hala* or ceramic *raku* to surprise and delight her friends at Rinerson Dorm; climbing to Mauna Kea's summit observatory to catch the sun's evening performance when it splashes a shifting palette of pastels across the shimmering Pacific horizon; then applauding the velvet night's encore magic show as star-trails sweep from Polaris to the Southern Cross, a father and daughter together reaching out to touch the glitter-freckled face of infinite sky.

And for Saturday, her last day, he'd hinted of a big surprise, maybe a festive *luau* in her honor, the celebration of enduring promise.

A mild thump, the squall of back-thrusting engines, and Rochelle found herself filing down the ramp, her carry-on clutched to her chest. The waiting crowd surged forward, people jabbering to family and friends, but she couldn't find her father—

"Rochelle!" called an unexpected voice. "Rochelle!" Mikalu waved from the side, that familiar blond mop crowning the face of a young teen who'd clearly outgrown the skinny boy she'd last seen less than a year before. "Hi,

Rochelle!" His voice, though somewhat deeper, still sang with gentle lyricism.

"Mikalu!" she greeted, glancing around for any sign of her father.

"Sorry, me is all you get," he said. "Your father, he come later. I bring you gift, say *aloha*." He lifted a *lei* of crimson and fuchsia, awkwardly placing it around her neck.

"Wow, it's beautiful. You must've spent hours on this."

He shrugged. "D'vines that grow flowers, they do d'hard part."

She arranged it across her bosom, sensing his awareness that she, too, had grown. "*Mahalo*," she added, amused to see him blushing.

"Is nothing. Come, we get your bags."

She found her hand in his as he led her toward the lower level. "So what silly business crisis distracted my father this time?"

He avoided answering until they reached the luggage carousel; then he turned to face her, a disarming sadness muting the sparkle of his eyes.

"What's wrong?" she asked quietly, serious now. "What is it?"

"Tapakiki. Your father, he is taking Poco and Lalani to see her."

"What happened? Is she okay?"

"No, she have big stroke in brain last night. She is very sick, in hospital now, maybe not live much longer," he added, a catch in his throat. "Papaii, he stay there already, sit with her all d'night long."

"Have you seen her yet?"

He glanced away. "No. So far, only family." He retrieved her suitcase, then led her to the promenade, patting his pocket and explaining, "Your father leave money, say fill our faces—eat now, I mean."

With that, she knew her exotic evening kneeling on *tatami* mats at Okiya Gardens had devolved to perching on patchy vinyl stools, chewing greasy corndogs and fries, her plans for a week-long sojourn alone with her father now wilting like so many forgotten blossoms in the *lei* she'd discarded the last time she fled this desolate outpost. Still, Rochelle understood the helplessness of worrying over a loved one, and though her brochures might remain packed away after all, at least her coming here now might afford the smallest chance to repay Mikalu and Pocomea for helping her the year before.

Mika barely touched his food, his dolor painting dark clouds across his eyes. "I worry 'bout Tapakiki," he explained apologetically.

"Mika, you're part of her family, too, aren't you?—I mean legally, with a custody agreement."

He shrugged. "Yah, but that's not like real family, not like you and Poco be soon."

"Me and *Poco*? What are you talking about?"

Mika's eyes widened, his face aghast. "Oh no, I say too much."

"How would Poco—? Are my father and Lalani getting married?!"

He grimaced.

"They are, aren't they? When is it?!"

"Please, Rochelle."

She grabbed his arm. "Talk, Haole-boy!" she demanded, remembering too late how he'd chafed at such teasing from local children. "I'm sorry, Mika," she said, sitting back. "I'm just freaking out right now."

"Me, too. We *both* gone all *pupule*, and now I wreck big surprise."

"It's planned for next Saturday, isn't it?" So much for a *luau*. "Is it a big elaborate affair?"

"Oh no, just family—and me, too. Lalani, she have pretty dress made for you, buy suits for us guys. I'm so sorry, not my business shooting off big mouth."

She stared at the table. "Then Poco *will* be my stepbrother."

"Not just that. He come be Poco *hanai*—adopted—"

"Well, I'm not letting anybody adopt *me*."

"I don't know 'bout that, but they say big hurry for Poco, make all legal for insurance, pay for big-dollar operation."

"Is something wrong with him?" Suddenly she felt very petty.

"Neck hurt all d'time, real bad by and by, sometimes can't hold arms up like diver's *okay* sign. Hilo doctor-man say maybe tumor, say Poco gotta go to Honolulu this Wednesday, get all *da kine* tests done for three days." He bit his lower lip. "I worry 'bout Poco all d'time, too, and now Tapakiki . . ." He closed his eyes, a young teen lost in the wilderness, that helpless-outsider feeling Rochelle knew all too well. She reached across the table, touched his hand—

"Rochelle!" Her father waved as he hurried down the concourse. She rushed out to meet him halfway, Mika trailing behind. Ramo DuFortier hugged her solemnly, forgetting his usual pronouncement about her mother's beauty and the angelic face of his little girl. To Mikalu, he said, "Thank you for escorting our Rochelle." He took her hand, tousling Mika's hair with the other.

"It is my privilege, sir," he said with no trace of pidgin.

They walked toward the escalator in silence, the distraction of unspoken questions cluttering their path.

As they approached the exit, she couldn't stand it anymore. "Daddy, will Tapakiki be okay?"

Ramo ignored her, leading them outside. They stood at the curb, waiting for traffic to clear.

"Will she?" Mika demanded, his face flushed. "Tell me!"

Ramo sighed, then ushered them past the cab stand, gesturing for them to sit on a bench. He took a deep breath and shook his head sadly. "She suffered another stroke, and they were unable to revive her."

"No!" Mika cried, panic in his eyes. He jumped up and ran down the side-walk.

"Wait!" Rochelle shouted, she and her father chasing after him.

Mika slowed to a walk until they caught up; then he stopped and stood staring across a field toward the sea, his fists clenched tightly, his face in profile twitching with tension.

"She died peacefully, Mikalu," Ramo said, reaching toward the boy.

Mika backed away from him, his eyes glistening, chest heaving with labored breaths. "But I not say good-bye! Tapakiki, she think I not want to come."

"But she was in a coma."

"I not say good-bye!"

Rochelle hushed her father with a hand on his arm. "You're right, Mika. You didn't get to say good-bye. Instead, you came here to meet me. For that, I'm grateful, but I wish it had been different."

He looked at her; then all the anger drained from his face. He lowered his eyes, his shoulders slumping, and he slowly nodded.

Ramo moved closer. "Mikalu, I need your help. Papaii and Pocomea, well, they are causing quite a scene. They wish to take her remains back to the valley."

"Yes," Mika said simply, "I will help them."

"No no, it is imperative that you help me *dissuade* them from this course."

"Why? Why you not want what Tapakiki wants?"

But Daddy, Mom wanted to be buried in France with Grandpa . . .

"It is not legal," Ramo explained to the boy. "The law today requires proper handling, and a licensed cemetery. I have offered to provide a splendid memorial in the gardens at Punalu'u, there close to your school. You boys and Papaii could visit anytime."

Mikalu turned away, his fists clenched again.

"Dad, why don't you get the car."

He studied them for a moment, then nodded and headed back toward the lot.

"Mikalu?" she said quietly.

"He not understand," the boy answered, turning to look at her sadly. "You not, either."

"Try me," she said, reaching to touch his hair without meaning to.

"Nā Wai-Nuikai follow ancient Hawaiian traditions—very secret. Lalani not even know. Tapakiki, she wants to rest with d'fathers in sacred place. She wants to go home."

Chicago is your home, Rochelle, but I still think of La Réole as my home. Someday you'll understand . . .

"I *do* understand," she said.

Her father drove up in a sleek black sedan, breaking the spell. Mikalu placed her bags in the trunk and joined her in back, settling in to stare forlornly out the window as Ramo pulled into traffic.

Rochelle watched him for a minute, not sure how to help; then she scooted forward and rested her arms on the seatback. "Daddy, what day will the funeral be?"

"I believe Tuesday," Ramo answered. "Lalani and I must take Pocomea to Oahu Wednesday. I regret you and I will have very little time together this vacation."

"I understand," she assured him, her mantra for the day.

She sat back and considered her options, Mikalu's frustration so palpable she found her own fists clenched in sympathy.

She leaned forward again. "It's legal to hold a wake in a private home, isn't it?—what some people call visitation."

"I suppose it is."

"They could do that part at Coulée Makai, right?—then have a burial service in Punaluʻu."

Mika turned and watched her, his curiosity piqued.

"Yes," her father answered. "In fact, that sounds like a fine compromise, if Papaii agrees."

She looked at Mika, and in that instant something passed between them, not a specific thought, but a feeling, a moment of shared trust.

Okiya Gardens appeared ahead, then passed quickly by, grand plans rendered moot by the greater scheme.

"Daddy, don't you think—I mean, for the next few days, wouldn't it be easier—?"

"What, sweetheart?"

"I think I should stay at Coulée Makai."

*   *   *

"Hawai'i boys . . ." she summoned quietly from the dark hallway. "Huh-wah-yeee boy-eees," she called louder, her mouth against the jamb, hoping not to wake Papaii.

Mikalu opened the door, blinking comprehension, Pocomea's soft snores keeping time with gusts of breeze through the open window.

"You come, Hawai'i boys," she whispered. "Soon daylight will chase stars across the sea."

"Um, yeah sure."

They met her outside, bringing pillow-cases, a flashlight, and two shovels. She led them down toward the beach, sand crabs skittering this way and that, a pink glow rising behind the towering cliffs standing sentry over the cove.

"Sneaky twine, it hides under Poco's bed," Mika admitted sheepishly, rolling his eyes. He jogged back toward the house to retrieve it.

"Why do you guys share that one bedroom?" she asked Poco as they set their supplies on a flat rock.

"Mika, he have his own room. You sleep in it," Poco said matter-of-factly, rubbing his foot in the dry sand along the high rocks.

"Was it his room last year, too, when I stayed the night?"

Poco nodded, reaching down to scrape deeper into the sand with his hands.

"But where's his stuff?"

"All moved in mine, give you plenty room, lotta space for Haole-girl who bring many pretty things." He turned his head, but not before she saw the tease of his smile.

"But he didn't know I'd be staying here this trip."

Poco looked up and smirked. "Just in case. That boy sure do hope all d'time. He one big hoper, that's saying d'truth."

Mika jogged back to join them, placing scissors and string on the rock.

"This here look dry enough," Poco pronounced, dusting sand from his hands.

They went to work, filling more than a dozen old pillow-cases each about a third of the way, Mikalu expertly tying them with nautical-looking knots.

Poco tried to hoist four onto his shoulders, but he winced and dropped them, his brow creased with anger, eyes betraying a hint of fear. He settled for holding one under each arm as they carried the first load back to the house, neatly stacking them behind a *lobelia* bush flanking the *lanai*.

"Can you guys get the rest? I'm gonna go shower," she said, realizing she'd just wiped grime across her brow.

She found the waterfall just as the first golden rays of morning sun burst across the sea, coaxing a faerie-tale rainbow from the pool's rising mist. She laid her robe and brush on a rock, fetched a towel and shampoo from the hidden tub, then glanced around self-consciously before peeling off her clothes. The open air made her feel very naked but somehow exhilarated as she waded into shallow water, the breeze stirring her hair and swirling around her young bosom as churning water crept up her thighs. She stepped under the shower, the icy bath taking her breath away, but she stood firm, quickly adjusting to the temperature, relieved it proved not nearly as cold as the spring that fed Coulée Makai's natural refrigerator up along the ridge. She waded over for a dab of shampoo, worked it into her hair, then spread it around her body before splashing back to rinse under the spray from a lower ledge.

And nothing tried to bite her.

Feeling clean and refreshed, she turned and faced the rising sun, her face peering out from the falls, liquid cascading over bare skin. The clearing awoke with a flurry of colors and song, *amakihi* birds and finches chittering the morning news as they flitted from bush to bush, butterflies dancing over a damp stretch of sand, a humongous dragonfly patrolling the perimeter as a platoon of giant camouflaged ferns slowly lifted their fronds to salute a new day. But the more she admired the serene beauty of this natural wonder, the more she realized the awful truth that Tapakiki could never again stand here in this very spot. The old Hawaiian woman had spent most of her life at Coulée Makai, according to Pocomea, a bride of fourteen pausing each morning to gaze over this lush valley, across the jigsaw-blue lagoon, between the towering cliffs toward endless sea, confident this is where she would always belong. Now Papaii and the boys wanted to bring her home.

Profound sadness crept up through her body, a melancholy no amount of water could rinse, so she took a deep breath and tried not to think of the grim tasks that lay ahead, concentrating instead on quickly donning her robe, having suddenly felt very naked and vulnerable again. She hurried down the path and found Papaii and the boys waiting patiently on the lower trail, all three clad in brand-new robes. They headed toward the falls as she walked down to the house, arriving at the same time as Lalani.

"Your father," the beautiful Hawaiian woman explained with a gesture, "he is *still* making calls on his cellphone." Rochelle could see him across the valley, standing alongside the roadway just through the open slot, his beloved phone pressed to his ear.

"Wow," Rochelle said, following her inside, "you look beautiful." And she did, adorned in dark burgundy, a skirted suit with blended jacket, matching jade clips pinning her long hair so it fell down her back.

"Thank you, Rochelle. I have dressed to honor my family."

"You must have left Hilo quite early."

"No, we lodged in Punalu'u."

"Oh. Um, why didn't you just stay here?"

Lalani closed her eyes and tilted her head, then looked at Rochelle appraisingly. "Have you chosen your clothing yet?"

"No, I wasn't sure. Would you help?"

Lalani smiled, following her into Mika's room to sort through various outfits and accessories. "I always wanted a pretty girl to dress up. I think this would look very nice, and appropriate for this solemn occasion." She indicated a dark blue pantsuit with French-cut jacket, then helped Rochelle into it, adjusting and smoothing, reminding the young teen of so many times with her own mother.

"I do not stay here," Lalani explained, "because this was my husband's home—Pocomea's father's—and when I lost him, I knew I could not support a family from here. Coulée Makai, it is not part of the real world. Out there," she explained, gesturing wide with her arm, "there are many demands, and money is most important. Now I am comfortable with my life, and this place is too—primitive, I would call it—and coming here reminds me of the life I lost so long ago." She turned Rochelle to help her with a hair clip, adding with a smile, "I could never convince my boys to leave, though. They are part of Coulée Makai, and for now, at least, it is part of them."

As Lalani stepped back to appraise the result, Rochelle blurted out the question she'd intended to leave unspoken. "Why do you call *both* of them your boys?"

Lalani sighed and sat on the bed, watching Rochelle carefully, measuring her words. "Mikalu, he is my boy, too, for I am the only mother he has known."

"Does he think of himself as part of your family?"

Lalani gazed at her lap, finally answering, "No. I do not let him. You see," she continued, looking into Rochelle's eyes now, "he is also his father's son, and I always hold some hope, for Mikalu's sake, that his father will come for him."

"But he won't. He's *not* coming. He's been gone from Mika's life too long."

"No, he is not gone," Lalani corrected, "but if I explain, this must remain between us." Rochelle nodded, not sure if she really would honor the request or not. "His father contacts me each time after two or three months to check on his son, but he will not talk to him until he is sure the promises he makes to his boy are the promises he will keep."

"Mikalu doesn't need promises. He needs truth."

"His father is engaged to be married to a woman in San Diego. He is seeking employment near her home so he will not have to live at sea for extended periods. Someday, he wants Mikalu to join them, to be a family again, but he cannot yet promise when that will be, so he remains silent. I have a big dark-haired boy whom I love very much, but I love my blond-haired boy, too, and I want it to be easier for him when the time comes that he must leave us." Lalani's eyes brimmed with unrealized tears.

"You want it to be easier for *you* to let go, too," Rochelle said, the truth a whisper swirling with a gust of window breeze.

Lalani nodded, then squared her shoulders. "Now I have much to plan. I trust Mikalu has revealed our pending marriage?" Rochelle just smiled. "I am not surprised. He has never been able to keep a secret, and sometimes I rely on that," she admitted, matching Rochelle's smile. "Then you must know of Pocomea's adoption. Please consider if you would like for me to adopt you, too. Whatever you choose, I will understand. Poco has never known his father, but you did know your mother, and I know I could never replace her."

"I think I prefer not to be adopted," Rochelle said suddenly, cutting through the awkwardness.

Lalani nodded. "I expected not. No longer are you a child, not like my boys, but rather someone who has begun to see herself as a young woman with her own place in the world." With that she stood and touched Rochelle's hair affectionately. "Still, I would have been very lucky."

Oh, Rochelle! I'm so lucky to have a little girl like you . . .

"But now," Lalani continued, "you should go wrestle that phone from your father, and I will lay out Papaii's and my boys' new suits so we can begin the argument about why they must wear them today."

"Your *boys* are very lucky—both of them," she said, catching Lalani's smile before she stepped into the blinding morning sunshine, feeling very mature, a young woman sure of her own place in the world.

I can't wait to see you all grown up!

Then she saw it, parked just across the footbridge, a dark and ominous hearse, two black sedans pulling in beside it.

She froze.

Four men in dark suits stepped out, then opened the back of the hearse and rolled out a shiny casket of polished wood, one very similar to Rochelle's mother's.

But I still think of La Réole as my home.

Mika rounded the corner, freshly scrubbed, his damp hair combed back, Papaii and Pocomea right behind him. All stopped and stared, the old man's face etched with helpless loss.

Someday you'll understand . . .

With stakes so high, she knew her plan better work.

Even more than Mikalu, Rochelle had become what Poco would call *one big hoper.*

*   *   *

Tapakiki looked beautiful, a tiny bronze-skinned woman laid out in the traditional blossom-patterned robe, her gentle face etched with deep grooves that spoke of wisdom and experience, laughter and love. Rochelle studied her until she could imagine the young bride from so long ago, and she knew the woman's heartache at losing her only son to the sea, and she understood one more reason Lalani's "boys" had chosen to live here with Papaii and their beloved grandmother.

The casket stood against the back wall of the big main room, surrounded by flowers, overlooking the beach and lagoon. People came to visit throughout the day, some of them friends of the Wai-Nuikais, the majority acquaintances of Ramo DuFortier.

Toward evening, a group of young teens arrived, schoolmates of Poco and Mika. Introduced to Rochelle with awkward politeness, they ultimately gravitated toward Poco, forming a small group off to the side, expressing sympathy for the loss of his grandmother. A red-haired *haole* girl hovered close to Mikalu, openly flirting with him. He looked uncomfortable, embarrassed, maybe even sad.

As the group prepared to leave, the girl asked him, "Do you *have* to go to the funeral tomorrow?"

Stricken, he lowered his eyes, then stammered, "Um, yes, I *want* to go. Excuse me," he blurted, suddenly fleeing outside and disappearing behind the house.

Rochelle hurried to follow, but stopped to watch a regal Hawaiian woman walking in from the open slot, a small boy in tow. Little Dabu sported new pants and shirt, his dark hair cropped short and combed neatly back. The teens came outside, each girl hugging Poco, the boys shaking his hand, all following him up the trail to see the waterfall. When the woman reached the house, Rochelle greeted her, introducing herself.

"I am Mrs. Taoke," she returned stiffly.

"And this is Dabu," Rochelle supplied, surprising her. She knelt before the boy, touching her own heart and reaching to touch his, smiling reassurance. Dabu smiled back and stroked her cheeks.

"Mrs. Taoke," Papaii said, stepping outside.

"Papaii, I come out of respect."

He nodded, leading her inside, Rochelle following discreetly. Her father and Lalani had disappeared to somewhere else in the house. Dabu headed straight to the casket, standing tiptoe to peer inside, his mother right behind him. Tears standing in his eyes, the little boy sniffled and whispered, "Dabu," as he touched Tapakiki's hand. Suddenly, he turned and buried his face in Mrs. Taoke's skirt.

She touched Tapakiki's cheek, her own eyes filling with tears, then looked to Papaii and explained, "My husband's father, he never have understanding with you, all his life. Your son and my husband, just like their fathers. Now my boys and your Pocomea, I fear the same . . . but Tapakiki, she one good woman, and she was my friend." A single tear crawled unbidden down her face.

Poco returned alone and sat forlornly on a divan. Dabu pulled away and hurried to him, the bigger boy gathering him in, each cupping the other's cheeks in his hands.

Papaii said, "Tapakiki always say Mrs. Taoke, she one good *wahine*, too."

"We all d'time meet in town on shopping days, hide this from our husbands."

"We know," Papaii said, a moment of understanding passing between them.

"We both wanted *nā 'ohana* to come make understanding someday." She gazed at her young deaf son, now snuggled in the big boy's lap, the little one's eyes half closed, contentment on both faces. "There is still hope," she said.

The funeral director and his assistants walked up the path and rapped on the door. Mikalu came up from behind and let them inside. Mrs. Taoke turned and touched Tapakiki's cheek one more time, then gently lifted her son from Poco's lap and carried him outside.

"I hope this arrangement pleases you, Mr. Wai-Nuikai," said the aged Hawaiian gentleman. "I value our people's traditions, and we follow them as best we can, but customs and the law have changed. I believe bringing Mrs. Wai-Nuikai here bestowed the honor she deserves."

"Thank you," Papaii said. "This we do for Tapakiki."

The director nodded, satisfied. "Do you prefer we take her now and meet at the cemetery tomorrow?"

"No, she will rest this night in her home."

"I understand. Then we shall come for her in the morning. There will be no more visitation?"

"Only ceremony at grave," Papaii said.

"Would you like a moment to pay your respects before we close?"

Ramo and Lalani came back, Poco joining them from the couch. All stood in a semi-circle and gazed upon Tapakiki. Rochelle felt dizzy, cold, adrift. Moments in time popped like flashbulbs, instants of surrealistic impressions, a smear of dried blood transposed across Tapakiki's face, crowds gathering to point and stare at Rochelle—

She gasped, then felt her father's arm around her shoulders, Lalani reaching to hold her hand, the protective adults steering her across the room. She watched through blurring eyes as Papaii gathered the boys to either side, putting an arm around each; the director carefully arranging the silk lining and closing the casket, then reaching behind the catafalque for an odd-shaped tool, inserting it into a slot at the end, slowly cranking a hidden shaft to seal the lid.

"Wai-Nuikai," Papaii whispered, the boys repeating it in unison.

"Do you want another opportunity to see her in the morning?" the director asked, "before we proceed to the cemetery?"

Rochelle stared at the device poised in his hand.

Papaii shook his head.

"Wait," Rochelle blurted, all eyes turning to her. "You don't know yet—maybe Poco, or Mikalu—"

The director looked right through her, his eyes appraising.

"Yes," Mika agreed. "We might."

The director still watched Rochelle.

Papaii nodded. "We will decide in d'morn."

An instant of recognition passed between the director and Rochelle; then he looked away, nodding to Papaii and carefully placing the tool in some unseen recess behind the catafalque.

Ramo and Lalani left soon after the director, just as the sun dipped behind Mauna Loa, deep shadows pooling in misty recesses down through the valley, the lagoon reflecting pale yellow streamers of splayed sunlight forming a dome that protectively covered the cove.

Papaii retrieved a small satchel from his room, then stood vigil at the casket while the boys hauled pillow-cases of sand into the room. Rochelle fished around for the tool, finally knocking it loose to clang on the floor. She reversed the director's motions, testing the lid until the seal broke.

Then she panicked, stepping back, clenching her fists. Poco and Mika moved around her, watching her patiently until she calmed before they opened the casket. First, they spread a large cloth—"*tapa*," Mika explained—painted with flowers and ancient symbols. They carefully lifted Tapakiki and placed her gently on the cloth. Papaii came forward and produced a palm-sized obsidian stone, carved and polished into the shape of an egg. He placed it in her hand, cupping his fingers around hers for a moment before closing his eyes and standing back. The boys folded the *tapa* cloth over her, then rolled her tightly into a cocoon. Undignified, crude, ghoulish—it all seemed at least inappropriate to Rochelle, if not grotesque, but not for her to judge. She'd decided to help, no matter what.

Poco secured the wrap by tying plastic strips before placing her on a hastily fashioned stretcher of *lau hala* mat; then everybody retreated to change into jeans, overshirts, and tennis shoes.

Mika rolled up his sleeves, and they set out, Papaii leading with one flashlight and the satchel, Rochelle bringing up the rear with another light and rolled blanket. That Mika could so easily lift his end of the load surprised Rochelle, his arms bulging with muscles she'd never noticed.

Papaii's bad leg slowed them sometimes, but he always pushed forward as they worked their way up the valley and sidetracked up several switchback trails to climb the northern ridge. Poco plodded methodically, too, except whenever he tried to lift the stretcher too high. Twice he had to stop and sit, his eyes scrunched tightly, brow furrowed with pain, the frustration over being a vulnerable link in their chain steeling him each time to move on.

Several hours and two smaller ridges later, the ground leveled and smoothed as if flowing glass had suddenly cooled, the surface crisscrossed with cracks and crevices and cylindrical pits where trees had burned as lava solidified around their trunks.

"We all big-time trespassers now," Mika cautioned, shining his flashlight around the desolate landscape, then clicking it off.

"National park," Poco explained. "Heli-choppers come make us hide in dark to keep Wai-Nuikai fathers' fathers' home secret, leave room in jail for *real* bad guys, not us."

Mika flashed his light along the first of a series of solid lava waves, each about six- or eight-feet high, breakers frozen in time, their surfers invisible phantoms fleeing the wrath of Pele.

"Ramo, he must never learn about this place," Poco said.

"Lalani, too," Mika added. "She thinks maybe she knows, but never for sure."

"I swear secrecy," Rochelle affirmed, the gut-wrenching secret of having killed her own mother gouging a hole more than deep enough to bury a few simple mysteries from others' lives.

Satisfied, Papaii came forward and removed a sprig of *ohelo*, placing it atop the nearest wave. "Pele," he breathed reverently, adding something in Hawaiian that sounded like a mix of praise and thanks.

Poco spread the blanket on the smooth glass, pushing it partially under the breaker. He and Mika positioned Tapakiki mid-blanket, parallel to the wave, leaving just enough room for the smaller boy to lie beside her before rolling under the narrow overhang and disappearing from sight. The blanket slid after him, pulled by unseen hands, stopping when Tapakiki disappeared, too.

An eerie glow shined from the opening as Poco lay on the outer edge and scooted himself underneath. Soon the blanket pushed out again. Papaii straightened it, then handed his satchel inside and gestured to Rochelle. Heart pounding, nearly exhausted from the trek, she found resignation easier to summon than fear, so she followed suit, Papaii right behind her.

She sat up in what appeared to be a cave, maybe four feet high, fifteen or twenty feet long. Poco sat at the back with his legs dangling into a slot that dropped seemingly into infinity. She scooted up to the edge and shined her light into it, discovering a stairway of sorts, a series of large, crudely hacked blocks leading down about fifteen feet into a tunnel.

"Lava tube," Poco said.

"Big lava flow," Mika explained. "D'outside get all cold and harden, middle flow out, leave tube. Whole island full of tubes."

"Places where *nā lapu* rest their bodies," Poco added.

"Ancient Hawaiian burial tradition," Rochelle said, recalling something from a brochure.

She climbed down first, afraid of bats that never appeared, wrinkling her nose at the musty odor that seemed to fade after several minutes. It felt cool, slightly damp, a natural mausoleum. She held a light for the boys while they lifted Tapakiki's stretcher down, followed by Papaii.

As the entourage headed several hundred yards up a slight incline, Rochelle found the sheer smoothness of the walls disconcerting, as if they had been polished by frequent flows. She stopped and froze, startled by the echo of their footsteps, suddenly afraid Pele might open the valve and release an incinerating pyroclastic deluge to unclog her island's arteries.

Then she felt silly for getting caught up in the mythology, for actually allowing the ancient superstition a persona.

As the passageway narrowed, a gradually deepening indentation formed a trough against the north wall. Where it reached several feet wide, it appeared to be filled with black sand. Crude niches had been chiseled every ten feet or so in the wall above it, each displaying a hand-crafted treasure . . . grave markers, she realized.

Papaii began to sing as they walked, Pocomea sometimes joining in. "*Mele*," Mika whispered, "—chant of d'fathers." He added his own mellifluous voice, stumbling over the words, his intentions nevertheless heartfelt.

They passed statues of mythic figures carved in jade, a series of nacre fishhooks arranged on a fish-shaped platter, stacks of varnished wooden bowls, elegant pottery glazed as black as the volcanic fields, hand-carved boxes inlaid with precious metals and polished stones, a *lei* of colorful blown glass, sea-turtle shells painted with images of beautiful birds, a traditional headdress of exotic feathers, a pair of onyx *papala*-holders . . .

Then they came to an empty slot.

The boys lowered Tapakiki, then retrieved two old shovels leaning against the opposite wall and spread the blanket. Shoveling the amalgam of sand and lava rocks onto it, they eventually reached bottom some four feet down. Rochelle held the flashlight, Papaii chanting louder as they lowered Tapakiki's wrapped form into the opening.

"*Ku'u ipo, ku'u mili mili*," he sang.

Poco whispered, "He say, My sweetheart, my beloved."

"Tapakiki *nahe nahe, mā kou hoʻohanohano ʻoe.*"

"We honor you, gentle and sweet Tapakiki."

"Tapakiki, *wahine o* Papaii, *kupuna o* Pocomea, *kupuna o* Mikalu, *aikane a* Rochelle."

Mika whispered, "He say she *my* grandmother, too, and call you friend."

Papaii fell quiet, then reached down and touched Tapakiki's cheek through the tightly wound *tapa*. Poco repeated the gesture, as did Mikalu, all three misty eyed.

Then Poco lifted his shovel.

"Wait," Rochelle whispered. She hurried forward and touched Tapakiki's cheek the same way, then stepped back. All three seemed very pleased with the gesture, Papaii reaching around her shoulders to gather her in for a brief hug.

As the boys carefully covered their grandmother, Rochelle experienced a profound sense of serenity, the opposite of what she expected from having to suffer through another funeral; and she thought it might stem from knowing Tapakiki had died in old age, not cut down too young by tragic violence, and the people who knew and loved her had conducted the service themselves in lieu of letting death's practitioners orchestrate some generic performance, and the box and the vault and the crypt had been discarded in favor of returning the body to her ancestors' sacred earth, and Papaii and Pocomea and even Mikalu would find solace in knowing they had honored her in life and beyond . . . and nobody, especially not Rochelle, deserved any blame.

When they smoothed the sand and stepped back, Papaii removed a box from his satchel, opening it to reveal a hand-crafted bird's nest woven from what looked like jet-black fiberglass.

"Pele's Hair," Mika whispered to Rochelle, "—lava that hardens into fine strings."

Careful to avoid cutting his hands, Papaii gently transferred it to the shelf. "My Tapakiki, she already holds our son close," Papaii said, and Rochelle thought of the obsidian egg he'd placed in her hand. "She leaves two grandsons behind." He placed a pair of smaller eggs in the nest, one black . . . and one yellow. "Watch over them," he whispered.

And Mikalu began to cry, Poco's lower lip trembling for a moment before his own tears broke free.

Despite knowing it wasn't her place to speak, Rochelle couldn't help herself. "She left you, too, Papaii."

The old man smiled as if reassuring a small child. "No, she waits for me." With that, he chanted one last time, then began to gather their things. The boys hastened to help, Rochelle holding the flashlight. As they turned to leave, she looked again, shining her light along the wall, pausing at the next empty slot opposite two old shovels, all waiting for another generation of Wai-Nuikais to join the fathers.

They set out into the darkness, using their lights only intermittently to avoid detection from wayward helicopters.

"What is *aikane?*" Rochelle asked Poco, as he helped her down a drop-off. "Isn't that when Papaii called me a friend?"

"That mean *close* friend."

She liked that very much. "So to say *my close friends* you say *ku'o aikanes?*"

"No, you not put *s* on end; you say more than one by putting *nā* before. *Nā aikane.*"

Mika climbed down behind them, adding, "When you say *my* and mean *always*, say *ku'u*, not *ku'o*. To say *my close friends*, not just now, but always, you say *ku'u nā aikane.*"

She pondered this during the long, exhausting trek back. Eventually, her jet-lagged body caught its second wind as sunrise teased the distant sky, so she hurried ahead to have time for a waterfall shower before the guys could catch up. She washed quickly, then wrapped herself in a towel and rolled her grimy clothes into a ball, calling the all-clear before heading toward the house. She closed the door to her room—to Mika's room—and doffed the towel, standing naked in the window breeze as she brushed her long tresses. The *amakihi* bird arrived at his customary perch to deliver the morning news, studying her curiously until she felt very immodest. Dressing quickly, she greeted the arriving guys and helped Mika prepare one of his sumptuous breakfasts. The bird joined them, chittering from a branch beside the *lanai*.

"*Amakihi*, he say Pele, she is pleased," Papaii pronounced, pouring some juice and passing the fruit. "Tapakiki, she always honor Pele's home, and now Pele will honor Tapakiki's bones." He smiled, then chirped back at his friend. Poco and Mika smiled, too, both surprisingly happy for the day of a loved one's funeral.

After a leisurely meal, Rochelle helped Mika carry perishables up to the spring cave, a quiet stroll without words, exhausted bodies floating in the slipstream of shared accomplishment.

They returned to find the funeral staff already inside. The catafalque stood away from the wall, positioned close to the door. The director knelt behind it, looked puzzled, then found the tool lying over by the wall. He retrieved it, staring very pointedly at Rochelle as he spoke. "Papaii, would you like to pay your respects one last time?"

"No. Tapakiki, she already have all my respect."

"I must open again to check for a proper seal," he said, watching Rochelle.

Pressured by his gaze, she breathed, "You already sealed it."

"One never knows what to expect in these secluded valleys of Pele's domain. It is best to be sure." He inserted the tool and began turning it.

Rochelle looked to Papaii, trying not to show the same panic already written on Mika's and Poco's faces.

The director walked around to the front, set the spray of flowers to the side, and studied the group arrayed behind the casket, his eyes stopping at Rochelle.

Papaii calmly told him, "You must honor Tapakiki."

He hesitated. The last-ditch effort seemed to pay off . . . but then he opened it and glanced inside. Holding the lid up, he looked from face to face, then fixed his stare on Rochelle again. Her mind spun with explanations, pleas, briberies, excuses—

"Yes," he said, "I must honor Tapakiki." His eyes never leaving Rochelle, he asked, "Papaii, have you honored Tapakiki?"

"Yes."

"Yes," Poco and Mika repeated quietly.

"Yes," Rochelle said, a catch in her voice.

He closed the casket, then sealed it and slid the tool into his jacket pocket. He and his assistants pushed the wheeled catafalque out onto the stone walkway in front, stopping just short of the sand. Rochelle retrieved the spray of flowers just as the director came back inside for it, both alone together for a moment.

"The old traditions," he said to her, "they are not your way."

"My way is to respect the people I care about," she said, his face registering a hint of surprise.

"Did you know Tapakiki?"

She glanced through the door, watching two boys and a gimpy-legged old man arrange themselves around the casket, Tapakiki's family preparing to help carry hidden bags of sand to a waiting hearse.

And she remembered an empty slot in the obsidian wall of a secret tunnel.

And she understood two small eggs protected by a nest of Pele's Hair.

"No, but I know Papaii and Pocomea and Mikalu . . . *Ku'u nā aikane.*"

*   *   *

Back to Coulée Makai after the funeral, Rochelle helped Pocomea sort through his clothes, packing for the trip to Hilo and on to Honolulu.

"I not worry," assured the big twelve-year-old without conviction, stuffing his duffel bag.

"Whatever you learn, it's the first step toward getting well," she said. He considered her words, then nodded, and she knew he believed her. She reached out and touched his cheeks, making him smile and blink several times.

Hearing her father and Lalani return from making cellphone calls across the valley, she met them in the front room, her eyes drawn to the open space where Tapakiki had lain surrounded by so many flowers.

"We have decided," her father said, "to be married on Oahu tonight. We cannot be sure Pocomea's tests will conclude before Saturday."

"Congratulations!" she said, not sure how else to react. She hugged Lalani, then her father.

"You may accompany us, if you wish," he said.

"But it's your honeymoon, and you'll be busy with Poco at the hospital."

"This is true," he admitted.

Lalani suggested, "You are welcome to stay here. We can arrange a limousine to the airport if we do not return before Sunday."

"Couldn't I just go home now?"

"I spoke with Mrs. Madison," her father admitted. "She says Mindy would love to have you, that they are planning an excursion to someplace called Greenfield Village. If that is your wish."

"Yes, that sounds like a lot of fun."

"Then you must pack now; we leave within the hour."

She heard a gasp, then turned to see Mikalu standing just outside the screen, a new *lei* in his hands.

"Mika—"

He turned and fled, so she took off after him. This time she would tell him good-bye; they had shared too much for him to run off and pout.

"Mikalu!" she shouted, falling behind the incongruous image of a boy in formal suit hurrying up the lagoon trail. Luckily she wore flats, but she'd clearly not dressed for this nonsense.

"Mikalu!" she called again, panting her way up to where he stood on the outcropping, his back to her, looking across the sea. "Why do you always run away?!"

"You run away more than me! Why *you* all d'time run back to Chicago?!" he demanded, refusing to turn and face her.

Miffed by his words, she explained, "That's where I *live*. I came to see my father, but now he has to go."

"Yes, I also have father with no time for me."

"You don't know my father," she accused, "and you don't know what yours is planning, either."

"My father, I know how he talk story. Papaii, he tell me what Lalani hears. He can't keep secrets no more than me."

"Then you should understand. Someday, *you'll* be running off to San Diego."

He shook his head, one fist clenched at his side, the other still clutching the *lei*. "All fathers d'same, 'cept some make promises, others keep mouth shut, face hidden, but they all d'time busy, all d'time have too many fish to catch."

"But what if yours quits his fishing job?"

He turned enough to roll his eyes at her. "I not talk about *fish*, Rochelle."

She sighed, noticing he pretended to look away but still watched her out the corner of his eye. "I just wanna go home," she said weakly.

"Just like maybe I go see Chicago someday, but I not belong there," he admitted, "so I come back to Coulée Makai."

And she looked at the boy standing there in the bright afternoon sunlight, his suit rumpled, collar damp, carefully combed hair already a wild tangle being teased by ocean breeze to resume its natural state; and she knew he would never live in some fenced-off suburban bungalow, waiting for his father to come home every night to help with homework and plan scout outings and tease him about all the girls who call. She noticed the slump of his shoulders, the protective way he still held the *lei*. "It's beautiful," she said, his eyes following hers to the delicate assemblage of flowers and fronds.

"I make it for you, celebrate rest of week, see more valley, show you underwater in d'lagoon."

"I do appreciate it," she said, reaching out.

He surprised her by pulling it away. "Now you cannot wear, must throw on d'water."

"Why?"

"Ancient custom. Those Hawaiians go all *pupule*, believe all *da kine* silly things," he mocked.

"What's it mean?"

"When you leave, you give *lei* to the d'ocean. If she keep it, that mean you not belong here, never come back."

"*Fine*," she pronounced, angry over the obvious rebuff. She snatched it from his hand and hurled it off the cliff, then felt embarrassed by her outburst. He turned his back to her and watched.

The current pulled it close to the mouth of the cove; then a wave lifted it, the backwash pulling it farther out. Another wave repeated the condemnation, dragging it almost beyond sight. A third wave made it disappear completely, halfway to the mainland for all she could tell.

"Good-bye, Rochelle," he whispered, his voice breaking.

"Mika—"

He darted around the point and clambered up rocks toward the summit where Poco liked to leave *ohelo* for Pele.

She rubbed her eyes and shook her head. "Bye, Mikalu," she whispered into the ocean's roar.

She headed back down to the house and quickly packed her things. At least she'd said bye this time, but it still didn't feel right, maybe because he'd not stuck around long enough to hear it. With more time, she would've changed clothes and climbed that darn cliff just to make him sit still and listen.

Poco tried to carry everyone's bags, but Ramo insisted on sharing the load. Rochelle and Lalani hugged Papaii, Poco blushing when the old man tousled his hair, and they set out toward the footbridge.

Then she spotted him—Mikalu, his shoes and socks on the rocks fringing the cove, his pantlegs rolled up so he could stand in the surf and gaze out between the cliffs toward open sea. She had him trapped, and she would make him hear the words after all. Promising to catch up in a minute, she veered off and worked her way around to the beach, slipping up behind him, then backing away from surf washing across the sand.

"Good-bye, Mikalu!" she called over the crash of waves battering the lower ridge. "Did you hear me?"

He said nothing, standing there vigilant.

"I said, *Good-bye, Mikalu!*"

He pulled his pants up higher, then waded through a rolling breaker and reached out, his tie dangling in the water. He retrieved something, lifting it high toward the cerulean sky . . .

The *lei* she'd hurled into the sea.

Triumphant, his eyes sparkling, he waved to Rochelle and shouted, "She give *lei* back, say valley rather keep *you!*"

CHILD OF THE LAND

Rochelle at 21

"Funeral-man, he not bring Papaii till after two, visitation at three," Mikalu said, parking his beat-up SUV alongside a pair of vans just inside the open slot. "These kids, they stay only for the morning, don't come again till another month."

"Still," Rochelle said, "he could've canceled just this once—considering the circumstances."

"Not Poco," he said, stepping out. "Not Poco's *nā keiki*."

"What's so special—?"

"You'll see," he said, taking her hand as she slid across to exit the driver's side, his grip both powerful and tender. His frizzy blond mop hadn't changed, but he sure had grown up. Buff without looking muscle-bound, he carried himself with a casual confidence she found refreshing after the posturing arrogance of so many young men at MIT.

And Coulée Makai sprawled before her, the patchwork hues more vivid than she remembered.

"Come," Mika said, leading her down toward the beach where she discovered Pocomea, towering above nearly a dozen children, pushing one of several empty wheelchairs across the sparkling obsidian sand. The big man looked up and waved, grinning broadly, then turned his attention back to a young Hawaiian woman lifting a small girl into the seat. An older Asian woman pushed a second chair into position and held it firmly while a boy with muscular arms pulled himself up, a maneuver of practiced skill and dignified grace. Twin dark-skinned girls crouched beside a water-filled tub, their faces suggesting Down's or maybe fetal alcohol syndrome, their attention unwavering as they followed the exploits of some briefly sequestered critter no doubt anxious to return to his home in the sea. Several boys, one on crutches, chased crabs with abandon; while a hairless blind girl methodically dug a hole with her plastic shovel, undistracted in her determination to reach China before noon. The smallest child, a Hawaiian boy barely old enough for school, paused from gathering a hodgepodge of strewn toys, waving his arms toward Mikalu. Rochelle realized he was speaking in sign, her rudimentary and unpracticed knowledge of the silent language barely sufficient to glean the lad's admonishment that Mika had already missed too much of the fun.

Then she spotted two rafts floating way out near the cliffs, right over the shallower section of coral reef. A native boy with snorkel and fins was treading water between them, holding them fast against the gentle waves. Each raft supported a smaller boy resting face down: one whose legs ended at the knees, the other with an arm encased in some kind of brace. Both wore life-jackets and looked quite comfortable as they peered through openings into the water, their heads supported by the padded face-rings found on tables used for chiropractic or massage.

"They work," she breathed, surprised by the rush of satisfaction from seeing her crude designs brought to fruition.

The snorkeling boy raised his head and glanced toward the beach, then signaled the diver's *okay* by bringing his hands together to form a circle in the air. The older woman motioned to come in, so he turned the rafts and propelled them toward land, one passenger kicking with finned feet while the other stroked with his arms.

"What did you use for view-ports?" Rochelle asked Mikalu as they stepped from crunchy lava rock down onto the satiny smooth sand.

"Plastic terrarium covers," he answered, smiling with pride. He led her to a smaller version of the same device parked above the tide line. Under the head support, waterproofed around the edges with aquarium sealant, he'd affixed a transparent hemisphere approximately eighteen inches across, an ersatz diver's helmet allowing perfect views into the depths, a personalized version of the glass-bottom boat.

Poco and the two women waded in to intercept their itinerant deep-sea adventurers, the big man pulling one raft, the other hoisted and carried by—

"Dabu?!" Rochelle exclaimed.

He beamed, then carefully laid the device beside the others, doffed his gear, and hurried to greet her.

Hello, D! she signed, much to his surprise.

Welcome home, R! he returned, the reference to home no doubt in conspiracy with Mikalu. *Now you stay always.*

Not for M and P—but maybe for you, she teased, sweeping him into a hug that made him blush and grin even more. Still very much a boy, his dark hair now shoulder-length, he nevertheless showed hints of burgeoning adolescence, his skinny torso already widening at the shoulders, the playful innocence of his face contrasted by a gently penetrating gaze, those dark eyes offering a glimpse of the young man just beginning to ponder his own place in the grown-up world.

Pretty clothes! he signed, way too impressed by the everyday piqué polo shirt and pleated twills she'd thrown on for the flight. Mika's new jeans and denim shirt looked nicer.

Pretty lady, too, Mika told him, both exchanging diver's *okay* hand-signals and wagging their eyebrows in a way that reminded her of horny-toad Todd. Somebody needed to hose them down.

Poco and the younger woman headed their way, so Dabu quickly signed from an angle his older friend couldn't see. *Make sure P go to hospital. We worry about him.*

"Hospital?" she whispered to Mikalu.

He grimaced and looked away. Suddenly her chest hurt, and the powerful *keiki* protector lumbering toward her somehow appeared very fragile, the challenges faced by these children too great even for his big heart, the invincibility of a caring man belying the truth that even he might once again need help.

Poco grabbed Dabu around the chest and pulled him close, threatening a noogie; then he stopped playing and gazed upon Rochelle, letting the boy wiggle free. "*Aloha*," he said tenderly, and for a heartbeat the valley held its breath.

"Pocomea," she said, and Poco smiled, and Coulée Makai sighed, a Hawaiian *nēnē* goose trumpeting its welcome as it descended toward the ribbon of stream.

"My friend Ginny," he said, also signing the words for Dabu. "She one big-time lawyer lady, also super volunteer at Dalla's *keiki* center. Dalla, she is best *keiki* director ever." He gestured toward the Asian woman, who paused to smile and wave before helping a boy into his chair. "And here is Rochelle, only MIT engineer in my *'ohana*. I call her Haole-girl, but not when standing too close 'cause she might go all *pupule* when I say that." He chuckled.

"I am very happy to meet the sister Poco teases so fondly," Ginny said with a slight bow, her exquisite oval face radiating a quiet serenity very different from the calculating ferocity of Ramo's attorney cohorts. "I am still preparing for the bar examination," she admitted, rolling her eyes toward

Poco, "but he would have me campaign for the position of attorney general." Her gaze lingered on him just long enough to reveal unmistakable affection.

"And I am just graduating this week," Rochelle admitted, faltering over how to sign the words—Dabu just patted her arm and smiled—"but Poco thinks I'm ready to design a utility grid that converts this whole island to solar energy."

"Your improvements to this valley *are* quite remarkable," Ginny pointed out. "Poco's dreams, maybe they are not so unrealistic after all."

"Come," Mikalu urged, "we will show her."

They gathered the children and gear, one boy hurrying ahead as the group worked its way up toward the ancient chiefs' houses, now blended completely into the terrain, overgrown with flowering vines and brush. Not until she stood before them could Rochelle see the conversion to fully equipped dive shop with changing rooms and showers. Poco and Ginny took gear to the dive racks while Dabu stored the rafts, shadowed and helped by the small deaf boy. The group split up and headed toward their respective locker rooms. Forgetting one boy had rushed ahead, Mikalu pulled Rochelle inside the men's to show off how he'd built her designs for solar-heated showers using water piped from the valley's highlands. The youngster squawked and executed the world's fastest towel grab. Mika apologized amid raucous giggles, quickly ushering Rochelle back out. Both exchanged knowing smiles, a shared memory only the two of them would understand.

By the time everybody made their way to the vans, Rochelle and Ginny had become fast friends. "My son was born without hearing," Ginny confided quietly, nodding toward the child tagging along with Dabu. "These field trips with Poco and Mikalu—they are, well . . ." A catch in her voice, words unable to convey how much she loved watching her son play, she searched Rochelle's face for understanding.

"Yes, I've *seen* what they mean," she answered, reaching out to squeeze Ginny's hands. They both turned and gazed across the valley, the place that used to feel like a trap now a vista of accessible wonder despite prosthetics and crutches and wheeled chairs, the voiceless community of a coral reef whispering to curious deaf boys learning new ways to listen, the mysteries of powdery lava dust promising secret subterranean realms to young explorers equipped with colorful shovels and pails.

"Please," Ginny whispered so Poco wouldn't hear, "be sure he goes to hospital. Mikalu scheduled no dive groups next week, no excuses for Poco to postpone. Poco promised, but sometimes he is very hard-headed."

"*Sometimes?*"

Ginny smiled, but not enough to erase the concern in her eyes. "You are right; he is *always* hard-headed, but . . ."

They watched as Pocomea gingerly hugged each of the children amid a chorus of "Bye, Poco! Bye, Poco!" led by one tiny conductor signing the same sentiment from his silent world.

"I will," Rochelle promised, suddenly realizing Mikalu must have sworn not to reveal the obvious return of Poco's back and shoulder problems, relying instead on her to notice, and for people like Dabu and Ginny to express their concern.

As the vans pulled away, Dabu helped Mika unload her bags from the SUV, both heading toward the house so she and Poco could be alone for a moment. Her adoptive brother had grown at least a foot taller than she, three times her weight, a giant bronze teddy bear with his trademark thatch of ink-black hair pointing every direction, tent-sized overshirt and drawstring pants barely covering his sumotori girth.

"Thank you for coming," he said, that tenderness in his voice touching her deeply.

"Oh, Poco, I'm sorry about Papaii." She stepped closer and let him gather her in for a hug, but she felt him wince at the effort of putting his arms around her.

"I tell Mika one big lie," he admitted, looking away, embarrassed. "I not really too big for lava tube, unless new lava cover top by now—it comes real close, by and by these days. Pele, sometimes she likes moving all d'furniture in her house."

"You know I'll help," she said, "but please don't hide that you're sick again, not when so many need you, Mikalu and your little friend Dabu and all those children . . . and Ginny."

Poco tried to conceal a sheepish smile by rubbing his nose, but his misty deep-set eyes betrayed him, lighting up at the mention of her name. "I promise, Haole-girl. Hospital, all is on schedule for next week."

She gazed into those eyes and found honor in his promise, and she believed him. "Okay," she whispered.

As they strolled toward the house, Poco asked, "So where is Haole-girl gonna live?—now that she one big engineer lady."

"I'm moving to Chicago, and I'm going to work with a wheelchair company," she added, surprised at herself, the image of children exploring a world normally beyond their reach still resonating in her mind. Every minute those boys enjoyed watching the reef had proven worth the two days she'd spent on those designs. "I could stay longer and go with you to Honolulu. Mikalu and I—"

"No," he said firmly. "No, please. I appreciate that way much, but this not easy to me, and I want to go by myself. Mika, he already make me all *pupule* trying to help."

She could imagine.

"Hey, I know," he said. "You take Mika, let him visit Chicago and help you move. Just a few days?"

"Well, sure, I guess. Yes! Okay."

"Good. That way I make sure he not show up at hospital. The ocean, she is too big, take Mikalu too long to swim from mainland. I finish my tests before he gets halfway." He smiled, the soft-spoken nineteen-year-old trying to put a whimsical face on what must scare him very much.

They stopped and stood quietly where the trail passed the beach, the sun on their faces, skittish crabs scattering this way and that. She noticed the only remaining evidence that a group of children had briefly staked claim to this sovereign territory: the small hole dug by the hairless blind girl, now slowly filling with seeping water.

Poco studied it a moment, then gazed wistfully across the lagoon toward open sea. "They are very generous," he said.

Rochelle listened to the crashing waves, watching how they broke across the coral reefs and floated up toward their feet, a series of diminishing ripples licking the lip of powdery black lava dust. A liquid tongue probed the edge of the small hole, washing away a crooked finger's worth of sand to form a small rivulet connecting this tiniest of man-made lakes to the great ocean beyond.

"Who's generous?" she wondered.

"Pele and her sisters. They trust us to share their home," he said quietly, "even give us this place to play."

"It's a wonderful playground," Rochelle agreed, more taken by the image of Poco's unabashed rapture than by the scenery he'd cherished all his life.

Then he glanced at where the hole had disappeared, now smoothed by successive riffles polishing the beach's satiny sheen. "And when our time is all gone," he added sadly, "they take it back."

*   *   *

Lava debris crunched beneath their feet, rising mist in shades of charcoal and ash swirling around them as they trudged through darkness. A massive thunderhead loomed above, rearing itself high into the night sky, puffing its chest and devouring stars like so many fireflies. The beast growled a summons to the fire goddess, grinding its teeth until crooked sparks flashed warning at the defiant volcanic dome, Pele's stronghold repelling another raging monster's advance. Suddenly Poco's flashlight beam cut a swath through the air, its tongue licking a trail of rock-candy sparkles across the obsidian rise, searching for the best footing lest they slip and fall.

"I can see better—*without* the light—blinding me," Rochelle huffed, reminded of their grim task, her mythic fantasy shattered.

"I take over now," Poco insisted, moving to wrest control of her end of the pallet.

"Not till the top—of this last ridge," she insisted, brooking no argument even as she struggled to hide her exhaustion. Mikalu had carried the other end—plus a satchel—without complaint since leaving Coulée Makai. Poco had tried, refusing to let Rochelle take a turn until he slowly succumbed to the excruciating pain of his shoulders and neck, actually dropping Papaii twice. She'd played the respect-for-grandfather card until he relented.

He clicked off the light, then stumbled and leaned against some rocks, pretending to adjust the scuba-dagger scabbard strapped to his calf. Mika wore his knife, too, at Poco's insistence, though his friend had refused to explain why. Poco's anger and frustration had gradually given way to uncharacteristic skittishness; eerie shadows and spooky sounds made him start, and he kept glancing back as if somebody might be stalking them. Rochelle tried to reassure him, but that failed miserably, making him angry again, ultimately leaving them both embarrassed.

They crested the final ridge, and Rochelle gasped at the unexpected sight. A photo-negative image sprawled before her, the colors reversed to paint a macabre landscape with a glowing orange stream snaking through ebony meadow, trees transformed to specters of volcanic columns, foliage caramelized in death throes. Tephra dust stung her eyes while sulfur fumes assaulted her with a rotten-egg stench.

Having earned his chance, Poco nudged Rochelle aside, easing the pallet from her grip, then yelped, staggering backwards and falling hard. He started to slide.

"Poco!" Mika shouted.

Rochelle reached to grab his collar, bracing her legs between rocks for leverage.

Mika dropped Papaii and lunged to grab her, to keep her from slipping.

Small stones rained inexplicably from the ridge up to their left.

Poco tried to hold on to a rock, but his arms failed him.

Mika wriggled his leg over the big man, wedged himself into an outcropping, fumbled with his flashlight.

A dark streak rushed toward them from the left, stones scattering in its wake, a phantom swooping in for the kill.

Poco clawed at his knife, got it free, swung the blade toward his attacker—but missed as a blur dressed all in black leapt over him and levered itself against his legs.

Mika's light exploded with brilliance, the beam swinging around to find—

"Dabu!" Rochelle blurted.

Panting from exhaustion, Poco lay back and grunted, "Taoke boy!"

Dabu squinted against the glare, looking very scared, his dust-smeared lips twitching in rhythm with a wordless guttural drone from deep inside his throat. Rochelle and Mikalu tried to help Poco up, but Dabu wouldn't let go. Rochelle had to take the boy's arm and get his attention, nodding assurance to break the spell.

It took some struggling, but Poco finally stood leaning against a rock, shrugging off any further assistance. *Go home!* he signed to Dabu, wincing with pain from moving his arms. Still, he managed to jab the air with his knife, pointing back the way they'd come.

Dabu shook his head. Gesturing toward Papaii, he signed, *I help you take him to—* something Rochelle couldn't understand.

Whispering unnecessarily, Mika asked, "He know about lava tube?"

"How you know?" Poco demanded, wincing again when he tried to sign the words. Mikalu filled in, acting as Poco's interpreting arms.

Dabu stepped back, but didn't answer.

"You talk, Taoke boy!" Poco demanded, Mikalu too shocked by his friend's behavior to translate.

Dabu understood well enough. He stood there like a child afraid to confess.

Poco took a menacing step forward.

His lip trembling, Dabu lowered his head but stood his ground. *I watch you time before*, he signed timidly, *come back later, find—* that gesture again, apparently his way of saying *lava tube*.

"Taoke sneak!" Poco pronounced.

"Poco!" Mikalu chastised. "Dabu your friend, brah—always tag along, ever since real little *keiki*." Turning to Dabu, he signed, *Still secret?*

Dabu nodded vigorously. *Your secret, my secret.*

"Go!" Poco ordered, pointing again.

Dabu scooted around him and grabbed one end of the pallet, obstinate. "Go!"

Rochelle butted in. "Poco, let him help. He knows already."

"No Taoke boys!" Poco raised himself high over the youngster and puffed out his chest, grinding his teeth until Rochelle expected to see sparks fly out his mouth.

Dabu's eyes welled with tears, but he stood firm under the onslaught, squaring his shoulders, defiant against the storm.

Rochelle picked up the other end, Mikalu stepping in front of Poco and shining his light toward the ground. "You no can walk, can you?" Mika asked him. "We leave you here."

"I can walk," Poco pronounced, proving it by heading down the trail, Mika staying close to grab him should the big man slip again. Rochelle couldn't help but smile; Mikalu knew exactly how to defuse his friend's tantrum, putting him on the defensive, giving him something to prove.

The breeze picked up as they crossed to the first of the solid lava waves, but not enough to clear the stench of thick sulfuric air lying in low pools waiting to be carried off over the mountain. The river of new lava grew brighter as they approached, liquid neon passing within a thousand feet of the tube.

Rochelle hesitated at the concealed entranceway, apprehensive about encroaching molten fire, images of burning bodies crying out in her mind, the fate of being entombed forever with Poco's ancestors a price too big to pay.

Dabu removed a sprig of *ohelo* from his back pocket, a paltry clump mangled nearly beyond recognition. He climbed atop the wave and laid it for Pele. Mikalu handed up a longer vine pulled from the satchel, glancing toward Poco for approval when Dabu placed it beside the other. Poco looked away, maybe angry, probably embarrassed.

She rubbed her eyes, making them sting from the grime. When she looked again, she found Mikalu standing close.

"It is okay," he whispered. "You wait here if you want."

She shook her head. "We've come to honor Papaii," she said, pushing around him to help Dabu spread the blanket.

They took turns sliding into the cavern, then carefully lowered Papaii's pallet into the deep crevice. The sulfuric stench disappeared, cooler air offering relief as they worked their way up through the subterranean tube.

They found the next open space and quickly went to work, Rochelle training the lights while Mikalu and Dabu shoveled. Once they'd removed enough sand, she helped them lift Papaii into place, finding a measure of solace knowing this was where he belonged. Poco remained off to the side, still having said nothing since he ordered Dabu to return home, still avoiding eye contact with the boy. Mikalu waited a moment, then gently covered Papaii with sand, while Dabu stood beside Rochelle, his head bowed.

Laying his shovel aside, Mikalu began to chant, Rochelle mouthing along from what she could remember. Dabu remained silent, but he lifted his head and watched Poco, who finally walked over and looked down where Papaii had been laid to rest. Almost reluctantly, he joined in the chanting, quietly at first, then louder, a single tear glistening on his plump cheek.

Mikalu removed what looked like a hand-carved jewelry box from the satchel and held it out.

Poco took it, then opened it to reveal thousands of exquisite red and amber and blue feathers. "Papaii," he said quietly to no one in particular, "he all d'time make friends with *amakihi* birds. Each time, they always leave him one feather. He collect them many years, ever since little *keiki*. He closed the box and placed it carefully into the open slot above the sand. "Now his friends, they help him fly home again, fly with Tapakiki."

"With Tapakiki," Rochelle breathed.

Mikalu echoed her. "With Tapakiki."

Poco started, realizing Dabu had eased in beside him. Poco looked away, his mien of anger back.

"Dabu, he just like *Poco's* little *amakihi*," Mika said quietly. Rochelle moved to the other side of Dabu, put her arm around the twelve-year-old's shoulders, and stroked his hair.

Poco shook his head. "Dabu, he all d'time be one Taoke boy. *Taoke!*" he repeated, virtually spitting the words.

"So?" Rochelle said. "So what?"

Poco looked at her, his eyes flashing. "Taoke all d'time go make *'aumakua* from Hilo-man, same Hilo-man who come talk to Papaii last week. Hilo-man, he say take money. He say let Poco and Mikalu keep putting scuba divers in lagoon, but let *nā* Taoke come make *kalo kuleana*—big grow farm. Papaii, he say no. He say *nā* Wai-Nuikai, they protect Coulée Makai, keep Pele's sisters happy."

Mikalu added, "Papaii, he get very angry 'bout that man, make Poco all *pupule*."

Dabu stood close to Poco, waiting patiently, nobody bothering to sign for him.

"Wipu and Pubo," Poco continued, his voice a snarl as he spit out the names of Dabu's older brothers, "they come back next day, make hard time for Papaii, only he not tell me till later. Wipu, he tell Papaii that Hilo-man say just wait, that Papaii be gone soon, that he talk to Lalani instead."

"Hilo-man," Mikalu ground out, "he can *burn* in Pele's house."

"Doesn't this guy understand you have ancestral ties to this land?" Rochelle asked.

Mikalu nodded. "Oh yah, he native Hawaiian, born here, live here all his life, but he not deserve to join *nā lapu* here. He knows Papaii one big chief, deserves respect."

Poco said, "Then tonight, we take my *kupuna* from his casket, wrap him in *tapa*, and I start thinking what Hilo-man say, what that means. Hilo-man and *nā* Taoke, they want Papaii dead; then Lalani come make big inheritance, get to say what happens to Coulée Makai, maybe let Hilo-man have deal."

Dabu watched him, his confusion obvious.

"Next day, Papaii fall, break head, same place he walk all his life."

Rochelle gasped. "Poco, what are you—?"

"Taoke boys come back, that's what I think—push Papaii down, come murder my grandfather."

Haʻulelau ʻAʻala, Ka Opio a ka Punawai

Sweet Autumn, Vernal Youth

Rochelle at 15

Shimmering sunlight rippled across a massive submerged brain, while purple oriental fans swayed in the gentle liquid surge and upside-down hula skirts concealed skittish trumpeters watching with wary eyes. Still gaining confidence in the dependability of scuba air, Rochelle practiced floating face-down on the surface, a tangle of BC straps and hoses, heavy tank on her back, watching Mikalu some twenty feet below. The wiry fourteen-year-old and his crest of wheat-colored sea-hair flowed between the coral heads, wending among razor-sharp antlers of elk and stag, a school of amber-striped jacks dodging his intrusions with swirling synchronicity.

A monstrously fat fish with big eyes and bigger lips kept sidling up beside young Rochelle, a friendly-looking feller no doubt trying to steal a kiss. She would shoo him away, and he would slink off with feelings hurt, only to return minutes later like a puppy-dog wagging his tail, confident that persistence would earn the friendship of this awkward newcomer with the shiny face.

Every glance revealed exotic new life: rocks waking suddenly to swim off into the deep, their cover blown by some meddlesome sneak; shrimps of crystalline glass materializing as the light tickled them just so, beady eyes and icky guts darting here and there in search of invisible meals; vividly hued tendrils sucking themselves into hidden tubes, shaking their fists at every challenge to the sovereignty of their submarine fiefs; exquisite shells exploring at snail's pace while impostors simply shimmied by on spindly crabs' legs . . . and fish!—more than Shedd Aquarium's biggest tank!

Wagging his finger under a ledge, Mikalu charmed a fearsome mottled eel, the razor-fanged denizen emerging curiously. Then Mika swam to a yard-high orange tube sponge, removed a small vial from his BC pocket, and released a fingering cloud near its porous skin. A puff of smoke! The filtering membrane had a quick taste before billowing the residue out its chimney stack.

Mikalu surfaced and suggested she try venting enough air to descend a dozen feet.

"You're *sure* I won't get the bends?" she worried for the umpteenth time.

"First dive, real shallow, no nitrogen in blood—nothing to get bent," he assured her. "We keep dive tables later when you go deeper, dive two or more times each day. You're ready for this; you clear mask real good, know how to equalize pressure in ears. I help you adjust for neutral buoyancy; then you feel like floating in sky."

"Yeah," she scoffed, "—without a parachute."

"Just back-up from one good dive buddy. Okay, *great* dive buddy," he corrected with a smile.

"You get me drowned, and I'll haunt you for the rest of your life."

"I burn *papala* for you, keep eyes peeled," he teased.

She gave him one of her patented Rochelle looks, then adjusted her mask, tested the regulator again, and tried not to panic as he released the air from her BC, making her sink toward the reef. She had to pinch her nose and blow to relieve the pressure, feeling herself slow to a hover as Mika spritzed air back into her vest. And she did float!—weightless, neither up nor down, suspended in liquid sky.

They exchanged *okay* hand-signs; then he led her on the grand tour, showing off exotic creatures she'd never have noticed without his trained eye. Soon she relaxed somewhat and let the surge carry her along, though she still tended to wave her arms too much. She admired how Mika maneuvered, the merest of subtle fin gestures sufficient to propel him with pinpoint accuracy. Sometimes he would tug gently at her vest, guiding her between obstacles, keeping her safe as she practiced the moves of a fledgling Rochelle-fish.

Then he led her through a crevice that dropped suddenly into bottomless blue. She panicked and swam back to hover above the ledge, finding irrational reassurance in having a place to land in case she suddenly fell. Sensing her anxiety, he motioned for her to wait beside an opening revealing a lower coral chamber, its floor dusted with lava sand and crushed shells. He pointed to himself and gestured over the edge of the wall, then into the hole with an upward motion. He tapped his watch and counted off ten seconds, followed by a questioning *okay* sign, wanting to confirm she felt safe. She nodded, then remembered to return the *okay*. He smiled around his regulator, then flipped upside down to watch her as he flowed down through the crack and disappeared into the abyss. She counted seconds in her head, delighted when he shot up through the hole right on time, presenting her with a beautiful cowry shell the size of her fist. She slipped it into her vest pocket, but Mika shook his head no, pointing at her eyes and the shell, then patting his heart and gesturing back into the hole. She understood: *Admire it, then leave it where it belongs.*

The air running low, they retraced their route toward the beach, the coral heads gradually ceding to the smooth obsidian sand, their big-lipped escort fish satisfied he'd conducted them safely home. Rochelle waved bye to the friendly guide, so Mikalu did, too, silly as it seemed . . . but she'd swear the goofy-looking fish paused and waved a fin, mouthing a silent "See ya!" before disappearing into the deep.

They doffed their gear just above the beach, rinsing everything in the cool stream before laying it in the shade of a *lobelia* bush. While Mikalu carried the tanks to a giant tricycle outfitted to hold eight of the silver torpedoes, Rochelle slipped behind the shrubs, peeled off her swimsuit, splashed fresh water on herself, then toweled off and slipped into shorts, t-shirt, and sandals. She walked out by the bike to wait while Mikalu rinsed and changed, and she caught herself wondering what he might look like standing there *au naturel*, cool water sparkling in the sunlight as it trickled down his body . . . but then she felt embarrassed, yet somehow, well . . .

"Gotta hurry," he said, jogging toward her. "Don't wanna miss Cho."

As they wheeled the tank-laden bike up toward the open slot into Taoke Valley, she looked back at the mosaic lagoon, the blotches of lurking coral reefs now lending new perspective to the familiar scene. "I can't believe such a place is, you know, right there. I mean, it's just—*right there.*"

Smiling, Mika said, "And Rochelle, today *you* belong there, too."

"Do boats ever come up into the cove?"

"Oh no. The coral, it is right below d'surface out there. Whole mouth closed off, 'cept for narrow slots where nutrients, they wash in, and silt, it wash back. Fishes, they come and go, but d'boats, they got no way in or out, 'cept over beach, and this is private land, deeded to Papaii."

"But you said when Poco steps off that cliff, he just *floats* in through the opening and up to the beach."

"D'ocean, she picks him up on top of wave, carries him over d'reef. Poco, he used to give me chicken skin, make me think he get all scraped; but no, never even one scratch. D'ocean, she lets him know he belongs here, thanks him for taking care of Pele's sisters' homes."

"You sound like you're starting to believe all that stuff."

He studied her for a moment, never breaking his stride, finally admitting, "Not exactly, but that not matter. These myths, they are just another way of looking at d'real world."

They walked in silence while she considered his words. "I'm worried about Poco," she said.

"Me, too."

"You think he's telling the truth, that he's still in remission? I mean, did you ask Lalani if this is just another six-month follow-up?" Hoping to see Poco again this trip, she'd been held up in L.A. with her father, arriving on the island too late to catch her adoptive brother before Lalani took the big thirteen-year-old for tests in Honolulu.

"I believe him. Poco, he'll be okay, by and by, go diving again in no time," Mikalu predicted, probably sensing her melancholy. "He got lots more reef to see."

"So how did you guys get certified?"

"Me and Poco, we use money earned from Monterey group, take classes in Hilo, buy all this gear."

"I'm surprised you even let outsiders dive here."

"Only 'cause they're big-time marine biologists. They explore lagoon, find three new species, teach me and Poco 'bout taking care of d'reefs. They even find lava tube two-hundred feet down. Me and Poco, next time they come, we go see it, too."

"Won't that be scary?"

"Sure, I get chicken skin, but now I know it's there, have to go see what's inside."

"I don't know," she said as they passed into Taoke Valley, a truck pulling up beside a field, kalo pickers gathering for lunch. "I guess I'm curious, too, but I'd be afraid of getting hurt."

She saw him studying her again, maybe deciding if he should respond. Finally, he said, "Take a chance, look inside; then you know d'truth. Being afraid all d'time, by and by, that's what makes people get hurt."

Sensing he'd spoken of more than hidden recesses buried beneath the sea, she quickly changed the subject, blurting the first thing she could think of. "This is a huge farm."

Looking disappointed, Mikalu followed her gaze up through the valley. "Too big," he said almost wistfully. "Many bad things, they are too big."

"How do they irrigate it all?"

"*Nā* Taoke, they build canals, dynamite rock, pour concrete, rape d'stream." He pointed at a rivulet passing under the bridge they'd just crossed. "This valley got no beach, just cliffs over ocean, used to have most impressive waterfall." She followed his gaze to where the water cut descending stairstep grooves into lava rock before disappearing over the cliff. "Now just one little tinkle, like Dabu going pee in d'ocean."

They walked in silence for a while, his allusion to exploring for the truth still weighing on her mind. The more curious she felt, the more determined she became to let it drop.

They reached a bus-stop on the road to Panalu'u just as a beat-up old van rambled up, an older Japanese man in cut-off jeans and ratty hibiscus-print shirt stepping out. He stroked his long mustache and grinned, a twinkle in his eye as he greeted Rochelle, followed by a knowing glance and wag of the eyebrows to Mikalu, making him blush. They traded the empty tanks for full ones from the van; then with a quick wave out the window, the tank man rolled off into a cloud of dust, and the diving team headed back through Taoke Valley.

Rochelle asked more about the irrigation design, questions Mikalu couldn't answer, so just before they reached the open slot, he parked the bike and led her up a trail traversing the inside ridge. He found a good vantage point where she could study the intrusive series of sluices and reservoirs cut into the valley floor, a patchwork of kalo fields rising in tiers more than halfway up the highlands. When she'd seen enough to be disappointed by the crude and inefficient design, they returned to the bike and found a pair of older teens blocking their way.

"Haole-boy, Haole-girl, they come make trespass on our land," the bigger one pronounced.

"C'mon, Wipu, you know we not hurt Taoke ridge," Mikalu said politely, his anger barely concealed.

"Pubo, he say you do." The smaller one, not much older than Mika, looked surprised at his brother's words, but quickly assumed his best menacing glower.

Mikalu stepped toward the bike, but Pubo pushed him back, Wipu moving closer to enforce the blockade.

Mika studied the situation, his fists clenched. "Nā Taoke, you all d'time play games. Whatchoo want?"

"You take bike, leave us tanks, ours now," Wipu said.

Mika glanced at Rochelle, then toward the open slot, a clear signal for her to walk away. Maybe too scared to move, definitely too angry to run, she remained frozen, not sure if speaking up would defuse the situation or exacerbate the macho posturing and hurt Mika's standing in this test of wills.

"No," Mika said. "No, I leave with tanks now, not belong to you."

"Okay, you take tanks," Wipu sneered, again surprising Pubo, "but leave Haole-girl with us." Pubo liked his brother's offer, grinning at Rochelle.

Mika glanced back at her, his face flush, shoulders tense, breaths deeper. He fixed his gaze on Wipu. "You think you one big funny-man, but this not playin'."

Wipu laughed, then eased around like he might move on Rochelle.

Emboldened, Pubo said, "I hear haole pussy, it not even pink—"

Mikalu nailed him, knocking him flat with three fast punches, then whirled on Wipu, who now stood between him and Rochelle, his back to her.

She backed up, knelt down, placed her hand on a softball-sized rock.

Wipu watched Pubo pull himself shakily to one knee, then laughed again and turned to reach for Rochelle.

Mikalu leapt on him, flailing like a madman, but Wipu landed a major punch in Mika's face, a loud thunk as the younger teen sprawled.

Wipu straddled him, grabbed him by the hair and lifted his head for another blow.

"Wipu!" Pubo shouted as Rochelle swung the rock, going for his head but weakening at the last second and slamming it into his shoulder.

He yelped, then whirled and caught her with an open-handed slap, spinning her as she stumbled, her head ringing.

Mika pounced on him again, a man possessed, berserk in the savagery of his blows. Pubo had to help Wipu get him off long enough for both to flee, and still Mika went after them until they reached the first kalo plot and bounded ahead, gaining distance.

Mika hurried back, favoring his left leg, his face bloody, clothes torn, elbow scraped, an uncharacteristic wildness in his eyes. He stopped before her, his breathing ragged, fists clenching and unclenching. "Are you—?"

"I'm okay," she said. "How bad is your leg?"

"I not hurt!" he blurted, his eyes flashing. He charged over to the bike and moved to wheel it back to Coulée Makai, pausing to wait for her without making eye contact.

They walked in silence, and every time she glanced toward him, he looked away. When they reached the stream, he parked the bike and stomped awkwardly up to the small pool, dropping very gingerly to his knees to splash water on his wounds, crimson streaks washing blood into the crystal water. He winced but said nothing, recoiling when she reached to help.

"Mika—"

"I'm sorry, Rochelle," he blurted, shame dripping in his words, his face turned away.

"Sorry? But you protected me! Mikalu, you're my hero."

"Don't make fun with me," he demanded. "I fail. I fail bad, let Pubo say bad things on you, let Wipu hurt you. I fail, Rochelle." He sounded like he might cry, his frustration overwhelming him.

"Come on, Mika, don't feel that way—"

He whirled on her, eyes blazing. "You not know how I feel. Don't say things when you not know!"

Surprised at her own sudden anger, she shouted, "Who do you think you're talking to? I'm the one who can't protect anybody! I let you get hurt!"

"You not understand. You never understand!"

"Mika, you—listen, you can't even begin to fathom how it feels to really fail someone, how it feels—how it—" She felt the tears coming, furious at her loss of control, determined not to show him her pain.

"You not know!" he repeated.

"I do know! I do— Oh God." A smear of blood streaked Mika's face, transforming him to a single vision of undeniable truth, the image of a broken and lifeless body, battered face, unforgiving eyes . . . "I'm the one who let her die," she whispered. She turned away and buried her face in her hands, no way to stem the tears.

And she felt him close, his arms around her.

"It's okay, Rochelle," he soothed. "Please don't cry; it's okay."

And she felt herself dangling over the edge, saw crashing waves begging to dash her against the rocks. "It's too late," she sobbed.

"No," he said. "No, it's not."

"It is too late—I can't—I can't stop it."

"Don't try, Rochelle."

"But it hurts."

"Then just let go."

"It's not that easy. What if— What if . . ."

"Don't worry," he said, holding her tighter. "I not let you fall."

*   *   *

Streamers of crimson and tangerine striped the sky, sunset hues dappling Pacific waters as distant clouds burnished the horizon line to a glowing sheen. The teens sat steeped in sheltering shadows, legs dangling over crashing waves. Rochelle kept her attention fixed on Mikalu, careful to avoid looking over the ledge. Bruised and bandaged, he gingerly smoothed his freshly pressed shirt, then picked at invisible threads on his new jeans.

"My mother," Mikalu said, "she die 'cause of me."

"Mika, you can't blame yourself for being born."

"Can, too. Blame, it not always have to add up, make sense. My father, he blame me, too. One time I ask about her, he get all angry, say she die for me. Then he get all weepy eyes, say I look just like her. He not let me hug him when he go, give me look all mean-like, push me away. That was last time he come. I never see him since."

"That's *his* problem," she said, inadvertently glancing down at the waves. She had to slide back some, her heart racing from the sudden image of Poco nonchalantly stepping off the edge.

"*His* problem? I not see my father four years now. That sounds like *my* problem, too."

"He's letting his grief get in the way of what matters."

"Me, I used to think he all d'time need someone *else* for blame. He leave her home, go off on fishing boat, not take care of wife. But then I think: he need money, have little *keiki* coming, all my fault again."

"But you're older now. You don't still feel that way, do you?"

"Feel? Sometimes, but now I know that's not right. Maybe she not take care of herself, not have money for doctor-man, no pre-natal care. Lalani, she say they were poor, no good education, live in bad place; but anybody can see doctor-man, be sure baby and mama both healthy. I want d'truth, so I'll get copy of d'report when I'm eighteen, find out what happen, find out who not make sure she okay."

"It might not be anybody's fault, Mika. You can't anticipate every bad thing in life. Like getting hassled by those Taokes this afternoon—" He tensed, but didn't say anything. "I was too scared to think straight, but you faced a bad situation and did what you had to do."

His hand went to the swollen gash on his brow, now salved with an herb paste and taped over by the ministering hands of Papaii. "I'm sorry I get so angry 'bout that. I too embarrassed, not want you seeing me scared, go all *pupule*."

"You got hurt saving me. I can't think of anything braver." She leaned closer, quietly adding, "Just like your mom risked getting hurt to save *you*. You didn't take her life; she gave you yours, and now you live in a way that honors her."

He looked across the sea, his eyes misting up, a newfound serenity in his face.

She closed her eyes and tried to imagine how he must feel. When she looked again, she caught him watching her with a tenderness not seen since she used to notice her mother gazing from across the room.

Just watching my little girl grow up before my very eyes.

"Thank you, Rochelle. You one good friend. Me, I trust you with *all* my secrets."

"I trust you, too," she said, but that made him look sad. "It's true," she said, puzzled by his disappointment.

He looked toward a pair of sea-birds dive-bombing the purple waters. "Not yet," he said wistfully. "Someday, I hope—but you not ready yet. I wait, first prove I'm your friend."

"But you are. I mean, we're nothing alike, and we live in very different worlds, but I look forward to seeing you, and I know you like it when I visit."

"But your secrets, they not feel safe with me."

"I'm not worried about you blabbing confidential information."

Mikalu rolled his eyes. "I not talking 'bout *locker combinations*, Rochelle."

No, he wasn't, but the words he wanted to hear would conjure her mother's face, the tender gaze forever gone, eyes now lifeless and unforgiving.

"I— I don't talk about that. It's not just you; I don't with anyone. I can't. It's too hard."

"Then tell me 'bout her life; save secrets till you're ready."

She closed her eyes, felt the rising swells of regret, her legs so heavy they threatened to pull her over. She pushed back from the edge, looked again, and reeled from an instant sensation of floating in boundless violet-and-magenta-stained sky; then she saw a tether, Mikalu, waiting patiently. The tension drained from her shoulders, and she tried to lie back, but the rocky ground hurt. Mikalu helped her up, urged her to a flat rock, sat close beside her.

"She lived with her mother, in the south of France, a village called La Réole." She looked toward the ground, so he did, too, scrutiny an uncomfortable stranger among friends. "She never knew her father—he died before she was born—but they managed with her mother's wages from a local distillery, and with the help of an old widow who looked after her during the day. But Grandma wanted Mom to have more opportunities, so they moved to Paris. Mom was very lonesome there; she got teased by kids at school, treated like a backwards country girl. Then Grandma met a wealthy businessman from Chicago who attended meetings where she worked. They fell in love, got married, and he brought Mom to live in the U.S."

My whole life changed, taken halfway around the world, a confusing place where I could never belong.

"How old was she?"

"Just thirteen, but she adapted, learned the language, grew to love Grandpa very much. Then Grandma died suddenly, a problem with her heart."

"Oh no. That is very hard for your mother."

Rochelle nodded. "And Grandpa spent the rest of his life proving how much he loved her, giving her anything she could want, sending her to the best schools, even selling his businesses so he could stay home more. He treated me the same way, setting up my trust fund, taking me places. I think he showed me just about everything you can see in Chicago. He so loved the city."

"Your mother and father, how did they meet?"

"As college students who married after graduation. Then I was born while Dad attended law school."

"He one big businessman now, too—travel a lot."

She huffed. "Don't remind me."

"I'm sorry."

"Oh, Mikalu, it's just an expression. Actually, with so many clients in the Pacific Rim, he *had* to open an office in Hilo. He tried to get my mother to move here, but Grandpa's health was deteriorating by then, so Dad commuted, coming home as often as he could. Grandpa thought she should go with her husband, so I think putting his house in *my* trust fund was his way of saying it's time for her to move on. I mean, he left everything else to Mom, so why not the house? It didn't work, though; she never left."

"Must be one good house."

"Oh, it's wonderful—three storeys, styled like a villa and surrounded by beautiful gardens. It's in an older section called Edgebrook, backing up to the river, very secluded and peaceful, lots of wildlife."

"You and your mom, you took care of big place all by yourselves?"

"Dad hired some servants to live in the guest house. Kala Ko was our housekeeper and cook; her brother Jackie handled maintenance and the grounds. You'd like them; they were from Hawai'i—Oahu, I think—so they talked like you and Poco. They were very sweet, always helping us out."

"Your father, he was away when it happened?"

She took a deep breath. A faint mist rose from the dark water, sienna haze mingling sea and sky. "He was in Honolulu, looking at office space, hoping a bigger city with more to see and do might entice Mom to move. To this day, I think he still doesn't understand why coming would be so hard for her. Sure, she grew to love many things about Chicago, but a part of her never left La Réole, something I didn't realize until she took me there when I was seven. She didn't want to move to some remote island, not to a another confusing and frightening place, to be an outsider among strangers."

"Your mother, she all d'time know where she truly belong."

"Yeah, I guess she did."

They sat there for a minute, listening to the waves. Finally, he asked, "How did it happen?"

"Oh, Mika, I knew you'd try to sneak up on me."

"I not sneak, Rochelle," he said, a hint of indignity in his words. "I try to make easy for you. That's okay; I know you trust me. You not have to answer, not for proving something to me."

Liking that, she felt the pressure lifting. "Don't you already know?" she asked quietly, glancing over to watch his face.

"Lalani, she say you not home when it happen."

She covered her face and shook her head. "I went with Mindy's family to Cedar Point—an amusement park—for the weekend. I should've stayed home 'cause Jackie and Kala were gone on two weeks' vacation, and Mom didn't want to be there by herself."

"You think it happen 'cause you not stay?"

She nodded again, and swallowed hard, her chest hurting now. The breeze paused, evening heat and rising humidity weighing her down, the air eerily still. "She got to where she was drinking too much wine after dinner. Sometimes Kala or I would have to help her to bed. I knew she needed me, but I was tired of being stuck home all the time, and I wanted to go— I wanted—" She shook her head and buried her face, the swells pulling at her, but she couldn't fight them right now, didn't have it in her, didn't care if they swept her away. "I thought she'd be okay. It was just two nights; then I'd be back."

Please don't leave me alone. You're my little girl; I depend on you.

"How did it happen?" he asked, touching her hand.

She stood and crept closer to the edge, looked down at the water, then backed away and closed her eyes, sensing Mikalu standing beside her. "She was on the overlook, a sort of balcony patio that opened off her bedroom on the top floor. It's surrounded by a stone ledge topped with different varieties of clematis vines growing from the rock garden below. She loved those flowers," she said wistfully. "My favorite was Sweet Autumn, the little white blossoms that look like jacks."

"Jacks?"

"The kids' game—you know, little star-shaped thingies; you catch a bouncing ball while picking them up. You have to gather every last one to win."

"These Sweet Autumns, they sound pretty."

"Oh they are, big gobs of them, always floating down to blanket the walkway when I shook the vine. Another kind was Odorata, big lavender blooms with a yellow starburst at the center, and a fragrance like vanilla extract. Mom thought the Mayleens were prettiest of all, with the biggest flowers, a glistening shade of pink that looked like satin. Mom used to say someday she'd stitch 'em together and make us matching Mayleen dresses."

"Your mom, she enjoyed beautiful things."

"Yeah, she used to gather clematis blooms every day, floating 'em in a big crystal bowl she had on the nightstand. But the Mayleens didn't grow as high as the ledge; and when she drank too much, she knew she couldn't get up and down the stairs to pick some from the garden; so I'd go, or sometimes I'd just lean way over the balcony to reach some."

"Oh no. Your mother, she try same way, lose balance?"

She nodded, then took a deep breath and headed back to sit on the flat rock, pulling her knees up and hugging them. "I came home and found the bowl half full, the glass doorwall open, the vines—the vines pulled loose and hanging, Sweet Autumns scattered across the ground." Her eyes filled with tears that spilled onto her cheeks.

Mika sat beside her, turning toward her this time. "Just one bad accident, Rochelle. That's all. You not know she might lean too far."

"I should have."

"But you say she understood 'bout wine, not try to go on stairs. You not think she make mistake like that."

"But she *didn't* know better when—when . . . It was more than that, okay? I should have . . ."

He waited quietly, his face so innocent and trusting, believing whatever she told him.

"She was hooked on painkillers, too," she blurted. "Okay? I *did* see her try to lean out once—when she was, you know, high from those things. She lost her balance and couldn't pull herself up. Kala saw her from below, shouted for me. I ran in and helped her up just in time."

"These painkillers, they can hurt many ways."

"Yes, and it's stupid to get hooked on them. That's why I made Kala swear not to tell anybody, and I kept it secret all these years. Mom didn't want anyone to know she was in so much pain. I should've known she'd sit there feeling sorry for herself, all alone while I was off having a good time."

"Doctor-man, he give her these pills?—not care if she catch addiction?"

"Her doctor didn't know. I think she was getting them from Mrs. Mac, a gossipy little charity booster Mom used to visit for lunch on Wednesdays in Sauganash. She always looked kinda stoned herself, and her *husband* was a doctor."

"Your mother, she showed you these painkillers?"

"No, she kept 'em hidden, but I saw her sneak something from a little jewelry box in her wardrobe, so I went back later and found them, then looked them up at the library and learned how dangerous they are. Without her knowing, I started counting them whenever I had the chance. If she only took one, I could go out with my friends that night. If she took two or more, I had to stay home and make sure she didn't fall down the stairs or something. Kala used to say go, but I knew seeing Mom that way upset her terribly, and it wasn't fair to expect her to clean up when Mom—" She caught herself, looked at Mikalu's sad eyes, and knew she'd said more than she intended. "Look, I don't want anybody to find out about the painkillers, especially my father."

"This secret, it is safe with me; but your father, doesn't he have police report? Autopsy, coroner opinion—he might already see d'truth."

Who was she kidding? She'd finally started to believe maybe he didn't find out, that he didn't know what a terrible job Rochelle had done looking after her mom, not getting help when she needed it most, knowing she had a serious drug problem, yet *leaving her to die alone.* "I don't— I don't know what the report says."

"Someday you find out, maybe not have to keep secrets from father after all."

She nodded, feeling queasy, determined to quit spacing out, to quit blabbing things never meant to be shared. "When I'm older."

"Maybe till then, you stop blaming yourself."

Her eyes welling with tears, she felt overwhelmed by possibilities, wishing he would quit being so understanding. "Maybe I *shouldn't* find out . . ."

"You 'fraid?"

She nodded, knowing this cop-out would be easier than admitting the rest.

"Me, I think take a chance, Rochelle. Look inside. Being afraid all d'time, by and by, *that's* what makes people get hurt."

She stared at him, wiped her eyes and looked again, then gazed off across the blackening waters, a pair of bright stars—or maybe planets—emerging amid the deepening sky.

"And trust people," he added, "—people like me."

"I already proved I trust you," she said.

He shook his head, then stared sadly at the ground. "You still keep secrets, something you not want me to know."

She jumped up and tried to argue that she owed him no explanations, that she'd already said too much, that she didn't appreciate him tricking her like this—but she just stammered, then turned and stomped away, breaking into a trot as she fled along the twilit lagoon-side trail. He kept up, not chasing her, just staying right behind her. She slipped once, and he grabbed her arm; but then he let go, let her hurry on without interference.

She veered left onto the beach and kept going, Mika still behind her. Where was the *I'm sorry, Rochelle?*—the *I not want to make you sad.* Nothing, not a sound, just keeping up with her.

She splashed into the surf, ruining her shoes, soaking the legs of her pants; and still he followed, his new shoes and jeans water-logged.

She whirled on him. "Why do you think there's something else?"

"I pay close attention to you."

"What do you want from me?"

"What you want, Rochelle. You want to say d'truth."

The sky behind him fanned out, blades forged in crimson piercing wisps of cotton cloud.

If you walk out that door . . .

Tears again, runny nose, a mind of their own.

You'll regret it; I promise you.

"She killed herself! Okay? Are you satisfied?"

He stood there, eyes glistening in the waning light, waves lapping around his legs, the valley quietly waiting.

She hung her head, deflated, rage vented to mingle with the water's rising mist. "She already tried once by taking a whole bunch of those pills. Kala and I had to make her vomit, then keep her up all night, afraid to call for help and humiliate her with a scandal."

He moved closer, waited.

Crying now, ashamed of betraying her mother's secret . . . "She warned me I'd regret leaving, that if something happened it would be— It would be my fault."

He took her hand and held it firmly.

"I counted fifteen pills before I left. When I found her—" She pushed the image from her mind and concentrated on the bedroom, the wardrobe, the jewelry box. She tried to stop crying, but couldn't catch her breath, and she needed to say it. "I wanted—I wanted to get rid of—the pills. I didn't want—didn't want anybody to know, but she'd taken—she'd taken all fifteen. I don't think—don't think she jumped—just wanted flowers one last—one last time—and—and it happened—it happened too fast—" Still sobbing, she cried, "I didn't want her—didn't want her to die. I didn't know—"

She felt his arms around her, buried her face in his hair, tried to erase the image of a broken and lifeless body, Sweet Autumn blooms scattering like jacks, no way to gather them all, the ball slipping from her grasp.

"Rochelle . . ."

"It's my—it's my fault."

"You made her want to die?"

"No, she was just—just so unhappy. Grandpa died—and she wanted—wanted to get a divorce—then she could—could move back to France—but it would never—never work."

"If you stay home all d'time, that would solve her problems?—make her sadness go 'way?"

Too many jacks spread out before her, all dancing in the breeze, so many beyond her grasp.

She lifted her head and wiped her eyes, struggling to stanch the flow. "No," she admitted.

You can't help, sweetheart. Please don't try.

"Your mother, she wants you taking her blame? All d'time? Rest of your life?"

She shook her head, Sweet Autumn blossoms swirling about her ankles, victory too elusive, so many jacks . . .

"She will forgive you?"

"I'll never . . ." She whispered, "I'll never know."

"Rochelle, you *will* know . . . when you forgive yourself."

"It's not that easy."

"But you can."

"How do you know?"

"Me, I am your friend, the friend you trust."

"It's still my fault."

"No, this fault, it is not yours. You all d'time try to gather so many pieces of guilt, hold them close. Me, I say just let them go. Let wind carry them far away, never touch you again."

"I don't deserve to get off so easy."

"To be *happy*, this is what you deserve."

"I—I can't."

"I tell you d'truth, show you how."

She looked into his eyes, recognized the tenderness she'd lost, and remembered how much her mother loved her.

"You trust me, Rochelle?"

"Yes," she whispered. "Yes."

"I never lie to you."

"I know, but—but it'll take some time."

"If I give you good reason, you promise you try, no matter how long it takes?"

She closed her eyes, and Sweet Autumn blooms began drifting away with the wind, one jack, two jacks, three, five, a dozen jacks at a time . . .

"Rochelle? You promise?"

"Yes."

"Then here is best reason: your friend Mikalu, he forgives you."

*   *   *

The *amakihi* bird insisted on rousing Rochelle. She felt rested and relaxed, liberated from the bad dreams that too often haunt her long after she wakes. She pushed back the covers, amused to feel an odd sense of intimacy from drowsing in the same bed where Mikalu slept nearly every night of his young life, an uncultured boy content to inhabit this austere room. Her trick today would be to protect the skinny ninth-grader's feelings, the deceptively smart and surprisingly educated Hawaiian wannabe obviously nurturing a budding crush that could never be allowed to blossom.

She slipped from her nightie and stood in panties before the window screen, uncowed by the admiring gaze of such a tiny bird. Slivers of sunshine pierced the dense foliage, buffing dew drops to a sparkling sheen, an iridescent beetle trundling from one miniature pool to the next. She took a deep breath, then sighed and rubbed her eyes. Mika could never grow into an ambitious and powerful man; he let people glimpse his heart through those innocent blue eyes, revealing simple passions with every unaffected smile.

She donned her robe and headed for the outhouse, the valley hers alone while Papaii and the boys slept, then strolled up the lower-ridge trail toward the waterfall, anticipating an invigorating shower while dawn's pink light crept down through the valley to rouse critters and kiss awake myriad blooms. She paused to gaze back at the lagoon, its water glassy calm, the satin beach and jigsaw reef framing a deep blue pool wherein lurked mysterious tunnels and lost treasures. She walked farther, the crescendo of rushing water echoing from the rising ridge, until a magnificent yellow butterfly appeared from nowhere and danced a silent recital in the air. The delicate pixie sashayed into the brush at her left, landing on a pink *lobelia* blossom. She eased closer for a better view . . . but startled it, causing her skittish friend to flutter toward the pond where it finally lit on a fat foot-soldier shrub armed with bayonet fronds.

And she saw Mikalu, his back to her, rinsing his hair under the falls . . . *completely nude.*

She gasped and stumbled, her heart pounding with sudden fury, lucky the roar of water covered her noise. She meant to back away and sneak off without him knowing, but she hesitated too long, and he turned around, running fingers through his hair, gazing into a copse of trees as rivulets of sparkling water traced the contours of his naked body. She froze, squatting behind the ersatz advance guard, afraid the slightest movement would alert him to her presence, hoping he would turn again toward the falls so she could slip away.

But he waded into the shallows and paused where golden sunshine burst through the canopy to caress him with a nimbus glow. Running his hands down torso and legs, he urged reluctant droplets back to their course, while a gentle breeze blow-dried dense strands of wavy blond locks.

She felt a warm rush rise through her body, her quickening pulse throbbing from the inside out. She'd seen web-posted photos of unclothed guys, even watched an explicit movie late one night during a Mindy Madison slumber party, but she never imagined a boy as young as Mikalu could look so much like a man. She meant to close her eyes against such unwarranted intrusion on his privacy, but then he turned sideways and she gasped, the sheer intimacy in profile too vivid to ignore.

He stepped up onto the low rocks, standing against the exotic backdrop, yet somehow blending into the jungle panorama. He crouched to retrieve his things from the hidden tub, and she stared with shameless abandon, trying to erase this montage of impressions even as she fixed every detail amid the vivid memories where fantasies romp and play.

He donned his slippers, quickly toweled off, ran a comb through his hair, then hung the towel over a branch before shrugging into his robe, that last instant of exposed flesh most teasing of all. Like a startled butterfly, he drifted up to the path and floated from sight, unaware the young woman he liked so much had violated his vernal trust.

She waited . . . listened . . . willed her breathing to calm, then stood and craned her neck to see down the trail, Mikalu long gone. She walked down to where he'd stood, reaching out as if to touch the very towel that had explored him so intimately only moments before, but she caught herself, feeling both embarrassed and foolish. She set her things on the rock, doffed her robe and panties, and waded into the exhilarating pool, clutching Mikalu's bottle of organic shampoo, feeling very naked as waterfall mist gathered on goose-bumpy skin and warm breeze nuzzled her own damp curls. She washed and rinsed quickly under the frigid spray, then moved to the exact spot where Mikalu had paused to brush the last clinging droplets free. Closing her eyes to picture the scene, she repeated his motions, her fingers drawing lines around the burgeoning curves of her unadorned form.

She shuddered, pulled her hand away, knelt with eyes still closed, and slowly splashed cool water on herself. She stood and raised her arms high, yielding to the whims of butterfly sky.

The sunshine swaddled her in a blanket of warmth.

The breeze whispered affirmation of her sensual essence.

A charm of finches heralded the womanhood she'd dreamed of even as a little girl.

And she opened her eyes to see the world renewed . . .

And discovered Mikalu!—standing right there in full view, gaping at her!

She dropped to a crouch, scrambling to cover herself. "What are you doing?!"

He stammered wordlessly, eyes darting to the towel he'd forgotten on the branch. Caught and exposed, he panicked, covered his face, then turned and fled down the trail.

How dare he spy on her, staring so boldly, gawking like a pervert in a porn shop . . .

A healthy teenage boy, she had to admit, accidentally stumbling upon the stuff of teenage fantasies, too stunned to disappear before she'd noticed him, before she'd discerned something in his face even more personal and private than his naked body.

She dried and dressed quickly, grateful her father would come soon to take her away, confident Mikalu would hide until then out of sheer humiliation, watching from some distant ridge as she passed through the narrow slot and left Hawai'i for at least another year, probably longer.

She walked the trail with leaden feet, short of breath for some odd reason, wondering how he could possibly explain himself were he so brave as to face her again before time painted layers of gloss over these memories of their former selves.

And she found him sitting on a rock beside the trail, waiting for her, his eyes red.

He tried to speak, barely managing "I'm sorry" before a single tear spilled down his cheek. Swallowing hard, he held his head high, shoulders square, taking full responsibility, accepting all blame, willing to suffer the harshest rebuke given the slightest chance he might make things right.

Her anger tried to flood back, but she recognized that truest of secret revelations in his face, and she knew this time he'd taken a chance and chosen to let her see.

And a moment of unabashed admiration from one so moved didn't really feel so embarrassing after all.

She stepped closer, and she realized maybe somebody so young really could feel more than a mere crush, and she finally understood why he always let her glimpse his heart through those innocent eyes:

Want it or not, it belonged to her.

"It's okay," she said. "I—well—Mikalu, I saw you, too."

Utterly surprised, he blushed furiously, stood up and blinked, sat down again . . . and finally allowed a hint of sheepish smile.

She reached for his hand, and together they walked toward the ancient stone house overlooking a pristine lagoon, the only home he'd ever known. Someday his own world would expand to encompass new places and new people, and he would grow beyond his tender feelings for the girl named Rochelle DuFortier, and he would fall in love again, this time with the kind of woman who would cherish him and his simple approach to life.

Rochelle could never take back what had passed between them this day, but given the chance, she couldn't be sure she would.

A magnificent yellow butterfly danced ahead, a moment's distraction from the awkwardness still swirling around two teens with a story best left untold.

She knew Mikalu most certainly would never again be the same . . .

But, then again, neither would she.

UA HELE LĀKOU, UA WAĪHO LĀKOU

SIMPLY GONE

Rochelle at 21

Mikalu let Pocomea and Rochelle climb from his battered SUV before pulling into the narrow space and popping the rear gate. She found something reassuring about him leaving his car at the airport; it meant he would return to Hawai'i after this whirlwind sojourn to the Windy City. He would drive the long-familiar route to Coulée Makai and find Poco already back from Honolulu, his lifelong friend reluctantly admitting that vertebrae-fusion surgery must be scheduled soon. They would sit on a rock in the pristine valley, gaze upon the sparkling lagoon, and swap tales of metropolitan insanity while the spectacular reef beckoned with a promise that of all places in the world, theirs would always be right there.

Just *right there.*

Rochelle wanted to cry.

Well, she didn't *want* to, but she worried about sending Poco off to face such a daunting challenge alone, his parents halfway around the world; and the anticipation of moving back to Chicago for a new life and new career had already exhausted her, the exhilaration of change tempered by the melancholy of saying good-bye to her adoptive brother, the stubborn soul even now insisting he at least carry his own flight bag. With no time to argue, Mika acquiesced, even letting Rochelle lug her own suitcase while he shouldered two carry-ons and dragged a pair of full-sized bags into the terminal.

Airports always depressed her, something about embarking on treks to new places inevitably requiring the old ones be left behind; or maybe deciding to skip graduation contributed to this awkward tenuousness, a fatherless ceremony denying the oft-fantasized closure one needs to move on; or maybe giving up Galway had lent her new appreciation for connections she could trust, a lovers' tour through Portiers and Angoulême and Bordeaux fading to all the romance and commitment of one's own fingers under the covers, of lonesome nights in the 'burbs thumbing through glossy village and countryside photos in the *Geographica*.

Sometimes people go, and sometimes they're simply gone.

"That roadwork, it made us very late," Mikalu said, setting the bags where walkways diverged. "I'll take ours down there," he suggested to Rochelle, "while you two say bye; then I follow Poco while you check us in."

She could see a long line, and knew she better keep this short—but then she spotted a familiar face! Jackie Ko, the family's groundskeeper, stood in line for the same San Diego/Chicago flight she and Mikalu would board. He was pushing two suitcases forward, big rectangular bags with diagonal red stripes like divers' flags. She'd never said good-bye to him or his sister, only returning to Grandpa's house to pack her things long after they'd vacated the guest house and moved on to other jobs.

"You may keep Mikalu," Poco said, his dark eyes sparkling, barely suppressing a smile, "—just let him come visit me at Coulée Makai sometimes, and you come visit, too."

"Five days in a frantic city, and I guarantee he'll be on the next flight back," she teased.

"The city, that is not why he'd stay."

"He'll be back, Poco, and I'll come see you more often."

"Five years, Haole-girl. Five years you not come, use college as one big excuse."

"I promise," she said quietly, trying not to cry. "But you—"

He held up his hand. "I save you lecture. I promise, too; get all da kine tests and take care of myself." He put his beefy arm around her, and she folded herself into his embrace, the tears coming now as he held her more tenderly than she could ever imagine for a man of his powerful size.

"You—you just *better*," she warned him, "and stick to your other promise, too."

"I know. Remember Dabu my friend; stay away from his brudders; let police handle investigation."

"Ten minutes," Mikalu's voice reminded them.

They stepped back, and Rochelle fished in her purse for a tissue, her nose all runny now. Poco glanced away and wiped his eyes. Mika rubbed his, too, too late to disguise that look of serene satisfaction one sees in the faces of mothers watching children play, of friends witnessing a special moment between those they love.

The guys hurried off the other way while Rochelle rushed to the check-in line, scanning the waiting crowd for Jackie or, hopefully, maybe his sister, too. The line moved slowly, too many people standing around blocking her view. Finally, bags tagged and gone, boarding passes in hand, she circled the group and spotted him sitting against the far wall.

"Hi, Mr. Ko," she said, standing before him, timing how long before recognition connected this vaguely familiar woman to the thirteen-year-old girl he'd last seen.

He looked up, surprised by the intrusion, his rugged and pock-marked Hawaiian features admitting puzzlement. "I'm sorry?" he said.

"You don't recognize me?"

He studied her, then shook his head.

"It's been eight years, and I've grown up since then."

Perplexed now, he glanced past her into the terminal, then looked at her again, then down the long hallway.

"It's me," she said, hiding her disappointment. "Rochelle! Rochelle DuFortier!"

"Rochelle," he said noncommittally.

Her disappointment weighed heavily, sudden emotional baggage with no place to stow. She'd spent countless hours with this man, learning all his tricks for keeping the physical plant of a home running smoothly, designing the underground sprinkler system he installed just weeks before tragedy scattered them in different directions. He'd repaired her bike, helped her put track lighting in her room, taught her how to prune roses, hugged her awkwardly that time she left for summer camp . . .

"I'm sorry—" she said, determined not to shed tears for people who pass through others' lives, only to forget.

"Rochelle!" called a woman.

She turned and barely had time to glimpse Kala before the now-chubbier Hawaiian woman swept her into a serious embrace. "Haole-girl, you're *all* growed up!"

"Kala! Kala Ko!" Rochelle managed to get out, a lump in her throat.

Kala reached around to poke her brother. "You not recognize our little Rochelle, all that time you teach her things in Chicago?"

Standing now, Jackie smiled, letting Kala hand her off for another round of hugs. "I just tease you, girl," he admitted.

"Do you still live in Chicago?" Rochelle asked, everybody grinning at each other.

Kala glanced at Jackie. "We did, but now we not sure where to live. Jackie lost job, mine not so good, so we come visit aunt in Hilo, then go try jobs in Honolulu, see if big money there gets in our pockets, too."

"I just came to see friends," Rochelle said. "Now I'm heading to Chicago, moving back. I'll even be in the old house again this fall."

Mikalu walked up, so she quickly introduced everybody just as the loudspeaker announced final boarding.

"We're on the same flight," Rochelle said.

Kala and Jackie glanced at each other. Kala said, "No, we just arrive, go see aunt."

"Oh," she said. "I thought— Well, I'd like to keep in touch."

"Yes," Kala said, her brother nodding.

"You know the address to Grandpa's house, but I won't be there till this fall. I'm not sure where I'll stay till then."

"We have no address, either," Kala said, spreading her hands.

"Well, my father is listed here in Hilo. As soon as you find a place in Honolulu, send him a note and I'll write to you, maybe call when you have a phone."

"Um, okay," Kala said. "Sure."

She hugged them again, then let Mikalu drag her to the gate just in time. They hurried onto the plane, stowed their carry-ons, and belted in.

"Wow," she said. "I'm glad I spotted them. Maybe I can hire them to take care of the house again—after I get some money together. Either way, it'll be nice to stay in touch after all these years."

Mikalu studied her, a sadness in his eyes, but he didn't speak.

"What?"

He shrugged.

She sighed and sat back. "You don't think I'll hear from them, do you?"

"No."

"I never got to say bye to them after, you know, back when it happened."

"Saying good-bye, finding the right way, this is very important," he said quietly, laying his head back and gripping his armrests as the jet engines roared to life, a novice flyer who'd never even been inside an airplane.

And she closed her eyes, the ache of losing everything in an instant swirling around her. She swallowed hard, determined not to hurt for people who pass through others' lives, only to forget.

"I didn't say good-bye just now, either," she said.

"No, but that's okay. I'm like that sometimes, too. You all d'time hope."

She sighed. "I guess I'm still, well . . ."

"Me, too."

Sometimes people go, and sometimes they're simply gone.

*   *   *

Cheeseburgers and greasy fries in a paper trough, little packets of ketchup, a plastic tray . . .

"All airports, they have food like this?" Mikalu asked, eyeing his meal suspiciously.

"Sometimes not this good," Rochelle admitted. "But hey, when in Rome."

"Then I try to fit in, act like native, not embarrass you," he said, rolling his eyes as he tasted a fry.

"You *are* a native here," she said. "Doesn't it feel weird to be back in San Diego, your hometown?"

"Airport not San Diego, more like sovereign territory, embassy plopped down in foreign land, not part of local community."

"This is true—but still, it's the closest you've been to home since you were a baby."

"You have funny notions of home, Rochelle. When I was *keiki*, my father's home, it *should* have been mine. Instead, I found place where people love me. If I am lucky, my home will always be where people love me, no matter how far I go to find it."

She sat back and considered his words. They certainly put a scuff in the shine of her moving to Chicago, the prodigal child returning as a woman, her former friends long past regular contact and mostly scattered across the continent. Still, she reminded herself, sometimes you have to go where you belong, then you find people to love, people who love you . . .

Mikalu continued: "My mother's grave, that is what's here, and my father, who may someday want to know his son after all. Yes, it feels weird to be so close to San Diego, but that's nothing like my feeling of leaving Hawai'i and coming here with you."

"Well—thank you," she teased. "I'm honored. Let's hope it's a fun ride. Remember to keep your hands and feet inside the car at all times."

"Hands and feet, these are not what get hurt." He scarfed a big bite of the burger, chewed tentatively, then shrugged and twirled a fry in the ketchup.

Rochelle chewed one of the fries, pensive for a moment. "*Would* you leave Hawai'i? I mean, move away. Poco said your girlfriend lives in Monterey."

"I *not* have girlfriend," he pronounced. "That Poco—big man, big heart, *big mouth*."

"It's not secret, is it?"

"No secrets." He wrinkled his brow at her. "Jenya, she is one important marine biologist, comes to Coulée Makai each time with group, sometimes by herself. We go see Hilo, have lots of fun. She say come to California, stay at her place, see how things work out, but she's only a good friend . . . best kept that way."

"Wow, Mika. She sounds like quite a catch: good job, her own place in a wonderful area, highly educated, shared interests like a love for diving, both ecologically oriented and preservation minded—"

He paused from eating to watch her. Scrutiny having seated itself between them, she took a bite and chewed nervously. "What? What are you thinking?"

"This man in Massachusetts, what was his name?"

"Galway?"

"I wonder, what was on his list?"

"That wasn't very nice."

"I'm sorry, not mean to say something bad. It's just, I never hear somebody make list like that before, made me wonder what you put on *your* lists."

"Don't you think Jenya sized you up before showing an interest?"

"I hope not."

"Why not? You're good enough for her; you have lots of positive qualities. Is that what's holding you back, thinking maybe you're not—?"

"Nothing holds me back, except when not enough reason to go forward."

Leaning closer to keep her voice down, she asked, "Are you two, you know, intimate?"

"Rochelle!" He blushed, then fidgeted with a fry. "We like kissing, play octopus with our hands, decide that's enough for friends."

"Maybe you'd feel different about her if you, you know, took the plunge. No pun intended."

"First, Rochelle, I not have problem thinking she's too good for me; she would be luckiest woman in the world if Mikalu loved her. Second, I already know how to fall in love *first*, even know how to wait long time before I get to show it all d'way. Do *you* go 'round . . . *plunging* so you can find love?"

"Ewwww, no—but I'm no prude. Geez, you sound like, you know, a virgin or something."

"Are you asking?"

"Um, no, I guess not."

"Then I not ask you, either."

"It's not like we're keeping secrets."

"No, no secrets. I'm wearing blue boxer shorts," he said, "but that's not secret just 'cause you not ask."

She smiled. "It *is* more than I needed to know."

"We have plane to catch," he said, glancing at his watch. "Windy City."

"Yeah, I've had enough of this culinary crap," she said, rolling her burger basket into a wad. They dumped their trash and headed down the concourse toward their gate.

"Yes," he said, "I *would* leave Hawai'i. I'd go anywhere."

"Even Tulsa?" she mused, more to herself.

"I'm wearing white socks, too," he said.

"Is that a fact?"

"Yes. The rest, you'll have to ask."

"I'll do that."

"When you're ready."

*   *   *

A loud buzzer sounded, and the luggage carousel at O'Hare hummed into motion.

"I think he *did* recognize me," Rochelle said, "but I don't think he was teasing. He felt uncomfortable, like he'd already left all that time he spent with my family in the past."

"That's probably so. Those two, they might feel guilty, too, not want to talk long enough for tragedy to come up."

"Yeah," she said, scanning for their bags. "They say tragedy can tear apart the strongest relationships—parents splitting up after the death of a child, friends made uncomfortable when another is suddenly stricken with terminal illness or crippled by an accident . . ."

"Here they come," Mikalu announced, their bags emerging from the chute. They elbowed their way forward and grabbed them from the track.

And Rochelle noticed a large one with diagonal red stripe. She paused and scanned the crowd, but saw nobody she recognized. The bag went all the way around, not having been claimed.

"Hold on," she whispered. Mika paused to watch her curiously.

No matching bag appeared, so it must have been a coincidence. Still, she waited, wanting to check the tag, afraid an indignant owner would accost her with accusations of theft.

Fifteen minutes they waited, nobody ever laying claim, until the crowd thinned out.

No owner, still only one red-striped suitcase.

She couldn't stand it anymore, so she stepped forward and scanned the tag, noticing an unfamiliar Chicago address and a single name:

Kalo Ko.

I MĀKAʻIKAʻI MALAILA

BEEN THERE

Rochelle at 16

Go Overboard! read the sign, a good name for an aquarium gift shop. Rochelle gazed around, not sure where to start, or what Poco would like. The world's biggest octopus watched her, a 3-D sculpture at least twenty-five or thirty feet across, with television screens for eyes. It looked rather silly, really, and so did most of the trinkets for sale, though she found herself drawn to some exquisite posters and glossy picture books. She'd been visiting Chicago's Shedd Aquarium as long as she could remember, but this time she enjoyed a new appreciation for the myriad images of marine life, having seen so much of it first-hand during last year's impromptu underwater tour with Mikalu.

Something about having been there makes it more real, she thought.

"There you are," Mindy announced, snatching postcards from Rochelle's hand. She flipped her long bottle-tinted hazelnut hair over a shoulder, barely glancing at the cards before setting them down.

"Where'd they go?" Rochelle wondered, not seeing the guys. She put the cards back in their rack.

"Zac went to the restroom, and Jake's checking when they feed the sharks."

Rochelle moved to shelves of figurines. "Well, Zac sure turned out to be a jerk," she said, eyeing some ceramics.

"Oh, don't be a snood," Mindy teased, wagging her eyebrows. "I think he's hot. Have you noticed?—he's either wearing boxers or nothing underneath."

"Duh! The way he keeps hitching up his trousers and posing? I think it's a rolled-up sock."

"He likes you, you know."

She moved to some puzzles and games. "He doesn't even pay attention to me."

"*As if!* He's been all over you."

"He'd *like* to be all over me."

"So how can you say he's not payin' attention?"

"You know, not noticing how I feel, what I'm thinking, responding to *me*."

"Well, he's no David Copperfield—he can't read your mind."

"Copperfield's an illusionist."

"What-ever." She tried on a cap, struck a jaunty pose, then put it back. "So what are you lookin' for?"

"Something for Poco's birthday—the big fourteen."

"How 'bout a shirt that says Goodyear?"

"That's not nice, Mindy."

"So sue me. I mean, he's as big as that squid, isn't he?" She gestured to the giant creature with TV eyes.

"That's an octopus, Mindy." Actually, some kind of octopus sounded like a good present.

"What-ever. You gonna see him and that little waterfall-peeper when you and your dad leave for the Philippines?"

"Just an hour at the airport in Hilo." The inflatable octopus looked too kidsy, not enough class.

"Oooo, you need to get this one for shower boy." Mindy thrust a moray eel sculpture at Rochelle. "See?—a dick-shaped snake sticking up from two hairy rocks."

Rochelle handed it back. "Here, I think *you* need it more. Take it home and play with it." She probably would, too.

"Why? I got Jake. Hey, this looks cool." Mindy handed over a brass octopus. About the size of Rochelle's hand, it showed intricate detail and the friendliest face, innocent eyes . . . Pocomea.

Zac walked up, then reached around and snatched the sculpture from Rochelle. "What's this for?" Proving all the more a jerk, the preppy punk with spiked blond hair tossed it to Jake, Mindy's acne-scarred team-wrestler boyfriend.

"She's picking a present for Poco," Mindy supplied.

Rochelle intercepted it on the toss-back.

"Oooo," Jake said, "is he that *love puppy* who's been writin' you every week about life in Cooler McHigh?"

Rochelle shot a look at big-mouth Mindy.

Zac grabbed the moray sculpture from its shelf. "Snake with a hard-on," he pronounced. "Kinda small, though."

Rochelle studied the octopus. It looked a lot like Pocomea, its face a study in childlike wonder.

"No," Mindy corrected. "That's his friend Mikalu."

"You're buyin' a present for some snood who sends you love letters?" Zac asked, amusing himself with eel-thrusting motions.

Rochelle looked at a bigger octopus, but it didn't have quite the same expression.

"Sharks don't get fed till three," Jake said. "But the dolphin show's in ten minutes. Let's grab a seat."

"Dolphins are why tuna costs so much," Zac explained, ever the fun factoider. "I saw it on Discovery or something."

"C'mon, Ro, let's go," Mindy said. She and Jake turned to leave.

"Save me a seat. I'll be there in a minute."

Oh joy, Zac stayed behind so he could lean against the display and hitch up his pants. "That big coral-reef tank is ninety-thousand gallons—can you believe that? I wanna see the sharks take a bite outta that scuba guy who feeds 'em."

"They only do the human-biting show on Sundays," she said, finding two smaller octopuses, lining them up to compare.

"What's the big deal? Just pick one, and let's go."

"I gotta pay for it," Rochelle said. "You hold me a seat, and I'll be right there."

"Okay, but if they're gone, you'll hafta sit on my lap." He took off, his mission clear.

Only one looked back at her with those Pocomea eyes, an easy decision. She paid for it, then wandered toward the Oceanarium.

But the coral-reef exhibit caught her eye, all 90,000 gallons of it. It looked small to her, but beautiful.

She moved closer and gazed at the panorama, almost feeling the gentle surge, waves lapping at her mask, the reef urging her to take a chance and release the air from her BC, to float in liquid sky.

A monstrously fat fish with big eyes and bigger lips sidled up to the glass, a friendly looking feller concerned she might not be having a good time . . .

Paying attention.

And a moray eel poked his head out from a crevice, undulating its lethal cobra challenge. Only one thing was missing to make the scene look completely natural . . .

A wiry teenage boy, with wheat-colored sea-hair, flowing between the corals.

They really had assembled a spectacular, mesmerizing display, and she appreciated it now more than ever before.

Something about having been there makes it more real.

NO LAUA NĀ NĀʻAU Ā NĀ MANAʻO LIKE

CONCORD

Rochelle at 21

A whirlwind of impressions electrified Rochelle the moment she stepped outside at OʻHare. Blaring horns and revving engines and hissing brakes and shouting travelers lent a syncopating rhythm to the scene, people coming and going, all connected to Chicago, this city at the center of the world. Waiting for the car-rental shuttle with Mikalu, she took a deep breath and tasted the fragrance of home, of fishy rainswept marinas and pungent chili-dog/pizza cuisine, of churning industry and springtime gardens, of ethnic-bakery hearths and traffic-jam exhaust. Mikalu simply wrinkled his nose at so many foreign odors, an obvious stranger in this strange land.

A shuttle ride, keys in the car, Rochelle behind the wheel, and Mikalu's excitement grew, anticipation dancing in his eyes. She'd once followed him on a tour of Coulée Makai, impressed by all the natural wonder, flattered by his gift of a *lei*; and now she relished returning the favor, introducing a way of life very different from any he'd known, watching him behold geometric vistas, maybe welcoming the *nouveau touriste* with a Bears t-shirt or the oblig-atory Cubs cap.

They stopped first at the police station, a frustrating ordeal of confusion and misdirection, finally managing to order one report copy by mail, rush fees paid in advance; and Rochelle recalled Pocomea's frustration with Hilo police, his suspicions of foul play, sympathetic detectives failing to poke holes in airtight Taoke alibis, the strain on his friendship with Dabu making it not worth pressing on.

The downtown skyline loomed against late evening's purpling sky, win-dow-lit checkerboard faces watching like a cortège of cliff-dwelling *nā lapu* guarding the waters of Lake Michigan. Swept along in the flow of traffic, they headed northwest to the suburbs, pulling over briefly to gaze upon the front of Grandpa's still-rented house, images of a fallen mother pushed aside in practice for someday reclaiming the home and gardens, Mikalu's sympathy left unspoken. They drove on to Sauganash, and Rochelle wondered if her mother had felt this way returning to La Réole, to the familiar face of an old woman waiting to greet her; just as Miss Dixon now stood in the townhouse doorway, their hostess welcoming new arrivals on behalf of the Windy City.

Delighted to see them both, the wheelchair-company conservator appeared more fragile than Rochelle remembered, this time relying on a cane for balance. Her place looked lovely, elegantly appointed, one wall festooned with family portraits, a beautiful young teenage girl standing expectantly before homework spread around the adjoining breakfast nook.

Pleased to meet Mikalu, Miss Dixon urged the girl out to meet their guests. "And this is my grandniece, Mauterre."

Mikalu gently squeezed her hand and bowed, a gentleman's acknowledgment of a proper young lady. "Your reputation, it is one of caring deeply for others," he said. "I am honored to meet you."

She managed to blush and smile at the same time, already charmed by this gentle man with the island tan. "You'll tell me about Hawai'i during your visit?" she asked.

"Coulée Makai, it is my second-most favorite subject."

"Should I ask about the first?"

He winked, suggesting, "I never say, but in time you may figure that out."

She liked him instantly, her dark eyes sparkling.

Rochelle's gaze drifted to a family portrait demanding her attention: Mauterre at maybe five or six, sitting in her mother's lap, father standing beside them. Instead of looking at the camera, he'd glanced protectively toward his stunningly beautiful Mediterranean wife and their adorable daughter. Rochelle knew better than to let her imagination run, and she tried not to picture *two* caskets lowering into the ground, to ponder how it must feel to lose both parents at once; yet those familiar swells of grief began pulling at her, her chest seized by that odd sinking feeling. She willed it away, determined not to dwell on how this innocent girl could possibly cope with so much tragedy.

"We are very grateful," Mauterre was saying, "that you've come to help with my father's designs."

"I've gained a new appreciation for the challenges so many people face," Rochelle admitted, adding with a hint of self-mockery, "but credit your great-aunt; she challenged me on a personal level—and I fell for it even though I knew what she was up to."

Mauterre smiled again, glancing toward the older woman.

"Yes," Miss Dixon said, "I've been meaning to apologize for that. You see," she explained, turning to Mikalu, "Miss DuFortier came after my business pitch had failed to recruit anybody else. I sensed an extraordinary empathy in her, so I shamelessly tried to play on her sympathies. That failed, too, but luckily for us she recognized that her talents *can* benefit others. Now I'm committed to helping our new development engineer succeed both at our goals *and* her own."

"Rochelle, she is undaunted by challenges," Mika said.

"We are counting on that," Miss Dixon declared. "Now, please let us find seats. I'm afraid I've reached my limit for leaning on this infernal stick."

Rochelle pointed out, "We still need to check in at the hotel—"

"Nonsense! You'll stay here, of course." Miss Dixon ambled toward the couch, lowering herself carefully as she explained, "We've prepared the guest room for Mr. Mikalu, and you'll have Mauterre's until he returns to Hawai'i. We made a pallet for her in mine."

After much debate, with Rochelle adamantly against Miss Dixon navigating around a sleeping youngster, they compromised: Mauterre would move the pallet to her own room.

Her words tinged with playful conspiracy, Rochelle told Mauterre, "Beware, I was pillow-fight champion of Rinerson Dorm."

Mauterre giggled, quipping, "I've been to slumber parties where police had to be summoned."

They chatted about Mikalu's impressions of Chicago for several minutes; then Miss Dixon admitted, "I apologize for leaving you early, but I'll need to retire soon. It seems I'm having another of my spells today." She touched her face, and Rochelle noticed her hand trembling. Mauterre hurried to the kitchen and returned with a pill and glass of water, helping her great-aunt hold them steady. Rochelle could only imagine how one so young must worry about losing the only person she has left.

"I know you're both jet-lagged," Miss Dixon said, "and probably feel like it's still afternoon, so I've chilled drinks and snack trays for supper, and left those designs stacked on the table. Mauterre can help you find your way around, but she does have homework to finish tonight—"

"I'm stuck," Mauterre admitted, sighing. "It's my weak subject."

"Life sciences?" Mika asked, glancing over at the text.

"The *botany* chapter," she said, wrinkling her nose at the odor of indecipherable gibberish.

"For me, it is my best subject. If I promise to make it easy, may I help?"

"Oh, would you? Please!" Mikalu would be her hero in no time.

Teacher and student headed in to blaze a trail through dense thickets of plant physiology.

"I hope you don't mind," Rochelle said, "but I put down this address when I ordered a police report. Tomorrow I'll set up a P.O. box—"

"Nonsense. You'll be staying with us awhile, so you might as well have all your mail forwarded here."

"Well . . . thank you. I'll—"

Miss Dixon waved her off. "I have one more bit of good news before I say good-night. I hired a manager who found some ways to increase both your salary and the budget for research and prototypes."

"Excellent," she said, "—about the research, I mean. How'd you find him?"

"Jodis is a retired gentleman who worked his way up from manufacturing supervisor to chief financial officer at a medical supply company. My nephew modified a wheelchair for his Parkinson's-impaired wife, padded armrests she could activate to grip her arms whenever they trembled too much. She and Jodis wanted to travel, but her condition worsened." She sighed, adding quietly, "He lost her three months ago. Now he wants to keep busy, and to give something back, so he agreed to work for a dollar a year with the proviso that at certain benchmark levels of profitability we donate equipment to needy children and elderly patients. He's already developed a plan to restructure our debts and restore us to modest profitability, at least until we introduce the new designs."

"That's fantastic. It gives us time to assure we'll exceed safety standards on the first application."

Looking very delighted, Miss Dixon admitted, "I believe you and Jodis will be rather impressed with each other tomorrow. Now, if you'll help me up, I must say good-night."

After escorting Miss Dixon to the bedroom, Rochelle spread out the designs and promptly found herself swirling amid possibilities, great ideas lacking completion, problems presenting challenges she believed could be vanquished. Mauterre finished her homework with a new appreciation for the natural world, taking an extra few minutes to guide Mikalu through his tourist brochures, making suggestions and agreeing to accompany him to the Field Museum after school. She hugged them both before slipping off to bed; then Mikalu sat with Rochelle, studying the drawings, offering impressively astute observations and several innovative suggestions. His eyes lit up at the last set, an amphibious wheelchair with lots of problems but even more potential.

"This device," he said, "it is good for staying in the chair, but very difficult for climbing in and out, even with help. This part needs to collapse and rotate down."

"Wow . . . But then it would need a motor."

"Just a small one back here, if you add counterweight there."

"But a weight would compromise buoyancy."

"Take these out," he said, pointing at extra cross-braces that would be in the way. "The weight, now it will help balance."

Modifications and refinements flooded her mind, but exhaustion had already begun its slow creep, two-way jet-lag spinning the hands on her internal clock.

Mikalu must have sensed it, because he gathered the drawings into a neat stack. "Good-night, Rochelle. Thank you for inviting me to see Chicago."

"Well, thanks for coming along. Since I'm skipping graduation, at least I'll get to spend some time with the one person who most encouraged me over the years."

Mika smiled. "Then I will save Shedd Aquarium to see together. You and I, we will celebrate with the big-lip grouper fish."

After exchanging good-nights, Rochelle changed in the bathroom, then slipped into Mauterre's room and sat on the king-size bed, studying the silhouette breathing softly under a pallet duvet. Thirteen looked smaller than she remembered, more fragile, more vulnerable. Nobody at such a tender age should ever know profound tragedy, learning so young that the very people who protect you sometimes can't even protect themselves.

She didn't like stealing Mauterre's bed, relegating her to the floor. Too late to change the arrangements, she sighed and lay back, smoothing her hair alongside the pillow and pulling the blanket up to her neck, feeling at once small, and fragile, and vulnerable.

"Rochelle?" Mauterre whispered.

"Yes," she said quietly. "It's me. I'm sorry—did I wake you?"

"No, I don't think so. I, um, wake up a lot sometimes."

"I did, too, when I was your age. Sometimes I had scary dreams."

"Really?" she said, sitting up.

"Yeah . . . You know, I'm not feeling comfortable about taking your bed. Can we trade places?"

"Oh no, you're our guest."

"Could we compromise then? I mean, would you feel okay about sharing?"

She hesitated, then meekly answered, "If you would."

Rochelle moved over, Mauterre lifting the sheet to scoot under. The young teen lifted her head and smoothed her brunette tresses down alongside the pillow, then nestled in and turned on her side. Rochelle recognized the gesture from a lifetime of practice, and she felt an unfamiliar burst of protectiveness, wondering if this might be just a hint of how a mother might feel.

"I have scary dreams, too," Mauterre admitted, her voice tiny in the darkness. "Please don't tell Auntie Dix."

"I won't, if you don't want me to, but talking to her might help. I lost my mom when I was your age, and I didn't have anyone else. My dad was away, so I lived in a dorm, and when I felt scared I kept it secret. You don't have to." And she didn't, either, especially with nothing shameful to hide—like being the one who let it happen . . . the guilt that *never* goes away.

"Yeah, but Auntie Dix already worries too much, and her heart isn't well." She hesitated again. "It was eight months and nine days ago when—when my mom and dad . . ."

Rochelle sighed. "You still feel like it just happened."

"Yeah . . ." Mauterre covered her face, ragged breaths suggesting a determination not to cry, sniffles betraying failure. "I didn't—I didn't want them to go, but they promised to come home soon."

Rochelle felt the lump rising in her throat, but she recognized something else, a reason not to drift into that most private realm of despair, a chance to put aside her own grief and help a child feel better . . . if only she knew how. She reached under the covers, found a trembling hand, and felt her squeeze back. "You know they didn't break their promise."

"They didn't?"

"Can you remember how much they loved you?"

"Yes."

"How it felt when they hugged you?"

"Uh-huh."

"How proud they were watching you grow into the kind of young woman you've become?"

"I think so."

"Remembering is how you bring them back home. They would never break a promise to you; it's just that they need your help now to keep it."

"I'll *never* forget them."

"Then they'll never leave you."

They lay quietly for a minute. "I'm sorry for—you know," Mauterre whispered.

"You never need to apologize for how you feel. I used to do that, but as I got older I decided that, well, if it's hard for others, then they should just leave me alone for a while and come back later." She didn't want to say how many never came back.

Mauterre's breathing gradually relaxed, the swells of grief allowing her respite. "Rochelle? Does feeling scared and hurting so much ever go away?"

She had to consider that. "Well, not exactly, but it gets—I don't know—*easier*, I guess—like you get more used to it. It doesn't sneak up on you so much, and when it does, you get better at deciding that right then isn't a good time to let it grab you. You learn to think about it only for a moment, then put it away for another time."

"I wish I could make it go away for good."

"Mauterre, it's hard to understand now, but maybe in time you won't want it to. I mean, sometimes feeling bad can turn into feeling good because of the good memories, and you'll know that what you feel is because you love them."

"Does it work for you?"

The truth? Would that be right? "I'm just starting to learn this myself; but yeah, it helps a lot."

Mauterre considered that. "I wish Auntie Dix wouldn't worry so much, but I guess I worry about her, too. Do you worry like that?"

"Oh yeah," she said, her thoughts drifting to Pocomea, wondering how his tests were going, the big man too stubborn to admit how much hospitals scared him.

They lay there in the darkness, a shiny-eyed clock ticking off the minutes, memories swirling about the room.

"Rochelle?"

"Yes?"

"Don't worry. We'll be okay."

"Yeah, I think so."

And Rochelle did believe it, that Mauterre and her Aunt Dix would muddle their way through; and like so many before them, they would find a way.

Mauterre faded into a world of dreams, her grip on Rochelle's hand softening.

Don't worry. We'll be okay.

And Rochelle felt very weary, a cottony serenity cushioning her world. Her last thought as she drifted off to sleep . . .

Mauterre wasn't talking about Aunt Dix.

*   *   *

Go Overboard! read the sign, and the world's biggest octopus watched with TV-screen eyes as a Saturday-morning crowd invaded his lair.

Mikalu laughed. "She is one big cephalopod."

"Is this the highlight of a trip to Chicago, or what?" Rochelle teased.

"This display, it seems right for the city whose river flows backwards," he returned.

"Oh c'mon, admit you're enjoying the sights."

"Very much. In just three days I have experienced more than I imagined. The culture here, it is world-class, with many impressive accomplishments, but I am sad to see how a vital estuary has been destroyed for no reason, the marshes drained and wildlife habitats bulldozed. All this could have been built ten miles inland, with only roads and rails to the water for shipping and recreation. Instead, I see dilapidated warehouses, slum neighborhoods, tire-filled vacant lots—all where Great Herons once nested. The birds, they lost their homes so people could pile used tires and trash bags closer to the Great Lake."

They strolled toward the giant coral-reef exhibit, Rochelle's favorite at Shedd Aquarium. "Unfortunately," she said, "cities like this evolved over the centuries, and not many urban planners saw nature as something to protect."

"Yes, money buys the power to choose, and there is little profit in caring for Great Herons."

They entered a cavernous room and gazed upon the massive display. Shimmering light rippled across a submerged brain, oriental fans swaying in the artificial surge. The undulating moray eel tracked a seashell trundling along on crooked crab legs, while Queen Barracuda hovered high, her watchful eyes surveying the minions of her realm.

"Ninety-thousand gallons," Rochelle breathed.

"Yes," Mikalu said quietly, "I agree—it is too small."

"You don't like it?"

"Me, I have many feelings, some good, some not so much."

"Millions of people come here, Mika, and this helps educate them about the environment."

"Yes, that is very good for the people . . ." He watched a pair of plate-sized angelfish glide by in a blaze of gold and iridescent blue. "—Just not so good for the fish."

"But these specimens are *very* well cared for, and protected."

"Oh yes, I agree, but as Poco would say, Pele and her sisters, they care for their children, too." A leather-shelled sea turtle breast-stroked through the scene. Bug-eyed fishes swirled away, then regrouped in the interloper's wake. "Imagine how it must feel, Rochelle, to be suddenly snatched from your home, taken halfway around the world, and left trapped in some confining place."

Rochelle hesitated, the most poignant of fleeting memories flooding her mind. "Fish aren't like people, though," she said. "People understand there's a bigger world out there."

"Not all, especially the children. Many know only their neighborhoods, and maybe places their families visit, but the natural world doesn't seem real to them, just images on TV, postcards and pictures in books."

The giant grouper fish appeared, taking particular note of Mikalu as if recognizing an old friend, a kindred soul. He eased up to the glass, so Mika moved closer, both gazing into each other's eyes . . . and something seemed to pass between them—unless Rochelle's imagination had run wild.

"These fish," Mika said quietly, "they think the ocean has trapped them in a tidal pool, so they wait patiently for the waters to rise and take them home."

The big-lipped grouper turned toward Rochelle and nodded sadly, then directed his attention back to Mikalu as if listening, a silent conversation swirling between two worlds.

Mika said, "I think he trusts us, maybe even understands. These aquariums, they are good for teaching, and for research in marine conservation, and for preservation. At the rate people kill reefs, someday this may be . . ." He sighed, quietly finishing, "All we have left."

The depth of his feelings caught her by surprise, but then she remembered that blond-mopped boy flowing among the corals, the passionate teen who'd been writing to her about the wonder of a tropical valley and its sheltered lagoon, the unique young man who'd grown in many ways to become one of her most enduring friends. "It's not too late, Mika. *We* know."

He reached out with one finger and waggled it just above the grouper's face. The big fish nodded again, then backed away and, with a wave of the fin, swam off. Mikalu turned to Rochelle, his eyes glistening. "And we'll not forget, will we, Rochelle? Not even if we move far away to help people who need wheelchairs, or just to be closer to those who matter most."

She tried to answer, but no words would come, none existing for what she wanted to say, a feeling so fleet it teased her before dancing beyond her grasp.

Her phone signaled an incoming text. She blinked several times and tried to make out the message:

EMERGENCY / HURRY BACK —MAUTERRE.

"Oh no. Miss Dixon . . ."

"We hurry," Mika pronounced, reading over her shoulder. He grabbed her hand and rushed her through the displays, out to the car. Taking the wheel, he steered into traffic and headed northwest toward Sauganash. Rochelle tried calling, but reached voice-mail.

"What if—" Rochelle said. "I mean, I don't know how Mauterre could deal with even more adversity. What if something leaves Miss Dixon unable to care for her? What then?"

"Please, Rochelle—we not know what's wrong yet. Wait and see first; then we find best way to help."

Rochelle tried to heed his advice, but she couldn't just wait; she had to anticipate. She'd always needed to anticipate, to plan for the best, and prepare for the worst. Even so, she'd been knocked down too many times by the unexpected, struggling to regain her footing with failed contingency plans, no lifelines, nobody to help.

Mika sped into the lot and parked at the curb. They hurried up the walk just as Miss Dixon opened the door. Except for leaning on her cane, she looked fine.

"Your father called," she said, stepping aside to let them in. "He urges that you return to Hilo as soon as possible—"

"Got 'em!" Mauterre called from her room. She trotted out, explaining, "I checked the net and got your reservations. You leave in one hour, with a forty-minute layover in San Francisco."

Miss Dixon thrust a slip of paper at Rochelle. "He asks that you call him in Sydney, wants to talk to both of you. This phone has a speaker button."

Rochelle caught herself trembling, so she handed the number to Mika. While he dialed and conferred with an operator, Miss Dixon explained, "He said you can work out of his house in Hilo while you're there. I'll have Jodis express the designs and your files there Monday, if you want, but don't you worry about us until things have settled down. Mauterre and I will—"

"Hello?" It was her father's voice over the speaker box. "Rochelle? Mikalu?"

"We're here," they said in unison. Miss Dixon ushered Mauterre into the kitchen.

Ramo hesitated, his breathing ragged.

"What is it, Daddy?"

"It's Lalani. She, uh . . . They operated this morning—morning here, I mean—and she . . ."

"No," moaned Mika quietly.

"She did not survive. There were complications, and the cancer had spread too much."

Mika whirled around and stared at the door, fists clenched, arms twitching, his flight reflex battling for control.

Rochelle felt herself floating, gravity pulling at her, the instant before plunging helplessly.

"I need to remain here for several days," Ramo said. "She agreed they could—they could—you know, study her, learn what they can. It is very rare, what she has—what she . . . had."

"Oh, Daddy, I'm sorry," she managed to say, now fighting to maintain her composure, worrying about Mikalu.

"Something else," Ramo said. "You need to hurry home—to Hawai'i, I mean. To Coulée Makai. It is Pocomea. He called from the Hilo airport just as I returned to our—my—hotel room. I told him the bad news, and he became extremely upset. He dropped the pay-phone, and I heard noises; then he came back and kept shouting 'I not say good-bye' and 'Why you take Lalani so far away?'"

"It's grief, Daddy."

"There is more, Rochelle. He dropped the phone again, then came back, and it sounded like he might be crying. He kept shouting, asking me if I knew what he learned in Honolulu—"

Mika whirled again, staring at the phone, panic in his eyes. "What? What he find out?"

"He said—let me remember his exact words—he said, 'I got it, too! Mine is back, too, all bad-like, get inside bones, spread all over.' He said the surgeon lied when he was twelve, that the operation must have failed to remove the entire tumor from his neck."

"Poco— We need to help Poco," Rochelle said, her voice breaking. She needed to take charge here, take care of business, handle things, help.

"Yes," Mika agreed. "Poco, he needs us now."

"More than that," Ramo said. "I tried to calm him, to explain we shall seek the best treatment, but he kept shouting, 'No treatment! Too late now! No treatment!' Then he vowed not to die like Lalani. He said he would die his own way, at home. Then he hung up."

Mikalu lowered his head. "Oh, Poco."

"You need to hurry," Ramo said. "I fear he might do something drastic."

KE AKUA HOʻOMALU ANA MĀLIE

GENTLE PROTECTOR

A mercurial streak on blurry legs, Dabu sprinted from Taoke Valley to meet Mikalu's SUV. He peered inside, unable to hide his disappointment, then hurried around to open Rochelle's door, greeting them both with his trademark wave, the other hand over his heart.

Poco not come with you? Dabu signed.

Speaking and signing, Rochelle said, "No, didn't he return home last night?"

Mikalu came around, adding, "He had shuttle ticket from airport, should be here."

Dabu shook his head, answering, *I sleep early, so maybe he came late and left this morning.*

They trotted across to the house, Rochelle wishing they'd considered a Plan B in case he really hadn't returned, but Mikalu found an obvious clue: Poco's still-packed suitcase propped behind his bed.

Dabu waved from the wardrobe, pointing at the pair of gargantuan running shoes Poco had worn to Honolulu. Missing were the ratty sandals Mika had persuaded him to leave behind.

We go find him! Dabu urgently signed before dashing to the front door.

They followed him out and scanned up into the valley, across to the towering cliffs, then as far as they could see along the lagoon-side trail, finally deciding Poco likely would be found sitting in his thinking place above the ledge where Rochelle learned the papala ritual so many years before. Dabu ran ahead, easily outdistancing them despite navigating the sharp stones barefoot.

They found no sign of Poco at the ledge, so Dabu climbed the ridge for a better view. He surveyed the other side, suddenly shouting, "Meeg-loo! Meeg-loo!" before disappearing from sight.

Mika and Rochelle picked their way around the outcropping, Rochelle asking, "What's he saying?"

"Dabu, he is learning to speak my name, but he not—"

They found Dabu staring at the ground, Poco's wallet and keys lying unattended near a sheer drop. Propped against rocks several feet away, a small framed portrait of Lalani gazed expectantly across the eastern horizon.

They knelt and studied the scene some forty feet below, jagged boulders relentlessly assaulted by surges of Pacific surf. Rochelle's eyes burned and blurred, making it difficult to see, the idea of possibly finding her brother's battered body more than she could bear, another suicide more than any family could survive.

"Poco," Mikalu said, "he know here is too much danger for jumping." His voice cracking, he added, "He know d'ocean, know she not protect him from here." Maybe he couldn't yet grasp that Poco had intended to kill himself, couldn't comprehend the numbing power of hopelessness and grief.

Dabu worked his way back around the lagoon-side ledge, climbing out on rocks, hanging over the edge, canvassing the area below.

Mikalu shielded his eyes from the sun to scan up the volcano-park side of the ridge. Rochelle joined him, desperately hoping against reason that Poco had left his personal effects below while climbing, nevertheless steeling herself for the inevitable: searching for her brother's remains.

"Meeg-loo! Meeg-loo!" they heard Dabu screaming.

They hurried around the cliff face and found him on his belly pointing over the edge at a limp body wedged in the rocks, Poco's blood-caked head twisted at an odd angle, legs bobbing in the reef-dampened surge that rippled incessantly up toward the beach.

"Poco!" Mikalu called. "Poco!"

"We gotta jump!" Rochelle said.

They raced back to the ledge where Poco always used to step off when he wanted to ride the waves. Dabu disappeared the other direction.

They studied the crashing breakers, trying to time a jump between swells, but they didn't trust the water, both ultimately too afraid to risk a leap of faith. Instead, they ran back along the lagoon and saw Dabu inexplicably zipping up the valley trail beyond the house. They reached a low point and climbed down close to the water. Mika sent Rochelle over the rocks toward a spot just above Poco. Already panting from panic and exertion, he stripped off his shoes and took a deep breath, then dove in and swam to the body of his friend.

"He's alive!" he shouted over the roar of crashing waves. He clung to a rock and cradled Poco's head.

Rochelle wedged her legs, then felt Poco's neck, barely detecting a faint pulse. "He's cold from exposure!"

"How we get him off here?!"

Rochelle spotted Dabu, clad in full scuba regalia, cutting a swath through the water while clutching what appeared to be several buoyancy compensator vests. He swam just past them, then slipped out of his gear and rode a wave back to grab a rock, swinging the tank up so Mikalu could slam it into a crack.

Rochelle grabbed the gear and found Poco's custom-sized vest.

All three clinging precariously, they carefully timed when the surges lifted Poco's arms so they could slip the BC around him.

Mikalu held his breath and squeezed underneath to buckle the straps while Dabu helped Rochelle position a smaller vest backwards around Poco's neck to protect his head from the rocks. Mika attached the octopus hose from Dabu's tank to the smaller vest first, inflating it slowly while Rochelle monitored to be sure it didn't cut off the big man's air. Mika pulled the hose free and attached it to the bigger vest, then paused. "When I fill," he shouted, "next wave, she lift him up. We must be ready."

Dabu motioned for Rochelle to climb down beside Mika, holding her hand until she found footing. Then he positioned himself sideways, his arms ready to lift Poco's head and push.

"Do it!" Rochelle called out.

When the next surge dropped, Mika squeezed the button, and three-thousand pounds of pressure ballooned the vest.

In rolled the next wave, lifting Poco as all three pushed hard to clear the rocks.

The vest hung on something, an inrush of water slamming them back.

They tried again, Mika barking his knuckles when he yanked the strap.

It worked!

Dabu held Poco's inflated collar to keep his head stable, kicking frantically to pull him away from danger. Mika and Rochelle jumped in and joined him. Soon they were riding successive waves to make slow progress up through the lagoon. Dabu broke free and swam ahead, turning to be sure they had Poco under control before cutting a diagonal line up toward the far side of the beach. He hit the sand and broke into a sprint, disappearing into Taoke Valley.

They managed to pull him up into the shallows, but couldn't get him completely out of the water. Exhausted, heart pounding, Rochelle tried to catch her breath. "Wait—wait. He might have—a broken back—something we'd make worse—"

Mikalu examined Poco's head. The water had washed away most of the blood to reveal a pair of deep gashes in a swollen knot at the crown. Bruises on his arms and legs testified to the battery of interminable waves against unyielding cliff.

A droning hum sounded from over the ridge, growing louder, bursting into a thunderous *thwap! thwap! thwap!* as a helicopter rose into view.

"Viku!" Mikalu shouted. "Viku Taoke!"

'Cano Airtours, advertised the chopper. It passed overhead, then circled and hovered above a flat stretch of lava rock just up from the beach, slowly descending toward the ground.

Dabu came running from the slot with long poles wrapped in cloth slung over his shoulder. He skirted the rotor blade and splashed into the surf, unfurling a camouflage stretcher as the chopper settled and cut its engine. The door slid open, a man and woman springing out and running their way.

My brother, Dabu signed to Rochelle.

"What happen?" Viku demanded while the young woman examined Poco. A much taller and very handsome version of the Taoke boys, Viku bore a striking resemblance to little Dabu.

"Poco—um, he fall off cliff," Mika explained. "D'ocean, she hold him against rocks."

"How long ago?" the woman demanded.

"My wife, Nona," Viku said, "—she one good paramedic." A plump native, she examined Poco with an air of practiced professionalism.

"We don't know," Rochelle said. "Could've been last night, or maybe this morning."

"We call for medi-vac?" Viku asked Nona.

She shook her head, looking closer at the knotty gashes. "Body-temp too low, in shock now. Too much exposure, no time."

"I take seats out," he said, racing back to the chopper.

Dabu and Mika spread the stretcher beside Poco and considered the Herculean task that lay ahead.

"Let the air out?" Rochelle asked.

Nona shook her head. "No, the vests, they keep him steady."

Viku worked feverishly unbolting seats. Mika and Dabu scraped sand from under one side of Poco, Dabu planting himself on the water side each time the surf surged so he could block silt from filling their hole. Rochelle joined them, helping Mika wriggle one side of the stretcher underneath. Once they reached halfway, they worked from the other side, painstakingly inching him into position.

Nona felt for Poco's pulse again, then shook her head and leaned close to check his raspy breathing. "Some obstruction," she said quietly. "He struggles for air."

"Are we gonna—be able to lift him?" Rochelle asked, her heart thundering, arms tingly from hyperventilation.

Viku returned, leaving several bucket seats scattered on the rocks.

"Where's Pubo—and Wipu?" Mika asked.

Viku shook his head. "They go hike yesterday, camp out, not come home yet."

Mrs. Taoke appeared at the open slot, waving her arms and pointing. Several native men—*kalo* pickers, Rochelle assumed—ran across the beach and splashed through the water just as Mika and Dabu gave one last pull, Poco now fully on the stretcher. Everybody gathered around, grabbing the poles like so many pallbearers, gently lifting the unconscious man with no small effort.

"Careful," Nona warned, holding Poco's head.

Dabu tried to help, but he was too small, only getting in the way, so he hurried ahead, clearing loose rocks from their path.

The canvas stretcher strained to its limit, but they managed to hoist Poco and slide him onto the chopper's floor, virtually filling the tiny space.

"I should go with him," Nona said, fixing Rochelle and Mikalu with a tender expression. "I must monitor, ready CPR if needed, open airway as last resort."

"We'll drive," Mika said, scanning the cramped interior, Nona needing space to work, "—and meet you there."

"Hilo Medical Center," Viku shouted from the cockpit before starting the engine.

"We take care of Poco," Nona assured them, climbing in and sliding the door shut.

The workers headed back toward Taoke Valley. Dabu ran up to the stream and jumped in, submerging himself for a fast rinse before sprinting back toward the slot and home. Rochelle and Mikalu rinsed the same way, nearly tripping over each other in their frenzied haste, agreeing that they'd find some way to change clothes on the road.

Just as they reached the SUV, Dabu came running toward them, still dripping, a wad of clothes and shoes under his arm, his mother not far behind.

"It's okay?" Mika shouted to her.

She nodded, placing one hand over her heart, the other touching her face.

Rochelle jumped into the back, the guys piling in up front, and they took off. She rummaged through her suitcase and came up with dry jeans and blouse, undergarments and socks, and two towels. She retrieved clothes and a towel for Mika next, feeling oddly intrusive sorting through his intimate apparel, emergency at least taking the edge off modesty, if not rendering it entirely moot.

"Eyes front," she ordered. Mika tipped the mirror up, then signaled Dabu, the boy nodding understanding.

She lay in the seat, managed to wriggle out of her clothes, dried off and dressed without getting the area too wet. Tapping Dabu's shoulder, she motioned for him to climb back. He handed her his clothes—shorts and t-shirt and shoes, but no underwear or socks—then climbed over in one graceful motion. She scrambled awkwardly into the front.

Dabu changed quickly, then announced, "O-gay riddy, Meeg-loo." Rochelle turned and looked at him with surprise, making him blush. She grinned and nodded, giving him the divers' okay hand-sign, coaxing a shy smile. Mika veered quickly off the road, slamming the car into park and jumping in back.

Rochelle took over driving, thinking about Dabu's words. She'd not considered that his school had probably been working with him on speech, and she wondered at how much trust it must take for him to reveal his rudimentary skills to others. Annoyed with herself for looking startled, she wanted to hug him and tell him never to be embarrassed about accomplishing the kinds of great things so many others take for granted. She imagined driving him to speech therapy, helping him practice in the evenings, sharing his pride with every tiny increment of halting progress; and she remembered that feeling of helping Mauterre sort through her grief. She wondered again if this is what mothers experience, and she dared test the fabric of this unfamiliar yet somehow exhilarating role, both thrilled at the notion that it might very well fit, yet scared of a world filled with wrinkles and spills.

When Mikalu climbed up front, she realized she'd missed that moment of keeping her own eyes front, of knowing he was completely nude right there behind her while she pretended not to think about it. She wondered if he'd thought of her while she changed, and she remembered that stunned look on his face when as a young teen he'd discovered her in all her natural glory.

It wasn't the first time she'd recalled that day, or wondered what might have happened had she been somewhat older and a whole lot braver, but Mikalu had since proven to be a true friend, the kind she could never risk losing. Trading some fleeting fantasy for the reality of a chance fling would sacrifice an enduring and sustaining relationship for a lie that must inevitably shatter amid the collision of two worlds.

"No cars now," Mika said, breaking her reverie—on purpose she suspected. "I take wheel, you slide under, no gas for a minute."

He'd slipped back into that childhood patois after impressing her with his more refined language in Chicago, but maybe she didn't care so much anymore what the Miss Dixons and Mindy Madisons thought of him.

I speak well when I need to. Around you, I thought, no matter.

No, it didn't matter, and she liked it when he simply sounded like Mikalu.

They completed the maneuver, then raced down the desolate highway much faster than she'd dared drive.

Quiet fell over the car, a palpable reminder of the emergency that had brought them together in this unlikely corner of the world. She tried not to recall the image of Poco's broken and bloody body wedged precariously against the rocks, his wallet and keys and portrait of Lalani left unprotected out there on a clifftop ledge, and she wondered how she'd failed him, how he could think fighting this disease wouldn't be worth the effort, how he could hurl himself into the void without spending at least one last day with his sister and friends.

I not say good-bye. I not say good-bye.

And the sister who'd not bothered to visit him for nearly five years felt waves of regret washing over her, and her eyes burned with tears, her nose suddenly runny. She glanced over at Mikalu and saw he wasn't doing much better, but nothing she could say would blunt the immutable truth swirling about them.

She looked to the back seat and saw Dabu curled up in a ball on his side, his face hidden. He looked so small, so fragile, so vulnerable . . . His body quivered, and she could hear him crying quietly, his voice a whisper. "No, Pogo. No, Pogo. Dabu dabu dabu . . ."

She leaned over and stroked his hair, no amount of words able to penetrate his silent world, just a touch, a reminder, a friend.

She felt Mikalu's hand take hers, and she held on tightly, burying her face against the headrest, squeezing Dabu's trembling shoulder.

"She brought him home," she said.

"Who?" Mika asked.

"The ocean. She wouldn't let him die, so she caught him, floated him out on the waves, brought him to Coulée Makai, set him on the rocks until we could save him."

Mikalu said nothing at first, and for an instant it seemed everybody agreed Poco would be okay.

"You not believe that, Rochelle."

And she didn't. "I want to," she said.

"Damn Hawai'i superstitions. I not believe, either."

And the battered SUV barreled down a lonesome highway in this isolated corner of a world that doesn't give a damn about its children . . .

A world where mothers tumble to their deaths, leaving broken and lifeless bodies smeared with blood for helpless daughters to find.

A world where a young woman given one rare chance to have a brother loses him before she learns to appreciate this unique and special gift.

A world where any blond-haired San Diego boy can grow into the kind of honorable young man who would do *anything* to protect his friend, yet must face the hard fact that nothing he does will ever be enough.

A world where one little deaf child can transcend the silence to forge a most unlikely link between two families, only to learn his gentle giant of a protector isn't big enough to save himself.

A world where the tiny voice of a little man quavers from the back seat, whispering through his tears . . .

"No, Pogo. No, Pogo. No, Pogo . . ."

KŌKUA

HELP

Graduation night passed with the interminable *tick-tick-tick* of the waiting-room clock, departure day dawning as blushing rose sunlight bathed the sterile walls. In another life, Rochelle would have been packed for France by now, rousing from sleep at the House of Hammond, anticipating her future with Galway, even as she bid adieu to an old bird named Keefie.

The *amakihi* bird, that's who was missing. He'd not followed them to Hilo Medical Center. With no song to herald the morning, this couldn't be Hawai'i.

Mikalu drowsed on the opposite bench, fists still clenched in helpless frustration, Dabu slumped against his shoulder, asleep. Viku and Nona had stayed awhile. Poco's friend Ginny came, too, driving through the night, everybody gathering in the parking lot while her little boy slept in the car. All three eventually had to leave, though—responsibilities and commitments, an early-bird volcano tour, morning shift at the urgent-care clinic, Sunday latch-key program for the *keiki* center.

Ginny had offered to drive Dabu home, but Rochelle couldn't bring herself to send him away, not while surgeons busied themselves drilling holes in his friend's skull, not without him learning if Pocomea survived the night. Ginny would bring his schoolwork on Monday if Mrs. Taoke agreed to let him stay at Ramo's house, trusting him to Rochelle's care.

And why not? Didn't the young Miss DuFortier have a spotless record of protecting others? How hard could it be to add a vulnerable child to the mix? Good ol' responsible Rochelle—she'd be lucky if he didn't suffer some horrible calamity during her watch.

Rochelle always admired how her mother could take adversity in stride, how she rose to any occasion, taking care of business, bucking up and seizing the reins . . . though later she would quietly crawl into her shell to swallow pills as insulation against an indifferent world. Mid-crisis, though, Mom was the one to turn to. Right now she'd be making plans: groceries for Ramo's house; phone numbers to keep people informed; a change of clothes for the boy—*Mon Dieu!* He's not even wearing socks! And did somebody send to

Honolulu for Poco's medical records? And when is Ramo returning? *You did call your father, didn't you?*

"Miss DuFortier?"

"Yes!" She wobbled to her feet, Mikalu suddenly beside her, Dabu right behind him rubbing sleepy eyes.

"You're Mr. Wai-Nuikai's next-of-kin?"

"Yes, I'm his sister."

"I'm Tessin Toddler, chief of surgery." A smallish Scandinavian-looking man clutching a clipboard, he looked very pleased. "We've relieved the pressure and reduced the danger of complications. The cold water likely saved his life; it slowed his metabolism and reduced the potential for cranial swelling that often proves more critical than the original injury."

"Is he awake?" Mikalu asked. Good, somebody could think to ask the right questions.

"I'm afraid not. Please understand, while we cannot predict how long he will remain unconscious, we are optimistic about his prognosis because his brain activity registers in the normal range."

"So he might recover completely?" she asked, a splash of sunlight bathing her in the golden glow of hope.

"From his head injuries, yes, he may. However, he'll face two other challenges. I'm afraid he suffered considerable lumbar trauma, a shattered vertebra and likely nerve damage; we won't know until further evaluation. Permanent impairment of the lower limbs is a very real possibility."

"No scuba . . ." Mika said.

Dabu tugged at his sleeve, so Mika began signing for him, catching him up on the news, the worried boy nodding solemnly.

"What's the other problem?" Rochelle asked.

"Well, I'm not sure how appropriate it is for me to say—"

"The cancer?"

"Oh, you know then."

"Yes, we got his message from Honolulu, but never had a chance to learn the details."

"We had his chart transmitted. They're terming it a 'second cancer,' an unrelated malignancy that surfaces long after a first cancer has been eradicated."

"How bad is it?"

"The tumor between his shoulders is crowding the spinal cord, already affecting the function of his arms. Also, there is a lesion on his left ulna—the arm bone here," he added, tapping the inside of his arm above the wrist. "He'll need the tumor removed, and probably more radiation or chemotherapy, but until he consents to a biopsy of the ulna, we cannot determine if the malignancy has spread."

"He didn't have that done?"

"He refused to schedule the extra two days."

"Oh, Poco," she sighed.

"His condition is stable for now," the doctor assured them. "You should go home and get some rest."

They thanked him and watched as he disappeared down the corridor. Dabu sat on the bench, rubbed his face, and closed his eyes.

"I'll leave my father's number with the desk nurse," Rochelle said.

"And I'll sleep-walk Dabu out to the car, open windows and let out stink of wet clothes," Mika said. He practically had to lift the exhausted boy to get him on his feet again.

Rochelle stood there alone for a moment, a respite from looking and acting strong, but she felt too numb, too weary to indulge in an ill-advised catharsis. She stopped by the desk, pleased by the reassurances of a very sympathetic woman, then headed out to find Mikalu waving their clothing in the breeze, Dabu asleep in the back seat.

"Size eight," Mika said, showing her Dabu's ragged running shoes. "Little guy, big feet already."

One big heart, too, she thought.

They drove to her father's impressive house overlooking the bay, retrieved the hidden key, verified Ramo hadn't called back yet, then located all three guest rooms before hauling their suitcases and wet clothes inside. They hustled Dabu to bed, then looked for the washer and dryer.

There were none. "Probably has a pick-up laundry service," Rochelle guessed. "Sounds like my father."

"Not Lalani, though," Mika said, "—except she change all *da kine* ways these last few years."

"We can deal with it later," Rochelle suggested, and Mika didn't need his arm twisted to agree.

They said good-night, gazed at each other for a lingering moment, then trundled off to their rooms, uncertain plans left undiscussed.

Rochelle donned her nightgown and slipped under the covers, exhausted . . .

But she couldn't sleep, not so much for worrying about Poco—his fate lay beyond her control for now—but more for how to organize the coming days, how to take care of a child, and a friend, and herself.

Her throat hurt, mouth suddenly dry. She slipped out of bed and crept quietly to the kitchen. The refrigerator stood empty except for a few staples, the cabinets woefully lacking anything nutritious. Kids need to drink milk when they wake up, she decided, and for some reason having milk there for Dabu suddenly loomed as the most important priority of her life—and *Mon Dieu!* He certainly needed a change of clothes!—at least clean socks and underwear—oh, and a toothbrush. And they needed groceries. What would the guys eat when they awoke hungry?

She found herself in Mika's SUV driving down to the Waiki Mega-Mart, then wheeling a rickety cart up and down the aisles, milk and juice and snacks and sandwich-makings and frozen dinners tumbling off the shelves. She took a deep breath and steeled herself, then dared to venture into that foreign territory known thereabouts as *Boys' Apparel*. Why couldn't Dabu be a girl? What did she know about shopping for boys?

She found some pants that looked nice, and some shorts, then a shirt, holding them up and picturing Dabu's size—making good guesses, she liked to think. She found some shoes on clearance, too—size eights!—much nicer than that decrepit pair she figured would self-destruct within the week. Socks proved more of a challenge, but one style had a chart on the package listing shoe sizes, so she triumphed over that part of the test.

Then she confronted a huge rack of briefs—and blinked. She knew the beast sensed her rising panic. She felt flustered, like she had no business being there, wondering if she'd embarrass Dabu. Maybe she should just leave them in the sack and let him discover them in private, 'nuff said.

But what size? The monstrous rack offered no handy charts, no open packages—not that she'd be caught dead holding up a pair to picture if they might fit him. Buying several sizes was an option, but she had to watch her meager funds, already having splurged too much. She looked back and forth, clutching a pack in each hand, and she felt dizzy, nauseated.

She leaned back against a pole and tried to imagine what her mother would do.

Look, Mom, only twenty-one and shopping for kids' clothes. You wouldn't believe how much has happened. You always called me your little planner; well, my plans don't seem to be working out.

She closed her eyes and tried to see postcard scenes from the *Train à Grande Vitesse*, but she found long stretches of desolate highway, a banged-up SUV speeding toward Hilo.

Oh Mom, you're missing it all. You're missing out on my whole life.

"You're new at this, aren't you, dear?"

"Huh?" Rochelle started, then realized she was clutching packs of underpants in the blinding fluorescent glare, no doubt looking like she'd had a seizure. "Um, yes. I don't know what size."

A petite, sun-burnished older woman, she smiled reassuringly. "How old is he?"

"Um, twelve, I think. Yes, twelve, nearly thirteen."

"Ah . . . A nephew, perhaps?"

"No, a friend." That certainly sounded weird.

"My grandsons, they are fourteen and eleven. They stay with me since my daughter, well, she's getting some help right now. How tall is your friend?"

Rochelle transferred the packs to one hand and held out the other at about Dabu's height.

"Regular, slim, or husky?" she asked, digging some photos from her purse.

"Slim, definitely."

She showed a picture of herself flanked by two handsome boys. "About like Scottie?" she asked, pointing at the younger one.

"Yes. In fact, almost exactly."

She smiled again. "I believe the twelve-to-fourteen will be fine. Besides, boys aren't insulted when you err in thinking they're bigger than they really are. Now, what else do you have?"

Rochelle let her rummage through the cart. "I'm sorry, dear, but these trousers just won't do. They're terribly out of style. And these shoes, too—that's why they're on clearance."

It took all of ten minutes to replace Rochelle's woefully inadequate choices. "I don't know how to thank you," she said, still embarrassed over being found gawking like a zombie at packs of underwear.

"Glad I could assist, dear. I can tell, you're helping somebody, aren't you?"

Rochelle nodded. "Yes, I'm—well, doing the best I can."

And she *was* doing the best she could. For Poco right now, that meant waiting, and trying not to let worry and responsibility overwhelm her. She'd taken care of everybody's immediate needs—places to sleep, groceries, clothes for the kid—and now she felt tired, really tired.

"You'll do fine, dear. I'm sure of it."

"I hope so."

"Just remember, everybody needs help sometimes. Even you."

Rochelle looked down at the woman's serene expression, gazing for a moment into her wise eyes, and she wondered at how people's lives change in ways they never expect, at the heroes who go on, caring for friends, protecting family, raising grandchildren, tapping inexhaustible reservoirs of love when it's needed most.

"Yes," Rochelle said quietly. "Sometimes I need help, too."

"Well, dear, then don't be afraid to ask."

*   *   *

Moonlight splashed creamy luminescence on the berry-patterned curtains as Rochelle sat in twilight thinking about get-well cards and watching Mikalu help Dabu with his school work. The studious pair worked side-by-side under chandelier glow at the dining-room table, a silent partnership solving mysteries of the universe. Mika finally closed the book and clasped the youngster's shoulders in one of those not-quite-a-hug guy hugs, Dabu smiling with pride.

One more, Mika signed to him, pulling a book into position. Dabu responded in mock anguish, pulling his hair with a voiceless wail.

Mika made the drinking sign, and Dabu responded by clutching his chest and lolling his tongue. "You want drink, Rochelle?" Mika asked, setting out three glasses before she could answer. Dabu flipped through the book to locate a challenging chapter.

Mika poured sodas and brought Rochelle's to the couch, pausing to eye the overnight parcel lying untouched in the opposite chair.

She couldn't tell him that tackling the wheelchair drawings would feel like accepting that Poco would never wake, that it would mean she'd finally decided to get on with her own life. "Thank you" was all she managed.

Mika knelt before her, looking up into her eyes. "We wait as long as necessary," he said quietly, glancing again at the package. "But all it means is you spend this time doing good for others. That's all."

"I will," she said, wondering not for the first time if he could read her mind.

He nodded, touched her hand, and returned to the dining room.

She would get to work in a few minutes; she just needed to relax a little and think about all those home-made cards the children had sent via Ginny, now decorating the hospital room: Poco lying face down on the beach while diligent *amakihi* birds built a nest of nuts and bolts on his lower back, a child's interpretation of yesterday's surgery to shore up his damaged vertebra with pins and rods; Poco pushing wheelchair-bound children across the sand; Poco floating rafts out to the shallow reef; underwater scenes, including the big-lipped grouper urging Poco to *Get Well Soon*; a crude sketch of scuba gear waiting on the rocks for Poco's return; and the one that for some reason had made Rochelle feel especially sad: Poco, tiny in the distance, watching from the far ridge, keeping an eye on the friends he could no longer welcome in person to Coulée Makai.

She closed her eyes and drifted awhile, then looked up in time to catch Dabu coming for his now-customary good-night hug. He never did it right, though; he was supposed to use that moment to find affection and reassurance from *her*, a ritual reminder that sleep is nothing to fear. But Dabu was too old for that, nearly a teen now, and smart enough to understand she needed the reassurance, too; after hugging her an extra few seconds, he always stepped back and gazed upon her face, enveloping her in his aura of serenity, then reached out and lightly touched her cheek, the other hand over his heart . . . and scampered off before she could say or sign or do something to embarrass them both.

Mikalu was straightening up in the kitchen, and she really didn't want him coming in to find the parcel still unopened, so she reminded herself again that moving forward didn't have to mean she'd given up on Poco, then carefully unwrapped the shipper and sorted through the pile. Mika came in just as she discovered an unexpected envelope: the police report about her mother's fall. After all these years, she would know if the world believed it really was an accident, or if her father knew the truth of her mother's suicide.

"You like me to leave you alone?" Mika asked, kneeling before her again.

She looked from the envelope to his face, recalling his words from so long ago.

Blame, it not always have to add up, make sense.

She asked, "Will you help?"

"Always, Rochelle. Always." He sat beside her, accepted the report, opened it, and held the documents on his lap. "You be okay, Rochelle? No matter what all *da kine* things these papers say?"

"Eventually, Mikalu. Eventually."

He watched her for a moment, then flipped past the cover page and found the cause of death: *Cranial trauma, accidental fall from 3rd floor balcony.*

Her eyes blurred with tears, and Mikalu waited quietly.

"The pills—they'll always be my secret," she finally said, not sure how much relief she could find in carrying such a burden.

"*Our* secret," Mikalu said.

She nodded. That did sound right, and it felt better.

"We should see everything now," he said, his hand on the papers, "then put this away."

She took a deep breath. "It . . . It won't answer the question, though. It can't." He looked at her, and she thought he might know what she meant, but she had to say it anyway. "Why—why wasn't I enough? I mean, she had *me*. Wasn't that enough reason—enough reason not to . . . ?"

"She forgot, Rochelle. She took drugs, and they made her forget."

"Yeah," she said with a sigh, "that's where I always end up." She wiped her eyes, reached for a tissue, and blew her runny nose. And she managed a weak smile. "Okay, let's get it over with."

He responded with that subtle, knowing smile of his.

"Victim discovered by daughter, Rochelle Voudette DuFortier, age thirteen." He looked at her, eyebrows arched. "*Voudette?*" If she didn't know better, she'd say he was smirking.

"Don't go there, Mr. Mikalu *Babyboy* Shulman."

"Ouch," he said, feigning a bee sting on the noggin. "How you learn about *Babyboy?* Pocomea, he give me 'way, right?"

"He told me that your mom wanted *Babyboy*, but your dad said all the kids would tease you. He wanted *Mikalu*, after his friend on the boat who died, and he thought everyone would call you *Mikey*."

"Please *don't* call me that," he said, repeating Dabu's feigned anguish, pulling his hair and this time giving voice to the wail.

"We'll put that one in our box of secrets."

"Thank you," he said, taking her hand and bowing in submission. "I owe you big-time . . . *Voudette*."

"All right, touché. Now, let's get through these papers," she said, grateful he'd helped her lift the tension.

"No witnesses," he read. "Daughter Rochelle was at Cedar Point with family of Frank Madison—names and address listed below—corroborated by interviews, ticket stubs, and photos of the trip."

"As if I were a suspect," Rochelle said, surprised by the detail.

"Just being thorough." He went on culling information from the report.

"Husband Ramo Rene DuFortier, separated, living in Hilo, Hawai'i. Corroboration—it lists Lalani and two men who were here for business meetings. They stayed with him and Lalani as guests in this house."

"Business—my father's favorite pastime."

"Housekeeper, Kala Ko, and gardener, Jackie Ko, siblings, were visiting their aunt, Tani Ko, in Hilo, Hawai'i—address below. It gives dates, looks like they were here for a week, Jackie arriving Wednesday, Kala Thursday. Corroboration: verified by Tani Ko, airline boarding passes, and car-rental records listing Jackie Ko."

"I wonder why they went separately," she said, lying back and smoothing her hair across the cushion.

"Maybe cheap tickets, fly standby, get bumped."

"Yeah, they'd be watching their budget. As live-ins, I'm sure the pay was low."

He read on: "No suspicious activity, visitors, or cars seen in the area." He added, "It names the neighbors who were interviewed, and it says no evidence of forced entry, then lists a detective and an officer."

"No prowlers," she scoffed, "—except the police. When I returned to pack my belongings, it looked like a whole platoon had tromped through the house."

"Toxicology report," he said quietly, pulling out a single sheet.

She sat up. "I thought they didn't do that."

Mika shrugged. "Remember, even with painkillers d'fall was still an accident."

"But taking so many should at least look like a *possible* suicide."

Mika was reading it and shaking his head. He looked up, puzzled. "No drugs," he said.

"Huh?" She leaned over to look.

He pointed to where it listed a blood-alcohol level of .03, the equivalent of a glass of wine.

Psychotropic Drugs: NONE. Other Drugs: NONE.

"She *did* get rid of the painkillers," Rochelle said.

"People who are addicted, is this what they do?"

"Yes, when they stop cold turkey. It's the only sure way to resist temptation. She regretted making me feel guilty, so she decided to quit while I was gone. That explains picking the flowers." Rochelle's enthusiasm swelled in waves, buoying her in ways she'd missed for many years.

"The flowers, they helped her celebrate remembering what was important," Mika said, riding with her at the crest.

"It—it was still a tragedy," she said, "but she made everything okay before it happened, and now I know." She hugged him, held tightly, felt herself trembling a little, but for once that seemed like a good thing.

"Now you know," he said.

"Yes, now I know."

Cranial trauma, accidental fall . . .

*   *   *

The call came just before seven Wednesday morning, a dreary day overcast with great roiling clouds stalking up Wailuku River to cast a pall over Hilo Medical Center. Mikalu roused Rochelle and Dabu, herded them to the SUV, then barreled down to the hospital, everybody rushing inside.

"He's medicated, and very groggy," the physician's assistant warned them. An older native woman, heavyset and wearing a flowery frock, she glared disapprovingly, a stern warning that she'd be keeping an eye on them. "You need to keep it short; let him rest."

She ushered them in, standing back to watch while they gathered beside the bed. Poco appeared no different, head bandaged, arms tethered to wires and tubes, trunk and legs webbed in strapped braces. The only evidence that he'd awakened was a tray with open milk carton, some gelatin, and a half-eaten oatmealy-looking concoction.

"We're here, Poco," Rochelle said.

"How-lee gir-ull," Poco said, his voice dry and raspy, eyes still closed. He swallowed several times.

The PA stepped forward and guided a straw from the milk carton to his mouth. He drank a little, then swallowed several more times.

Mika said, "You give us much *pilikia*, you know, but now we're all glad you wake up."

"They drill hole—in my head—Mikalu," he said.

"And let some stubbornness leak out, I hope," Mika said. "You got plenty left, though, brah."

Poco managed a hint of smile. "I have one big dream," he said, his voice improving slightly.

"You were unconscious four days," Rochelle said.

"One *big-big* dream, then," Poco said, his humor rising. "I dream Pele's sister—d'ocean—she float me on d'waves, say I ride long enough, say she take me back to Coulée Makai now, say Pele needs me. I told her leave me on d'beach, but she say I might drown, leave me on rocks, wait for Mikalu and Haole-girl, they come help me."

"Dabu," Mika said, "he help, too."

"Dabu," Poco, said, "he one good friend."

Mika signed Poco's words for Dabu, the boy visibly moved. "Dabu, he's here now, too."

"Dabu?" Poco opened his eyes, squinting against the bright glare.

Dabu stepped forward and placed a hand over his heart, the other reaching to touch Poco's hand. The big man squeezed the boy's fingers. "Good clothes," Poco said, Rochelle signing the words. "D'pretty girls, they all wanna be Dabu's friend."

Dabu smiled proudly, a gesture Rochelle had seen every time he passed a mirror and noticed his cool new appearance.

The PA waggled her finger at them, then slipped out, tapping her watch.

Rochelle said, "Dabu's brother Viku helped in the rescue, too."

"No!" Poco snarled. "No Taoke boys!"

Startled, Dabu stepped back. Nobody needed to sign what Poco had said.

"Viku and Nona," Mika said, "they fly you to Hilo, save your life."

"Taoke boys, they belong in jail," Poco spat. "Wipu and Pubo most of all. D'police, did they catch them yet, lock them up?" Poco acted as if he might try to sit up, then settled back, wincing with pain.

"Let's not worry about that now," Rochelle suggested, reaching out to squeeze his other hand. "You'll pop your pins and throw a rod if you get any more excited."

Poco calmed some, Mika giving Dabu the *okay* hand-sign.

"All right," Poco said, "Don't call police; I get better first, then go get Taoke boys myself."

"Well," Mika said, glancing at Rochelle, "that sure is one big goal, one good reason to get all better."

"Yes," Rochelle said, "and we want you to think about going for the treatment in Honolulu, too. We need you around for a long time."

Mika subtly told Dabu that Poco had decided not to kill himself, Dabu nodding enthusiastically.

"You have lots to live for," Rochelle added, "—us and Ginny and all your *nā keiki*."

"Yah," Poco said, "and to protect Coulée Makai."

"That's right," Mika said, buoyed by Poco's newfound will to live. "D'valley, and d'lagoon, they need you. Pele's sister, she was right."

"So you've decided to get the treatments then?" Rochelle asked.

"Yah, I already decide that in Honolulu."

"But you checked yourself out," Rochelle said.

"I get chicken skin," Poco said, "—already have plane ticket home, decide to wait for when Mikalu comes, too—maybe even Haole-girl, if she not too busy, and Dabu if school out then."

"We get chicken skin, too," Mika said, "but we'll come to Honolulu and have chicken skin together."

"That's right," Rochelle agreed.

Dabu nodded and pointed at his chest, sensing the drift of the conversation. Mika explained with some quick signs, and Dabu nodded more vigorously, signing, *I come, too.*

"So you didn't decide—" Rochelle started. "Um, you didn't come home intending to—I mean, not until my father told you about . . . about Lalani."

Poco looked downcast. "I sorry for that. Please tell Ramo I sorry, not mean to say bad things, all *pupule* 'cause Lalani—" He had a catch in his throat, his voice raspy again. "—All sad 'cause I not say good-bye."

"You know she'd want you to take care of yourself," Rochelle said.

"Yah," Poco admitted. "She worry all d'time 'bout me and Mikalu."

"Poco," Rochelle said, her own voice suddenly quavering. "Poco, please promise you'll never try that again. Don't make us worry, too, okay?"

"Try what, Haole-girl?"

"You know, ending it all."

"You mean kill myself?"

"Well, yeah."

"I *never* do that! Coulée Makai, she needs me. I not *that* much *pupule*, you know."

"But— Are you saying it was an *accident?* You *fell?*"

"You think I *jump?*"

"Well, you took out your keys and wallet, and what about the picture of your mom?"

"What picture?"

Mika said, "The one you left up on the cliff."

"I not do that. I was taking nap when I hear noise, wake up and find note by front door. It say come meet on *papala* cliff. I think Dabu leave it, so I go, but nobody's there. Then I hear noise around ridge. When I go see, somebody throw sand in my eyes, then hit me in d'head, and I fall down."

"Somebody *ambushed* you?" Rochelle asked, incredulous.

"Yah. I say, 'I break you face, Taoke boys!' But then everything explode like *papala* with not enough oil."

"You got hit a second time," Rochelle said.

"Yah. Then Taoke boys, they push me in d'water, hope I drown."

"They pulled out your keys and wallet first," Mika said, his ire rising, "then go get Lalani's picture." He clenched his fists.

With nobody signing for him, Dabu looked upset, confused by the angry faces.

"Did they say anything?" Rochelle asked.

"No," Poco said. "They too chicken-shit, 'fraid I get up fast and find 'em."

Mika chimed in, "Now 'cause Lalani die, they have no chance she might say use Coulée Makai for one big *kalo kuleana*. They know Poco not agree, so they make like Lalani's death is reason Poco go all *pupule* and kill himself."

They all stared at each other for a minute, Dabu's lower lip trembling, Mikalu's fists clenched in frustration.

Rochelle shook her head. "But how would they know Lalani died?"

BEYOND THE RIDGE

Rochelle and Mikalu dropped Dabu at home, then parked and crossed the valley. They paused to stare at the carved-*koa* door, its ornate handle worn smooth by generations of Wai-Nuikais who made a home of the ancient chiefs' *hale*.

"I can't believe nobody's ever installed a lock," she said.

"Never needed one. Coulée Makai, it has always been safe. We have locks on our dive shop, protect expensive gear, but not even *nā Taoke* ever violated the sanctity of *hale 'ohana*—till now."

"You think there's any chance of getting prints off the handle?"

Mika wagged his finger at her reprovingly. "Three times you promised Poco you not call d'police."

"*Yet*," she said. "I said I wouldn't call them *yet*. It was the only way to calm him down. Besides, *you* didn't promise."

"Poco, he thinks you meant us both. That's d'truth that matters. Besides, I already use door that night I drove back to pack our clothes and things: twice carrying bags to car, once bringing Poco's wallet and keys and picture from d'cliff, and again to go check compressor at dive shop. I not expect Poco to wake up d'next day and say prowlers came in to leave a note, steal Lalani portrait."

Rochelle sighed and pushed the door open, Mika following her inside. She checked the trash where Poco said he'd tossed the note. "Nothing," she said, disappointed.

"See?" Mika said. "You call those detectives again with nothing but Poco's accusations, they think he just cries wolf."

"I'll talk him into letting us file a report, but it would help if we had something to back it up."

"Divers are here," he said, glancing out the window. A van had pulled into the open slot across the valley, long-haired *haole* men in Farmer-Johns unloading scuba gear.

"Hmmm . . ." Rochelle said, following him outside, "I think I'll see if Mrs. Taoke is back yet. I'll assure her Dabu is welcome to return with us to stay in Hilo, then see where the conversation leads. Maybe I can learn something useful."

"Be careful," Mika warned. "You're one smart lady, but *nā Taoke*, they might be dangerous if they think you know Poco got pushed."

"I will, but I feel dishonest continuing to hide it from Dabu. He'll be hurt when the police get involved and he figures out we already knew. I'm already hard-pressed to explain why we still haven't told him his best friend's mother died."

They crossed the footbridge and greeted the divers, a quartet of lanky beach-bum types sporting expensive, high-tech gear. Mikalu introduced everybody, updated the visitors on Poco's condition, then explained he'd be staying in Hilo during their three-day octopus-filming expedition, but that he would leave them access to the air compressor and showers.

"Spear guns?!" Rochelle blurted, spotting several of the onerous-looking trigger-handled tubes with razor-barbed steel shafts affixed to their sides.

"Only for the Kona coast," Mika assured her.

"We just store 'em here," said one of the divers, "whenever we know we're coming back in a few months."

"Poco would shoot 'em at us," said another, "if we so much as got 'em *wet* in *this* lagoon."

"This is a private marine sanctuary," the first said, everybody nodding agreement.

As Mika led them toward the dive shop, Rochelle walked through the slot and up the gravel road bisecting Taoke Valley, then hesitated outside the ramshackle house. Misshapen plaster-board and corrugated-tin additions had grown like barnacles on the original shell of lava stones and mortar, *kalo*-farm prosperity obviously not having been invested in home improvements.

Dabu startled her, racing out to take her hand and lead her to the door. Mrs. Taoke waved off Rochelle's apologies for the intrusion, then invited her inside. A contradiction of stiff demeanor and flowing hibiscus-print *mu'u mu'u*, the Hawaiian matriarch winced when Rochelle's gaze drifted to the grotesque-looking man staring at a portable TV, one foot soaking in a washtub, the other missing from a stump of leg propped on cushions. Covered with bulging veins and odd scars and several gaping sores, he looked sick, possibly gangrenous, his once-bronze skin tinted green like the patina of tarnished copper. A half-full bottle of liquor sat open on the rickety table beside him.

My father, Dabu signed without recognition from the man, apparently not expecting any.

Mrs. Taoke ushered her son and Rochelle to a shabby but immaculately clean dining area, pouring glasses of juice as they took seats around the table.

They began by trading concern over Poco's condition, expressing optimism for his recovery, then embarrassing Dabu as they alternately gushed over what a fine young man he was becoming. Mrs. Taoke relaxed quickly, pouring more juice and warming to her visitor.

"I'm curious about the enmity between your family and the Wai-Nuikais," Rochelle said, no longer signing for Dabu. "—Why they haven't gotten along for so many generations," she added, sensing she might have used an unfamiliar word.

"That go way back to d'chiefs," Mrs. Taoke said. "D'land grant gave roadway rights across Ki'Patu and Taoke lands. *Nā* Ki'Patu, they already related to *nā* Taoke by marriage, so they not care when our fathers pass on their land; but both *nā 'ohana* angry 'bout *nā* Wai-Nuikai crossing to Coulée Makai. *'Ohana* Ki'Patu, they want to get paid each time. It turn into one big fight, and one boy from each family get killed. *Nā* Ki'Patu, they long gone now, sell land, move away; but sons of Taoke and Wai-Nuikai make bad words to each other ever since. Papaii, he one good *kāne*, try to make things better; but that end very bad, only make things worse again."

"That was when your son drowned?" Rochelle asked sympathetically.

Mrs. Taoke nodded sadly. Dabu reached out to hold his mother's hand. Though nobody signed for him, he was paying close attention, the light in his eyes charged by currents of emotion swirling in the static air.

"What was his name?"

"Timu, my first *keiki*—and all are boys ever since," she added, stroking Dabu's long dark hair.

"Timu became friends with Papaii, just like Dabu befriended Pocomea?"

She nodded again, her eyes glistening with memories, Rochelle unsure if she'd intruded too much. "Same age, too—twelve, just like Dabu. Timu, he all d'time wanna learn how Papaii step off cliff and let d'ocean bring him to d'beach. My husband, he tell Timu *No*. He say d'ocean, she knows only *nā* Wai-Nuikai belong in Coulée Makai. But Papaii, he tell Timu stop stealing corals and show d'ocean he take care of her children's homes, then she take care of him, too. Papaii, he say Pele and her sisters, by and by, they welcome *all* d'peoples who take care of Coulée Makai."

"Papaii was a good man," Rochelle said.

"Yah," Mrs. Taoke agreed. "And Tapakiki, she one good friend, too."

"Why did Timu try jumping off the cliff without Papaii showing him how?"

"Timu, he break promise to Papaii that morn and take cowry shells from d'lagoon, bring them to me for presents. I tell him take them back, but he say no and run away, so I send Viku—he just nine then—but Papaii, he catch him and get very angry, think little Viku was taking d'shells that crabs need for homes. Viku, he get all weepy eyes, say Timu did it; so Papaii, he send him home and go looking for his little friend. Papaii, he tell us he find Timu up on d'cliff; but Timu, he jump when he sees Papaii coming. Papaii, he dive in and search; but d'ocean, she . . ." Tears welled in her eyes, a lone droplet breaking free to zig-zag a glistening trail down her wrinkled cheek.

"You know it broke his heart," Rochelle said. "Pocomea told me Papaii always talked of little Timu, sometimes sitting up on the cliff and gazing at the water, his eyes all weepy, saying the ocean didn't understand that Timu really was a good boy who just needed a chance to learn." Rochelle's own eyes blurred, and she felt Dabu squeezing her hand.

Mrs. Taoke wiped her face, then sat up straight and shook her head. "My husband, he think Papaii push our boy, go accuse him of murder. Kono'au, my husband's father, he still lived here then; he talk story 'bout nā Wai-Nuikai killing Taoke boys, try to poison my sons' heads with all da kine hate. Little Viku, he not believe them; he already old enough to know Papaii always been one good kāne; but Wipu, he listen too much, get older and go make trouble for Pocomea all d'time. Pubo, he one quiet boy; but he all d'time follow Wipu 'round, get in up to his ears, too. Little Dabu, he born after Kono'au die, make good friends with Pocomea before my husband learn to talk story with his hands, before he fill Dabu's head with hate."

"Mrs. Taoke, do you think Wipu—or any of your sons—might still do something to hurt Papaii's family?"

She shook her head. "That time you and Mikalu climb up on ridge, when Wipu and Pubo make fight over scuba tanks, my boys come home all bruises and bloody lips, hide from me all shame-like. When I find Pubo, he get all weepy eyes, tell me what happen, feel real bad. Then I go find Wipu and whack him with stick till he get weepy-eyes, too, tell him no more bother Coulée Makai. Both boys, they make one big promise; and when Viku find out, he say he whack 'em, too, if they break it. I believe they still keep their promise."

Rochelle thought that for Pubo that might be true. But Wipu . . . "Did you hear about Lalani's cancer?"

Mrs. Taoke nodded sadly. "Yes. Dabu, he bring us all d'news. I chant *mele* for Lalani, ask *nā lapu* to bring her home safe. She be all right, by and by, you'll see. Poco, too."

A low rumble sounded through the window, growing into the unmistakable *thwap! thwap! thwap!* of Viku's helicopter coming in to land. Dabu put a hand on his chest, apparently feeling the vibration. His face lighting up, he rushed out to greet his brother.

"Lalani is very sick," Rochelle said, "but we all appreciate you asking the spirits to help her."

"Lalani, she one good *wahine*, let Pocomea and Mikalu stay here at Coulée Makai with Papaii, even when she need to leave for school, get job."

"Were you ever tempted to leave?"

"Almost had to, by and by. Needed money for boys' school clothes, and to pay taxes; that's why Hilo-man's deal look so good at first."

"It doesn't now?"

She shook her head, muttering, "No" without offering to explain.

"What's Hilo-man's name?"

"D'nai'i. D'nai'i Ko'opea." It didn't sound familiar.

"I've noticed your sons don't work the farm established here."

"No, they want nothing to do with him. We use his money one time for Viku's helicopter, help oldest boy start business, think we get lots more for younger boys, too; but Hilo-man, he rip us off."

"So even if he paid them extra, Wipu and Pubo wouldn't, you know, help him out, do odd jobs?"

"No, my boys, they hate him, still angry he steal their land."

"Does Hilo-man ever threaten you, or act like something violent might happen if he doesn't get his way?"

"No, he not need to; he already gets his way. But after police come 'round to ask about that time when Papaii fall, I wonder if Hilo-man try scaring him to make deal in Coulée Makai."

"If you don't mind me asking, how *did* he take advantage of you?"

"He wanted to buy whole valley to make *kalo kuleana* above d'road, and to put apartments down by cliffs over d'water, but we say no, need land for our sons to live someday. So he make deal with my husband, sell only d'land between road and water for money to get Viku's helicopter, plus get one free apartment for each boy after they get built. For d'land above d'road, they make lease for twenty years to grow *kalo*. Hilo-man, he buys all supplies and pays workers, gives us twenty percent of profit, except he cheats us by selling *kalo* for less than everyone else. Viku, he say Hilo-man gets kick-back, or maybe his friends own wholesaler, help keep our share small. We all d'time have to clear more land, make farm bigger, just to get enough money for living here. Those apartments not built yet, either, and now Viku already married, and Wipu and Pubo ready to move out, too, got no place to go."

Viku came in with Dabu. He greeted Rochelle warmly, asking about Poco's progress, everybody sharing the obligatory guarded optimism.

"I wish my father could be here for him, too," Rochelle said, "but he's still in Sydney with Lalani."

"Is she getting better?" Viku asked, concerned.

"I wish I could say," Rochelle deflected, still preoccupied wondering how much the promise of quick apartments might motivate Wipu and Pubo to do Hilo-man's dirty work.

"We all hope she's okay soon," Viku said.

Rochelle took a drink from her juice, stalling while she decided how to proceed. She didn't want them to learn the truth about Poco's "accident" from the police, thus revealing her duplicity in conducting a personal investigation. That might alienate the family again, risking Dabu's access to Poco at a time their friendship might very well matter most. Finally, she turned to Dabu and signed, also speaking aloud: "D, now I tell you and your mother and brother something you do not know." She repeated what Poco had said about the attempted murder, but left out his accusations and reference to a note. Mrs. Taoke appeared shocked, eyes wide, unable to speak. Dabu jumped to his feet and paced around the room in angry frustration, his fists clenched in a perfect imitation of Mikalu. Viku stared at the table, his mouth set in anger, maybe formulating his own list of suspects.

Dabu turned to Rochelle and signed, *Nobody came that day, no cars, no people.*

She signed and asked, "Can somebody come from the other side of Coulée Makai?"

"Yah," Viku answered. "It's just three or four miles to Hawai'i Belt Road and the town of Pahala. Rough ground for sure, some climbing, but good hikers could."

"You said your brothers were hiking that day," she said, trying not to sound suspicious.

"Maybe they see something," Mrs. Taoke suggested. Good, she didn't realize Rochelle still had serious doubts about her middle sons, especially Wipu.

"Could we ask them?"

"They go up there again today," she said. Then to Viku, she asked, "You take her? Go see what they know?"

"Sure, but where they camp is other side of d'road, up into Pa'auau Gulch."

"You go anyway," Mrs. Taoke said, still clearly upset. "I not feel safe till we know what happen. Too many *kalo* workers 'round here, people I not know. Maybe Wipu or Pubo, they see one go in Coulée Makai other days." Rochelle hadn't considered that. Sometime in the past, Poco might have tangled with somebody stealing coral or cutting *lau hala*, making an enemy who waited patiently for revenge. She'd have to ask Mikalu.

I go, too, Dabu signed, his mother nodding approval.

Mrs. Taoke watched from the doorway as all three walked to the chopper and boarded.

"My brothers," Viku said while checking his instruments, "they're all in love with two sisters who live in Pahala. *Nā wahine*, they got one mean father, so they go camping in gulch, meet my brothers there, spend the night."

Of course. Both in their twenties, the Taoke boys' idea of exploring nature would mean more than chasing butterflies in secluded ravines. She caught herself studying Dabu as the chopper's engine roared to life, wondering what kind of limited opportunities he might have for someday meeting that special girl who would deserve his heart, the boy from an isolated home, attending separate classes, moving through a silent world.

As they lifted off, she swallowed hard, pinching her nose and blowing to pop the pressure in her ears. Viku flew over Coulée Makai and hovered just upstream from the lagoon, offering her a spectacular view either direction: stairstep waterfalls stitching a carpet of rising valley pleats, the obsidian-sand beach now appearing lava-dust gray under the yellow-wash of afternoon sun, Mika supervising a group of divers wading in to stalk wily octopuses lurking among spectacular reefs, the ancient stone house hunkering down to blend seamlessly into the valley's natural terrain, honeycombed solar panels bellying up to the rainforest bar to drink springtime sky, but nary a sign of flexible pipeline hiding in ridge-top shadows as gravity urged sparkling water from the upper falls into an eco-friendly dive shop and house.

As Viku rose above the north ridge, he shouted over the engine's cabin-muted roar: "Can't hike in from the north ever since caldera became active." Heading a couple miles that way to show her, he pointed across the series of frozen waves concealing the secret Wai-Nuikai lava-tube burial ground. A thin snake of smoking orange liquid slithered down from a bubbling cauldron, passing alarmingly close to the hidden tube's entranceway before veering northward again and disappearing into a valley, its final destination marked by rising steam billowing along the shifting shoreline.

"Could the lava ever overrun Coulée Makai or Taoke Valley?" she shouted back.

"Nah. Ridges too high. See?" He pointed. "More than two-hundred feet. Pele, she would have to blow up d'whole island to make lava that deep. Besides, she's getting tired of this house, already building a new one on d'ocean floor hundreds of miles south."

Rochelle noticed he was slipping back into his childhood patois, and for the first time she thought about all the children's voices—the deep-south small-towners drawling tales at county fairs, rust-belt minorities rapping their own brand of urban folklore in asphalt corner lots, second- and third-generation immigrants repeating the histories of elders who've never quite left their homelands behind—and she marveled at how these youngsters grow up speaking the hybrid languages of their families and friends, only to practice hiding these colorful distinctions when it comes time to make their impressions on a bigger world.

Viku showed her the various hikable routes westward, a rugged terrain splintered by streams stairstepping down layers of ancient lava-rock sloping away from Kilauea, the newest of Pele's mythical homes, a present to the people of Hawai'i. The higher ground leveled out quickly, its sparse vegetation forming floral-paper patterns, the village of Pahala a neat little bow tying the ribbon of highway that stretched across Pele's gift.

Viku followed a practiced route up through a deep gorge where canyon walls reached skyward and dense foliage clung precariously to unlikely precipices. The chopper slowed, dropping lower over a series of deep pools strung like midnight pearls along a silver chain of cascading stream. Several people appeared from under the canopy of trees, waving their arms. Viku turned and flew the quarter-mile back to a flat area dotted with tufts of whitish grass, carefully landing the chopper and powering down. Within minutes, two bronze-skinned young men appeared, climbing a rocky slope to the ersatz helicopter pad. Rochelle stepped out, and they froze, looking at least surprised, if not outright guilty.

"Haole-girl," breathed the older one. She instantly recognized him as Wipu.

"*Rochelle*," corrected Pubo, the boyishly cuter brother of a strikingly handsome pair.

Dabu took her hand and led her to where they stood, gallantly offering silent introductions, oblivious to her suspicions about his brothers. She wondered how long he would be able to preserve that innocent trust, and what inevitable events would finally shatter that childlike capacity to find a heart in the dark eyes of a giant stranger, two families' last best hope for someday forging a new friendship.

"Will Poco be okay?" Wipu asked.

Rochelle shook her head. "We don't know, probably not," she admitted more frankly than when speaking to Mrs. Taoke and Viku earlier. "His back is broken." She watched them carefully, trying not to be too obvious. Wipu looked angry at the news, Pubo lowering his eyes, a sadness in his features. "I wish somebody had found him sooner."

"Little Dabu," Wipu said, "—he not know Poco come home yet, or he would be over there, come get help from Viku right away."

"Do you know if anybody else was around that day?" she asked.

"No," Wipu said, "we come here for two days, not see nobody."

"Have you seen Lalani around this week?" she continued.

"No," Wipu said.

"Ramo and Lalani," Pubo said, looking up at Rochelle again, "—they come back from Australia?"

"I haven't seen them yet."

"We hope she get all better," Wipu said, and Rochelle wanted to believe him.

"Have you heard what really happened to Poco?"

"What d'you mean?" Wipu asked.

Rochelle glanced toward Viku, but he stood there quietly, not betraying anything. "Poco says he was lured up on the cliff, then knocked out and pushed in the water." She wouldn't mention the note, leaving that detail for the police to keep up their blue sleeves.

"I *told* you Poco not fall," Pubo blurted to his older brother. Then to Rochelle: "I not believe it was accident. Poco, he knows every cliff, not make stupid mistakes."

She asked Wipu, "Do *you* think it was an accident?"

"That's what Viku tell us, only thing that makes any sense. Poco, he one big boy, maybe sit on edge, then rocks break loose."

Pubo said, "I wonder at first if he hurt himself on purpose, all weepy eyes 'cause Papaii die; but Poco, he not like that, not make Lalani suffer, not with friends like Mikalu." He leaned closer to Rochelle. "He not make bad feelings for little Dabu, either."

"Then who go push Poco?" Wipu demanded, his anger growing. He was either innocent or putting on a good show.

"Do you have any ideas?" Rochelle prodded.

He shook his head. "Damn *kalo* workers not always good people, drink too much—but what beef they have with Poco?"

"What about Hilo-man?" Rochelle asked. "Could he be involved?"

Pubo turned to Wipu, both considering the idea. Finally, Wipu said, "I not think so. He only come every first of month, two weeks ago last time. I know he go talk to Papaii then, come back and say bad things. We go tell Papaii, make sure he know Hilo-man not honest."

"But we not see Hilo-man since," Pubo added.

Wipu went on: "Next time he come, though, I break his face, say don't talk story to me, find out d'truth. He not keeping his bargains. If he thinks we go along 'cause we're afraid, we show him *nā* Taoke, they not afraid of nobody."

"I do worry 'bout Mama now," Pubo said, glancing away.

"Yah, and little Dabu. If some *kāne pupule* go 'round killing people, we gotta stay home, watch out for *'ohana*."

Pubo asked Rochelle, "Little Dabu, he okay to stay with you Hilo-side for now?"

"Yes," she said. "He's very welcome, and it's good for Poco that he visit the hospital every day."

"Good then," Pubo said, Wipu nodding agreement. "Keep Dabu safe for now."

"We go pack up," Wipu said. Then to Viku: "You come back, pick us up, one hour?"

Viku nodded vigorously, and Rochelle noticed his adrenaline seemed to be rising, too, the Taoke boys rallying to a cause.

"We make plans with Mikalu," said Pubo to his brother. "Watch both valleys, see what's going on."

They promised Rochelle their help, then took turns squeezing Dabu's shoulders before hurrying off to pack their campsite. Viku powered up the chopper as Dabu handed her inside like a little gentleman, Rochelle lost in her thoughts.

Viku rose even higher this time, affording her a view of rugged terrain stretching beyond the horizon, an island much bigger than she'd ever imagined, the tiny town of Pahala looking so tenuous as it clung precariously to the windswept lava expanse. She traced possible routes across the unprotected corner of national park, picturing caravans of determined settlers seeking footholds in a new world, just as Visigoths had once settled her mother's beloved homeland in the south of France.

The chopper crossed the series of magma-repelling ridges and hovered for a moment over Coulée Makai, an elongated Soldier Field flooded at the low end and stretching westward up to the cheap seats obstructed by highlands mist. She'd once felt trapped here, afraid she might never escape, yearning to be rescued through that narrow slot into Taoke Valley, the canyon walls a barrier looking not quite so daunting from the vantage of soaring independence. She'd grown to consider this isolated valley a haven, a safe place to visit, the refuge protecting her brother and her good friend Mikalu and all the critters they cherished as members of Pele's family. Now it all looked fragile and vulnerable, the walls that once conspired to imprison her suddenly insufficient to repel invaders, the faces in the cliffs watching helplessly as thieves and killers streamed over the ramparts to sack Pocomea's ancestral lands and murder those Rochelle held most dear.

Even if they didn't know Lalani had died, whoever lured her gentle brother to a dangerous ledge at least had the knowledge that Coulée Makai would be deserted, and that Poco would return alone that day while his friend Mikalu was still thousands of miles away. Poco had made Mikalu promise not to tell Ginny about the hospital trip, so that left only one person on the island who would know all the details, surely an innocent pawn used by people who wouldn't give up now just because their first attempt failed.

She lay back and watched the worried expression of Poco's young friend as he stared at his lap, fists clenched in frustration.

And she remembered Mrs. Taoke's answer when asked about Lalani . . .

Dabu, he bring us all d'news.

'O NĀ MAKA KA WAHINE

SHE IS THE EYES

I am Rochelle . . .

She opened her eyes and stared back at the darkness, lost for a moment until she kicked off the sheet and touched her face, making herself real again.

I am Rochelle Voudette DuFortier.

Sometimes she felt trapped in the body of a stranger, this time trapped here in Hilo while an impostor was off living her intended life. Maybe the other Rochelle had jetted to France after all, Galway joining her for lazy afternoon strolls along the cobblestones of La Réole's Rue Deloroit; or maybe she'd remained in Cambridge long enough to attend commencement, her father applauding proudly before whisking her off to Indonesia or the Philippines in search of engineering challenges; or perhaps she'd completed her move to Miss Dixon's and joined the daily Chicago commute, single-handedly launching a new era in wheelchair-assisted mobility even as she saved the family business for one orphaned child.

Ever since her own mother's death changed everything in one wrenchingly tragic instant, Rochelle had cultivated the reassuring predictability of meticulous planning, each day a step toward achieving ever more ambitious goals, every accomplishment a check-mark on the master list. She liked to review her planner before sleep each night, setting her auto-pilot for that early-morning push, knowing what to expect being the only way to relax.

But that hadn't worked in weeks, and it wouldn't again tonight.

She donned her robe and crept toward the moonlight-washed front room, a place both familiar and somehow not, then stepped onto the veranda, half-expecting to find she'd awakened in a new realm—Tulsa maybe, or the fabled Timbuktu. A pair of stout trellises greeted her, each struggling to shoulder spilling bracts of pale magenta and purple bougainvillaea. Hilo spread out below the railing, a luminous fishnet of twinkling thoroughfares stitched to the sloping volcanic soil, at once both an ancient city holding fast against Pele's lavaform tantrums and a modern metropolis braced for the next raging tsunami hurled by an impudent goddess of the sea. Rochelle's father loved this place; he'd chosen to live here even before Lalani taught him to love its people.

Shouldn't staying at your father's house feel like coming home?

I am Ramo DuFortier's daughter.

She gazed northward toward Hilo Medical Center, but shimmering moonlit mist drifting from Rainbow Falls obscured her view. She hoped Poco was sleeping well. His pain medication seemed to help, but she couldn't be sure, so determined he was to hide his suffering, those briefest hints of panic betrayed by his eyes whenever he looked quickly away. Rochelle needed to return to Chicago soon, but she vowed to visit Hilo more often in the coming months, maybe for a long weekend or two. She would show support for her family in this time of grief, at least while her brother recuperates.

I am Pocomea's sister.

She wandered inside and noticed a radio on the kitchen counter. Keeping the volume low, she tuned it to a station featuring traditional Asian music, then closed her eyes and recalled a story she'd once read. The melodies swirled around her, conjuring the picture of a young Japanese girl kneeling on a *tatami* mat, an apprentice *geisha* diverting her gaze from powerful men as she poured their *sake*. The flicker of colorful paper lanterns danced in her innocent eyes, revealing the pride of a young teen learning to serve others, but concealing the deepest melancholy of a delicate child far removed from her family's village, her mother's face but a fleeting wisp among fading memories . . .

Rochelle reached out to touch the girl's face, but it dissolved to an image of handicapped children waiting patiently on the beach at Coulée Makai, the lagoon's exquisite treasures just beyond their reach, their view obscured by sheafs of unfinished mechanical drawings scattering on the waves. Rochelle touched her own face and returned again to the kitchen in Hilo, then noticed Mikalu had left those design sketches spread across the dining-room table, a chair pulled out, waiting. She'd been drifting too long, ignoring responsibilities amid the paralysis of circumstance beyond control.

She liked Mikalu's idea for a collapsible seat that could rotate down and deposit its user onto the ground or into water, but it would never work for anybody bigger than a small child. She would have to add too much weight and extra power to make it viable for adults . . . unless!—unless a bigger motor and battery pack also acted as the seat's counterweight! The additions would have to move with the seat during rotation, but if she had them lock while in the up position, then a simple gear-and-clutch assembly would allow a powertrain to drive the wheels, too. A waterproof housing, plastic gears, rubber seals . . .

Three hours later, she looked up at the clock. Soon Ramo would return to his hotel room from the medical center near Sydney, expecting her to call. That would leave just a few hours of sleep before visiting time at Hilo Medical. A list stared at her from the table: information needed from Jodis about available materials, specs on the five styles of motors already in stock, vendor costs for several alternatives . . . She would ask her father how to gain access to his downtown office, plus any passwords she'd need to access his engineering programs and transmit secure files to and from Chicago. After rubbing her eyes and stretching, the sleepy R&D specialist studied her rough design again, a significant departure from Mauterre's father's sketches, but a workable application of his concept, plus Mikalu's suggestions and her own innovations. For the second time since completing her degree, she felt proud of her skills, having accomplished something very important this night.

I am an engineer.

Heading toward the bathroom to wash her face, she noticed Dabu's door standing ajar. A slash of window-cast moonlight cut across the boy's slumbering form. Sprawled face-down in brand-new Waiki Mega-Mart undies, he'd somehow managed to kick the sheet down and twist it around one foot, leaving himself exposed to the cool breeze. She eased quietly to the window and pulled it partly closed, careful not to wake him, then remembered sheepishly that he dreamt his boyish dreams in a silent world. Mrs. Taoke must have peeked in like this many nights, wondering how a mother best helps her young son face the challenges of disability, resisting the need to protect him even as she knows he must learn to make his own way.

Rochelle gently untwisted the sheet, then pulled it over him and paused to listen for the gentle rhythm of his soft breaths, finally reaching out to stroke his hair before slipping into the hallway and pulling the door to. No engineer in the world could design the foolproof plan for keeping a child completely safe during brief visits, let alone year after year. How could a single parent get through each day knowing even the most unlikely twist of fate might leave her boy or girl subject to the whims of strangers, an orphan swallowed whole by the system? It takes two to care for a youngster, Rochelle decided, and a support network just in case . . .

Could I ever be a mother?

Off to the bathroom, she washed her face, then paused to study the mirror, those ever-familiar eyes looking back from a newly tanned visage now framed by Lalani's decorative appointments, hummingbirds and hibiscus blooms against fields of nacre and powder blue. Poco's mother must have stood here many nights, gazing back at the image of a woman who missed her son even as she believed he belonged at Coulée Makai, and who loved Mikalu even as she secretly hoped someday he'd leave her for the father he needed more.

Why did Keefie adopt Galway and horny-toad Todd, then insist they call her *aunt?* Were these vulnerable boys selected as mere civic projects for garden-club approval? Or simply the unfortunate foci for Keefie's obsession with control? She'd turned Galway's love for building things into a career of chasing after stock options under watchful relatives' eyes. She'd exploited Todd's need to belong, punishing his loyalty to Rochelle. Mikalu had shown that need to fit in, too, and matched it with a heart as big and deep as the sea; but Lalani had nurtured his, fostering his friendship with Poco, encouraging that lone misfit boy—all blond hair and *haole* skin—to claim their ancient Hawaiian world as his own. For an instant, Rochelle regretted never letting Lalani adopt her. Afraid it would feel somehow like denying her real mother, Rochelle had failed to recognize that Lalani loved Mikalu too much to let him forget the very people who gave him life. Lalani would have cared about Rochelle that much, too, and even helped her keep alive the memory of Gina DuFortier, but the headstrong young teen had foolishly thought she didn't deserve that kind of love. This she could still see in those unchanging eyes watching from the mirror, and now she'd lost Lalani, too, without ever having given her a chance.

She sighed and turned out the light, stepping into the dark hallway, quiet strains of Japanese harps drifting from the kitchen. She peeked in at Dabu again, finding him sprawled crossways, the sheet kicked down and twisted this time around his other foot. Resisting the urge to slip in and cover him again, she smiled with the admission that he would be all right. She'd given him plenty to eat, a safe place to sleep, a good-night hug . . . the important stuff.

Surprised by light spilling into the hallway, she found Mikalu standing by Lalani's dresser. His back to the door, he was gazing at a portrait of the elegant Hawaiian woman posing with "her boys" on either side.

"What are you doing up so late?" she asked from the doorway.

"I ask you d'same," he said without turning. "You and me, we're both restless tonight."

"It's time for me to call my father."

"I know. I go back to sleep in a minute."

She moved beside him and studied the picture. The boys looked maybe eleven or twelve, no older than when they'd tried to teach some *haole* girl how to cope with her own mother's death.

He rubbed his eyes, then spoke quietly, still not turning. "I not say good-bye, Rochelle. I not say good-bye to her." He turned and searched her eyes.

"Lalani was holding you close when the time came," she said. "She knew how much you loved her."

He lowered his head, staring at the floor. "Yah, Dabu tell me like same, too. I know that's true, by and by, but sometimes it doesn't feel that way."

"You'll say it in other ways when Daddy brings her home."

He looked up. "Yah, but can we honor her with lava tube? Poco, he wants this very much, 'specially since d'sea take his father and never bring him back. But Lalani, she is your father's wife—his decision, and we can't tell him about d'tube."

"I think he's a bit too proper for that anyway, so let's just do what we've been doing. He'll honor her with a grave in the cemetery, and we'll know she's joined with Papaii and Tapakiki and Poco's fathers' fathers."

"Poco, he will be pleased that you help us with this." He gazed at the picture again.

"It's not just for him."

He looked into her eyes, then nodded. "Thank you, Rochelle."

And she hugged him.

She didn't mean to. It just happened, but when they stepped back and half-grinned sheepishly at each other, she knew she'd found the reason he couldn't sleep, and she'd given him the confidence that finally allows gentle rest.

I am Mikalu's friend.

"G'night, Rochelle," he said, pausing in the doorway for one more glance at the photo. "You are right about Lalani; she knew. Still, I wish I told her; then maybe I not be all wake-up wondering about what's already d'truth." He looked at Rochelle, weighing his words carefully. "Me, I need all *da kine* practice telling people how I feel." He allowed a hint of smile again before turning to go, his parting words: "I best work on that—before it's too late."

She stared at the empty hallway, wanting to say something, but not sure what that might be, so she grabbed her phone and headed out to the veranda. Five minutes and two helpful operators later, she reached her father in Sydney.

"They will finish with her tomorrow," Ramo said, his voice betraying uncharacteristic weariness. "They are learning much about this rare form of malignancy, but cannot explain why the Honolulu clinic failed in determining it had spread so far."

"Is that the same place Poco's been going?"

"Yes, but now that my confidence is shaken, I prefer he seek treatment elsewhere. I—" He hesitated, his voice breaking. "I have fallen in love twice, and I have lost them both. You are all I have left of your beautiful mother, and Pocomea is all I have of Lalani. Now I fear I might lose him, too."

"Don't worry, Daddy, he'll be all right, one way or another. When you get back, we'll talk to him about other options, but for now I'm not sure when or if he can be moved."

"Has he improved since yesterday?"

"Yes—remarkably, in fact—except for the paralysis. So far there's nothing to suggest he might regain use of his legs."

Ramo sighed. "Does he still assert that Taokes pushed him?"

"We avoid that subject for now."

"What do *you* believe?"

"Well, I—I guess I don't know *what* to think."

"You know, the Wai-Nuikais have for generations blamed just about every kind of misfortune on Taokes. Rochelle, you would be shocked by how distraught Pocomea sounded during our phone call, how dangerously rash, even hysterical. Maybe he committed this foolish act out of grief over Lalani and fear of his own illness, and now he is embarrassed, finding it easier to blame an age-old enemy than to admit—maybe even to himself—that he suffers from his own mistake."

"Well . . . maybe, but I'm wondering if he'd had some run-ins with vengeful *kalo* workers, or maybe that man who wanted to lease the valley for farming."

"Surely Mikalu would know of any enmity with laborers—or even with that farm broker. I met him once when he came to pitch Papaii, and though he impressed me as possibly dishonest, I cannot imagine why he might now resort to violence. Has anyone notified the authorities about Pocomea's accusations?"

"No, he insists we shouldn't."

"His reluctance suggests he might regret having assigned blame. Please consider what is best; a police investigation likely would exacerbate a conflict that has persisted between these two families far too long, and uncovering the truth may humiliate Pocomea."

"I guess I can see why he'd want to save face—if he really tried to kill himself."

"Rochelle, you cannot imagine the kind of despair that would drive someone to attempt suicide."

God, if he only knew how much she understood it, how much she'd felt it, a secret she'd kept from him for eight years. She gripped the rail, its varnished wood slippery with pre-dawn dew.

"We should focus on the future," he continued. "Let us not make the mistake of allowing him to dwell on this tragedy."

She heard the regret in his voice, and for the first time realized he must blame himself for not recognizing her mother's depression in time to intervene. He, too, had struggled with his own secret for eight years, wondering if he could have done more to save her.

"You're right," she said. "In time, he will tell the whole story to Mikalu; then we'll decide what to do."

"Good. For now, our priority must be to plan Lalani's funeral."

"Mika wants to hold a wake at Coulée Makai."

"Mikalu's wishes are as important as Pocomea's," Ramo said, much to Rochelle's relief. "Unfortunately, the clinic warned me that, uh—" He hesitated, faltering in his customary business-like approach to confronting challenges. "Their studies have been rather, uh, invasive, which negates any possibility of an open casket."

Gina DuFortier's casket had remained closed, too, a three-story plummet to unforgiving flagstones having battered her beyond the mortician's skills. Death should appear peaceful, its victim at rest, a serene soul floating away on gentle pillows of clouds, caressed and cradled . . . "Still," she said, "the *keiki*-center people and others who might not be able to get to Hilo should have a chance to pay their respects, too."

"The grave-side service will be there at Punalu'u."

"Yes, but that's formal. People need a chance to, you know, gather in advance to share their feelings." She'd never really considered the machinery of grief, like the roles played by counselors who came to her school after that girl's suicide, holding sessions where friends and strangers alike fluffed a group pillow to help each other cushion the blow.

"We could hold visitation in the valley that morning," he suggested, "then conduct the service later that afternoon—"

"No, Daddy. Don't make it feel rushed. It needs to be like Tapakiki's and Papaii's."

"Leaving her there overnight," he said, waiting for Rochelle's response. Could he suspect?

"Yes. Overnight."

"I understand," he said, and she wondered if he knew the truth, if Lalani had told him she long suspected that Wai-Nuikais steal their dead and whisk them into the night, burying them in Pele's subterranean catacombs so *nā lapu* will know their bones rest close to the island's heart. "I guess I could lodge for one night in the valley."

She felt panic rising. "Oh, Daddy, you *never* spend the night there."

"That is true, but it feels somehow disrespectful to leave her."

"Mika and I will stay, and it shows *us* respect to entrust us with that role."

"Yes, I can appreciate the importance of such a gesture. But what about Pocomea? Unable to leave the hospital, he will have no opportunity to pay his respects."

She tried to find the words, finally admitting, "By doing this the right way now, Poco will be pleased, and we'll have the rest of our lives to honor her together."

Silence fell over the line, satellite transponders waiting anxiously for his verdict. "As you wish, Rochelle. I always trust you to do what's right."

"Thank you, Daddy."

"Are you and Mikalu still staying at our—at my house?"

"Yes, and Dabu, too."

"Who is this Dabu?"

"You know, the deaf Taoke boy—the twelve-year-old."

"He is staying with you in Hilo? Why?"

"To visit Poco with us. We go three times a day."

"Pocomea welcomes visits from a *Taoke?*"

"Oh yeah. They're great friends; plus Dabu works for him and Mika helping run the dive shop, taking out groups, assisting when Ginny brings all the kids."

"Ginny is the woman Pocomea has been dating?"

"Yes. She drives out here from Punaluʻu with her little boy most evenings and joins us at the hospital—"

"This boy is not Pocomea's son, is he?"

"No, but you wouldn't know it seeing them together. They adore each other."

Ramo hesitated a moment, then said, "Well, if Pocomea is friends with one of the Taokes, then he will likely change his mind about accusing the boy's brothers. I am glad we agree to give this some time."

They discussed Ramo's arrangements for returning with Lalani's body, setting visitation for two days hence, burial the following morning.

"Good-night, Daddy," she said. "Get some rest."

"Not yet," he said, his words a long breath of exhaustion. "Not for a long time, I fear."

"Please try."

"I will. Good-night, Rochelle."

After they disconnected, she realized she'd forgotten to ask about getting into his office, then decided instead to seek out a local place offering business services.

She set the phone down, stretched and rubbed her shoulders, then leaned against the rail and gazed at the first hints of sunrise framed by sprays of bougainvillaea. Mikalu should have drifted off to sleep by now, his rest cushioned by the confidence that Rochelle would help him honor Lalani through traditional burial. Dabu would be sprawled across his bed, leg twisted in the sheet, vulnerable but trusting of any who might tiptoe by to check on a boy who's too old to be fussed over and too young to leave on his own. Ramo would be sitting in his hotel room making lists, organizing each step in the process of grieving a lost love, desperately trying to impose order on a world where too often none exists.

And Rochelle would stare back at those eyes in the mirror one last time before sleep, wondering who'd stolen the life she planned, and how she would live the one she got. What had become of the little girl whose mother dressed her to alert the world Rochelle stood in their midst?

As the cresting sun cast new light on Hilo and its weary guest, this much she knew to be true:

Rochelle would pass up stock options and a high-paying career in the ball-bearing polymer industry for a chance to improve the lives of those who must rely on wheelchairs for personal independence.

Rochelle would be counted on to fly halfway around the world to help her brother honor ancient family traditions.

Rochelle would respect Mikalu's love for Lalani and support him through his grief, understanding that he, too, had lost the only mother he ever knew.

Rochelle would confront even the most dangerous Taoke to protect her family's safety, and remain quiet if necessary to protect their pride.

Rochelle would love her own father with undying devotion, but mourn the years he'd let her grow up too far away.

And if she ever dared to have children of her own, Rochelle would know if her daughter teetered secretly on the brink of despair, or if her son cherished an unlikely friendship born of discovering he and some little deaf boy understood each other long before learning to sign the words.

Rochelle had squandered a year planning some illusory future with Galway, believing he embraced her desire for exploring the world, only to discover it was her own world he refused to embrace. And Rochelle had squandered more than a decade seeking in others that which she'd always most wanted to find in herself.

The eyes in the mirror had known this all along, a secret they never dared reveal. They knew the young woman gazing back would have no choice but to give up some list of steps toward a plan of carefully plotted expectations for a vision now blurred by the whims of circumstance and fate.

Let that imposter continue living Rochelle's intended life . . .

Gina's daughter rather liked the uncertain challenge of improvising in a world with no guarantees.

I am Rochelle Voudette DuFortier.

Nā meheu a pepa, nā ʻapuka ā mē nā kaʻao

Paper Trails, Tricks and Tales

Morning

Rochelle drifted between sleeping fitfully and waking to the world of beckoning responsibilities, her dream a fleeting impression of standing amid wilting violets, surrounded by people all frozen in time. She couldn't find her mother in the crowd, a shifting montage of faces familiar but somehow frightfully wrong. Then something distracted her, words in the air, a list. She tried to ignore them, but the very effort rendered her much too aware.

Locate business services (hotel, maybe?), transmit specs to Jodis, visit Poco at 8:30, call funeral director, order flowers, place notice in paper, contact keiki-center staff, compile list of Lalani's friends . . .

The sound of running water gave way to knob squeaks and a pipe moan as somebody shut off the shower, probably Mikalu getting ready. Noises from the front room suggested Dabu was up and about, his motor revving, the boy who could doze like desert sand refusing again to let the first rays of daylight filter through windows unchallenged.

"Meeg-loo! Meeg-loo!" Dabu called.

Unfamiliar voices.

Rochelle donned her robe and hurried down the hallway. Mikalu burst from the bathroom, wrestling a t-shirt and fastening his jeans.

A pair of middle-aged, bronze-skinned strangers stood in the front room, the door wide open.

"I am so sorry," the woman said, gesturing toward Dabu. "We are trying to explain—"

"He's deaf," Mika said, moving between Rochelle and the intruders, his wet hair hanging every which way. "Explain to us, please." Still looking a bit frightened, Dabu moved to Rochelle's side.

"You are guests of Mr. DuFortier?" the lady asked. A plump Hawaiian barely five feet tall, she appeared too gentle to pose any serious threat. A lanky older man in wire spectacles held her arm, looking embarrassed about having startled everyone.

"I'm his daughter," Rochelle answered.

The woman's eyes lit up, the man's features softening. "Rochelle!" she said, her eyes darting to a framed grade-seven photo on the shelf. Mikalu's body relaxed some, but he stood his ground. "I never think of you all grown up." She touched her own cheek. "I am Carmi; and my husband, he is Jonn. Twelve years now I clean d'house for Lalani, and d'office and his car for your father. Jonn, he has tended to the gardens and repairs, but most times we are helping each other." Jonn put his arm around her, nodding agreement. Mikalu turned and signed an explanation for Dabu.

Rochelle introduced everybody, Mika and Dabu shaking Jonn's hand.

Carmi moved closer, her dark eyes sparkling, and took Rochelle by the hands. "No wonder your father, he is proud of such a pretty daughter." Turning toward the others, she added, "And you, Mikalu, many times I hear Lalani speak with love for her yellow-haired boy." She reached out and touched his face, everybody in a circle now, all warming to the flickering glow of growing familiarity. Her voice tentative, Carmi asked, "Lalani? And how is she?"

Mikalu's eyes dropped, his hand on Dabu's shoulder.

Rochelle shook her head sadly, a new wave of grief rising. "She didn't make it," she answered quietly, avoiding the stark words *She died* that would've been, for some reason, so much harder to say.

Carmi gasped, her hands to her mouth. Jonn pulled her close, putting his arm around her. Rochelle and Mika glanced at each other, every telling of the awful truth inevitably feeling like they'd just learned for the first time.

After Rochelle explained the funeral schedule, Carmi said, "We will come to Coulée Makai, but cannot come to Punalu'u. You see, it is that day we leave for d'mainland."

"How long will you be gone?" Mika asked.

Jonn removed his glasses to rub his eyes, his wife answering, "We are moving there. Today, this is our last time to work for Mr. DuFortier. We tell him this just before he leave with Lalani. This morning, we already clean his office, come now for house, leave d'keys when we go." She produced a ring with door and car keys, handing it to Rochelle.

"We have granddaughter there," Jonn said, putting his glasses back on and producing a photo of a sleeping newborn from his wallet. "We not even see her yet." The proud grandparents gazed at the baby's tiny face, each already indelibly bonded to this child they've never held.

"Our son's wife," Carmi said, "she get good job in Kansas two years ago."

"Topeka," Jonn said, smiling as he added, "—sounds like Hawai'i name."

Carmi chuckled, rolling her eyes. "This Kansas, we know it is very different place, but we find way to make it home."

"We come be d'babysitters," Jonn said, wagging his brows.

"It's always better," Mikalu said, "to live close to your family."

"Topeka," Jonn repeated impishly, "—Hawai'i without d'ocean. We teach 'em to grow d'*kalo*."

They chatted for a few minutes; then Rochelle hurried off to shower and dress, grabbing her satchel and schedule planner for the road. Leaving the housekeepers to their work, she and the guys zipped over to the hospital and found Poco sitting comfortably in bed, watching his portable alarm clock, a smirk on his face.

"Haole-girl! Oh no, she come seven whole minutes *late?*" he asked Mikalu with mock incredulity. "We make island *wahine* of her yet."

She ruffled his hair and kissed his cheek, then stepped back to let him shake Mika's hand, his other arm grabbing Dabu for an impromptu noogie. "Not today, valley-boy. I'm leaving these two for an all-guy visit while I run some errands."

"Haole-girl, she never change—busy all d'time. Good thing we like her, by and by." Then more seriously, he asked, "You go make funeral plans?"

She glanced at Mika. "Yes, and for the lava tube without my father finding out."

"We know all d'time you think of a way," Poco said. "*Mahalo.*"

She patted his arm. "Also, I want to track down our old housekeepers from Chicago. If I catch them still visiting their aunt, I'll see if they can stay until I ask my dad about hiring them to work here."

"You go be d'busy *wahine*," Poco said, brushing her off playfully. "Us *nā kāne*, we sit around all bachelor-like, drink beer and talk about d'pretty girls." His fairly lewd gesture involving voluptuous breasts garnered a giggle from Dabu.

She left them all pretending to hoist brews, Mika leading with a drinking song, Dabu rocking and tapping his feet in time to their bobbing heads. A nurse peeked in, then wandered off shaking her head.

Rochelle drove to Ramo's office, a tastefully decorated suite atop a three-story office building in downtown Hilo. Lalani had kept a list of key passwords and e-addresses posted beside the reception-area computer, so Rochelle quickly set up some files, scanned her wheelchair documents, then called Jodis in Chicago as she sent him a string of attachments.

"Good," he said, confirming receipt. "That gives me something to do. I'm growing bored overseeing a company that practically runs itself. I'm ready for the challenge of expanding."

She listed some software she would need for computer-aided design.

"That'll be here by the time you return, and I'll have this data to you in one hour." He expressed his sympathy about Lalani again, adding that Miss Dixon and Mauterre wanted to know where to send flowers.

She gave him the name of the funeral home, then thanked him and hung up. Steeling herself for the inevitable, she called the funeral director to arrange services and burial, feeling somehow disrespectful consummating such a wrenchingly final act by using Lalani's own fax equipment to sign the contract. Afterward, she found herself sitting numbly at Lalani's desk, the momentum of this early-morning push already spent.

Three small framed photos watched from beside the blotter, one each of Mika and Poco posing in cap and gown, the other of Rochelle standing on Longfellow Bridge with sunshine blazing her wind-tossed hair.

She studied the graduation pictures and detected something unspoken in Mikalu's sapphire eyes, and in Pocomea's deep browns. These guys weren't gazing blankly into the lens of a camera; they were looking right at Lalani, at the woman who encouraged their education every step of the way, the mother they counted on to cheer at commencement, the one who knew to step in when "her boys" needed help, and to step back as they learned to make their own way in the world.

Personalized notepad, a vase of silk flowers, hummingbird figurine, nacre doo-dad box . . . Lalani had claimed this space as her own. Ramo DuFortier had lost more than his wife; he'd lost the heart and soul of his business, too. She had shared both of his worlds in a way Rochelle's mother either would not or could not. He would need more than house- and groundskeepers to help him get his life back into a daily routine adding check-marks to the master list.

She sighed, then pulled the police report from a pocket in her satchel and copied Aunt Tani Ko's address onto a Post-it before packing her papers and heading for the door. She paused with her hand on the knob and looked around, finding herself drawn back to the pair of graduation shots poised patiently on the desk. People cherish such keepsakes, even braving the flames to rescue them from burning houses, but the person who'd kept "her boys" close for so many years now could never return. Lalani had watched over those confident faces too long to leave them, well, vulnerable like this, so Rochelle retrieved them. She would find them a place; that much she could do for Lalani.

But something else distracted her as she tried again to leave: her own picture still sat there, alone now, no longer one of three. It was just a photograph, the emulsified print of photons scattered through a plastaic sheet of ionized gelatin-suspended silver-halide crystals, one single moment in a changing life captured and mailed to her father before being co-opted by his wife. Glancing toward her father's office door, she considered moving it to his desk, returning it to the only person she'd counted on all her life.

But this belonged to Lalani, and Lalani was gone.

Sheepishly, she slid it into her satchel and locked the door behind her.

Driving westward several miles beyond town, she got lost and had to backtrack, but eventually found Tani Ko's place squatting in the sunlight beside an open *kalo* field. A primitive stone *konohiki*, it had benefited considerably from renovations like a modern roof and double-paned windows, pavement and modest landscaping. A heavyset older native woman lounged in a faded recliner on the covered porch.

Standing to greet her visitor, she stood nearly six feet tall, her frock vividly purple, her wide nose turned up to look like an oversized button. Acne scars framed a warm and friendly smile, but her bloodshot eyes kept glancing away, betraying a somewhat distracted confusion.

"Yes, I'm Tani. Who are you again?"

"I'm Rochelle. I'm looking for your niece and nephew, Kala and Jackie."

"Why, Kala and Jackie, hmmm . . . Oh, they go home already."

"But I thought— Did they move to Honolulu?"

Ms. Ko looked around, spotted her recliner, then settled into it again. Rochelle stood awkwardly for a moment, then sat on a bench alongside the railing. "Somebody, they go move to Honolulu?—that's what you say?"

"No, I asked if they *did*—Jackie and Kala."

"Oh, I not think so. Jackie, he stay San Diego-side. Kala, she go back home, too."

"Where does she live?"

"Huh? Oh, Kala, she stay Chicago-side. That's on d'mainland," she added for clarity. "Who are you again?"

"Rochelle. Jackie and Kala used to work for my family in Chicago—for Ramo and Gina DuFortier."

"Oh yah, Ramo DuFortier. He one good kāne." She craned her neck to look toward Rochelle's rental car as if expecting Ramo to emerge.

"You say Jackie doesn't live in Chicago anymore?"

"Jackie? Oh, he never live Chicago-side. He stay San Diego ever since d'Navy. Gina DuFortier . . . she d'*wahine* police come ask about that time?"

"You mean eight or nine years ago?"

She shrugged, then seemed distracted by a beetle trundling across the porch. "I not remember when; long time is all I know."

"You mean right after she died from a fall."

"Yah."

"The police asked you if Jackie and Kala visited that week."

"Yah, I know all about that."

"You told them Jackie and Kala were here when the accident happened."

"They was—just come here from Chicago."

"But you just said Jackie never lived in Chicago."

"They not ask about that," she said impishly, glancing around as if worried about eavesdroppers.

"Ah," Rochelle said, her heart pounding, "then you did a good job not telling what really happened."

The older woman grinned broadly, bobbing her head with pride. "I keep secret."

"But you can tell *me* now. What was it?"

"Jackie, he never live in Chicago."

"But I know he did. I lived there, too. I saw him every day." She'd seen copies of his airline ticket and car-rental agreement attached to the police report, too.

"You think so?" she challenged, smiling like she'd gained the advantage in a wit match.

"Yes, I do," said Rochelle, her curiosity wavering between anger over some nebulous conspiracy and pity for a woman obviously suffering dementia.

Ms. Ko pulled herself up, then wandered casually into the house, motioning for Rochelle to follow. The front room shrieked of purple, from violet carpeting and lavender walls to dark burgundy upholstery and knick-knacks in all the hues between pink and blue. "Jackie," she said, "he d'one hooked on drugs, by and by, ever since d'Navy." She stepped to a low table crowded with framed photos, pushing them around until she found one of herself posing with even younger versions of Jackie and Kala on the pier at Hilo Bay. "This is who you mean?"

"Yes, that's them."

She shook her head, grinning conspiratorially as she tapped the picture. "Kala, she come visit me two weeks that time; then both go see Jackie in prison, San Diego, leave right after this picture."

"I don't understand—" Rochelle started, but Ms. Ko had produced another photo, two young Navy men posing in their Cracker Jacks, Jackie and . . . Jackie again.

"Brothers?"

"Twins. Donny," she said, pointing to the one at left, "he d'one go live Chicago-side with Kala, work for Mr. DuFortier."

"But he called himself Jackie."

"They do that all d'time, ever since little *keiki*, play games with each other's name, try to get d'other one in trouble—or *out* of trouble."

Rochelle knelt and sorted through the other photos, several confirming how interchangeable the brothers appeared. "*Jackie* and Kala are the ones who visited you this past week," she said.

"Yah."

"And *Jackie's* never been to Chicago."

"Just d'one time, I think—go see Kala, ride up on tall building, then come visit me and say make sure I remember who come."

I just tease you, girl, the real Jackie had said after not recognizing Rochelle at the airport.

Rochelle asked, "Has *Donny* been here this past week, too?"

Ms. Ko looked puzzled. "Whatchoo mean?"

"Where does Donny live now?"

"Why, here. He live here all d'time, ever since Chicago. He gone all day now, come back tonight. You want to wait?"

Rochelle stood up, clutching the photo of two identical sailors, her feet sinking in violet carpeting as the purple room swirled. She focused on the double image, either face appearing to be Jackie—Donny—the man who'd repaired her bike, helped her install track lighting, taught her how to prune roses, hugged her awkwardly that time she left for summer camp . . . unrecognizable now, a familiar stranger.

"Who are you again?" Ms. Ko asked, looking very confused.

"I'm Tani," Rochelle said, setting the picture down and easing toward the door.

"That's *my* name, too!" she gushed, delighted by the coincidence.

"Yes, that's right. I must have the wrong house." She stepped through the door onto the porch, Ms. Ko watching through the screen.

"What should I tell Donny?"

"Oh, can you keep a secret?" Rochelle asked.

Ms. Ko laughed. "I keep d'good secrets."

"Then don't tell him I was selling magazines."

"I not buy any," she said as Rochelle headed toward the car.

"Nope," Rochelle called back, "you didn't buy any from the lady selling magazines."

Rochelle backed out and headed straight for Hilo Medical, hands gripping the wheel, mouth clenched. She parked around the side and closed her eyes, trying to calm herself, but failing as a hint of fear crept around the fringes of anger and suspicion.

Did you know this, Mom? Why did Donny use Jackie's name? Was he there that day?

She wrapped herself in the silence, alone with no list and no one to guide her. So many times she'd looked into her mother's eyes and seen all a young girl need understand of the world . . . or so she thought.

She wanted one more chance, just one brief moment with her mother again to uncover the truth, and maybe to promise she would always honor her in word and deed.

But that moment would never come, and Rochelle couldn't even picture her mother now, the shifting image lost in a crowd of imposters, each face familiar . . .

But somehow frightfully wrong.

*   *   *

"My father got duped," Rochelle told Mikalu, keeping her voice quiet as they entered Hilo Professional Center's first-floor lobby. Dabu stayed close to her, just as he had since she showed up at the hospital unable to hide her agitation.

"But that?—it is not his fault," Mika countered. "He not know d'brothers, they play switch."

Rochelle signed in at the security desk, the other two adding their names as visitors.

Waiting for the elevator, she told Dabu, *Somebody tricked my father. I am angry.* As the doors opened and they stepped inside, she explained to Mikalu, "You don't understand; my father is infallible. I know that sounds like a daddy's girl speaking, but he's always scored on every deal he ever arranged.

I've heard him talk about how to outmaneuver people who are trying to gain the advantage. To think the Ko's deceived him, and to what end I don't even understand—" She growled her frustration. "They lied to my mother, and to me, too, in our own home."

He gripped her shoulder as the third-floor doors opened, fixing her with a gentle look. "But this trick, it not work on you, after all—not now. You found out d'truth."

"But I still don't know *why* they did it," she said, calmer now as she let them into the suite.

Mikalu pulled a chair beside Rochelle's while she accessed her secure link to Jodis and opened a phone line. Dabu busied himself studying the myriad framed aerial photos and artists' sketches of real-estate developments Ramo had brokered throughout Asia.

"Thanks," she told Jodis. "This is exactly what I need."

"Too easy," he told her, "but you're welcome. Tell me you need the dimensions of a snipe, and I'll go catch us one and measure it myself."

"I'll bet you would, too, but right now I need some advice." She explained about the switch game Jackie and Donny had played, obviously with Kala's cooperation. "What kind of records should I look for?"

"Well, each should have an employee or contractor file, depending on how they were paid. It's a basic human-resources package: application, résumé, references, background check, withholding declarations, and so forth. There'll probably be a payment record in there, too, especially if your father used a payroll service. If he paid these people as independent contractors, you'll need to go through his account statements or check ledgers. I assume he uses lots of consultants and contractors, so he might be, you know, fudging a little, charging them to one or more project budgets, which should have separate records. Keep in mind, too, that he might not have paid them directly, but rather through another business they worked for."

"Like a maid service."

"Precisely. Then his records would only show invoice payments. The last resort, of course, is to plow through his own company and personal tax records.

"I hope it won't come to that." She thanked him and closed the line, then looked at Mika and took a deep breath.

"I'll help, if you want," he said.

She nodded. "Let's start with these." She indicated four squat filing cabinets in Lalani's area. They pulled their chairs closer, then found them locked.

"Wait," he said. "I see Lalani open these before." He fished around under her credenza and came up with a ring of small keys she'd kept concealed. After trying a few, they managed to get them open.

What they found proved rather boring, indeed—mostly shipping records, vendors' sales kits, supply orders, and mundane business paperwork—until Mika spotted a set of development files.

"P-Corp," he read, "TVE, Buki, Shi-To, Myanmar—"

"I remember him complaining about all the political wrangling involved with that one," she said.

He continued, "Pyang, Thai-STK, and SMTC."

"Singapore Majesty Towers Complex," she said. "I've heard him refer to SMTC because I own a piece of it."

Mika pulled the folder up enough to peruse a few pages. "Yah, that's d'name."

"Well, there's nothing here," she said, closing the last drawer. Mika closed his, too, and followed her through one of two opposing doors into Ramo's office. Dabu joined them, and became instantly entranced by a scale model of the Singapore project mounted on a low table. Dropping to his knees, he studied the intricate details of so many little trees and cars surrounding twin towers, while Rochelle unlocked all the file cabinets except the one no key fit. They skimmed through reams of legal contracts and disclosure statements and financial and presentation packages and too many other things, none of which looked like what she was after. Then, in the bottom drawer, she found several files stacked in an open space, all looking like they'd been tossed in, waiting to be re-filed later. Most related to Lalani's illness: insurance paperwork, information on treatment centers around the world, medical summaries . . . Ramo had done a lot of legwork trying to assure his wife the best possible care.

Wai-Nuikai, Papaii said the label on another, *Probate* across the front.

Rochelle Trust read another. Opening this one seemed reasonable, not an invasion of privacy or confidentiality, so she took it to Ramo's polished teak desk and sat in his oversized leather chair. Mikalu could barely contain his curiosity until she invited him to look over her shoulder.

On top was the original and a half-dozen copies of the Power of Attorney she signed shortly after her eighteenth birthday, authorization for Ramo to continue making transactions on her behalf. Next were several series of ledger pages, then tax returns, deed and title and rental agreements and tenant payment records for the house she inherited from Grandfather, and finally miscellaneous documents like canceled bank drafts and stock certificates. She flipped back to the ledger entries.

"Wow," Mika said, "your father, he start education fund for you right after birth." He was correct; that section showed a series of deposits into three accounts over nearly eighteen years, each moved in and out of various mutual funds and certificates until withdrawals began her freshman year at MIT. "The money was depleted by halfway through my senior year," she said. "Daddy must've made up the difference."

Next she looked through her trust-fund ledger, which was established right after her grandfather died. It showed the inheritance of his house, valuated back then at $565,000. She flipped ahead to see last year's estimate of $1.46 million.

"Wow," Mika said.

The trust also showed a cash deposit of $1.5 million from Grandfather's estate, reduced to $1,094,664 after tax liability.

"Wow," Mika said again, his elocution rather pointedly succinct.

"When he was sick, Grandpa told me he was leaving Mom more than seven-million dollars, with a small amount set aside for me. I thought he meant *small*," she said, a lump in her throat as she remembered how he'd gripped her hand and tried to talk through profound pain those last weeks of his life. She'd sat with him for hours, sometimes with her mother, sometimes in separate shifts, reluctant to leave even when his breathing slowed in those rare periods when he slept a few uninterrupted hours.

Dabu carefully slid the table away from the wall so he could inspect the towers model from a new perspective.

"Your father," Mika said, "he do one good job investing your money." They flipped slowly through the pages, tracking quarterly updates showing her money moving in and out of various projects, the numbers always growing, even after tax liabilities. By the first quarter of this year, her million-odd dollars had grown to three lucrative investments: $450,000 in SMTC—the Singapore project he'd expected to sell off this month until a fire set their timetable back—$140,000 in TVE, and $2.9 million in CMDC.

"TVE is small," she said. "It seems like I could have just cashed out of that."

"And go see France all d'summer long," Mika said, reading her mind again.

"Yeah, but it doesn't matter. You needed me to help with Papaii, and now with Lalani, and Miss Dixon needs me to get Mauterre's company into new products as soon as possible."

"TVE . . . That was in the file out front," he said.

"Let's see what it is."

Dabu followed them out, growing restless when he saw them dig into the drawers again. He went to the other closed door and called, "Ro-zhill," indicating his curiosity.

"Conference room," she said, trying to sign it but having to settle for *place where people talk*. She nodded that it was okay for him to explore, so he pushed the door open, his face lighting up at the first glimpse of another development model.

"Here it is," Mika said, pulling the TVE file. He opened it, then sat back and handed it to her.

"Taoke Valley Enterprises, Incorporated," she read aloud.

"*Kalo* farm?" he asked, looking confused.

"I doubt it. Hilo-man has a deal with them for building apartments along the coast, so maybe my dad's been brokering it to investors."

She flipped through the records, Mika moving beside her now. Then she gasped and set the papers on Lalani's desk, sitting back and rubbing her eyes.

"What?" he asked.

She pointed at the company-president's name on the articles of incorporation.

D'nai'i Ko'opea.

Mika looked puzzled.

"Donny Ko," she said, recognizing Aunt Tani's address.

His jaw literally dropped.

"Or as Mrs. Taoke calls him: *Hilo-Man*."

"Ro-zhill?" Dabu said, standing in the conference-room doorway looking confused. He pointed inside, so they followed him.

On the conference table stood the huge model of a magnificent development project, hotels and condos and restaurants and gift shops, a boardwalk around the pristine obsidian beach . . .

"CMDC," Mika ground out as they all read the plaque:

Coulée Makai Development Corporation.

E PUHI I KĒ AHI ANA KA LĀʻAU

BURNING TREE

Like a budding twig discovering the reach and grandeur of its own branch, Dabu sat across from Rochelle at the dining-room table, earnestly charting his family tree. Mrs. Taoke's time-worn chest of mementos and documents had proven a treasure trove of data for her son's ambitious school assignment. From ancient chiefs' trade declarations and scrawled inscriptions on the leaf pages of musty old books, to embossed original birth certificates and big brothers' crisp new laser-printed diplomas, every clue revealed a rich heritage steeped in history. Rochelle kept busy conducting her own investigation into the past, sorting and stacking a lifetime's worth of business records into various piles, her own story reduced to a series of impersonal flow-charts plotted neatly on a discount Mega-Mart graph-paper pad. Mikalu kept busy topping off their mugs of soda, preparing dinner in the kitchen, and helping Dabu organize his notes. Such a disarmingly simple and contented moment in time, this would be the last night all three spent alone like this in Ramo's house.

Needing a break, Rochelle stood and stretched, then tousled Dabu's hair and wandered in to watch Mika stir a simmering concoction. "You're enjoying Dabu's project," she observed, leaning against the counter.

"Yah," he said, sniffing a spoonful of the dark liquid. "One inscription, it tells of d'time Chief Puʻulai trade his three daughters for three boats so Chief Taoke's sons have wives. Then he go to Chief Napanea Wai-Nuikai and ask if Puʻulai boys can test d'boats in lagoon. Wai-Nuikai, he say okay, but warn them not to go out to d'reefs. They try anyway; and d'ocean, she break up all three boats and drown all d'boys. Chief Puʻulai, he blame Taoke for bad boats; and Taoke, he blame Wai-Nuikai for making d'ocean so angry."

"Then a century and a half later," she said, "a Taoke—little Timu—drowned in the same spot."

"And now Dabu's father, he think Papaii give Timu to d'sea for revenge." He began chopping mixed vegetables with the deftness of an accomplished sous chef. She'd enjoyed watching him revel in the luxury of a modern kitchen these past few days, his penchant for adding flair to their meals something Rochelle had grown to appreciate enormously. Clearing his throat, Mika added, "I wish I knew this much about my own history. I used to think no matter."

"Well," she said, "maybe it doesn't. I mean, it's interesting, but there's always a chance of learning things you don't like."

He poured some olive oil into a wok, then added the chopped vegetables, a colorful medley hissing and popping its protest against the searing heat. He studied her for a moment. "You are learning more you don't like from your father's files?"

She tugged at a thread on her jeans. "Like 'em or not, they're things I already should've known. It seems like my family history is mostly a series of clandestine business deals—proprietary secrets sealed in secret files."

He stirred the sizzling food. "You still feel bad about calling d'locksmith to open that other filing cabinet?"

"No . . . I guess I feel even more entitled to this info now. My father's dealings always seemed like something separate from Mom and me, something exclusively *his*; but it's my money, too, and my future as much as my past. It's Mom's inheritance, and Grandpa's life's work, and even Daddy's parents' bakery, which they left him despite a huge falling-out back when they tried to make him work there instead of going to college. Now all this is wrapped up in Poco's family history, too, including the legacy of Chief Wai-Nuikai, and the place *you* call home."

Mika slivered some fresh scallops and fish fillets, then tossed them into the mix and added capers along with chopped herbs and dashes of spice, international flavors to accent the blend of traditional Hawaiian and Asian fare. "All these family, these people, at least you know they care about you. That's why they leave you something to be sure of good future."

She watched quietly for a moment, then admitted, "But it looks like my father cared more about financing his projects than investing for my needs." She sighed and rubbed her eyes while he arranged crunchy noodles on their plates. "Mika, I should be able to take a couple years for myself right now, a chance to explore the world before I settle into a career—*if* I feel like working. Having money is supposed to be about possibilities, but I'm not the one in charge anymore; my life is turning out nothing like I planned."

Mika finished spooning the stir-fry onto plates, then turned to face her fully. "That's not right, Rochelle," he argued, his face surprisingly intense. "*You* make d'choices, and you all d'time *do* make right ones. You decide to come help Poco and me. You decide to help d'wheelchair place for Mauterre. You decide to honor Lalani—to honor what Lalani—" His voice broke. Looking embarrassed by his outburst, he shook his head and began ladling sauce over the food.

"Yes, Mika, I always try to do right by the people I care about. It's just, well, the choices always seem to fall between options I never expect."

He looked up and offered a knowing smile.

"Yeah, I know," she said, rolling her eyes.

"Okay," he said, pouring their drinks, "I not state the obvious."

They carried everything to the breakfast nook overlooking sprawling *lobelia* bushes that dripped with pink blooms, the backdrop a tangerine sunset firing a crooked laser outline of the western ridge. Dabu appeared instantly, his nose calibrated to anticipate Mika's culinary triumphs. He took the seat between them—his customary spot—the last time Poco's three musketeers would share a meal here together like this. Everybody tasted; then Dabu nodded enthusiastically and patted Mika on the back. Rochelle had to agree, repeating the silent gesture and earning grins from both the chef and his younger patron.

After eating quietly for several minutes, Rochelle paused and said, "I think I'll put the files back when I'm finished tonight, and not mention to my father that I went through them—not yet, anyway."

Mika nodded. "You find something he might get angry that you know?" he asked, polite if not subtle.

"Well, he obviously made it a point not to tell me the CMDC project has been in development for nearly ten years." Mika put his fork down, dumbstruck by the revelation. "He's not only invested most of my inheritance in it, but nearly all of his own fortune, too."

"How did he spend so much? They not build anything yet."

"Actually, they have. That new power station near Pahala was financed by CMDC, as was an upgrade of the water-treatment plant. Millions of dollars in sewer, water, and gas lines have been laid right up to the ridge behind Taoke Valley. Add to that the cost of surveying, engineering and architectural planning, environmental-impact filings, plus the political stuff like zoning and winning favor with local and state power-brokers, and you've got a huge investment now depending on completion. All that's left is site preparation and actual construction, which is slated to begin this winter."

"Wow," Mika said, sitting back and wiping his mouth. Dabu watched out the corner of his eye, glancing back toward Rochelle with a hint of surprise and concern. As always, the perceptive youngster was acting as their mood barometer, registering the prevailing emotions that swept through their little pseudo-foster family.

"My father also bought up a lot of local land, including most of what lies just beyond Taoke's ridge, plus several large parcels between here and Punaluʻu. It looks like he's expecting an explosion of development in the area."

"*Nā* Taoke, they not know about these plans, either, I think."

"I agree."

He considered this, then quietly asked, "And Lalani, you think she knew?"

Rochelle studied him for a moment, his gaze dropping to the unfinished meal.

"She was d'office manager," he said quietly. "She know all d'time."

"I found out for sure when I read her, uh . . . her estate plan."

He looked up, searching her eyes. Dabu sat back and watched. "Her will?"

She nodded.

"What it say?"

"She left everything to her husband—my father—except for thirty-thousand shares of CMDC stock. She wanted that to be split between you, Poco, and . . . me." She felt a lump rising, an odd sensation of having been, at least in one small way, Lalani's daughter after all. "They're to be held in trust by my father until sufficient profits can be used to purchase each of us a prime condominium overlooking the lagoon. The trust also provides a guarantee that you and Poco will be allowed to operate one of the watersports concessions, which would include everything from snorkeling and diving to personal watercraft rental, if you guys want."

Mika's eyes glistened, but he kept his composure. Dabu reached up and squeezed his shoulder. Feeling awkward, Rochelle set down her fork and watched an iridescent beetle exploring the *lobelia* blooms.

Mika rubbed his face, then returned Dabu's shoulder squeeze and took a deep breath. "I not want this condo," he said, "and Poco not want it, either; and Rochelle, you not even want to live in Coulée Makai at all. How can we stop this, now that Lalani is gone?"

Rochelle shook her head and gazed beyond the *lobelia* where a descending melancholy bruise was purpling the sky. "I looked through Papaii's will, too," she said.

Mika's shoulders slumped, his gaze falling to the plate again.

"He left the entire valley to Lalani."

"And she left all but the stock to your father," Mika breathed.

Rochelle nodded sadly. "The man who's already invested so much in developing it . . . is now the one who owns Coulée Makai."

*   *   *

Shaking their hands solemnly, Ramo showed several business associates to the door. He thanked them for stopping by, promising to keep busy and call as soon as he felt up to it. Mikalu talked with Mrs. Taoke near the closed casket, his button-down oxford shirt and silk tie still crisp after a long day. Dabu was taking great pains not to muss his new outfit as he knelt to inspect the cards tagged to myriad floral tributes, a botanical extravaganza spilling down the hallway and into the kitchen. Ginny bundled her little boy into his jacket while sharp gusts of bitter wind howled warnings from the eaves and rattled impatiently against window panes.

"Little Dabu, he stay as late as you want," Mrs. Taoke told Mikalu, glancing toward her son. She cupped Mika's face in her hands, her own eyes glistening as she looked deep into his. "You're one good *kāne*, Mikalu; I know this all d'time. Lalani, Papaii, my friend Tapakiki, they always be part of you, by and by. They all d'time love you."

Mika nodded sadly while she held him for a moment, no words necessary.

When Dabu suddenly appeared at her side, she turned and told him, *You help your friends*, then tousled his hair and headed toward the door, patting Ramo's shoulder as she passed. Declining Mika's offer of escort, she paused to touch Rochelle's face, then hurried outside and disappeared into the roiling dusk.

Ramo thanked Ginny for coming, nodded to Dabu, and retreated again toward the kitchen, a lost man still trying to protect the last remnants of his coveted privacy as he reeled from yet another catastrophic loss. Rochelle watched him go, then joined Mika in seeing off their last visitors.

"Rather than going to the funeral," Ginny said, pulling her son close, "we'll drive to Hilo and spend all day with Poco."

"That's wonderful," Rochelle said, Mika nodding agreement. "Instead of grieving alone, he'll be with friends—but how will you get around the limited visiting hours?"

"I am not easily deterred," she said, and Rochelle believed her, the beautiful young Hawaiian woman's gentle demeanor notwithstanding. "Besides, if the nurses insist we leave, I'll invade the chief medical director's office." With a twinkle in her eye, she explained, "He is a friend of my family."

They all traded hugs; then Mika hefted the little boy piggy-back for a ride across the valley. Ginny followed them out, glancing back at Rochelle with an approving smile and wink.

Rochelle slipped down the hallway and watched her father sip from a pint of gin at the kitchen counter, his gaze fixed on an explosive arrangement of lilies and glads perched on the table.

With Sympathy.

Without turning, he nodded to acknowledge her presence, then closed his eyes.

Rochelle recalled watching her mother in those hectic days before Grandpa's funeral, sometimes catching her watching back, both reading each other's thoughts, stepping in with the right words or a simple touch when needed most. Going on without him at the center of their lives seemed unimaginable, too painful even to consider, so of course that's all they could think about. Staying up late the night before his service, both vowed to remember him always, young Rochelle never suspecting for an instant that far too soon the job of remembering would fall to her alone.

Now her own father stood before her, wrapped in shadows this blustery night before Lalani's funeral, drifting in his own lonesome world. He could never tell Rochelle what he thought, nor would he ask how she felt, the enormity of another wrenching tragedy looming between this father and daughter who never learned to find each other in simpler times. Maybe she should have stayed in Hawai'i all those years ago, trading away the reassuring familiarity of friends and school and the bustling city Grandpa had given to "his girls," taking a chance instead on the possibility of growing closer to this man who'd given her life and loved her always, no matter how far away . . .

Or of knowing for sure that standing silently on opposite sides of a grief-filled kitchen is the closest they could ever be.

She moved toward him and tried to speak, but no words would come, so she smoothed her skirt and picked at phantom lint on her blouse.

He lifted the bottle again, hesitated, then capped it without drinking, sighing as he placed it in the cupboard. "Thank you, Rochelle," he said, his voice uncharacteristically small. This time he turned toward her, and the powerful man she'd admired all her life looked more vulnerable than she ever imagined, the lines in his face somehow deeper in the twilit gloom, his eyes robbed of their trademark confidence.

And she hugged him.

She didn't mean to; it just happened.

"Daddy," she said, "maybe we could— My time will be more flexible now, and I'll be coming to see Poco—"

He nodded. "That would be good."

"It's my fault that we haven't—"

"No, it is mine."

"We have so much to talk about."

"And we will."

They considered each other for a moment. She wanted to ask about secret deals, but couldn't—not tonight.

"I must go now," he said, and she knew he was right. Following him to the front room, she offered to walk him to the car, but he declined. "I will thank Mikalu when I pass him outside." He waved to Dabu and headed for the front door, pausing just long enough to say, "Good night, sweetheart" before disappearing into the darkening night.

Rochelle stood there a minute, then felt Dabu's hand in hers. She looked down and saw that he'd understood, even without hearing their words. He squeezed, then glanced toward the casket, reminding her of obligations and responsibilities.

By the time Mika returned, they had stacked the sandbags on a tarp near the casket, placing a neatly rolled *tapa* cloth to one side. Rochelle dreaded this moment, not sure how Lalani would look, afraid of exposing Mika to a gruesome sight that would haunt him forever. Shunting the guys to another room, she removed the tool from its usual place behind the catafalque. Her hands trembled near the end, but she finally managed to break the seal. Taking a deep breath, she looked inside.

A neatly zippered body bag lay nestled respectfully in the customary position. Unsure about the industry standards, she suspected their funeral director had included the sealed bag specifically for their benefit, there being very little pretense now regarding their plans. She breathed relief and thanked him silently, then called the guys out to help.

All three stood before the casket, a chance for Mikalu to steel himself, until mood-barometer Dabu signaled the group's readiness by pulling the *tapa* cloth into position. Rochelle and Mika carefully lifted Lalani's remains onto the traditional shroud, then gently wrapped her and secured the loose ends. Dabu helped them fill the casket with sandbags, then retrieved the makeshift stretcher; but Mika shook his head and disappeared down the hallway, returning with Poco's oversized backpack and several extra canvas straps. Rochelle sealed the casket and helped Mika rig a makeshift truss so he could hoist Lalani onto his back.

"It not look dignified," he said quietly, "but we can move much faster, by and by, especially in this wind."

"The dignity lies in honoring her the best we can," Rochelle said, satisfying Mika with the sentiment.

All three having dressed for the elements in jeans, long-sleeve knits, and tennies, they set out. Each aimed a flashlight, Dabu carrying a duffel, Rochelle positioned to help Mika if he stumbled. Wind ripped at their clothes, sandblasting them with lava-field detritus. An intermittent crescent of moon strained to reveal the ascending path, its patchy light quickly blotted by creepers of darkling clouds casting ominous shadows across the obsidian terrain. Columns of ancient lava rock shrieked like haunted-graveyard ghouls, while hollow moans echoed warnings from unseen denizens lurking amid the parapeted ridges. Mika never stumbled, his purpose driving a dogged determination to push on, his strength and stamina amazing Rochelle.

Faster than usual, completing nearly all of their trek required approximately an hour. They were just starting across the last flat stretch when Dabu and Mika suddenly stopped and Rochelle felt ice-cold water soaking her sneakers. Playing their flashlights around, they found themselves standing in a stream several inches deep. Its source appeared to be a stairstep waterfall cascading from the huge bubble mound to the west, an underground mountain spring probably forced to the surface by recent seismic shudders, its brief flirtation with open sky ending where it disappeared into a crevice some hundred yards to the east. The last series of rising lava-rock furrows lay just ahead, the concealed lava tube well above the water level, apparently safe from seepage.

"Let's climb," she said, Dabu taking the lead over this last bit of tricky terrain.

As they approached the secret lava-tube entrance, the air barely a hundred yards beyond it glowed in patches of eerie orange light.

"D'lava move closer!" Mika shouted, his voice nearly lost in the din. "Pele, she is carving new lines in the rock around her home."

Rochelle considered the burial tube's proximity to this encroaching threat, concerned the island might suddenly rumble with a gaseous chthonic retch, a pyroclastic exhalation incinerating them in its dark bowels.

"We should go see," Mika shouted, reading her mind again as he waved Dabu down from the mound he was climbing to place a sprig of *ohelo*. "Lalani, she would want to be sure it is safe before we enter d'lava tube."

They carefully slid Lalani's shrouded body under the ancient volcanic breaker, then scaled the series of low waves and worked their way around the densest part of the thicket, tripping through snarls of coarse vines that snaked down through narrow, ankle-twisting grooves. Reaching the ragged edge of a new ravine, they stood looking down at what appeared to be a dry riverbed some twenty feet below, its banks a series of cracked and crumbling ledges. Some thirty yards either direction, gaping holes in the crust exposed a subterranean lightning-fast rush of lava, an active tube sluicing liquid fire like steel pouring from a foundry's blast furnace. They picked their way up through thick vegetation for a closer look, the stench of sulfur burning sinuses and watering their eyes despite the scrub of misty sea wind howling across the plateau. A tattered carpet of vines hung over the lip, brown and blistered from the heat, thick bony arms locked in helpless death throes where they'd reached desperately to rescue their tender blossoms already long sacrificed to Pele.

"*Pāhoehoe*," Mika said, describing the 2,000-degree molten rock gushing from some 37 miles below ground, its ultimate explosive clash with the sea still characterized by many as Pele's handiwork for expanding her waterfront widow's walk.

At maybe a dozen yards across, these holes were dwarfed by a larger one farther up the rise, a rimmed crater boiling and splashing, its southern side bordered by an oblong mound of hardening lava stretching more than a hundred yards in their direction. Creeping slowly, the beast shed pebbles like dandruff, its hide cracking to bleed orange light, then healing just as quickly as it inched down the slope.

"That slow lava, it is called *'a'ā*."

Rochelle had studied enough geo-thermal physics to appreciate how this satellite caldera acted as a pressure-release keeping the Wai-Nuikais' ancient burial tube relatively safe—for now. She turned to gauge the protection of those moonlight-washed ridges dividing this area from Coulée Makai, the highest at more than 250 feet. Viku Taoke was right: only a catastrophic eruption powerful enough to wipe out much of the island would threaten Poco's ancestral valley, an extremely unlikely scenario for this dying volcano whose "hot spot" had already moved hundreds of miles south to build the undersea foundation for Pele's next fire-island home.

She turned back to the exposed tube of rushing lava and gasped at the sight of Dabu picking his way down along the fissured ledge for a better view.

"Dabu, he careful 'round d'lava," Mika assured her. "He come leave *ohelo* for Pele."

The boy placed his sprig atop a short column overlooking the river, then hefted a large rock and crept closer to the searing flow. He heaved it into the lava, jumping back just as it got swallowed in a brief flash of flame, a puff of phosphorescent gas marking its demise. Reading the concern in Rochelle's face, he nodding dutifully and picked his way back up to his friends.

"I'm satisfied," she pronounced. "Nothing worth doing is without risk." Mika nodded agreement, then gestured for Dabu to lead the way back.

After taking turns sliding in through the open slot, they lowered Lalani to the tube's floor and carried her up the incline to the area just beyond Papaii's grave. Dabu assisted Mika with digging; then Rochelle helped lift the body into place.

And Mikalu paused, looking down at the zippered body bag, his eyes filling with tears.

Rochelle gently turned him and pulled him close, his head on her shoulder so he wouldn't have to watch while Dabu carefully covered the woman who'd raised this blond-haired *haole* as her own. Mika wiped his face and stepped forward, chanting *mele* as clearly and passionately as Poco would, Rochelle joining briefly during the parts she remembered.

And the lava tube fell quiet, Pele's living island reduced to echoes of gusting wind reverberating from the narrow entrance slot.

"I forgot something for d'shelf," Mika said quietly, fists clenched, sudden frustration twisting his face.

"I brought something, but I wasn't sure . . ." She reached into her duffel and produced a tribute she thought embodied the kind of life Lalani lived: three small framed photos, one each of Lalani's "boys" posing on graduation day, the other of Rochelle watching from Longfellow Bridge. "She looked at these every day," Rochelle said, handing them over.

Mika smiled, his glistening eyes glowing in the backscatter from their flashlights. "She all d'time hold us close."

Dabu took Poco's picture from him and placed it on the shelf, then stepped back.

Mika handed Rochelle's to her, then briefly studied his own before stepping forward to place it next to Poco's. He stood back, pleased by the simple gesture.

Rochelle stared at the raven-haired college girl, searching for any hint suggesting this framed keepsake deserved to spend eternity helping Lalani's "boys" watch over her.

But she couldn't find it.

She couldn't find it in the image of a reluctant stepdaughter too busy to come "home" for visits, nor in the distracted face that never truly earned those desktop honors as an equal one of three . . .

But she did find something else when she looked into those eyes.

She recognized Pocomea's sister.

And she remembered she'd always be Mikalu's friend.

And she finally discovered what Lalani had seen so many times in this photo of a stepdaughter left behind: Rochelle could be counted on to look out for the young men those "boys" had become.

She held it close for a moment, then placed it on the shelf, one of three.

As they turned to go, Dabu glanced back and spoke from his silent world, words echoing what they'd each come this night to say . . .

"Bye, Allani."

*   *   *

Wind ripping at their clothes, lava dust stinging their eyes, the exhausted trio crested the last ridge and followed their flashlight beams down into Coulée Makai. The intermittent washes of moonlight now revealed a chorus line of dancing trees along the trail, each straining to break free and fly away. Down at the lagoon, overarching waves slammed the beach-fringing rocks, shimmering white-capped breakers scrabbling futilely for handholds even as successive surges conspired to pull them back into the sea.

They paused at the fork between home and the footbridge leading across the valley. Mikalu offered to walk with Dabu, but got waved off with a hint of big-kid-now chagrin, so everybody stood awkwardly for a moment before Rochelle signed her thanks and hugged the boy. Mika offered to shake his hand, then surprised him by turning it into another hug. They stood there and watched him go, his flashlight beam crossing the footbridge and heading up toward the open slot into Taoke Valley.

Leaning into the wind, they headed for the house, arriving to find the door ajar—

And Ramo waiting inside.

"We need to talk, Rochelle," he said, his brow furrowed in a way she'd never seen. He'd changed into slacks and a pullover, too, a casual look quite rare for him.

"Okay," she said, glancing toward Mika.

"In private," Ramo said, also eyeing Mika. "At my hotel."

Mika obviously disliked the idea, but Ramo must have an important reason to return this late the night before Lalani's funeral.

"I'll be back in a few hours?" she asked, quickly slipping into dry deck shoes and grabbing her purse.

Ramo nodded impatiently, avoiding Mika's increasingly challenging glare.

"Don't wait up," she told Mika, trying to reassure him without saying the words. "I'll let myself in."

"Yes, I imagine you are tired," Ramo told him, pointedly surveying their bedraggled appearances. He didn't ask where they'd gone for so long in this stormy weather, or how they'd gotten so dirty. Could he suspect?

Ramo donned a twill overcoat and led her outside, closing the door firmly. Mika watched from the window.

"What's this about?" Rochelle shouted over the wind.

Leading her down the trail with a penlight, he answered, "I met with one of my associates when I returned to the hotel. He had come directly from my office." He watched for her reaction as they walked. Getting nothing but a look of *And?* he added, "It seems you, Mikalu, and your little Taoke friend have been there, and somebody accessed my files."

A branch whipped her like a mean school-marm's switch while gritty dust tried to wash the words from her mouth. Ramo's "associate" must have checked the sign-in log at the front desk downstairs. "I was setting up a link for transmitting wheelchair data, but then Dabu found your CMDC model," she shouted.

The moon appeared, its eerie glow revealing more of the anger in Ramo's eyes and clenched mouth. "That was confidential," he shouted back.

Hoping to disarm him, she avoided the obvious challenge, instead playing along. "CMDC looks very ambitious. You must think there'll be enough clients to support it." *Duh.*

"Volcano tourism is de rigueur, as is island retirement among the nouveau riche; but foremost I intend to establish a burgeoning business center linked to Hilo, a central hub between North America and the Pacific Rim. I expect *more* than enough clients."

"But there's no airport south of the park," she shouted back.

"Twenty-minute helicopter shuttles crossing an active volcano—the commute is an extraordinary selling point."

They crossed the footbridge, its planks soaked by surges of frothy lagoon water rushing up through the stream. "Lalani must have known Poco would be against it."

"She agreed it would provide needed security for his future—and for Mikalu's, as well. Their little scuba enterprise will never prove lucrative; this development will make them wealthy."

"A paltry ten-thousand shares each?"

As they reached his Lexus, he turned and shouted angrily, "You had *no* right to read my wife's will."

"I'm named in it, too," she countered.

"Those ten-K shares will be worth five- or ten-million dollars to each of you someday!"

He jerked out his keys and chirped the door locks, gesturing for Rochelle to walk around and get in. As she opened the passenger door, Dabu suddenly appeared from nowhere, offering to return the flashlight he'd taken from Mikalu.

Mom said H-I-L-O man came with your father, he signed, *—don't know where he went.* He glanced up into Taoke Valley, then toward the slot into Coulée Makai, shrugging his shoulders.

"Thank you!" she shouted into the wind, tossing the flashlight onto the front seat. *Sneak and tell Mikalu,* she signaled, waving the "M" sign atop her head, a bushy-hair reference Dabu used in place of spelling Mika's name. *I will return soon,* she added, torn between wanting to find out more from her father and sticking around to confirm Donny Ko was here for something to do with the *kalo* farm.

"You're welgum," he said, nodding and strolling back up toward his house, no doubt intending to backtrack once they drove out of sight.

She climbed in and closed the door, relieved to be out of the wind. "It was Papaii's land," she said as he started the engine and pulled out.

"He would have agreed," Ramo said, dismissing her with an argument she could never win. "Besides, it was likely to belong to Lalani by the time we broke ground."

"Then Papaii conveniently died after Lalani got sick," she said, ashamed of her words even as she said them.

"What are you implying?" he demanded as they left Taoke Valley and pulled onto the main road toward Punalu'u.

"I'm sorry. It's just—it seems like such a risky plan. Since Papaii wrote the will when his son married Lalani, he specified his son, then Lalani, then *any grandchildren*. If Papaii or Tapakiki had outlived Lalani, then it would by-pass her estate and go straight to Poco—who would *never* allow this to go forward no matter how much you've already spent."

"Had you not been so stubborn, Lalani would have adopted you. Then you, too, would have been a grandchild covered by Papaii's will. Now that Poco has cancer—"

"How dare you!"

"Look, Lalani *wanted* to look out for you—you and that . . . Mikalu. The old man was even talking about adding you two to *his* will. I just never got around to it, which means *you* have a very weak claim and Mikalu has virtually none."

"I can't believe Lalani would betray Poco like that, cutting secret deals to destroy his valley."

Ramo shook his head, turning to drive along the coast toward his hotel. "You simply do not understand."

"Well, it's moot now. Lalani inherited it and left it to you, and you'll do whatever you want with it."

His expression one of puzzlement, he turned into the hotel lot. "You must not have read the will thoroughly," he said.

"What do you mean?"

"It includes a standard survivorship clause. Didn't you see the boiler-plate? A successor must outlive the decedent by six months to be eligible for inheritance."

"Lalani didn't outlive Papaii by six months," she said, surprised by the twist, "so the valley *is* Poco's."

"Not yet," he said, parking away from other door-dingable cars.

She pictured Poco undergoing grueling cancer treatments, Mika left behind to protect their home. "You married Lalani *and* adopted Poco, which means you're next of kin for both."

He opened the door and gestured for her to step out, which she did reluctantly, a merciless gust of wind whipping her suspicions into unspoken accusations. Crossing the lot behind him, she pictured Poco's broken and unconscious body washed into the lagoon, her brother pushed onto jagged rocks and left for dead. Questioned later, the Taokes appeared not to know

Lalani had succumbed to her illness; they had no reason to lure Poco to the cliff and leave the framed photo with his wallet and keys . . .

Rochelle froze.

Ramo turned and regarded her. "So, I hear you visited Tani Ko," he said. "How did you even learn about her?"

Donny Ko must have been in touch with Ramo after Lalani died. He could have known why Poco was so distraught! "You know what Donny's been doing!" she blurted.

"Doing what?" Ramo asked, spreading his hands.

"What happened to Mom's pills? Was Donny there that day?"

"All I know," he said, carefully measuring his words while fixing her with sympathetic eyes, "is that stealing human remains is a serious felony, but of course I would protect my daughter from such outlandish suspicion. Hey, is it true those lava tubes hold exquisite treasures, tributes to the spirits, priceless artifacts dating back centuries?"

Mom said H-I-L-O man came with your father—don't know where he went.

She clutched her purse, felt the cleaning staff's keys tucked into an inside pocket. "Poco *was* pushed," she said.

He stepped toward her, his brow furrowed again.

"What is Donny Ko doing here?" she demanded, pointing behind him. He turned to look.

And she took off running, yanking the keys from her purse. She unlocked the doors, pawed one open, then jumped inside and locked it.

Ramo pounded on the window, fishing for his own keys.

She fumbled with the ignition, got it started, and jerked the shift into reverse.

He jumped away just as the car lunged backward.

She slammed it into drive and punched the gas.

Ramo ran toward the hotel lobby while she careered from the lot and raced toward Coulée Makai.

Never slowing, she swerved onto the access road, scattering gravel as she gunned it through Taoke Valley, then skidded to a stop just inside the slot. She jumped out and ran down to the footbridge, fighting the wind as she hurried across and up toward the dark house, no sign of activity inside.

Movement from the left caught her eye, Dabu bursting from the converted dive shop. Spotting her, he ran her direction with some kind of gear tucked under his arm. Meeting him halfway, she could see a flashlight and two of the spear guns left by divers the week before.

"Ro-zhill! Hilo-man and Meeg-loo go o-fer the ridge!" He pointed up toward the north. "He not see me, but Meeg-loo did, wafe his arms so Hilo-man not know he tell me they go lafa tube." Breathing hard, Dabu was difficult to hear and understand over the wind. "He got gun point at Meeg-loo."

She grabbed one of the spear guns, instantly discerning how to load and fire it, then held it under her arm and signed, *Go tell Mom call police, bring help*.

He shook his head frantically. "No time! No time!"

She pointed urgently, ordering him, *Go!*

He backed away and shook his head, obstinate, and she knew he'd follow her, no matter what.

Stay apart, she insisted, turning to head up the ridge.

Understanding, Dabu threaded his way up a parallel course through brush some thirty yards west, the flashlight left off, both relying on moonlight through gaps in the clouds.

As they crested the rise, wind gusted and howled furiously. Rochelle looked back in time to see a hotel van race into the open slot from Taoke Valley, her father jumping out and heading toward the footbridge.

Working her way down toward the national park, she could see no sign of Mikalu or Donny Ko. They must have passed over the next ridge, already heading across the lava fields.

Rochelle picked her way over the smaller rises, then broke into a careful jog, stumbling through vegetation, tripping over cracks, barking her shoes on pumice debris. She could make better time whenever the moon briefly appeared, but had to slow again as serpents of cloud slithered through her light, shifting shadows skulking across the terrain, hurried along by impatient winds. Still she pressed on, lungs burning, legs rubbery, eyes stinging. Every time she feared losing Dabu, she would glimpse him to the west, a phantom darting from one lava pillar to the next, this child of the land tracking intruders for one critical chance to protect his friends and family.

She tripped and went down, caught in the bushy arms of a scrubby shrub, losing her spear gun. She managed to back out, Dabu suddenly materializing to help her up.

"You o-gay?!" he shouted, his words carried off into the wind.

She found the spear gun and got to her feet, squeezing his shoulder and giving him the diver's *okay* sign. He waited for her to navigate the obstacles, then hurried off to the west, his silhouette drifting along a shallow ravine before jumping a narrow section to disappear among the riffles of solid lava sea.

She assumed he was keeping close, but didn't see him again until she splashed through the new stream and approached the series of rises marking their secret entrance. Dabu was climbing atop one, waving his arms, then turning to point toward the bright orange glow. She'd assumed Mika would lead Donny Ko away from the burial tube, but surely not into the deadly molten maelstrom.

She motioned Dabu away, so he dropped into a gulley and trotted down to the right before skittering over the rocks, keeping an eye on her as she headed toward the flowing lava. She paused and crouched where the brush yielded to a flat, open stretch, then scanned the area, detecting no sign of either Mika or Ko—

There!

They were picking their way through crisscrossing vines, heading straight for the creeping wall of ʻaʻā that sheds pebbles from its cracking skin. Ko followed Mika from a half-dozen paces back, his pistol leveled waist-high, their images shimmering in the orange-lit heat.

Keeping low, she worked her way left, careful to avoid Ko's notice, blending into the shadows.

Mika led him into a dense thicket of shrubs and vines, both slogging methodically through knee- and thigh-high snarls, a looming mass spilling like Medusa's snakes from over a large rock near the lava river's bank. Mika bent and pointed into the tangle—

Then disappeared!

Ko lunged after him, tripping his way through the brush.

Rochelle hurried across the open area, slipping along the ragged fringe of vinery carpet.

When Ko peered into the dark hole, Mika leapt up from beside him and heaved a rock at his head. Ko twisted to prevent the full impact, but still went down, his pistol flying free.

Now within twenty yards, Rochelle jumped into the mass of vines, pulling herself forward just as Mika pounced, Ko flailing desperately. Mika knocked him backwards and dove after the gun, but Ko grabbed him, both struggling until Ko came up with it. Mika kicked him in the chest and leapt to the ravine's edge. Ko reeled from the blow, but managed to swing his arm up to aim. Mika whirled around—

And stepped out!

"Mikalu!" Rochelle screamed, but the wind snatched her words and carried them howling across the mountain, and the man who embodied loyalty and friendship vanished into the depths of Pele's hell, the blond-haired boy who'd written her a thousand letters lost forever in an instant.

Ko scrabbled to the edge, searching, arm shielding his face.

Rochelle clawed through the tangle, vines twining her legs, the nightmare of sleepless nights bursting through to steal her waking world.

Ko leaned out farther, his gaze drawn to the left.

She yanked her leg free, straddled a snarl, crawled desperately, slipped and twisted her arm, pulled herself up and pressed forward.

Ko stood upright.

Close enough now, Rochelle aimed the spear gun—

And Ko leaped, disappearing from sight.

There must be a ledge, but the heat . . .

She crab-walked across the brush, balancing on three points, her spear gun held aloft like the challenging pincer of a male fiddler.

The heat hit her first, like opening an oven, the lava a red-hot element warning reluctant chefs to steer clear. The wind screamed in her ears, sulfuric stench inflaming sinuses and watering her eyes, so she held her breath while dropping to the ledge, pointing the spear gun away to prevent stumbling onto the deadly barb.

She hurried around an outcropping and wedged herself into a crevice to escape the furnace blast, pausing to survey the scene. Mika had somehow reached the other side, now climbing downstream along a precarious series of rises, Donny Ko not far behind. Only one place this high up appeared possible to leap, a chunk of hard rock jutting most of the way across, the last few yards cracked and broken away, liquid fire not more than thirty feet below. The temperature would be unbearable, but somehow the others had survived it, so she took a deep breath, then ran and vaulted, banging into sheer embankment as she cleared the abyss.

She climbed quickly, the rocks too hot to hold more than a second or two, the spear gun slowing her down. She got her head above the next ledge and gasped for breath, rubbing grimy tears from her eyes, then pulled herself up and followed the men, billowing steam and gases obscuring her view.

Movement caught her eye, Dabu in the crevice now hurrying to the crossover, a determined boy too small to risk the deadly jump. She motioned him back, signed, *Please don't*, and touched her heart. He rubbed his eyes and backed away, turning to pull his shirt over his mouth and nose, then nodded and hurried back the way he'd come, continuing downstream along the widening ledge.

The rocks jutted out like shards of porous glass, growing sharper where deep lacerations laid traps for unprotected flesh. She ripped the sleeve from her overshirt and wrapped her free hand, pulling it tight between two fingers before tying it around her wrist. Her footing precarious, she inched along, nearly losing the spear gun when a piece broke off and bounced several times before skittering across the lower ledge and plunking into the raging lava.

A patch of thick, gnarled vines hung in her path, whipping in the wind, hiding the handholds even as they promised safety lines that could never be trusted. She pushed them aside and climbed higher, the jagged rocks broken by deepening fissures where the mound veered left, cooled ʻaʻā sculptures piled like river ice before the bow of a Great Lakes breaker.

Ramo appeared across the shore, Dabu naively leading him toward the drop-off and pointing at the crossover. She tried to wave them off, but had to cling to the rock face, her warning undelivered. Arms throbbing, she pulled herself up onto the next jut and gasped for air, spitting acid from having to breathe through her mouth.

Leaning out into fierce gusts of howling wind, she spotted Mikalu climbing down toward the lava some hundred feet ahead, navigating tangles of vine clawing at him like rabid fans reaching up from a head-banger mosh-pit crowd. Ko appeared above him, pausing to aim—

Crack! echoed the shot.

Mika jumped lower, grabbed onto a rock.

Crack!

And the mound began collapsing!

"Mikalu!" she screamed, her words lost in the roar as he tumbled and disappeared amid the rubble. Ko tried to turn back, but he slipped and fell, clawing at the vines, her view obscured by searing gases from boulders tumbling into the flow.

The wall screamed as new cracks splintered through the rock. Rochelle tried to withdraw, barely escaping when the jut broke free and exploded below, shards raining into the molten river. Blazing heat seared her back as she clung to the rock face beside that miserable thatch of hanging vines. She could barely hang on, seeing no direction to escape.

Then her foot slipped, and she clawed with the other hand, grabbing a hold, looking down in time to watch her spear gun career off the rocks. It came to rest beside the lava, fiery splashes coating it with smoking black glass. She looked up, the sky lost in a swirl of nauseating fumes, everything beneath her falling away, the entire world suppurating into a seething liquid morass.

She started to slip, but pressed tighter against the sheer drop, the vines mocking her plight.

Please, take me home.

And there stood her father, up along the ravine toward the churning caldera, searching the rocks for any route toward her. Fixed between her and the popping orange light, his image transformed to a shimmering silhouette, hair ablaze with a fiery corona.

She'd been here before, in her dreams, waiting for the man who always turned his back and walked toward the isolated road, the only escape, the only way home.

The dream flooded back, everything so real, her father and . . .

And the form atop the ridge.

It was Mikalu. That form atop the ridge had always been Mikalu, the gentle soul praying that Rochelle be given one more chance to pursue her destiny.

Me, I am your friend, the friend you trust.

But Mika was gone now, lost in Pele's violent tantrum, consumed by her fire. Like in the dream, he would never have a chance to reach down and pull her up.

And she would never have another chance to reach out for him.

Heat curled the hairs on her exposed arm, burned and cracked her nose, her eyes stinging through tears.

Qu'est arrivé à votre mère? Rochelle, whatever happened to your mother? Qu'est arrivé?

So many times she'd tried to add her mother to the picture, to imagine the victim's triumphant resurrection, a reunited family's jubilant celebration . . . but she'd always failed, the indelible clarity of a broken and lifeless body dashing all hope.

She looked back toward the blinding fire again and found the face of her father, an eruption of licking flames trying to consume him. Closing her eyes, she searched for her mother . . .

And a single memory flooded back, a woman's face, that hint of smile that always inspired confidence, her eyes still glistening with a sustaining promise of love.

Never had Rochelle seen Ramo as clearly as she now remembered her mom.

She dared to open her own eyes again, that shimmering silhouette of her father now in total eclipse, casting the coldest of shadows across her very soul.

Mom had never left her all those years ago—she could never lose her. It was Ramo she'd lost, the fantasy of a father she never had.

Rochelle recalled the sheer panic of feeling alone in the world, and she couldn't help but cry. She cried for the man she'd tried so hard to love, and for the mother she could never again hold close.

Her foot slipped again, but couldn't find purchase this time, her aching arms ready to explode, the young woman who once dared think she wanted to die remembering how it felt to be so very afraid.

She reached and touched the vines, the wind roaring its relentless warning, lava taunting her with its hissing, hungry laugh.

Any second now she would lose her grip, desperately grabbing the vines that surely must tear loose, and she would know that briefest instant of floating free before plunging to the rocks and slamming mercilessly into oblivion.

One last look toward her father, the man she could finally see . . .

And he was gone.

In his place, a woman stood in the fiery corona . . .

Her mother, Gina Naroux DuFortier, there all along.

The vision nodded and shimmered into the light.

And Rochelle trusted her, believed in her, knew she must take a chance. Reaching out tentatively, she touched the tenuous vines, gripping them, testing their sustaining power, and she pulled hard. Grabbing with the other hand, she climbed slowly, legs kicking at the rocks, hand over hand, higher, lungs bursting, higher, higher.

And she did float.

She floated the hard way, hauling herself inch by inch to the edge, a leg up, pulling with all her might, rolling over onto her side, gasping for air.

She had to find Mikalu, or at least know she'd tried, then get Dabu back home, attend a funeral, go see Poco, tell her brother who'd already lost so much that his best friend had honored and protected the Wai-Nuikai lava tube with his last breath.

She struggled to her hands and knees, retched and spit, coughing up tephra-clotted sputum. Staggering to her feet, she lifted her head to the sky and witnessed a massive thunderhead rearing high to puff out its chest and devour stars like so many fireflies. The beast ground its teeth and bellowed gusts of warning, crooked lightning sparks flashing taunts even as it robbed

Rochelle of the moonlight desperately needed for navigating the deadly terrain.

She leaned out and gazed over the edge, the lava more than fifty or sixty feet below the broken rise. Keeping her back to the ravine so her eyes could adjust, she eased sideways toward the avalanche scree. Her foot slid into a crack, barking her ankle as she stumbled into the brush, but she pressed on and within minutes found herself towering over the debris of a massive collapse.

Holding a squat shrub, she knelt and peered into the jumble of rock, spotting a shock of blond hair hanging below a sharp jut, curly locks glowing an eerie, undulating orange reflecting the lava splashing onto boulders below.

She considered various routes, reluctantly deciding the best chance depended on reaching the lower ledge directly above the lava, coming at Mika from below. Taking a deep breath, she moved quickly, pausing a half-dozen feet below her friend to wipe her eyes, preparing to scale the jagged outcropping that cradled him so precariously.

She tried several handholds, but couldn't find the leverage to shift her weight up. Finally, she managed to wedge her hand into a slot and push with one foot, the other barely reaching a crack where she jammed her toes.

Somebody grabbed her leg!

Donny Ko had her, pulling hard and nearly dislodging her. He held tightly, his face bloody, rage in his eyes.

She kicked, but he held tight, yanking harder. She kept kicking, but nearly lost her hold, so she tried jerking her leg free, trying desperately to haul herself out of reach, but he wouldn't let go. She felt with her other hand for loose rocks, anything—but he yanked again, twisting, her face pressed against the rock.

Swish-thunk.

He shuddered, a garbled scream carried into the wind. Losing his grip, he turned to look, a glistening metallic arrow protruding from his leg, the hazy image of a Hawaiian boy across the ravine aiming again, one spear left.

Ko roared and lunged at Rochelle—

Swish-thunk.

He let go and twisted, falling to his knees, gripping the new spear protruding from his abdomen, reaching behind with one hand to hold the shaft. He fell to his side, thrashing about as he teetered over the edge, hazy waves of heat distorting the rictus of his face. Rochelle scrambled down and grabbed for his leg, trying to pull him away from danger, but he kicked at her. She tried again, snagging his shirt, but he flailed with his arms, then squirmed free—

And dropped.

The lava swallowed him with a bright flash, belching satisfaction with a hideous spurt of noxious gas.

She tried to look closer, but the heat drove her back, and she saw the image of Dabu standing across the flow with one hand over his heart, tears streaming his orange-lit face. He pointed up into the rocks, toward the shock of blond hair.

Mikalu.

She wedged her arm into the crevice and pushed, lifting herself to the jut, freezing when the rocks to her left grumbled and shifted slightly. The entire scree could collapse at any time, sweeping her and Mika into the hot lava.

"Mikalu!" she shouted into the wind.

She heard a sound, but couldn't tell if he'd moved, eddies of wind teasing his hair like the broken feathers of a fallen *amakihi* bird. She hooked her fingers around the oblong protrusion above his head, terrified of possibly dislodging it, but seeing no other way. Pulling herself up, she let one leg hang unsupported, a knee against the wall, and got her face over the top just enough to see part of the back of his head.

"Mika!"

"Ro—chelle," he answered faintly. "Hard to breathe—pressing on chest."

"Are you hurt?" she shouted.

"No, I—think not—just can't move."

She studied the arrangement of stones, diagraming it in her mind. Three pressure points supported the large rock poised to crush him. She would have to slide him out into open space with virtually no leverage.

"Watch out," he said, his words barely audible. "Donny Ko—"

"He's dead," she assured him, that horrible image flooding back. She needed to focus.

"Your father—he come?"

"He's around here somewhere," she said, calculating how far she would have to swing out to get around and under the big jut that prevented him from tumbling down the slope and over the ledge into fiery river. If she slipped . . .

"Donny Ko—" Mika struggled for breath. "He tried—to kill me—"

"Don't talk now, Mika," she ordered. "Conserve your air. If you pass out on me, you won't be able to help."

"You know I—get chicken skin," he admitted.

"I'm afraid, too," she said, maybe too quietly for him to hear over the roar. The gases burned her eyes, tears streaming her grimy face.

Now or never.

She pressed her hand against a small knob for friction, then swung her legs around, reaching with the other hand—

And missed.

Legs flailing, she twisted and swung her body.

Again, and again.

And her foot caught the tip of a rock. She pressed hard against it, her hand a lock-down pressure point, until she managed to wedge her other foot into a crack. She groped with her free hand and found a hold, then tested the inverted tripod she'd created with her limbs, finally letting go with the other hand.

In one fast motion, she was up. Pressing her shoulder against the outcropping, she managed to shift her weight and find footing, bringing her shoulders just above the opening where Mika's hair swirled in the wind.

He lay squeezed into a narrow groove between the jut and a flat, coffin-sized rock above. A smaller one sticking out from the pile acted as a brace, holding its end up just enough to save Mika's life. She couldn't tell what other supports might be down by his feet. His head was pressed against the glassy pumice, facing away from her. Broken rubble, loose soil, plant matter, and other detritus filled the space around his neck.

She picked out the larger pieces, scooping and digging, clearing as much as she could, all the while talking to him. "Are you gonna be able to help, or will I have to pull you out by myself?—don't answer. Good thing you've got all that hair—but you may lose some if I have to tug *real* hard." She wanted to reassure him, to keep his spirits up—without betraying her own heart-pounding terror. The truth was, she couldn't be sure of freeing him, and one small shift in the rocks would likely kill him.

"Rochelle!" called a voice from above. Dammit, Ramo was working his way down the scree.

She frantically motioned him away. "Don't! Get off there! You'll get us killed!"

He kept coming, stopping at a big drop some thirty feet up. "Is he alive?" he shouted.

"Go back!"

"Leave him! Get out of there. I sent the boy back for help; you and I are the only two here. We will say you tried; nobody will know!"

She hurled a stone at him. "Get off the rocks!"

He dodged it, his eyes blazing orange fire, face shifting in eerie moon-strobed shadows. He turned and climbed back up.

Once she'd removed as much debris as possible, she asked Mika, "Can you wiggle anything?"

"Just my stupid head," he said. "I breathe easier now," he added, but she knew it might not last. "Thanks."

"I'm going to try pulling by your neck," she explained.

"You're not pulling my leg," he said, his voice quavering despite trying to make light of a bad situation.

One hand around his chin, the other cupped behind his head, she braced against the jut and gradually increased the tension of her pull until she was straining with every bit of strength she could muster. He shifted upward about an inch, but wouldn't budge any farther.

"It's my feet," he said without a hint of complaint for the pain she must have inflicted. "The rock, it is across them, can't bend enough for heels to clear.

She stroked his hair, wiped his forehead, desperately searching for a plan, tears of helplessness mingling with the sulfur stinging her eyes.

"It's okay, Rochelle. I know you try, but it's way too dangerous for staying here. You get help. I wait, promise not to go anywhere."

"I'm not leaving you," she said, crying now, no way to hide it from him.

"You're not safe, Rochelle. I heard Ramo say leave me. You get away."

"No, Mika. I'm not leaving without you. I've got to clear your feet. You keep shouting at me; let me know you're all right."

"You one good friend, Rochelle."

"*Ku'u aikane*, Mikalu."

"*Ku'u mili, aikane.*"

She touched his cheek, then wedged her foot, got a firm handhold, and swung out, then under the jut, gaining purchase on the first try. She managed to walk her hands around the overhang, heat rolling in waves up her back. Hanging briefly beyond the crumbling ledge, she dropped to the narrow spot below where Mika's feet would be trapped.

She studied the rock formation, estimating stresses, calculating every possible chain reaction should any piece be disturbed. Finally, she decided where she had the best chance, carefully gripping a flat stone about two feet across, then taking a deep breath and working it free.

She braced herself as it tumbled down the slope, bounced, and disappeared into the lava with a sigh of gas.

Nothing else moved.

"You okay, Rochelle?"

"If you are!" she shouted into the wind, already peering into the hole she'd formed, considering her next move—

"Ro-zhill!"

She started, nearly losing her footing. Dabu was picking his way along the ledge from the left.

Father said you left, she signed.

"No," Dabu answered aloud, the wind making him difficult to hear. "I read lips. *Get help*, he said. I acted like I go, but not really leave."

He must have leaped the lava river, risking his life.

Please go up, she signed, motioning back the way he'd come. *Danger*.

He locked eyes with her, and she knew nothing in this unforgiving world could ever be powerful enough to make him abandon his friends. That Taoke stubbornness honed through generations of razor-sharp *'ohana* animosity had been transformed by a mere child into the kind of faithful loyalty most people could never achieve. He would choose to join his long-lost brother Timu amid the *nā lapu* before living another day knowing he'd given back less than he would expect from Pocomea or Mikalu . . . or, she liked to think, from Rochelle.

She pulled him close and hugged him, feeling his slight body tremble almost as much as hers.

Quickly explaining the task, she insisted he stay back enough to flee should the wall collapse. He knelt and peered into the hole, shining his much-needed flashlight inside while her hands wiggled some bowling-ball stones loose. She couldn't see well from her angle, so he touched her leg and motioned where her fingers might find places to grip. One came loose, rolling down slightly, but she had to hold the other one up to keep from smashing her hand. Dabu crawled closer, reaching as far as he could, and gently pulled the first rock out, then jumped back, ready to escape as she let the second fall into the opening.

Nothing happened.

Rochelle shifted back on her haunches and wiped the grime from her eyes, her sleeve caked with tephra dust and tear-soaked mud.

Dabu shined the light up there again, lying flat on his stomach for a better view. He sat up and, using his wrist and fingers to depict Mika's foot and toes, showed her the pinning rock's position. She pressed her face to the ground and followed the light to evaluate the chances, finally deciding the best hope would be to ease it sideways, then flip it over Mika's right foot and let it fall while desperately hoping the debris above it was small enough to avoid dislodging the brace.

Motioning Dabu back, she tried every angle to press her arms up that high, but couldn't reach it. Taking a deep breath, she steeled herself, then pushed her head and shoulders up into the hole, claustrophobia wrapping her in its constricting embrace, the stark realization that even a shift of inches could pin her hopelessly for a slow, agonizing death.

Her fingers touched it, clawing gently as they searched for a place to grip, failing at every attempt. The beam stayed with her, but she couldn't tilt her head up enough to see. Maybe she would fit better trying upside-down . . . She withdrew and rubbed her face, thinking.

Dabu wanted to squeeze in there, she knew, but he respected her enough to seek approval with a simple gesture toward himself and the hole, waiting quietly for her to agree. She looked around, but could find nothing she might use to pry the rock free, an engineer caught in the field without her tools, no time to draw up a plan for client approval. They locked eyes, and in that instant she could see the man little Dabu would someday become, a strong but gentle Hawaiian *kāne* who would slay dragons with one hand while gently cradling a child with the other. How many times had she stood before the mirror back when she was his age, searching her eyes for the woman who never would have dreamed of digging deadly lava from the slopes of an active volcano?

She wiped her runny nose and motioned for him to turn around, then knelt behind him and gripped his legs just above the knees, showing him how she intended to hold him, prepared to yank him free at the first hint of danger. Standing again, she took his hands and covered his face, then tucked his elbows in at his sides. He nodded understanding, seeing the importance of protecting himself, the warning that his elbows might hang on a rock one more vivid reminder of the deadly risks he faced.

Positioned on his belly, he pushed the light ahead, carefully wriggling up into the hole, his head disappearing into the narrowest section, followed by his shoulders and torso. She held his legs, keeping her own braced to pull with all her might.

Muffled scrapes signaled he'd gone to work, the light flickering as he moved it around to check his progress. Pebbles rained down, her hands throbbing with tension, arms like coiled springs ready to trip at the slightest tremor.

The rocks groaned, shifting slightly. She tried to ease Dabu out, but he wouldn't budge, resisting her.

"Is o-gay, Ro-zhill! Don't pull!"

Thunk. Had he dislodged it?!

"Is o-gay!" he called again.

She wanted to shout, to beg him to tell her what was happening, but he toiled in silent determination, trusting her to pull him to safety even as she struggled to trust him to minimize the risk.

"Meeg-loo feet is looze now!" he announced.

"Rochelle, he got it!" Mika confirmed.

Dabu worked over onto his side and wriggled his butt up against the rock where he could brace for pushing Mika's feet. "Meeg-loo is moving now! Go help him, Ro-zhill!"

She hated the very idea of leaving Dabu in this crushing worm hole, a hair-trigger trap barely wider than his slight body, but Mika might have no other chance. She had no way to warn Dabu again to be careful, thinking this must be how it feels for a worried mother to know her child is out somewhere in the world, a pocketful of parental lectures never quite enough to guarantee safe return. She squeezed his legs, then patted them . . . and left. She left knowing she could never forgive such foolhardy miscalculation if Dabu got hurt trying to save his friend.

She leaned out and grabbed the jut, then swung around below it in what now seemed a practiced move, hoisting herself into position. Mika's shoulders had emerged a good eight or ten inches from the narrowest part of the slot, but not enough to free his arms. She grabbed him around the chin and head, bracing her legs, and gently increased the pull, feeling Dabu pushing from below.

Mika inched farther, a little more, almost to his elbows, one arm free—

And the rocks shifted, several tumbling toward the boy.

"Go help Dabu!" Mika shouted.

Rochelle let go and scrabbled over the top, no time to worry about the coffin-sized slab pinning Mika's chest.

One formidable chunk thunked onto the narrow ledge, blocking their carefully dug hole, Dabu swallowed alive.

"Ro-zhill!" he called, unmistakable panic in his muffled words. "I'm o-gay! You there?! Help, Ro-zhill!"

She grabbed the boulder and pressed all her weight into it, barely budging it. "I'm here, Dabu," she grunted, her words cast to the wind, no way for the scared boy to know she'd returned to save him.

Twisting her body, she braced her legs, pressing a shoulder against the side, knowing if it gave way all at once she might tumble behind it into the lava.

She strained, moving it a few inches.

Again, a few more.

Again, and it gave way all at once, her head and shoulders following it over the lip, dangling precariously in the hot gas. Fire reached up to singe her face and hair, but she'd hooked the toes of one foot into a crack, her ankle locked in a life-saving grip. She got an elbow on the ledge, then hauled herself up in time to hear the hillside grumble again. Dabu had worked his feet free, squirming desperately to extricate himself. She grabbed his ankles and turned him face up, pulling his mud-caked body carefully down and out, pebbles raining in his wake.

And the ceiling collapsed!

She shoved him to the left, leaping after him.

"Mikalu!" she shouted.

Dabu fled, Rochelle right behind him, both climbing above the crevice as that coffin-shaped rock slid down right where they'd just stood.

"I'm out!" Mika shouted, his words barely audible above the furious roar of angry winds. Boulders tumbled toward him, the rockpile shifting and giving way.

Rochelle kept moving, Dabu in the lead. Mika fled the other direction, climbing the scree, now out of sight around the bend.

Plop! Sssss! Plop! Plop! Sssss! Like flaming seltzer, the lava hissed approval while the hillside fell in on itself, an avalanche rushing into the narrow ravine, relentless neon waves splashing high into the night sky. Molten rock surged over the invaders to form new Class V rapids and a sheer drop deep enough to swallow a ten-man raft.

Rochelle and Dabu found themselves clinging to the wall. He tested the twist of blister-brown vines, pulling himself up just as new cracks began splintering the rock face, threatening to hurl them both over the fifty-foot drop.

As soon as Dabu cleared the edge, he turned and leaned over to urge her up. She tested the vines and took a deep breath, no choice but to trust them again, then started climbing hand over hand, her legs kicking against the rocks, toes seeking cracks, hauling herself over the edge, Dabu pulling her to safety.

"Mikalu!" she shouted into the night, frantically gesturing that symbol of a wild-haired *M* Dabu always used for naming his friend. He helped her up, then led the way, jogging through darkness, stumbling over vines and shrubs.

"Mikalu!" she repeated.

"Meeg-loo!"

The wind blasted them with gale force, the words ripped from their mouths and hurled into the void.

The broken ground trembled, so they worked away from the lava, seeking sure footing to get around to where Mika might have escaped—or be trapped again, maybe not so lucky this time.

They searched for what seemed forever, then spotted the silhouette of a man moving toward the ravine.

Dabu tripped and fell, disappearing into the brush. She pulled him out, got him on his feet, and pushed past him.

The man was standing, lifting a rock over his head, now dropping it over the edge. A hand reached up and grabbed him around the ankle, jerking him off his feet.

Rochelle hurdled the scrub, getting there just in time to watch her father fall and slip from sight.

"Daddy!"

She leaned over and looked, her eyes burning with the sulfur and heat of liquid lava not more than fifty feet below, Mika clinging one-handed to the vines while trying to hold Ramo at the same time. Ramo was clutching the vines, too, struggling against the younger man, trying to knock Mika's hands loose so he'd fall.

The lava rose up, splashing and igniting the blistered tendrils, a whoosh of sparks swirling in the eddies of wind, rising high into the shimmering sky.

She warned Dabu away, dropping to her belly and extending her hands.

Ramo looked up, fury in his eyes.

Mika tried to climb, but his adversary held him back. They struggled until Ramo got Mika by the hair, jerking his head backwards. Mika rabbit-punched him in the ribs, freeing himself long enough to scramble up the vines. Rochelle grabbed him under the arms, his leg up now, rolling him onto his side to clear the edge. She reached down for her father—

And gobs of vine began tearing away!

Ramo dropped a few feet, clawing wildly for handholds as detritus scattered across the burning river, countless miniature lights flashing everywhere it ignited, each consumed in the briefest instant of blazing glory. The lava reached higher, flames spreading like wildfire up the dense tangle, whipped by the wind into a raging frenzy.

And the gusts suddenly died, the air falling still.

Flaming debris swirled up over the precipice and rained from the sky.

Rochelle leaned out as far as she could while Mika gripped her legs with the fiercest protective determination. Ramo extended a hand toward his daughter, a man always just beyond reach—

And lost his grip!

He flailed his arms, plunging with a silent scream into the merciless fire, a bright gasp of gas sealing his fate.

The vines exploded into a trillion glowing embers, whirling dervishes dancing around a helpless trio who'd lost the one man who could never be saved.

Mika pulled Rochelle and Dabu close, holding them while she cried, the trembling boy's grimy face streaked with his own tears.

Fiery sparkles skipped across the ground like scattering jacks, too many for any player to pick up in a deadly world where surviving is the game, where failing to see clearly one's own opponents can exact the ultimate penalty.

The burning embers of Rochelle's former life would swirl around her for days, following her to the hospital where Pocomea wept for the family betrayed by a man he'd tried so hard to love, for the *haole* sister he did love even as she watched the last remnants of her innocent trust die in the unforgiving flames.

And the embers would swirl amid the flowers at Lalani's funeral, astonished mourners recounting the tragic tale in sympathetic whispers, a sand-filled casket lowered beside the empty plot of a husband claimed by Pele's wrath.

And Rochelle watched those very same embers begin transforming into delicate white blossoms floating from the sky as she paused on Ramo's Hilo porch listening to the scared voice of a thirteen-year-old girl crying over the cellphone . . .

"What is it, Mauterre?" she urged quietly over the static. "What's wrong?"

"It's—it's Auntie Dix. She won't wake up, and they won't let me go home without an adult, not unless you come back right away."

And a swirl of drifting Sweet Autumn blossoms ignited in Rochelle's heart, a fire raging against the hopeless plight of every child who must wake to face another day feeling lost and alone in the world.

And the last fading embers turned to ash as she stood there gazing across the sea, promises whispered to the one who most needed her now.

And Rochelle DuFortier left Hilo for home again, gone before the dust of grief and regret could ever have a chance to settle at her feet.

Ke one e ho‘ololi ana

Shifting sands

Mid-August, ten weeks later

Slashes of window-blind sunlight striped a silk bouquet of lilies and carnations. Mauterre unpacked some beauty supplies and leaned over to brush her great-aunt's hair while Rochelle worked on her laptop in the customary corner chair. The comatose woman lay still, unresponsive since the day her grandniece came home from school and found her unconscious on the floor.

"We have good news, Auntie Dix," the young teen said quietly, setting the brush aside. She pulled her own long brunette tresses back behind her ears and sat on the edge of the bed. Rochelle joined her on the other side, reaching down to squeeze Miss Dixon's hand. "The temporary guardianship has been extended indefinitely. I can stay with Rochelle as long as necessary—until you come home."

"She's quite a nuisance," Rochelle added with a wink to Mauterre, "—always underfoot, but she's good at sweeping cinders from the hearth."

"I have to be, or she'll feed me scraps of moldy bread and keep me chained in the cellar."

"You're not fooling her, you know," Rochelle sparred with Mauterre. "She knows the condo has no cellar."

"Well—locked in the closet then."

They both smiled, as much for themselves as Miss Dixon, a trapped woman registering brain activity but with no way to smile for herself.

"Tell her the other news," Rochelle urged.

"I get to go to Hawai‘i!—for five days. Rochelle got permission for me to leave the state. I'm gonna meet Pocomea, and see Mikalu again."

"I have business to take care of out there," Rochelle explained, not so much because she believed Miss Dixon could understand, or could even hear her, but for Mauterre, who nurtured this tenuous connection faithfully.

"But don't worry about the wheelchair company while we're gone," Mauterre assured the sleeping woman. "Jodis got us another big account yesterday, and we've added a second shift just to keep up with Osteo-Bright's

orders for Rochelle's new version of the motorized DAK-5. She's developing so many new models that we've hired three designers to help, and Jodis
is looking for someone to build prototypes in-house so we don't have to
spend so much contracting out."

"Jodis is a business wizard," Rochelle said, not quite comfortable with
praising her own contributions. "You really made a good choice there; and
with your grandniece constantly looking over his shoulder—"

"He's teaching me *everything!*"

"—I wouldn't be surprised to see her working up a plan for buying out
our parts suppliers."

"Only the big ones," Mauterre kidded, smirking.

"Don't worry, though—I make her shut off the computer sometimes,
and coax her to go out to play or read a book."

"I've been writing a story, too," Mauterre said. "I brought it so I can read
to you today."

"I'll be over here working," Rochelle said, her cue she would leave them
on their own for a while. She took her seat and loaded the draft file her new
associate-engineer Brian had just completed, attachment specs for the amphibious wheelchair incorporating Mikalu's ideas.

"It's called 'Garden Friend'," Mauterre began. Her unfinished tale had
been started a dozen times, each version a variation on the concept of one
little girl who visits an exquisite botanical wonderland every day to see her
friend reflected across the surface of a cattail-fringed pond. She can't hear
the friend speak, or even find her face whenever a frog jumps and ripples
the water, but she knows the surface will always grow still again, and if she
waits her friend will return.

Rochelle found herself watching dust motes swirling in the air, tiny
specks disappearing and appearing again as they danced through slashes of
window-blind sunlight. Images of her own mother had drifted in and out of
Rochelle's thoughts the same way over the past few months, sometimes elusive as they faded beyond the light, other times so vividly clear as to seem
real. Recalling her father had proven much too easy at first, stark images of
his furious face intruding at the most awkward times, Rochelle well practiced
at chasing them from her mind.

Even bad men can love their daughters, Rochelle, Mika had said, urging her to
find some way to reconcile so many unanswerable questions with what she
did understand about the man she'd always called Daddy. *And will always be
okay that a daughter loves her father, no matter what.*

Rochelle tilted her head back and closed her eyes, rubbing the crick in her neck. For months—maybe for years—her mantra had been: *In crisis, deal with facts.*

Do what needs to be done—now.

Ever since Mikalu's call late one night asking her to come help bury Papaii, and even now fighting the system for legal authority to protect and care for Mauterre, her life had proved one crisis after another, responsibilities and obligations leaving her no time to second-guess the hard choices she had to make.

Is not all emergencies all d'time, by and by, Rochelle, Mika had explained. *At night, you wake up, and for just a minute before you remember so many things, you find out how you really feel.*

Even so, too much of what she felt had amounted to sheer frustration, especially in trying to develop a plan for dismantling Ramo's estate without hurting those who had trusted the man.

"Don't worry," Mauterre was whispering to Miss Dixon, her faerie-tale told, "we'll come back to see you after five days."

Rochelle rubbed her eyes, then opened them and looked. Mauterre sat very still, tears standing in her eyes, gazing at Miss Dixon's serene face. She lowered her head, chin trembling, a lone tear crawling down her cheek. Rochelle had learned not to rush over and hold her every time grief crept up like this, sometimes letting it run its own course, reserving some of those hugs for the happy moments, too.

"I want to know if she can hear me," Mauterre said quietly.

They'd talked about this many times, so Rochelle remained quiet.

"I know there's no way to tell, and you say at least maybe she feels that I'm here, but what if she can't?"

The discussion had never gone this far, Mauterre always having been satisfied with the possibility.

Rochelle set the computer aside and pulled her chair close. Mauterre fidgeted, fingering the spot where a teardrop had darkened a perfect circle in the denim leg of her jeans. Rochelle reached toward the young teen's hand, extending her fingers to cover it, but not quite touching. "Can you feel me?" she asked, sensing her tentativeness.

Mauterre sat very still. After a moment . . . "Yes," she admitted, curious but unconvinced.

Rochelle pulled her hand back, watching until Mauterre looked up, those dark eyes glistening with extraordinary depth. "I'm a part of you now, Mauterre," she said quietly, but with relaxed confidence, "—aren't I? You know this, whether I physically touch you or not."

Mauterre nodded. "I'm—I'm part of you, too."

Rochelle offered a hint of smile. "I know this, even when you're asleep. And *you* never forget, either, even when you're asleep, even when I don't touch you . . . even if I couldn't touch you . . . because you know."

Mauterre nodded again, glancing away, lost in thought. "You think Auntie Dix knows."

"Yes, I do. Your Aunt Dix knew this might happen, so she made arrangements with Jodis for us to live together in her home, and for your financial support, because she counted on me to look out for you, and she counted on you to be okay, no matter what."

Lalani had trusted Rochelle's father to look out for Pocomea and Mikalu, never suspecting for an instant the man she married might try to hurt her "boys." Rochelle had struggled with reconciling how Ramo could earn people's absolute trust, yet betray them in the worst possible ways. It sometimes left her wondering if she could ever again fully trust another . . . but because others *could* place their faith in her, that meant surely she could dare again to believe, for to live without confidence in those she loved would be far worse than any deception a man, woman, or child could possibly conceive.

"She knows I love her," Mauterre decided, "and that I always will."

Rochelle smiled knowingly. "And she knows you would come see her, no matter what."

"Because she needs me here?"

How many people needed Rochelle? How much could she do? Why did she keep trying, even knowing she might fail?

Rochelle reached out and pulled her close. "No, Mauterre, not because she needs you . . . it's because you're the kind of young lady who needs to be here for her."

*   *   *

"Ro-zhill! Here, Ro-zhill!" Dabu called as Rochelle and Mauterre entered the terminal, an extended lay-over in San Diego making them more than two hours late. He rushed forward to greet her, then skidded to a stop like some exaggerated cartoon character, gaping at the sight of Mauterre, a farcical moment missing only the humorous sound effects.

Rochelle ushered them away from the crowd, then hugged Dabu until he blushed, stepping back to sign, *Where is Mikalu?*

He glanced toward Mauterre, looking away just as quickly. *Calling Ginny,* he responded, pounding the letter *G* like a gavel, a reference to her career as an attorney.

Curious why he'd chosen to sign rather than speak, but not wanting to put him on the spot by asking, she introduced her young ward. *This is M-A-U-T-E-R-R-E. Say it like M-A-W and T-A-R-E.* "Mauterre, this is my excellent friend Dabu."

Mauterre reached as if to shake his hand, but Dabu flinched, so they settled for polite waves. He didn't try to pronounce her name.

"*Aloha,* Miss DuFortier!" Mikalu announced, rushing over to grab Rochelle in a bear hug, twirling her round, practically lifting her off the floor. "And *aloha* to the captivating young Miss Dixon," he added, grabbing the clearly delighted young teen in a similar hug, her feet definitely leaving the ground. "We made you each a welcome *lei,* but leave them in d'fridge, not knowing when your plane finally arrive. Come, we get your bags." He hustled them toward baggage claim. "Rochelle, you are late for one big meeting already. They all wait, not want to come back later."

"Good. I want it over with so I can relax for Poco's homecoming tomorrow."

During the brief wait, Mikalu assured Rochelle the parts she'd sent to build a custom wheelchair for Poco had arrived intact; then he praised Dabu's help in prepping Ramo's house for their visit. Rochelle echoed similar accolades for Mauterre's assistance in assembling portfolios and organizing visuals for the meeting. They managed to have both youngsters blushing by the time everybody exited the terminal.

"You need freshen up?" Mika asked Rochelle, surveying her somewhat rumpled travel clothes.

"No time. Just drop me off and I'll dance in my civvies."

"Okay, then I take these punky teenagers, go see Poco one last time in d'hospital. You call my cellphone when you're ready, by and by."

"Yeah—ready to flee, screaming like a mad-woman," she added.

They drove to the building that used to house Ramo's office, the entire third floor now occupied by the law firm where Ginny was fast-tracking her way toward a full partnership. Dabu insisted on helping her carry the materials up, so Mika waited in the battered SUV with Mauterre, both wishing her luck, Mika adding a wink and confident smile.

A young Asian woman met them as they stepped off the elevator, thrilled to see Rochelle had finally appeared. She led them to a large conference room at the end of the hallway, then hurried off to load Rochelle's presentation file.

A room full of people greeted her, more than a dozen men and women of various nationalities, most dressed considerably more business-like than the late-comer who'd called this meeting. Her mother would have clucked disapproval of such undignified presentation, Rochelle mused fondly, but she would understand. Dabu placed the box on a table cluttered with snacks and drinks and paperwork, then scooted back out before anybody could make eye contact with him.

"I'll be right back," Rochelle apologized, following him out to the hallway. She stopped him from leaving, turning him to face her. *Thank you, my good friend. Remember: Be yourself.* She emphasized the latter. *Be yourself.*

He nodded. "You're welgum," he said quietly, looking a bit sheepish as he scurried off.

She took a deep breath and stepped back into the arena, hungry lions watching in predatory anticipation.

Ginny took the lead in introducing everyone: two older men, partners in her firm, one Asian, one Hawaiian; an assortment of eight speculators who had invested with Ramo in the Coulée Makai Development Corporation—they ranged from a fiftyish bleach-blond woman wearing too much make-up to an elderly Filipino, his lanky frame bent over a cane, a wise and knowing smile—two venture capitalists recruited by Jodis, scrubbed young men sitting stiffly in wool suits; the island's portly economic-development director, an observant native who could pass for Pocomea's brother . . . and Mrs. Taoke, looking very relieved to see Rochelle, her plain dress somehow elegant in stark contrast to the stuffy group.

Rochelle headed straight for her, taking her hands as she rose, surprising her with an embrace that melted some tension from the room. The economic director stepped forward and presented Rochelle with an exquisite pink flower in an onyx bud vase, a robust welcome from the man she'd called for help so many times over the past two months. Then Ginny's bosses competed for who would hold Rochelle's chair, one on each side as she took her place at the head of the table. Ginny was passing around the binders when her assistant signaled the visuals were ready . . .

And Rochelle couldn't help but think of her father.

This was his world she'd co-opted. If only she'd inherited—or taken the time to learn—some of his business savvy, she might feel more confident right now. Ramo reveled in the challenge of a deal, a master at steering negotiations, the ultimate pitchman who could sell anything . . .

And fool anyone.

It wasn't Ramo's expertise Rochelle needed right now. It was the integrity he'd never achieved. She believed in what she hoped to accomplish, and she believed in herself, the young woman who needed no tricks or sleight of hand to perform in scrutiny's blinding glare.

"Thank you, everyone, for coming today, and for waiting so long. My late father's will has named me the sole living heir of his estate, including his stake in CMDC. Some of you know—or may suspect by now—that the development he envisioned is no longer possible. The property known as Coulée Makai has *not* been acquired by our company, and there appears to be virtually no chance it will ever become available." She knew the latter to be a gamble that Poco's remission would last the additional fourteen weeks he needed to survive Papaii by six months and claim the deed. "The Wai-Nuikai heir refuses to consider either selling or allowing even modest development—for any price."

The tension had returned, backs stiffening, pin-drop silence so ominous that Rochelle could listen to her own pounding pulse.

"I hope we can reach agreement today," she continued, "that will expedite restructuring our goals without costly challenges or other delays." That certainly didn't sound reassuring.

They all watched, shields up, death rays set to obliterate. The blond woman looked around, then offered her assessment: "Good luck, honey."

"First," Rochelle said, gathering steam, "I pledge to make my father's personal assets available for settling any claims." That earned a few looks of relief, the rest an assortment of piqued curiosity. They knew she could complicate probate, and probably succeed in limiting the estate's liability to Ramo's stake in the company. Investors leveling charges of fraud would probably make things even worse, possibly putting them all in the position of bleeding their own precious pints to cover the exorbitant cost of suing a turnip for blood.

Squeezed into an ill-fitting suit, a beefy rugged-featured man tossed his pen on the table and sat back, declaring, "I might not be interested in dissolution. Maybe I just might want to see this thing through."

"I certainly hope so," Rochelle said, earning a quick smile from the blonde, "—but I want all of you partners to have that option, so let's begin by considering the company's current value."

She turned to the first page, a list of assets, everybody's eyes drawn to their own binders. Mrs. Taoke followed suit, glancing around tentatively, a mischievous twinkle in her eye.

"The bulk of company funds has been invested in infrastructure," Rochelle explained, "all of which are virtually unrecoverable. This page itemizes what's left, which is fourteen percent of your collective investment." She still had them, she could tell, none remotely interested in taking such a loss. "The next page lists my father's personal assets, which include the estimated value of his house here in Hilo and the considerable property he purchased in the area between Taoke Valley and Pahala. This adds approximately thirty more, for a total of forty-four percent recovery." She glanced toward the venture capitalists, their cue.

One obliged, saying, "And my firm is prepared to offer forty-four cents on the dollar cash for the shares of anyone who prefers not to wait out liquidation."

"I've done worse in fast food." The blonde shrugged, feeding a stick of gum into her mouth. "I've also done much better by not getting cold feet."

"I propose an alternative," Rochelle said. "I would like to exchange my father's property for additional shares, and bring in new partners." The capitalists looked, well . . . hungry. "If that's agreeable, I will transfer to the company some options I've recently negotiated for additional property. I also recommend we offer shares for the Taoke family to include a large portion of their valley, which is adjacent to a parcel bordering Punaluʻu Beach."

Mrs. Taoke looked from face to face, a regal air of confidence gracing her wizened features, her status as a serious player now established.

"I also propose," Rochelle added casually, "that we designate the firm of Nipiton-Okamata to manage . . ."

She clicked on the first projection—

"The Pocomea Business, Technology, and Science Center!"

An artist's rendering of a sprawling complex appeared, a breathtaking blend of sweeping modernistic architecture accented by traditional Hawaiian motifs. She paused for a beat while the clearly impressed group caught its collective breath, a million questions hanging in the air.

She clicked the next image.

"And Taoke Golf & Beach Resort!"

Shots followed of oceanview condos and apartments clustered along the cliff and climbing the southern ridge, all overlooking a magnificent 36-hole course covering the areas already cleared for *kalo*, the upper valley left in its natural state except for a nature center marking botanical tours and a lone road climbing to Pocomea Center visible in the highlands toward Pahala.

"And now I present . . . Hokele Wai-Nuikai!"

Stretching down the outside of Taoke's ridge, a layered hotel offered bay views and a trail down to the northern edge of Punaluʻu Beach.

"A thriving eco-tourism industry!"

Sketches of helicopter pads at the hotel and Pocomea Center showed people queued up for *'Cano Airtours* excursions to the national observatory and the world's most active volcano. Then several photos depicted visitors who looked suspiciously like Dabu and his brothers, plus Mika and several young ladies, all hiking "the lava walk."

Another series showed startling scenery up through a stairstep gorge, sparkling waterfalls and pristine pools, breathtaking expanses of raw cliff face, trails through exquisite natural displays of blooming flora.

"My God," the blonde gasped.

"Where is this?" demanded the beefy skeptic, suddenly very intrigued.

"Pahala Valley," Rochelle offered matter-of-factly. "Ten minutes from Pocomea Center."

She cut to artist's renderings of condos and luxury homes along the lower cliffs, views up into the stunning expanse without cluttering its natural splendor.

"We can include all this?"

"My father already owns some of it. The upper reaches are protected by the land conservancy. For the rest I've negotiated options, either for our company or for other investors if we don't reach agreement."

"What about Coulée Makai?" asked the beefy guy. "Won't this make its value sky-rocket, an even more attractive parcel for other developers—or *you*—to come in and compete with us?"

"The most important aspect of this project, its very *character* and trademark, will be an emphasis on conservation, on protecting the unique ecosystem that makes the Big Island an unparalleled jewel in the Pacific. I want to remain a partner, represented by my friend Ginny's firm, to keep this focus clear. Pocomea Center—" She clicked past the Pahala shots, Mikalu's inspired photography already having worked its charm. "*Our* Pocomea Center will include a science complex for public and private interests to study everything from volcanology and geology to medicinal-plant pharmacology. In that spirit, the heir to Coulée Makai has agreed to designate the lagoon as a marine sanctuary and will continue to offer limited scuba excursions, especially those emphasizing oceanographic study." She clicked to a shot showing a dive shop on the Taoke Valley side of the ridge, offering access through the open slot. "Likewise, the entire valley would be available with certain restrictions for botanical study, an ecological preserve with permanent occupancy limited to the Wai-Nuikai ancestors' home." Several images followed, reminding everybody why they'd been attracted to Ramo's project in the first place. "To be clear, Coulée Makai is not included in our development, and the family will refuse all offers of shares or other compensation so as to avoid any obligations involving the valley or lagoon."

"We don't need it, honey," the blonde pronounced as she looked through her binder at photos and legal/business data expanding on what Rochelle had shown. "That would just be extra frosting on a cake that's already looking damn sweet."

The beefy guy announced, "I'll be taking a serious look at how the shares will be distributed, and I need guarantees on the level of capitalization, plus a few dozen default clauses so I don't wind up back here in five years looking at cents on the dollar, and some occupancy-intent agreements to prove we won't go begging for tenants, and a thorough investigation into the Nipiton-Okamata firm's capabilities—no offense," he added to Ginny's bosses, both nodding with quiet confidence.

Rochelle listened to the buzz as everybody started calling out their concerns, pens flying across note pads, binder pages fluttering like butterfly wings, Nipiton and Okamata swarmed by hungry Happy-face Spiders all spinning webs of contractual legalese. She saw Mrs. Taoke holding her own, goal-tending against shots aimed at expanding her valley's role; and she caught Ginny's eye, Pocomea's devoted friend nodding approval of Rochelle's pitch, a cautionary glance toward the frenzy admitting that a stroll through molten lava might be easier than reaching consensus.

The elderly Filipino hobbled toward her, touching her hand as he offered a mischievous smile. "So far you have three of eight committed to exploring a possible agreement, Miss DuFortier. It might require many months, and the attorneys may ultimately dissuade us, but there is a modest chance we might eventually choose to move forward."

The blonde sidled over, interjecting, "You done good, honey. Listen, I can't say if this thing'll fly or not. It looks a lot riskier than what your father sold us, but you're offering something he never could."

"What is that?" Rochelle asked, wary of the implications.

"Well, we figured he'd make that Makai thing work 'cause he stood to rake in a lot of dough, but you're willing to give up the cash, so the way I see it, you're working for something you care about a whole lot more than linin' your pockets." She glanced around, then leaned closer, her voice lowered to a whisper. "You're lookin' out for people, the people who trust you."

"That's why," Rochelle admitted, "I want you to think carefully before committing to this."

"Hell, I'm already thinkin'. Bottom line is: if I decide to become a partner, it won't be because I've decided the world needs another golf course. It'll be 'cause I'm bettin' on *you*."

*   *   *

"It's all downhill from here," Rochelle said, cresting the ridge with Mauterre, both sweaty and grimy after hiking all morning under the hot sun.

"We've got twenty-five minutes to spare before Poco wants us back," Mauterre declared, focusing her camera for a shot across Coulée Makai. "Without these pictures, *nobody* would believe I got so close to *real* burning lava."

The lagoon's surface shined like riffling glass, the ocean beyond it unusually calm. Small in the distance, Pocomea sat on the beach in his brand-new custom all-terrain power wheelchair, gazing off toward the reef marked by a pair of divers' float-flags. Dabu stood beside him, one hand on the big man's shoulder. The chair had proven a remarkable success—better than Rochelle expected her retro-fits to perform—able to sport Poco all around the valley, even up the outhouse trail Mika had smoothed with natural-looking black concrete. Still, for the native *kāne* who'd learned to cherish his family's beloved undersea realm by the time he was old enough to splash in its lapping waves, the limitations of paraplegic paralysis never appeared more daunting than at this very moment, reducing Poco to a mere spectator who could only dream of joining Mika and those divers in the weightless world where any healthy human-fish, no matter how big, can always swim free.

Though too young to be certified dive master, Dabu would normally be out there assisting with the group, an invaluable team member who knows the lagoon, handles crises with aplomb, and communicates in sign language with Mika to share potentially life-saving observations about the strengths and weaknesses of each diver. That he'd chosen to remain behind with Poco today spoke silent volumes about the shy teen who'd tended uncharacteristically to disappear over the past four days whenever Rochelle and Mauterre drove in from Hilo.

The divers all surfaced and began snorkeling toward the beach, Dabu meeting them in the surf to assist with their gear.

"Let's hit the showers before they get up here," Rochelle suggested, leading Mauterre down the trail. "Be warned: it's a musty, mossy old stone room, despite the very nice carved-*koa* benches installed by Mika."

"It can't be *that* bad," Mauterre said. "I *am* glad we stayed here instead of Hilo last night. It was kind of an adventure."

"Then let's see how you feel about chasing lizards from the shower. At least you don't have to freeze in the waterfall like I did when I was your age."

As they climbed down the rocks, Rochelle found herself recalling that day she caught Mika standing naked in the waterfall pool, and she wondered how he would look out there now, his golden skin glistening with chill droplets. She'd have to mention this to him later, maybe embarrass him a little, hopefully get a laugh.

"We should both use the women's shower," Rochelle said, a subtle test to avoid intruding too much on Mauterre's modesty, "—in case the divers get here soon." She grabbed the pack of clean clothes and supplies they'd left at dawn on their way to tour Pele's fiery sanctuary.

"I gotta go to the bathroom first," Mauterre said, continuing along the upper path. "I'll be right back."

Glad she'd given Mauterre a chance to stall, Rochelle undressed quickly, shooing a pair of lizards before stepping into the solar-heated spray. She intended to hurry so Mauterre could have some privacy, but wound up closing her eyes, lost in the flow, picturing Mika blushing and stammering as if he happened upon her again like that sunny morning so many years before. She drifted with the image for a moment before realizing somebody had entered the room. Already barefoot, Mauterre was slipping out of her t-shirt and walking shorts.

"This is the bio-degradable *organic* stuff?" she asked, sniffing one of the bottles on a stone ledge. "It smells nice." She turned on a spigot and rinsed herself, adding the shampoo to her hair.

Rochelle glanced over discreetly, amazed by how this bright-eyed eighth-grader—whom she knew had only recently become a young woman—could still look so much like a mere child. Rochelle vividly remembered the tumult of being thirteen, the mad rush toward adulthood, that naïve eagerness to sacrifice the innocence and simple grace of this fleeting moment in life, not realizing it can never be captured again. Mauterre tried too hard to be responsible all the time, but that was Rochelle's job now, a choice she'd made and would always honor. Unfortunately, she'd neglected to remind her young charge to cherish the freedom of childhood while she could, and to carry that sense of wonder and adventure into every stage of her life . . . good advice for a burgeoning adolescent girl, and for the still-kinda-young guardian who sometimes found herself peeking in at night to watch her sleep.

Rochelle dried quickly and pulled on clean clothes while Mauterre rinsed and brushed her long hair. "No need to hurry," she said, stepping into blinding glare just as the group of six older men led by Mika and Dabu arrived. Poco brought up the rear, his four fat tires chewing their way up the rocky trail like an army tank oblivious to minor obstacles such as gravity and those other pesky laws of physics. Dabu stowed the tanks while Mika hit the shower. The divers rinsed their gear in a large barrel before heading in for a good de-salinating body-scrub. Dabu glanced about warily, then signaled Poco he was leaving, a quick wave to Rochelle as he tried to retreat.

Poco intercepted him with a lightning-fast grab.

"Not so fast, Taoke boy," he teased, giving him the wait sign. When Mika came out in shorts and tank top, pulling a comb through his wet hair, Poco pointed at him and Rochelle, then announced, "Me and Dabu, we come make one big surprise for you two, but he not know I think up surprise for him and Mauterre already."

Mika rubbed his face sheepishly, then shot a glare of mock accusation toward Dabu. "What you *hapa* guys cooking up now?"

Poco pulled Dabu close and gave him a noogie, then released him and continued to sign while speaking. "Diver group, they plan taking me and *nā keiki* to hotel in Punalu'u, treat us for one fancy lunch, come watch these shy teenagers play on d'beach, no place for 'em to hide."

Dabu looked positively mortified, even more so when Mauterre strolled out to pronounce, "Cool."

"And what this other surprise?" Mika asked, trying to smirk despite looking very curious.

"Me and Dabu, we make picnic for you two, only chance you have time for saying hi without *nā keiki* and one big bad-ass wheelchair-*kāne* underfoot all day long."

The men started coming out, their wetsuits replaced by shorts and garish hibiscus-print Hawaiian shirts. "We're in on it," said the shaggiest, his gray beard and frizzy Jerry Garcia 'do shiny in the bright sunlight. "Consider it a thank-you to the greatest dive master anywhere—and we've been down with the best all around the world." His companions echoed the sentiment, all shaking Mika's hand before heading down the trail.

"Bye, you guys," Mauterre said to Mika and Rochelle as Poco ushered the young teens down the trail, Dabu glancing back with a *Help me!* look so obvious that hands or mouth could never do it justice with mere words.

Rochelle and Mika tried to follow, but Poco turned and blocked the path. "Picnic thataway," he said. "Is up to you to find out where." He put it in low gear and buzzed down the trail, leaving them standing there looking at each other.

"Well," said Mika.

"I *am* hungry," said Rochelle.

"Me, too."

So they strolled farther up into the valley, Mika taking her hand so casually she didn't even realize it at first. Eventually, they felt the mist and heard the quiet roar of the waterfall, turning the bend to find their surprise waiting in the clearing: a large picnic blanket spread in the grass, two coolers along the side, a bottle of wine chilling between rocks in the sandy shallows, and a huge inflatable duck floating in the pool.

And butterflies!

Poco and Dabu had placed several dishes of sugar water around the clearing, attracting a profusion of gold and azure butterflies, delicate pixies fluttering about and perching to drink, their wings undulating in the gentle breeze.

And dragonflies, too, iridescent choppers hovering here and there before zipping off into the sky.

And hummingbirds! She'd never seen them here before, a trio shimmering in shades of ruby and emerald, flitting from one blossom to another amid the hanging tendrils of pink *lobelia*.

"Poco and Dabu, they go all *pupule* on us," Mika breathed affectionately. "I saw these coolers in d'van, big plan all along."

"Poco and Dabu," she repeated, resisting the urge to get all weepy eyes over such a simple, heartfelt gesture.

They opened the ice-packed coolers and found plastic tubs stuffed with sandwiches and snacks, a jug of the green nectar that had wowed Rochelle during her fist visit to Coulée Makai, and a *lei* for each of them, exquisite pink blooms with crimson stars at their centers. They spread the food around, laughing at themselves for reveling in such luxury, feeding each other morsels and talking about whatever fluttered through their minds.

"I think it's so cute," Rochelle said, "how Dabu is shy around Mauterre."

"I think so, too—at first," Mika admitted. "But Poco, he explain that last night, say Dabu get all red-face 'bout being deaf. Kids at his school know him already, all got something makes them different. But Dabu not like talk with his voice around strangers, think he sound like some big retard, 'specially after he go field trip to Panaewa Rainforest Zoo where Hilo kids make all *da kine* fun of him."

Rochelle hung her head, saddened by having misunderstood her young friend. "I should've taught Mauterre basic sign language, made it easier for them to know each other—but I've just been too busy to think. God, Dabu is one of the most impressive young men I've ever known; to think he's embarrassed learning to overcome challenges most of us never have to face both hurts and makes me furious."

"Yah, that Dabu, he could run whole dive operation while I take nap, only he not legal yet, is all."

"Mauterre would find so many things to like about him, but now with us leaving tomorrow there's no time left."

"You got another chance: Thanksgiving break. Come back and celebrate. Poco turn twenty that week, and pass six months to be owner of Coulée Makai all legal-like. We party till Pele come say be quiet 'cause d'volcano can't hear itself roar."

"Excellent idea. I just wish we could get together again sooner."

Mika shrugged. "Mauterre, she got school, Aunt Dix to visit, very important. Me, I got Poco, need my help every day, too private for letting strangers come do things best between friends. Dabu, he got school, too, and he not big enough to lift big *kāne* by himself anyway, so I gotta stay here, look out for Poco."

"Thanksgiving then—and we'll stay nearby in Punalu'u since the Hilo house will probably be sold by then."

"We'll see 'bout that. Mauterre, she like it here in d'valley last night, have good time."

"Yeah, it's been a good trip. I just wish I'd found a way to settle the CMDC mess before I head home."

"Too many lawyers, lots of stipulations and clauses—just give it time. Maybe we celebrate that, too, when you come back."

"Here's to next time," she said, lifting her wine mug for a toast, Mika smiling and echoing the sentiment.

They ate more of the snacks, then packed the coolers and leaned back against them, both gorged. Butterflies and *amakihi* birds flitted around the clearing, late-afternoon sun cutting long slashes through the trees, a rainbow sparkling in the waterfall mist.

"This is the most beautiful I've ever seen this place—except for once," she mused slyly.

Mika closed his eyes, soaking up the rays. "Oh yah? When?"

"That time I stumbled upon this handsome yellow-haired boy standing completely nude right there in that pool."

Mika glanced over, suppressing a mischievous grin. She did manage to get a hint of blush from him. "All I think of is coming back to find some *haole* girl splashing 'round all naked like she own d'place."

"You liked it," she teased, poking him in the ribs.

"I think so—hard to remember. Me, I got so busy freaking out, I forgot to look close—stay 'wake many nights after that, trying to get that picture back in my head."

"You *did* get it back, didn't you?"

He closed his eyes again, and just grinned.

"Ahhh, we were just kids then," she said, laying her head back.

"Not so, Rochelle. Very young, yes, but old enough to know it turn out okay 'cause we're good friends, make us even better, by and by."

"You know, we *are* adults now—we've grown up."

He looked over with mock nonchalance, surveying her from head to toe. "Yes, I notice," he said, glancing back toward the falls.

The spray looked so inviting, reflections of sunlit trees undulating across the pool's surface, a giant duck teasing them with its goofy gaze. Rochelle wanted to play, to laugh and splash and feel the water on her skin, to admire Mika unabashedly in his most natural form, but it would be too risky, too awkward if he got the wrong idea and tried to cross that important line between friendship and becoming lovers . . .

"You know, Rochelle," Mika said, turning to face her. "All these years, I never write you more than two letters 'less you write back."

She had noticed, all right, even testing it a few times, only to wind up feeling bad for making him wait so long, then writing him even longer letters in return. He'd always taken his cues from her, pushing only when she truly wanted to understand something important. "As many as you felt like sending would've been cool, but I did appreciate you understanding about my busy schedule." She looked toward the waterfall again.

"You know," he said, "if you wanna play in d'water, I like to play, too, 'specially with you; but if you worry too much how I behave, then I rather just sit here with you. Worry, it gets so big, it fills us up, no room left for fun."

He had read her mind again, and he was right. She did want to frolic without a care in the world, but she couldn't really be herself unless she had faith in him. She wondered, what is faith if not untested trust?

She lifted the *lei* from his neck and set it aside. He repeated the gesture, taking hers.

She stood.

He stood.

She said, "You know I don't want this to get out of hand."

"Worry-wart."

She kicked off her shoes and fingered her top. He kicked off his sandals and removed his shirt.

She hesitated.

He rolled his eyes. "Tell you what, silly girl—I go swim alone; you hide by bush over there and spy on me."

In one swift motion, he tossed his shorts and boxers onto the blanket and splashed into the pool, his tan-framed *haole*-white booty shining in the bright glare. He reached down and splashed water on himself.

She hooked her fingers in the waistband of her own—

And he turned around and waved, then fell backwards, submerging himself in the deep end.

And she gasped.

The dancing butterflies now fluttered in her belly, a warm tingle spreading up through her body.

It was now or never . . .

Off came the shorts, then her top, a cool breeze stirring the soft curls between her thighs.

A quick run—and *splash!*

Very self-conscious at first, chagrined every time Mika caught her openly admiring his handsome form, she finally managed to relax and not feel so modest after a while, sort of *natural* like the *amakihi* birds flying sorties in the mist and perching along ledges to ruffle their feathers with cool, crystal water. Mika tried several times to ride the big duck, finally staying up for several minutes before it flipped and dumped him unceremoniously into the drink. Rochelle laughed a bit too much, earning a challenge to perform better. She never did, but she wanted the record to show that she *would* have—an assertion subject to considerable disagreement—had her adversary not "cheated" by slithering up from beneath the surface to tickle her foot.

Eventually they found themselves standing in the shallows, swiping water from their skin, ready to take a break.

He caught her watching several droplets cling for a moment before they fell from his—

"You get my back?" he asked, turning around.

She wrung out his hair and gently wiped her hands across his shoulders, then down over his shoulder blades, following the small of his back. After hesitating just for an instant, she kept going, lightly tracing the contours of his buttocks, detecting only the slightest quiver, a catching of his breath . . . and she smoothed her way down his legs to the ankle-deep water. Standing again, she lightly pinched his butt-cheek.

"Now I wait for *two* letters in d'mail, Rochelle, before I send you *one*."

"You have that backwards—" she started. "Oh!" So she pinched him again.

He turned and smiled, then reached up and carefully wiped the water from her arms, moving his hands down her chest, following the curves of her breasts with only the slightest brush across her firm nipples, and continued down her belly, now below her navel, his touch a feather trailing goosebump tingles. She gasped and flinched, so he flattened his hands and kept them still, a moment for growing easy with his presence, the current flowing uninterrupted. He spread his hands apart and carefully circled her pubis, chasing droplets down her legs.

He moved around her slowly, a stroke here, a brush there, a hint of polish for the cherished statue of Venus. Behind her now, he began at her neck and repeated his liquid massage down her back . . . except he brought his hands together at her buttocks, caressing her cheeks a few seconds, just long enough to make her gasp again, his own shallow breaths betraying a sense of intimacy she found more reassuring than worrisome.

She wanted him to feel the way she did, or she might risk suddenly finding herself standing naked in the cold wind, feeling very alone.

"Come, we dry in the sun," he whispered, taking her hand, "—still be careful how we show our friendship."

He led her to the blanket, pulling it several feet toward the water to catch a slash of rays, then placed the *lei* around her neck again, watching her with those sparkling sapphire eyes as she placed the other around his. The fragrance of stunning pink blooms with crimson stars at their centers swirled around them before mingling with the cleansing mist.

"I not hurry to put on clothes, Rochelle," he said, "—long as you wanna play." He was watching her eyes, which made her feel less naked.

"Yes," she said, utterly failing to articulate anything meaningful. Needing to catch her breath, she sat on the blanket.

Mika followed, rolling her clothes into a pillow so she could lie back. He rolled a pillow for himself, then lay beside her, holding her hand . . .

And closed his eyes.

She watched him for a moment, her gaze ranging down his exquisite body, suddenly realizing there could never be anything more beautiful, more natural than this San Diego boy who'd grown to manhood in concert with the living world that even now embraced him and his Chicago-bred visitor as equals.

She closed her eyes.

"This is best kinda fun, Rochelle. You are one special *wahine*."

"I can't imagine doing this with anyone besides you," she said, the sun's warmth kissing her skin, water droplets tickling where they trickled in retreat, the breeze breathing through her long tresses and soft curls. "I was so self-conscious at first—I mean, what if Dabu and Mauterre had come walking up the trail and seen us skinny-dipping like that?"

"Me, I think they get surprised at first, then happy they find out grown-ups don't all d'time forget how to feel good d'easy ways. I go swim Oneloa Little Beach couple times with dive group, 'nude beach' they call it, everybody hanging out, by and by, no clothes on. Whole families come there, little *nā keiki* and big-eye teens, too; and I notice how the young ones, they forget about cares right away, run off laughing and having fun while d'grown-ups, they look around first, have to think about it, finally give up d'worries, wind up having just as much fun. They hafta remember sex not the only way to leave d'clothes off around friends."

"You just go there 'cause you like watching all the beautiful young women, I'll bet," Rochelle teased, her accusation sounding more serious than she intended.

He rolled his eyes, then studied her face for a moment. "I tell you d'truth, Rochelle: I look at *every* pretty *wahine*, but not for so long."

"Why's that?"

"I all d'time look somewhere else, 'cause she's not d'one." He watched her, his face so earnest.

And the tension returned, hovering between them like a hummingbird.

He sighed, shoulders hinting at a shrug, a tinge of embarrassment so palpable she could taste it . . . yet he didn't look away. "But you know that already, Rochelle. You know that long time, by and by."

She took a deep breath. "I'm worried that . . . this might change things."

"Then we put clothes back on, eat more Poco food, chase butter-flies—even if they not let us catch 'em. You know I never lie to you, Rochelle, so I promise you one thing: no risk in whatever you decide, 'cause nothing ever change how I feel about you, not since I twelve years old. Only thing changing now is how many ways I show you. You know I pay attention to you, only show it d'ways good for both of us."

"I just wish I had your—I don't know—confidence, I guess."

"You think I not get chicken skin?" He smiled. "You know how many times I re-write those letters when I was thirteen, fourteen . . . nineteen?—get all *pupule* 'bout what you think? Same way I get chicken skin over diving so deep in d'lagoon, still haven't seen d'lava tube down there. I know I see it someday, by and by, but only when I'm ready."

"It doesn't bug you not knowing what it's like down there?"

He smiled again. "But I do think I know, so I wait, make sure I not get hurt. I went up on Poco's cliff last week and thought about jumping in, see if d'sea, she bring me back, prove I belong here; but then I get chicken skin thinking nobody knows what happen to me if she let me drown, Mikalu just disappear one day like he run away. Instead, I walk around d'valley, finally decide I do belong, wonder why I get doubts when I stand up there looking at d'waves."

"Because that's when it's do or die time—literally, in this case."

"Yah, same way with you, by and by. You know things already, too, like that moment you wake at night, before you remember so many responsibil-ities in Chicago, and me so far away taking care of one big wheelchair-brah. So what if you're not ready yet; it's okay, I promise. You decide when it's do or die, don't dive down to d'tube or go up on d'cliff to jump 'less you're sure. Don't worry 'bout me; I wait my whole life for you."

And she kissed him, on purpose, no hesitation.

And he kissed her back, cradling her in his arms, but he wouldn't press himself against her, waiting for her to come to him, asking her to show him where they might go together.

She traced a line down his chest, and she felt the liquid cascade of his hand moving down hers, the base surge of fingertips igniting untested passions, newly effluent moisture guiding their explorations, searing ripples radiating like *nuée ardente* as she helped him learn to probe the caldera depths, both lingering in anticipation of joining together at the peak.

She stroked his body, making him shudder and gasp as she caressed his growing fire, and he held her tighter, pressing against her thigh, refusing still to take her, like he might, in one swift motion.

No man had ever touched her this way. Rochelle's boyfriends had always led, guiding her up their own shortcut trails to the summit. Only Mika ever seemed to walk hand-in-hand beside her, both exploring together, the journey most exquisite, a destination unimportant.

Rochelle had always given herself over to her lovers, only now discovering she might become part of something bigger, one of the butterflies dancing around Mika's hair, waterfall mist tickling their skin, *amakihi* birds heralding the day, insistent breeze humming as it caressed swaying trees, Mika's soft blanket anchored by faith to the slopes of a living mountain floating upon a sea of molten fire.

And she trembled as he held her, Mika still waiting, *showing* her in ways she never dreamed possible even as she stood at the precipice facing a plunge she could never take alone.

And she remembered what she always knew in those moments of waking at night, that instant of realizing she'd dreamed of the blond-haired San Diego boy again, the blissful confidence in knowing he's the one who loves her even when she can't admit she loves him, too.

And the waterfall roared as she guided him closer . . .

And the *nēnē* goose honked insistently from a distance.

But Mikalu hesitated, that goose honking incessantly.

She felt him trembling, so she squeezed him hard, both afraid of what that annoying bird might mean.

And the urgency of a car horn just kept echoing up through the valley.

"Oh no," Mika whispered. "Poco might be hurt."

"Mauterre," she whispered back, responsibilities cascading over her very soul, "—she's never swum in the ocean."

And they stumbled about, pulling on clothing, afraid but ready to face the truth together.

He took her by the hand, both hurrying down the trail, and she knew he would never let her fall.

A van had parked in the open slot, somebody beside it, reaching in to honk the horn. Several cars were pulling in, people spilling out.

It was Ginny, waving when she sighted them.

Rochelle and Mika rushed down the main trail toward the footbridge, hand-in-hand, exhausted and out of breath as they crossed and climbed toward the open slot.

People had gathered around the vehicles, clutching portfolios and bottles of champagne, the group Rochelle had pitched for a new development deal.

"Everybody's ready to sign!" Ginny announced, hugging Rochelle. "Hmmm . . ." she added quietly, stepping back with a sly grin for her and Mika. "Sorry about the commotion. Poco said you were picnicking somewhere in the valley, and we need Rochelle's signature before she goes home in the morning."

She hurried to the van to retrieve a satchel of papers while the beefy guy unloaded a cooler and stacks of lawn chairs from the back of a pickup.

The blond woman came up and smirked at Rochelle. "You gave a helluva pitch the other day, hon, but for now when you get the chance, you might wanna turn your shorts around—you got 'em on backwards." She wagged her eyebrows at Mika, reaching up to pick several leaves from the back of Rochelle's hair.

Nipiton and Okamata, both dressed in jogging suits, each took one of Rochelle's hands and grinned. "They say your father," Okamata explained, "always held big party for signing an important deal. Is it okay with you and Mr. Mikalu that we come celebrate?"

Nipiton chimed in, "Not that we have much chance of making everybody leave too soon."

Everybody turned to watch the venture capitalists, who looked like a couple of MTV spring-breakers in shorts and Hawaiian shirts, helping beefy guy carry the coolers and chairs down toward the footbridge, another investor following with tiki lamps on eight-foot stakes. Mrs. Taoke waved before hurrying up toward her house, good news to share with family.

"You're very welcome," Mika said, Rochelle nodding, still trying to catch her breath.

The crowd hurried to their cars to unload no-telling-what.

Ginny came over patting her satchel. "I'm sorry we interrupted your picnic, but at least you can go home knowing you have a deal."

And the valley buzzed with life, Rochelle and Mikalu standing together as the world swirled around them.

She looked into his sparkling sapphire eyes, and he smiled, reaching up to touch her cheek.

"Yes, Rochelle," he whispered, "you go home tomorrow, and see how much you know."

Ka puka ana o kā lā a ka heʻe

Octopus sunrise

Thanksgiving break

Hello, D-A-B-U, Mauterre greeted, arriving in Hilo this time armed with a rudimentary but practiced knowledge of American Sign Language. Mikalu hugged Rochelle, then Mauterre, then Rochelle again. On a roll, he went ahead and surprised Dabu with a hug and a noogie, pretending to glance around for anybody else to grab. Rochelle laughed, glad the skycap hadn't passed within reach. Dabu barely managed to sign-return Mauterre's greeting before Rochelle buried him in a motherly embrace, reluctant to let him come up for air.

After claiming the baggage and verifying arrangements for delivering a freight shipment, the foursome piled into Mikalu's SUV and headed for Hilo Medical. "They're refilling Poco's pain-kill pump," Mika explained, "—good chance for getting him out d'house a while."

Entering the hospital waiting area, Rochelle recalled the desperate helplessness that gripped her the night she sat right over there with Mikalu, fearing Poco wouldn't survive his plunge from the cliff. The antiseptic odor filled her lungs, leaving her queasy, heart pounding in rising panic.

"You need some air," Mika said, watching her carefully. He stood and asked the teens to wait for Poco, taking Rochelle by the hand. Dabu moved to the farthest chair, trying to look anywhere but toward Mauterre.

"Don't worry, she won't hurt him—much," Rochelle said as Mika walked her outside. They found some benches surrounded by myriad yellow flowers in a quiet area, Rochelle thankful no ambulances burst onto the scene wailing urgent desperation for the injured and ill.

"The hearing," Mika said after a minute, "it not go well?"

"The doctor withdrew his evaluation when Miss Dixon had another attack the night before. It's been adjourned till next week while he does another, but the attorney assured us it's just a formality, that we'll be able to withdraw life-support as soon as the order's signed."

"And Mauterre?"

"She seems to be handling it better than I am. Right after the *big* attack last week, she touched her aunt's cheek, then told me she was gone. We hadn't even seen the medical report yet; she just knew. She only cried for a minute; then she wanted to go, looking back one last time as we left. It seems important for her to believe the person lying there suffering all that indignity is no longer Auntie Dix. I guess it's important for me, too. Otherwise, I don't know how I could consider just letting somebody die."

"It is helping her complete one very good life; and Mauterre, she is ready, by and by, because she knows honoring d'body is part of honoring d'memory."

"She's already talking about funeral plans. She mentioned the pearl-and-jade brooch Miss Dixon wore the first time I met her. It was a favorite gift from Mauterre's parents just months before they died, so she wants her to be wearing it during the services. It's remarkable how little things can come to symbolize so much at times like this."

"Mauterre, she think of this now because she not busy being afraid. You do that for her. She's very lucky having you, Rochelle," he said, reaching out as he stood. "You feel better already? Go check on Poco?"

"Yeah," she said, taking his hand as they headed in. "At least I think I'm ready. I'm worried I'll get upset when I see how he looks."

"Just watch his eyes," Mika said, holding the door. "You always find Poco there."

The nurse was wheeling him out. Rochelle steeled herself, but still felt that stomach-churning weightlessness as if falling helplessly, so she gripped Mika's arm even as she tried to smile.

Poco must have lost at least a hundred pounds. He wasn't skinny yet, but the treatments had robbed him of his imposing bulk, and had stolen his trademark thick black hair, leaving him bald, without eyebrows or even lashes. Mauterre stepped forward first, a moment for Rochelle to calm herself.

"Hi, Li'l Haole," he greeted, lifting one hand to wave, his shoulders un-nat-urally rigid.

"Hi there, island brah," she returned, smiling broadly before leaning over to take his hand and kiss his cheek. He kept his head back against the rest, and Rochelle realized seeing him not be able to reach out to a child was harder to accept than any of the ravages caused by radiation or chemotherapy.

"Come, Haole-girl—you not break me, by and by," he teased Rochelle.

Desperately trying to stem her tears, she took his hands gingerly, then leaned close and kissed his cheek, lingering for a moment while he kissed hers.

She wanted to turn away lest he see her cry, but she couldn't. She didn't dare make him feel bad about his appearance, and she desperately needed to look into his eyes as Mika had urged.

And she did find him there.

She found that mischievous sparkle, the man who'd beaten a coma, the brother who'd gazed back at her from the web-snaring traction of a hospital bed and telegraphed a silent *I still here, Haole-girl. I still here.*

And single tears crept undeterred down each of her cheeks.

"Good," said Poco quietly, "we got that outta d'way, by and by, so let's go home." He winked and offered her a goofy smirk.

And made her smile.

She stroked his bald pate and stood up. "You wouldn't have it any other way."

"Course not, Haole-girl. Count on d'truth from you—all d'time. Hey, you got plenty hair; you come make me one big loan?"

"No, brah," Rochelle mimicked, "we all busy getting used to you that way already." He just grinned.

They wheeled him out to the SUV; then Mika helped scoot him into the passenger seat, belting him in while Dabu collapsed the chair and stowed it in the cargo area.

"Haole-girl ride up front with us," Poco pronounced, "—make *nā keiki* ride together in back, no place for Dabu to hide."

"Now don't be picking on Dabu," Rochelle tut-tutted as everybody piled in.

"I not pick on him. He one good friend, come early today while Mikalu sleep, read me *National Geographic* out loud, one big treat 'cause I been asking him practice on me—best present ever. Now Mikalu, he go all day, pretend he not know it's my birthday."

Rochelle slapped her forehead. "I plum forgot, too. Oh well, it's not over yet; we'll find a way to celebrate."

"Haole-girl and Li'l Haole come see me—present enough."

She squeezed his hand. "Damn straight."

Mika pulled onto the highway.

"How they doin'?" Poco asked quietly.

Mika casually checked the mirror, whispering, "They're signing, and he's teaching her some new ones."

"Good," Poco said. "Sometimes all they need is chance, no *big* people getting in d'way. Now, Haole-girl, tell me all 'bout you thinkin' have *two* jobs."

"A couple I know from MIT want me to join their start-up in Boston developing *haptics* technology, cutting-edge computer-interface peripherals. Where mouses move in two dimensions, haptics devices operate in three, and they provide tactile feedback, too, incorporating *feel* as well as position. For example, an engineering stylist could design a car by moving this device to create a digital simulacrum on a high-res screen. It's only an image, but he can feel it with his hand, and it offers resistance when he pushes against it. He can shape the object from outside, or click off, push his hand through the shell, then click on again and press outward from the inside."

"But how can you feel TV picture?" Poco asked.

"You know how movies only flash a couple dozen images per second? That's enough for the brain to perceive continuous movement. Well, it takes only about one-thousand force-feedback pulses per second against the hand to be perceived as continuously touching an object."

Mika interjected, "Sounds like good for d'artists, too."

"Sure, create a digital sculpture with your hands, then have it robotically rendered."

"So you and Mauterre move to Boston?" Poco asked.

"No need, brah. Haptics data can be transmitted via the internet. I can *touch* something happening anywhere, so I offered to participate from a satellite office if I also get first-rights to all assisted-living applications."

"Helping people with disabilities?" Mika asked.

"Exactly! For example: imagine a substantially paralyzed young mother who can move only her hand, or maybe her foot. A haptics system with the right robotics could make it possible for her to use these tiny movements to actually lift and care for her baby, to hug her children and husband, and to *feel* them in ways never before possible. And she could better care for herself, and cook for her family, and create things beyond what can be typed on a keyboard—" She was getting caught up in her own enthusiasm. "Well, anyway—it's just so, well—"

"Yah," Mika and Poco said together.

Mika added, "It sounds like one big opportunity to make d'career you were born for."

Rochelle nodded, relieved and pleased they understood how important this was to her. "It's an incredible way to help people who most need it, and it has the potential to make Mauterre's company *the* cutting-edge player in the world market." A little louder for Mauterre's benefit, she added, "And even though Mauterre's proving an excellent apprentice, I keep having to limit her computer time and chase her off to practice just being thirteen."

Mika glanced in the mirror. "They're ignoring you."

Poco summed up, "Sounds like she got thirteen down already."

They rode quietly for a while, Rochelle still holding Poco's hand. Mika slowed as they passed the Pahala area while Rochelle and the teens craned their necks to scan the bustling site preparation and early construction. Pocomea Center was becoming a reality, and Rochelle knew that the love she'd seen in her brother's face when she first told him about it would live with her forever.

"Three more days," Poco said, "and Coulée Makai, it is ours, legally mine. Maybe we have small *luau* that day, invite Ginny and some friends, celebrate saving d'valley and d'lagoon."

"We will, Poco," Mika said, "—promise."

They turned into Taoke Valley, passing through stacks of crates—irrigation materials, erosion dampers, and so on—plus grading equipment already at work shaping the area that used to grow *kalo*, hints of a spectacular golf course with nesting ponds and roosting trees taking shape.

As they pulled into the open slot, Poco's face lit up. A banner stretching between two poles on the beach proclaimed *Happy Birthday, Pocomea!*

Scores of people came from every direction: Ginny and her son, the *keiki*-center lady and all her little charges, partners in the Center project, dozens of divers—some in from the mainland—friends from his and Mika's school days, Mrs. Taoke and her son Viku, the old Japanese guy who used to fill their tanks, and many of the local merchants who'd known Poco's family for generations. Several tables covered with food and coolers lined the walkway, beach and lawn chairs scattered about.

"Whatchoo do?" Poco said, his voice cracking with emotion. "Watchoo do?"

"Not forget one big birthday," Mika said, "—that's what. Twenty years old, it mean not a teenager now, hafta show everbody how Poco, he finally growed up."

The crowd had the door open now, Dabu unloading the wheelchair, Mauterre busy collecting hugs from Ginny and her boy. Poco situated in his seat, everybody pressed forward for a turn at touching his hand or patting his shoulder, the mob finally moving toward the valley, an entourage parading the man of honor down toward the beach he'd always loved. Poco smiled broadly, his eyes misty, and for the first time Rochelle had ever seen, he seemed lost for words.

Hours passed too fast to count as the sun tilted and slid like melting butter toward the volcano, a silly hat protecting Poco's pate, snacks passed around, cups filled and filled again, a thousand stories about the Wai-Nuikai boys—yes, the *haole* one, too—twenty years in the life of one man shaped by a place and touched by the people who shared it.

Tired and jet-lagged, Rochelle found herself flagging at one point, resting against a large rock jutting from the sand. Mauterre had wandered off with Viku for a look at his helicopter, Mikalu helping supervise youngsters splashing in the surf.

She looked around for Poco, realizing she'd not seen him for a while. She walked up into the rocky area and looked around, people still celebrating all around her, one of the mellowist parties she'd ever seen, that laid-back Hawaiian lifestyle.

She felt somebody take her hand, Dabu sensing concern. He led her up along the stream past a small pool, toward a copse of *'ōhi'a* trees. From there, she could see Poco's chair parked at the base of the ridge, Ginny on a rock beside him, her head against his shoulder, their arms linked. Her little boy was curled up in the big man's lap. All three had their eyes closed, the sun bathing them in a golden corona from across the mountain.

And she saw something she'd never seen before, a glistening streak down each of Poco's pudgy cheeks.

Feeling like an intruder, she looked down at Dabu to signal they should leave.

He nodded before she could recall the signs, taking her hand and leading her back toward the beach, and he finally felt confident enough again to speak to her aloud:

"Pogo, he got one big heart."

*   *   *

Dense blots of cloud climbed the pinnacle of Mauna Loa, jostled by gusts of wind, competing for the best views in anticipation of another day's imminent flaming demise. Tiki torches lined the Coulée Makai beach, guttering amid slashes of long shadow as the retreating shield of sun fired volleys of laser bursts across the eastern sky. The lagoon sparkled like glitter, its waters shimmering with a golden glow as it absorbed the last splash of sunlight, fattening its plankton and algae to feed the feathery fans of ravenous midnight coral polyps.

Two men carried a dismantled crate from the open slot, the delivery truck long gone. A half-dozen remaining divers piled gear on the sand, then joined Rochelle and Mauterre—both in new wetsuits—plus Ginny and her sleepy young son to watch Poco test his new amphibious wheelchair. Clad in flowery swim trunks after a brief evening nap, the big man beamed with new-toy pride as he tested its controls, practicing the maneuver of powering its seat outward to form a horizontal platform, then lowering himself to the ground. Dabu and Mika were lugging Rochelle's body-length ADPV platform down from its hiding place in the dive shop.

"What's that?" Poco demanded, his eyes wide.

"Assisted Diver Propulsion Vehicle," Mika answered. "That's what Dabu and I test all week while you sleep, by and by."

They set it on the sand, Poco watching while they strapped 3000-psi tanks to either side and inflated a series of buoyancy-compensator bladders that lined the padded shell. They flipped up handlebar-styled controllers and activated the battery packs, testing four shell-encased plastic propellers linked by flexible tie-rods from each corner.

"It's your birthday present from Rochelle," Mika said.

"You make this, Haole-girl?" he demanded, his face rapt as he realized the possibilities. "You give this for my birthday?"

"Yes," Rochelle said, thoroughly enjoying the moment, "I designed it, anyway—and trust me, it's very crude right now—but your actual present is getting back something you lost for a while." She swept her arm across the lagoon, and Poco followed her gaze, already losing himself in the water.

Mika was attaching an octopus of hoses, including a regulator attached to a collapsible wand placed where the viewport had been on Rochelle's kid-tested snorkel rafts.

"Wow!" Poco said, barely able to contain himself. "What this baby can do?"

"It's got four independent motors with thrusts of fifty-two pounds per, and a ninety-five-minute running time from sealed rechargeable batteries. Each swivels one-ninety degrees, operated by these joysticks with button controls for linking them, and there's full reverse. The best part is they're fully throttled variable-speed motors with the option of ten pre-sets. Oh, and look: it has headlights, too."

"We hold lagoon races," Poco gushed, "—paint sponsor logos on there."

"You not beat one fast HydroSpeeder," Mika cautioned, "but this do lot more for people with limitations."

"I looked at what's on the market," Rochelle explained, "and most forms of DPV are practical only for traveling, but they rely on the diver to maneuver his own body once he's arrived at the dive site. This is for fine-tune exploring, especially since you can adjust for neutral buoyancy and simply hover with the currents. You don't have to wear scuba gear, either. This one's an *Assisted* DPV, the prototype of what we're calling "The Poco-Diver," because the platform acts as your scuba apparatus. All you wear is a mask—with snorkel for when you surface. Once we strap you in, everything from your regulator and second-air to the tanks are already in place."

"We go now," Poco decided, an over-sized puppy itching to romp and play.

"You need practice, Poco," Mika warned him.

"We test in d'open water first, then go see d'reef. Get dark soon, catch d'predators coming out to hunt."

Rochelle explained, "Once you get the controls down pat, you can go out with only one or two buddies, but for now we're going to treat you like an aircraft carrier surrounded by tactical support divers, ready to help you maneuver."

"It's real easy," Mika said. "Dabu and I, we learn to do tricks after only one time."

Ginny hugged Poco, explaining, "We must leave in a few minutes; it's my night to babysit some of the children, but we'll watch until you get out there." Her son signed something Rochelle couldn't understand, Poco responding in kind as the boy climbed up and gave the big man a hug, earning a gentle pat on the back.

Dabu signed to Rochelle: *M-A-U snorkeling on surface; I will stay with her, watch and be ready for emergency.*

Rochelle flashed the diver's *okay*, winking at Mauterre, who looked very pleased by the gesture.

"Okay," Rochelle said to Poco. "Drive yourself in, a couple feet deep at least."

"You sure d'chair okay?" he asked. "Who I kidding; Haole-girl design this thing. I drive it across d'ocean floor, go see San Diego." He blazed his way into the surf, stopping when the riffling water covered the wheel tops, submerging himself waist-deep. "Wait," he said. "We bring couple *'ōpae* for d'cephalopod?"

Mika gestured to Dabu, then tossed him a small mesh bag. Dabu took off up the small stream, disappearing into the brush around the gear-rinsing pond.

Everybody's equipment strapped on, underwater lights and glow-sticks dangling from their lanyards, the divers helped Mika position the ADPV next to Poco's chair, Rochelle holding a two-piece wetsuit. As if he'd practiced the maneuver, Poco used his hand controls to collapse the seat, extended himself horizontally, then slowly lowered it until only his face and belly broke the surface. Dabu returned with several squirming shrimp-like critters in the sack, securing it to Mika's lanyard. Then the two of them gently wrestled the wetsuit onto Poco and helped him don his mask and snorkel. Poco lowered the platform the rest of the way, rolling himself face-down without assistance while they slid the ADPV underneath him. A quick spritz on the buoyancy valve brought it up, lifting him above the water.

"Test the regulator for position," Rochelle instructed. Confirming Poco could breath comfortably from the compressed-air tanks, she and Dabu strapped him in, then floated him out to about a dozen feet of depth, the sandy bottom rippling in constantly shifting patterns of sunlight.

Poco practiced with the controls for about ten minutes, "swimming" in all directions, reversing and pausing, quickly developing a feather touch.

"Whenever you're ready," Rochelle said, "test the buoyancy. I want to see you take it down, go neutral, then bring it up slowly." She needed to be sure he wouldn't sink too fast or, worse, pop up like a cork from fifty or sixty feet, risking the bends from rapid decompression.

First he turned toward the shore, tilted his head up, and waved to Ginny and her son.

"Bye, Poco!" Ginny called back.

Her son waved, too, and for the first time Rochelle ever heard, shouted out loud. "Bah-bah!"

Poco mastered buoyancy quickly, then refined his finesse with the propulsion. The big-lipped grouper fish came to watch, at one point enjoying a sort of dance with Poco as they circled each other, pausing to mouth silent how-doo's.

Ridge-cast shadows began mottling the surface, and Rochelle knew it was time to head out, better to let him practice at depth before it grew so dark they had to rely on lights.

The friendly grouper fish escorted them, pausing to look back several times, flipping his fin in a way Rochelle would swear must be a gesture meant to wave them along.

And they arrived at paradise, exquisite coral gardens fringing the lagoon shallows, swirls of jacks and snappers and silversides whirling around Poco's entourage in an iridescent haze. The fading sunlight rippled across a massive submerged brain while purple oriental fans swayed in the gentle liquid surge. Upside-down hula skirts concealed skittish trumpeters watching with wary eyes as the itinerant pod of air-breathers drifted by.

Rochelle tried to watch Poco, but he proved so adept at controlling his movements, so in tune with his surroundings and so respectful of the rule never to disturb or damage this calcified kingdom, that she found her gaze simply following his, seeing this exquisite beauty through new eyes. Poco noticed rocks suddenly waking to swim off into the deep, shrimps of crystalline glass materializing as the light tickled them just so, vividly hued tendrils shaking their fists at this benign challenge to the sovereignty of their submarine fiefs, art-deco shells trundling at snail's pace while impostors simply shimmied by on spindly crabs' legs . . .

Something about having been there makes it more real.

She looked up at the silhouettes of Dabu and Mauterre watching from above, both aglow from weary sunshine kissing the surface good-night, their ease in the water, a subtle flip of the fin, the slightest gestures with their hands, floating more carefree than Rochelle ever dreamed possible that first time Mikalu introduced her to the reefs of Coulée Makai. Sometimes Mauterre showed a remarkable capacity for riding the currents of tragedy, but too often those riptides of fear and insecurity nearly pulled the young teen under. More than once Rochelle had found herself awake late at night, afraid she could never live up to the confidence and trust that kept Mauterre's head above water. Soon Miss Dixon would be gone, and Rochelle's legal status as guardian would grow even more tenuous, the only choice a full adoption so the leviathan system could never rise up from the depths to swallow Mauterre whole. Just weeks out of college, still too young for a such a commitment, unmarried and with no practical child-care experience . . . the caseworker hadn't proven very encouraging that one time Rochelle dared broach the subject. Maybe she'd simply underestimated Rochelle's tenacity, her determination, her loyalty to one who had become family.

Poco turned on his headlights, those schools of shiny fish disappearing into nooks and crannies as nocturnal marauders emerged from hiding. He spotted a large spindly-legged crab and tracked him for a minute, then turned his attention to Mika, who was wagging his finger under a ledge to charm the fearsome mottled eel undulating its lethal cobra challenge.

All at once Poco turned toward Rochelle, lifting his head to look right into her eyes, and through the lenses of two masks and the diffusion of a yard of water she recognized the boy who'd called to her that dark night so many years ago.

Only this time, he was her brother.

She knew this, had even felt it on many occasions, but it never seemed more real than at this moment.

Thank you, he mouthed, maybe not understanding he'd done more for her than she could ever do for him.

When she gave him the diver's *okay* sign, he took his mouth off the regulator again and smiled before resuming his breaths, then moved closer and turned to float beside her, reaching with his fingers to entwine hers for a moment, squeezing with all the gentle strength and power one big Hawaiian man could muster. Reluctantly, he let go to grab the joystick again, giving her one last knowing look, thanking her for being the sister he always wanted.

Then he gestured something to Mika, an unfamiliar sign with wiggling fingers. Mika gave him the *okay*, so Poco led the group down along a lower shelf, dropping to a depth of nearly fifty feet, then threading up through a narrow crevice into an open area. He turned to face the coral, everybody gathering around him, and focused his attention on a dark crack, its slender opening not more than a few inches wide. He reached forward with one hand and tapped at the entrance to this tiny cave, then waited.

Azure patches of creeping darkness descended around them.

He tapped again.

Several flashlights came on, illuminating the area around the crack, none trained directly on it.

Mika moved closer, transferring the lanyard to a clip by Poco's left hand, then backing away.

He tapped again.

A tentacle uncurled from the dark recess, feeling around for a moment, followed by a second.

And a big wary eye looked out, glowing like a cat's.

Poco waited.

Several more tentacles appeared, one reaching up to touch the intruder's face mask.

Then all at once an octopus emerged, a small one maybe two feet from tip to tip, swimming directly to Poco and wrapping itself around his head and right hand. It probed about, touching and exploring, its eyes watching Poco's through the mask.

When it discovered the sack containing two ʻōpae shrimps, it set about trying to open it, the temptation of tasty treats too great to ignore. Poco helped a little, using one finger to loosen the drawstring. That was all his cephalopod friend needed. It reached in and snatched the smallest of the shrimps, pulling it underneath his body for a quick snack, then retrieved the other, holding it in one tentacle as it wrapped another around Poco's face and mouthed a silent *Thank you* before swimming away, disappearing amid a garden of tube sponges.

Almost fully dark now, the corals came alive with feathery polyps, crabs and eels out prowling openly under the flashlights' blinding glare.

Mika gave Poco the *air* signal, and the entourage reluctantly began working their way home, two searchlight beams from the surface following them, Dabu and Mauterre escorting from above.

The grouper made another appearance, joining them like one of the gang, swimming alongside Poco until they reached about ten feet of water. Then the giant fish backed away, one last look for his night's most honored guest, a final flip of the fin before he disappeared into the darkness.

Poco managed to maneuver himself into the new wheelchair with minimal assistance, then began jabbering boisterously, recounting every detail of what they'd seen, a man so happy Rochelle wanted to cry.

"So," she said to Poco when he stopped talking long enough to catch his breath, "you and that octopus must go way back, huh?"

"Oh no," he said, "she come be a new one."

Surprised, she asked, "Hasn't she been here for years?"

"No, never see her before. The octopus, its time is very short, one year maybe, sometimes two. Each time one dies, new one comes along."

"How'd you know to find her there?"

"Because that's d'best lair, place where good octopus belong. Each time, I like come make friends."

"Well, this one seemed to like you."

Poco smiled knowingly. "That's 'cause she d'smart one. She d'one knows how good this place is."

*   *   *

Rochelle lay awake in the pre-dawn hours, her body still on Chicago time, her mind racing with memories of that first night she spent in this very bed. The lantern's probing corona showed that Mikalu's room had changed very little over the years, the man who still called it home not so very different from that earnest boy who so long ago refused to let her be consumed by grief.

Nightmares had awakened her that night and many nights in the years after, but now what invaded her sleep was worry . . . worry over another young grief-stricken teen, the brave girl slumbering fitfully in the far room, the orphan who still sometimes called out for her mother in the night.

Rochelle closed her eyes and listened to muffled murmurs through the crude slat walls, hints of Poco's struggles against another bout of pain. The lifelong friend who often droused beside his bed had awakened instantly to help, but nothing he could do would ever again be enough. Mere sympathy for the fact of another's illness, she understood, must pale before the true commitment of living with it day after day.

"Rochelle?" whispered Mikalu from the hallway. "You wake in there?"

She slipped into her robe and opened the door. He was standing there in shorts and tank top, his fists clenched in frustration. "Is Poco okay?" she asked.

"I not sure," he said, concern quavering in his gentle voice, "but he not look so good. I say we go hospital, but he say no. You talk to him?"

She followed him and found Poco propped in bed, drenched in sweat, the lantern's light carving eerie shadows. His amphibious wheelchair sat positioned level with the mattress in anticipation of reluctant assent. With Mika hovering like an anxious parent, she sat beside him and placed her hand on his warm cheek.

"I hope he not wake you up, Haole-girl," Poco said weakly.

Ignoring that, she quietly admitted, "We're worried about you, Poco."

"I know," he said, his breathing raspy and shallow. "Mikalu, he worry all d'time, by and by—but I okay. It just d'pain, comes at night, gets better after while."

"Is it worse this time?" she asked, sympathetic but serious, dealing with facts first, emotions later.

"No," he assured her. "It's just hard for Mikalu 'cause he wanna make it stop."

Mika clenched his mouth and glanced away, and Rochelle could see the toll he'd paid for friendship and dedication, his brave façade starkly transparent in the dark hours before dawn. She knew a trip to the hospital would offer no relief, their only option being to sit with him while he rode it out one more time. She never should have let him scuba dive after partying all afternoon, that nap too brief to replenish his waning reserves.

"We're just trying to figure out what's best," she said.

"I know," he said quietly. "I not like to see you and Mika hurting 'cause of me, but having you both here, that makes it easier—don't ask me how."

"I'm afraid we pushed you too hard today."

"Not so, Haole-girl." His eyes sparkled in the lantern glow. "Was d'best day in months: you come see me, bring Li'l Haole, get d'whole 'ohana back together again, throw big *luau* for all d'friends—*and* give me back d'reefs." He smiled, barely hiding a wince.

Mika stopped fidgeting long enough to retrieve another hand towel, kneeling to dab the perspiration from Poco's face and arms.

"I like to think of it as giving *you* back *to* the reefs," Rochelle kidded. "Now, what else can we do?"

"How long we hafta wait, Mikalu?"

Mika checked his watch. "Next dose in forty-five minutes." He eyed the small pump attached to Poco's arm, then looked away.

Poco asked Rochelle, "Then how 'bout some fresh air? Sit outside awhile, come back in and sleep when d'medicine chase pain away?"

Rochelle hurriedly dressed while Mika helped Poco move to the wheelchair. They draped him in a sheet as protection against the breezes, and wheeled him outside into the luminescent night.

"Over by d'lagoon?" he asked.

They started down the main walkway, then veered onto the ascending path overlooking the water, parking him between two large rocks where they could sit on either side.

Nearly full now, the shaved disk of moon hung right over Punalu'u, the long Taoke ridge bathed in milky glow, Coulée Makai a shimmering panorama floating in open space. They followed Poco's gaze as he surveyed the familiar scene. To the right, the ribbon of meandering stream stitched a zigzag seam up the velvety carpet floor, a series of embroidering waterfalls rising toward the pleated outskirts of Kilauea before disappearing under a veil of highlands mist. The stream spilled onto the fringing horseshoe beach, glistening like a quilt of melting glass as it riffled across obsidian sands and emptied into the secluded cove. Breakers crashed through the narrow inlet a quarter-mile to their left. Shadows across the sheer faces of towering cliffs revealed a cortège of sad expressions watching from amid the rocks. The scene whispered with patrolling crabs tracing lines in the powdery lava sand, night marauders hurriedly scouring detritus to prepare the beach for another sunrise, a new day, a moment never again to be taken for granted.

"Rochelle?" Poco said, his sonorous voice drifting through her reverie. He'd never called her anything but Haole-girl.

"Yeah, brah?"

"You one good *kaikuahine*," he said quietly. "That mean sister to brother."

"Thanks, Poco. You're lucky to have me," she teased.

"Yah," he said. "Just like my brah here. Mikalu, you one good *kaikua'ana.*

"Hadda say *older* brah, huh?"

His shoulders shaking with a silent chuckle, Poco couldn't hide his impish grin. "You all d'time look out for me, big brudder—just like I try teach you be Hawaiian, all yellow-hair, not need my help after all."

Mika looked away, lost for words, finally musing, "Hard to call you *little* brah when you so much bigger than me."

"Size of d'heart, that's what matters, by and by. Like yours, Rochelle—what you gonna do 'bout Li'l Haole? Huh? You get stuck 'cause nobody else taking care of her?"

"No, and you know better than to even imply that. I'm gonna fight like hell to adopt her because I don't want anybody ever to take her away from me."

"That sounds like *my* sister, by and by. I just wanna hear you say it."

The night sky faded to blotches of purple stain in the east, a pink glow lighting the horizon's backdrop while tendrils of crimson and gold licked the surface of the water. A blue haze crept above the valley in anticipation of the sun's dazzling appearance.

"Li'l Dabu," Poco said, "—he one good friend, too, prove how *nā* Taoke and *nā* Wai-Nuikai all d'same peoples, Pele's *nā malihini*." He reached over and pressed the pump attached to his arm, closing his eyes for a minute. "I sure lucky Pele let me stay here," he said, his voice fading. "This is good . . . I like sit here with my *'ohana*."

Rochelle twined her fingers in his, Mika gripping his other wrist.

After a minute, Poco opened his eyes and looked across the beach again, the recognition in a hint of smile briefly crowding out the pain in his face. Climbing down from the distant rocks, unaware of anybody watching, a young teenage boy clad in ratty shorts and tank top paused to gaze up into the valley, patches of rolling fog fleeing the probing lances of dawning sunshine. He dropped to the sand, his bare feet leaving an ephemeral trail of prints as he strolled to the lapping water. He splashed along in the shallow surf, engrossed by the view, pausing to eye the fringing reefs. Taoke's youngest had come to greet a new day in the place he'd first learned to trust the big Wai-Nuikai boy from across the ridge.

A *nēnē* goose erupted from the rinsing pond, skipping across the lagoon until it rose high in the sky, circling the inlet several times before veering out over the sea and disappearing up the coast.

Watching it carefully, Poco asked, "So, Haole-girl, you put your grandfather's house on sale yet?—decide on staying in d'auntie's townhouse?"

"No, Poco," she said, rolling her eyes, "—not yet. But at the rate I'm going, I may have to."

Surprised, Mika asked, "Why so?"

"I may need the money. Everything else is either gone or tied up in Pocomea Center. Getting the adoption done could prove costly, plus I want to set up my own haptics-research office without obligating Mauterre's company, at least until I'm more confident it's a money-maker."

Poco chuckled. "You make it so, Haole-girl, then open one big design place in Pocomea Center someday. By then you and Mika both own Coulée Makai."

Mika's back stiffened, Rochelle's pulse suddenly racing.

"You not talk like that," Mika insisted.

"C'mon, you two," Poco said. "You know my time short, and I worry 'bout who gets this place next, need t'keep in d'family, leave it for d'ones Pele trust for protecting it."

Rochelle felt a lump rising in her throat, her eyes misty.

Mika tried to protest. "C'mon, Poco, you be round long time—"

But Poco kept talking: "Two more days, *kaikua'ana*, and I finally get d'say-so that you can stay. You keep taking good divers out; let Dabu work here, too, make sure he grow up one good *kāne*. Rochelle, you come visit, bring Mauterre, maybe decide stay someday, find out what Mika, he already knows." He refused to make eye contact with either of them, instead watching a flurry of *amakihi* birds swirling around the stream, some splashing in the riffles. An iridescent dragonfly hovered nearby to survey the scene before resuming his morning patrol.

"You not worry 'bout that, Poco," Mika said.

"Have to, brah. Ginny, she say my legal-will not good till two more days, or d'state try to get d'land, try hold one big auction."

"But Rochelle, she is next of kin already, even now," Mika insisted.

"Mine, no matter. Papaii, he still d'owner. Now is almost six months after he join *nā lapu*; but Rochelle, she is only his son's widow's second-husband's adult daughter, not adopted, never named in Papaii's will. Ginny, she says not much chance t'win that, cost lots of money, all politics 'bout *haole* who not even live here. But don't worry, in two days I fix everything. After you take me to d'lava tube to join my ancestors, rest take care of itself. I one smart octopus."

Mika suddenly stood, turning to face the cliffs behind them, rubbing his eyes. He glanced at Rochelle, and she knew he needed to say something, had struggled for the words that still would not come. He took a deep breath, then turned and touched Poco's cheek before sitting down again, looking across the lagoon. Not now, he must have decided. Another time . . .

Dabu still stood at water's edge, gazing toward the east, unaware he was being watched. A sound from behind betrayed Mauterre's presence, the sleepy girl finding a seat on a rock up near the house, entranced by the view.

"Today, Poco," Rochelle whispered, "—this morning. That's all that matters right now."

"Yah . . ." he said quietly.

They sat for a while, the splash of distant waterfall echoing between the ridges, butterflies dancing in the briny breeze, giant ferns rising to attention, awaiting inspection.

All at once, a laser-shot of fire appeared at the horizon, its blinding beam washing over Dabu and tickling whorls of mist rising from the water. A tiny lizard eased up onto a shard of lava to watch the dawn, a Hawaiian Happy-face Spider creeping along in the shadows at their feet.

Poco tensed a few times, his pain still resisting the soft quilt of medication, but in time he relaxed a bit, his breaths softening, Coulée Makai welcoming him to another day.

The sun eased higher against the sea, its light flowing like liquid, rising amid the valley's rocks and trees. Poco turned his head to the west and watched the mist dissolve into sky, his valley teeming with life, stairstep waterfalls hurling rainbows that soared like distant kites.

Rochelle imagined taking him on another tour of the place where he'd lived his entire life: the large copses of crimson-bloomed *'ōhi'a lehua* trees lording over supplicant *mau'u* grasses; blossom- and berry-laden vines of *ohelo* reaching out with an offering to Fire Goddess Pele; *pū hala* trees lifting their can-can skirts to pose on spindly legs, pineapple-like curlers in their hair; the sacred *maile* plant, its almond-shaped leaves hosting a mid-morning brunch for the pale yellow arachnid with a wide red-lipped grin; hanging pink tendrils of *lobelia* professing their love; *'akala* raspberries ready to squish between hungry teeth; the rare *palila* bird pausing to drink from a riffling pool; the Wai-Nuikai waterfall where countless generations bathed in the purest waters from a living mountain . . .

Poco turned his head to face the sun, settling back into his seat, and finally relaxed completely as the warm light found their little group, swaddling them in its reassuring embrace.

Rochelle looked back and saw Mauterre standing now, her eyes closed.

Down on the beach, Dabu lifted his eyes to the sky.

Poco took a long breath, releasing it slowly into the gentle breeze.

Water splashing his feet, Dabu covered his face with both hands. *Amakihi* birds lighted on the sand and watched as Taokes' youngest dropped to his knees and bowed his head, his slight body suddenly wracked with sobs.

Why would he cry?

Confused, Rochelle looked to Mika, but he was crying, too, tears streaking his cheeks as he placed the big man's hand back in his lap.

"Poco?" Rochelle whispered, but only the wind answered her . . . then the subtle moan of crashing waves, and the helpless chitter of *amakihi* birds, and the sad stare of an iridescent dragonfly returning to confirm the awful truth.

Mika reached up and closed his brother's eyes, gently stroking his bald head. "Bye, Poco . . ."

And Rochelle desperately squeezed her brother's hand, searching for any sign he'd not left her, not now, not this way.

"I never tell him 'bout d'lava tube," Mika wept, "—too late for burying him there, all covered up forever."

And the *nēnē* goose returned, circling the cove before heading up into the valley to spread the news, its mournful cries the grief of Poco's ancestors at the passing of Wai-Nuikai's last son.

HOʻOHANOHANO KA ʻOHANA, Ā MĒ KA NAʻAU IHO

HONOR THE FAMILY, HONOR THE HEART

Card-waving potted plants and a profusion of posturing flowers all held their collective breath as Rochelle and Mikalu stepped up to face the casket, Dabu and Mauterre on either side. Carefully closing its lid, the funeral director turned toward them and bowed his head for a moment. Then instead of moving to seal it, he looked up and quietly asked, "You will allow me some minutes for paying my respects to Pocomea?—for all of ʻOhana Wai-Nuikai?"

Mika bowed his assent, so Rochelle added, "We'll wait outside; please, take your time."

"Have you *tapa* cloth?" he asked.

Mika hesitated, glancing toward Rochelle. Sensing her wordless assurance, he signaled for Dabu to fetch it. Rochelle looked to the director again, and something familiar passed between them, the understanding they'd shared that day so long ago when he discovered their plan to honor Tapakiki in the ancient family tradition.

The director's assistant entered with a plain cardboard box as Dabu laid out the *tapa*. Mika led the group outside and rubbed his eyes, then gazed up at the small clots of wadded clouds drifting across bright, late-afternoon sky. Viku Taoke watched from against some rocks across the valley, up near the open slot. When Rochelle held one finger up in the air, he signaled *okay* and settled back to continue waiting.

"Dabu?" Rochelle spoke and signed, "will you walk with me?"

Surprised, he nodded enthusiastically, joining her as she promised Mika and Mauterre they'd return soon. Heading up the path to the dive shop, she invited him to sit with her on a stone ledge.

Looking directly at him, she both signed and carefully enunciated the words so he could read her lips. "Dabu, you know our plan probably will not work, and it is very dangerous."

He waited for her to continue, a mien of stubborn determination barely masking his dread of what she might say next.

"It is safer if you and Mauterre stay behind—"

He started to sign urgently, but she took his hands and placed them in his lap, then touched his mouth and looked right into his eyes. He glanced nervously down the trail before speaking aloud. "*Please* let me help."

"Only if you make two promises."

"Anything," he said, and she believed him.

"You grew up here, so you know how to climb lava rock and avoid the hot splashes. Mauterre is not used to this place. I will be too busy to watch her, so you must promise to help protect her from danger."

"You know I *always* do that, Ro-zhill. I not hafta make extra promise."

She nodded, pleased by his response. "Also, you must *listen* to me. I know you cannot listen here—" She touched one of his ears. "But you can with these—" She touched next to his eye. "—And this." She put her hand over his heart. "I am the boss on this project, so I decide how much we try, and when we give up. We cannot honor Poco unless we keep each other safe."

Dabu sat up straight, an Eagle Scout prepared to declare his oath. "I promise, Ro-zhill. You count on me."

"Good. Now I ask a favor."

"I do anything for you, Ro-zhill."

"This is for Mauterre."

He looked curious, attentive.

"She is trying very hard to learn sign language. Please do not make her feel bad just because she is not good yet."

He looked aghast. "I never make fun of no one, 'specially not Muh-tare."

Rochelle pretended to ponder that a second, then posed a question: "Would it hurt your feelings if she refused to try because she was afraid you *would* tease her?"

The very notion did hurt his feelings, that much was clear. "I'm not like that, Ro-zhill. You tell her."

"I don't need to, Dabu; you already show her. That is why she trusts you." Rochelle watched him carefully. "You know what? Mauterre would never make fun of someone, either—but she has no chance to prove it."

Dabu started to say something, but he suddenly realized her point. He looked at his shoes a moment, then up into Rochelle's eyes, his own glistening with raw emotion. She recognized the little boy who used to cry "Da-bu da-bu" when confused by a frightening, silent world, that vulnerable child even now still cradled protectively in the heart of this young man sitting before her. "I'm sorry, Ro-zhill," he said. "I worry too much what people say."

She reached out and took one of his hands, shaking her head. "Don't apologize for being afraid. Some people *are* mean, but you will never find the good ones unless you take a chance. Talk with your hands, your mouth—no matter, long as you speak from your heart." She paused for him to consider her words, then added, "Your friend Poco taught you that. He took one big chance on a *Taoke* boy."

Dabu smiled, his eyes brimming. "Poco one good Wai-Nuikai."

"And he left *me* one good Taoke friend, too."

She found herself holding him for an instant before standing and wiping her face, Dabu dabbing his own with a sleeve. She took his hand again and walked him down the trail to find Mika and Mauterre sitting on rocks near the house. Dabu hesitated, then approached Mauterre. Mika tried to look casual about wandering over to Rochelle, both pretending not to watch.

"Ro-zhill says we can go," Dabu told her. Sure, the way he enunciated was a bit unusual; he simply sounded like Dabu.

Mauterre stood up, surprised and clearly relieved. "I am glad," she said, signing and speaking at the same time.

"We hafta stay together, look out for each other."

"Good—I was kinda worried about the hot lava." She smiled that beatific smile of hers, the one destined someday to make men empty their wallets in florist shops and jewelry stores.

Dabu smiled back, his newfound confidence as solid as the rock beneath his feet. "Don't worry. Nobody gets hurt with Dabu."

The director came out and stood before Rochelle and Mikalu, his assistant heading toward the footbridge. "I left something for your journey. Thank you for allowing me to serve your family as my fathers' fathers have for many generations." He fixed Rochelle just briefly with that knowing look, then pronounced, "Truly, you are both what we call *kamaliʻi ʻāina*—children of the land." He bowed slightly, then waved to the youngsters and headed for the bridge.

Watching him go, Rochelle sensed how much that meant to Mika, and she caught herself enjoying the compliment, too, trying it on, testing the fit. Then she noticed Viku disappearing through the open slot, so she broke the spell and announced, "We have about five hours of daylight. Are we up for this?" A silly question, she knew, as they rallied around her, everybody charging into the house.

And there stood the casket with a lone sprig of *ohelo* on top, Poco's final offering for Pele.

Dabu retrieved a small duffel from the bedroom and carefully placed the sprig inside, setting the bag over by the door. Everybody scattered to change into jeans and long-sleeve knits, Dabu collecting their jackets for his bag. They quickly rolled out a small tarp and stacked it with sandbags from the rear *lanai*, then waited solemnly while Rochelle opened the casket, all surprised to discover Poco had been placed inside a body bag, the zipper left open just enough to confirm he'd been carefully wrapped in *tapa*, the last Wai-Nuikai prepared for his journey to join the ancestors.

A *thwap! thwap! thwap!* sounded through the valley as Viku landed on the beach and powered down. He entered a minute later, bringing the surplus stretcher that had helped save his neighbor's life nearly six months earlier. He and Mika lifted Poco onto it, then carried him outside while Rochelle and the youngsters quickly filled the casket with sandbags. Dabu grabbed the duffel as they headed down to the chopper.

The seats had been removed earlier, leaving room to lay Poco on the floor, everybody piling around him to brace themselves for the trip. As the chopper powered up, Viku handed Rochelle a small box from which she distributed work gloves, face masks, and protective goggles. She traded knowing glances with Dabu, confident her crew's youngest "workers" would need no reminders about their safety gear.

As they lifted off, Mauterre looked a bit green around the gills, but Dabu held her hand and kept her attention on him until she relaxed enough to watch the series of towering ridges pass below. When they entered the national park, a narrow belt of forest gave way to sparse patches of green clinging to the barren lava field like loose toupees, thatches of vines stretching into clumsy comb-overs. The layered swirls of glassy rock looked like the icing on a stale birthday cake decorated with clumps of candy flowers, each candle a lava pillar where some ancient tree had succumbed to Pele's fire.

Viku circled the tube area to afford Rochelle a better view. A pair of strapping young Hawaiian men—Wipu and Pubo!—leaned patiently against the Bobcat dozer. Two large wooden crates sat nearby, one side pried off each, generators and other equipment scattered about, a 55-gallon fuel drum set back several-hundred yards from the work area. They must have spent all day airlifting the gear she'd requested from the Taoke construction site. She hoped the Park Service hadn't noticed the extra activity, or at least had chosen to ignore it for now.

As Viku circled again, Mika looked toward Rochelle and subtly shook his head. He'd seen it, too, the newest trickle of orange lava having widened to at least twenty or thirty feet in just two days, completely blocking their access to the burial-tube area. The creeping wall of 'a'ā now covered the upper stretch, oozing shallow streamers of smoky black phlegm that layered the frozen waves, obliterating the cave entrance. All hope of success dashed, Rochelle knew she nevertheless had to let everybody try, that honoring Poco now lay in working together despite the odds.

If only she could guarantee nobody would be injured . . . or worse.

Viku set down on a flat overlook, then shouted, "I hafta go! If they see me land in d'park, I lose my permits, maybe my license!"

"Thanks, brah!" Mika returned, shaking his hand, Rochelle waving her gratitude.

The passengers quickly lifted Poco out, Dabu grabbing the duffel.

"I hike back!" Viku shouted before lifting off. He banked toward the ridges and disappeared in the glare.

Wipu and Pubo hiked up to join them, masks around their necks, goggles pushed up on their heads. They stood awkwardly before Mika for a moment, the blond-haired *haole* finally pronouncing, "Dabu, he got three good brudders."

Liking that, Wipu announced, "Pocomea, he got one good friend, one good sister." Pubo nodded agreement. The tension broken, everybody started shaking hands. Then Dabu stepped forward and introduced Mauterre, his brothers clearly surprised and pleased to hear him speak among outsiders.

The Taoke men insisted, so Mika stepped back while they hoisted his friend. Rochelle closed her eyes and savored the moment, wishing Papaii and his own little friend Timu could be here to see 'Ohana Taoke come to honor 'Ohana Wai-Nuikai.

They wended down the tortuous trail, Dabu staying very close to Mauterre, then paused to place the body on a small rise before turning to survey the scene. Already too aware of the dismal odds, Rochelle found herself gazing toward Mauna Loa where great blots of purple cumuli gathered to watch, gusts of wind moaning laments for those who would ignore Pele's warnings to keep away.

"Let's do it," Rochelle said, leading them to the equipment for a quick survey of tools ranging from shovels to lanterns. She had ordered everything except what they needed most: a crateful of miracles . . . a big one. Any question of her crew having committed for the long haul were settled when Pubo broke out a cooler brimming with sandwiches and cold drinks, then a sack of snacks and . . . toilet paper. Rochelle held up a roll and looked around.

With Wipu snickering, Pubo led everybody behind the crates to where a deep fissure some six inches wide dropped into an underground void. Mauterre looked puzzled, so Dabu stepped over it, one foot on each side, gesturing downward as if to squat. Mauterre looking horrified, everybody laughed, coaxing a sheepish grin from the mainlander Poco had affectionately called Li'l Haole.

Pubo announced, "We put crates in front so *nā wahine* have one big private powder room!"

"Thank you," said Rochelle graciously. "Not even volcanoes can hold it forever." She went on to explain her plan, asking the Taokes if they still thought it worth a try.

"We kick lava ass," Wipu declared.

"What he say," Pubo agreed.

They hauled a generator, two pumps, and a ton of fire hose up to where the spring water poured out from a fissure, then linked several hundred feet to each pump, capping them with high-pressure nozzles. Mika made a fuel trip while the Taoke men followed Rochelle's instructions meticulously, unrolling and positioning one about halfway down the slope, the other all the way to where the tube entrance had been buried.

"You two," Rochelle said/signed to Dabu and Mauterre, "are in charge of the water source." She showed them how to start the generator, then the pumps, opening the valve on each just long enough to prime them. "You may have to keep adjusting the pressure so we don't lose suction. Watch the generator fuel, and make refill trips with only *half* a can; I don't want extra sitting this close to the fire. When you have time, pile rocks around the pumps to make sure we don't pull their intakes away from the water source. Also, watch for steam coming this way; it may be hot enough to burn your skin and lungs." She wanted to ask if they understood, if they thought they could handle it, and to warn them to stay safe, but she dared not, counting instead on Dabu's promises and similar oaths coaxed from Mauterre the night before. Instead, she watched quietly while they went to work, already a team, both clearly proud of such important assignments.

Rochelle left them and led the men down to the buried tube entrance, pointing to where the *'a'ā* wall inched forward. "We need somebody to concentrate water on the front, sweeping from there to back here. Move slowly so it has time to crack and break between passes, and stay away from that corner; it's the stress point where we want the lava to shift. Treat it like you're herding a stubborn beast."

"I tame this bitch," Wipu announced, stepping forward to claim the hose. Rochelle almost believed him, and she knew he'd be here all night trying, even if he failed. With a quick signal to the valve-tenders, Wipu began streaming the wall, explosions of steam lunging toward the sky.

"I take d'other one," Pubo announced.

"Then I get the jack-hammer," Mika called.

She led them up to where the caldera's newest lava channel flowed under the *'a'a*. Pointing at the opposite bank's low point, she said, "Let's try to divert it there. Pubo, you cool along this edge with fast sweeps. Concentrate on building a sort of gate just below the drop-off, but don't let that area over there get wet. Mika, you break off chunks of the wall here, and Pubo will spray them as I doze them into the fire. It's like building a dam across a hot spring using chunks of ice—we have to move fast before each layer melts away."

They set up another generator, then a compressor to run the jack-hammer. When Mauterre opened the valve, Pubo started spraying the near shore. His arcs were too wide at first, but he adjusted and began making steady progress adding quarter-inch layers to a burgeoning levee of cooling rock.

Mika hauled the hammer up on a fissured lava jut at the base of a cooled section of *'a'a* wall and set about battering it into chunks a foot or two across.

Rochelle hiked back for the Bobcat, pausing to watch everybody's progress: the youngsters piling rocks around their pumps, firefighter Pubo unflinchingly intent as Mika tumbled boulders right behind him, Wipu facing down the monstrous behemoth like a lone Chinese student challenging a caravan of military tanks. Boiling streamers of dense white steam sparkled in the intermittent sunshine, clots of plum-colored cloud scattering to make room in the sky. For the first time, she dared to believe, fueled by hope and possibility as she fired up the Bobcat for a jolting drive up to Mika's burgeoning rock pile.

Pubo's first attempt at building a levee had already collapsed, so he moved a half-dozen feet upstream, Ro signaling her approval.

She raised the Bobcat's blade about six inches and began pushing the pile of broken rocks into a long row just above where Pubo worked. She motioned for him to wet them down, then began tumbling them into the fiery deluge. Most disappeared, but a few stuck to the edge, Pubo cooling them as much as possible. The lava gushed up and over the barrier, a small stream starting the wrong direction, but Pubo bombarded it and managed to divert it back within its banks.

They repeated the process at break-neck speed for twenty minutes, making slow but frustrating progress. Viku showed up, taking over for Pubo so his brother could stretch. Rochelle offered Mika a break, but he waved her toward Wipu below, working his way up a crack he'd fashioned in a ten-foot-high chunk of basalt.

Bam! bam! bam! bam! the hammer drummed. Suddenly Mika jumped out of the way, dragging the jack with him. The wall groaned, then splintered and cracked open, a pile of glassy boulders tumbling down. Mika grinned with satisfaction, then went right back to work.

Pubo took over in the Bobcat, so Rochelle scanned the young water team above, Dabu raising his arms over his head to form a circle, the long-distance diver's *okay*. When Mauterre raised her arms in the same signal, too, Rochelle headed down to check on Wipu.

He was having a ball, whooping like a bronco-buster, wrangling the great beast, constantly blasting across its wide expanse. He'd managed to stop its forward progress, but the skin kept cracking on the wrong side, spurting coagulated fingers of black slag to ooze down from glowing orange wounds. They needed at least one more hose down there, if not several.

"You need a break?" she asked.

"Only one minute," he announced, "just for stretch, not too long. I got her pissed now, make her ready fight me."

She took over the hose, amazed by the sheer strength and stamina required to control it. The pressure would ease slightly for a moment, then come back full force, Dabu and Mauterre already having mastered teasing every possible drop from the source. She looked back at where the spring had once flowed across the plateau, the rock barely wet, robbed of its precious water.

"I ready now," Wipu insisted. He was itching to climb back into the saddle. "I go 'nother hour; then you send Viku down, show him little brah not so *iki* now." He grinned, so she clapped his shoulder and left him to slay the dragon, another *whoop* signaling he'd pounced back into the fray.

Viku had made some real progress building the levee, but again part of it collapsed, merely making him all the more determined. Rochelle walked higher and scanned the target stretch, considering her options. Hitting on an idea, she hurried back and began directing Pubo in lining up boulders about a foot from the edge, three deep. Mika shattered another large section, giving them plenty to work with. It took about half an hour, with the sun hanging low over Mauna Loa, but finally they were ready.

Pubo traded places with his brother, taking the hose again. On Rochelle's signal Viku drove the dozer down along the edge, snow-plowing them in one fast sweep, the inner boulders tumbling into the searing flow while the outer ones formed a stone wall along the edge.

Lava began splashing onto it, thickening as it hardened, now layered several feet deep. More leaked over the other bank, forming a narrow stream that trickled northward above the wall of *'a'ā*, but it wasn't nearly enough to divert the main channel.

Rochelle looked up and saw Mika standing up on the *'a'ā*, directly above the raging river of fire, still in mask and goggles, but shirtless now, glistening with sweat, muscles bulging. He'd dragged the hammer up there to the end of its air hose. She tried to wave him down, but he pretended to ignore her, calculating the best spot. He braced himself and began pounding along a crack. Energized anew, Pubo concentrated on building the barrier just below him, Viku quickly feeding more rocks into the pile, the lava splashing dangerously high.

Bam! bam! bam!

Crack!

A massive chunk the size of a Sherman tank gave way, Mika leaping clear at the last second, now clinging to the rocks, his leg supporting the jackhammer.

The chunk fell straight in, damming where it had been disappearing under the wall, fiery liquid splashing the rock face, Mika's arms protecting his head, his body narrowly escaping gobs of smoky black goo plopping all around him.

Pubo trained the water just below him, knocking down the lava spray until Mika could scramble away.

Viku quickly pushed more rocks against the chunk, a pool of liquid fire now rising before their eyes—

And it broke free, cascading down the other side, then along the *'a'ā* wall toward the low spot several hundred feet away.

Pubo kept playing the water across the ledge, reinforcing it as the level dropped, then concentrated on solidifying where the new embankment steadily diverted the lava river.

Viku climbed out of the Bobcat to watch, Mika joining him.

The lava formed a pool down there against the wall, filling the depression and growing steadily deeper.

"Come on," Rochelle urged it. "Come on!"

Pubo played the water directly into molten rock at the curve, spawning iridescent tornadoes that spun feverishly skyward, gathering storm clouds circling ominously to welcome reinforcements.

The lava pool began churning in the middle, a whirlpool suction, the level slowly dropping. Mika and Viku high-fived each other, but Rochelle wasn't satisfied yet, not until she knew where it was going.

She watched the sloping field beyond the other side of the creeping wall, but found no sign of the liquid's escape. It could be disappearing into an underground cavern that might collapse the entire area, or maybe feeding an unseen lava tube and racing even now toward the ocean . . . or it might be flowing back toward the burial tube, heating the ground, undermining its support, laying a deadly trap for any who might foolishly enter the subterranean lair.

And a faint orange light shone from beyond the wall, glowing brighter, then brighter yet, finally revealing a neon streak snaking its way across the field, seeking a new route to the ocean.

They all cheered and jumped around like idiots for a minute, clapping Pubo on the shoulder, waving their arms toward the jubilant teens watching from above . . . then they got back to work, pushing rocks, reinforcing the wall, making sure the flow couldn't reverse itself and reclaim the original course.

Once Rochelle was satisfied, they moved the hose to below the edge of the wall and sent a surge of boiling water down the cooling riverbed. Like the smoke from an old locomotive, a line of billowing steam chugged eastward, the water spreading steadily farther and farther before boiling dry.

The men moved the generator, compressor, and hammer down closer to where the tube's entrance had crusted over, but couldn't yet cross the suppurating morass. Pubo drove the Bobcat back up for refueling while Rochelle and Mika fetched the tools and some cold drinks.

When the water temperature dropped to merely warm, Rochelle signaled the teens to shut off the pump, then joined Mika in moving the lower portion down to just above where Viku had taken over for Wipu, the younger Taoke lying flat on the stone floor, exhausted. The wall had come no closer, but it continued to ooze down the wrong side, refusing to back away and break free toward the north. Surely two hoses would make the difference, she tried telling herself, tentative hope easier to summon than blind confidence. They'd already accomplished more than she truly expected, and of that they could be proud.

The sun dipped low enough to kiss the distant flanks of Mauna Loa, stingers of red and yellow agitating the bruised clouds, a flash of heat lightning sparking their anger. Mika and Viku were hauling equipment across the solid riverbed now, setting up. Pubo drove down in the Bobcat, picking up Wipu along the way. Rochelle knew they would lose their light soon, so she headed back to the crates and retrieved the flashlights, plus sandwiches and drinks, hiking up to check on the teens. They thanked her politely, then rather pointedly suggested she might prove more useful down below, all's fine here, thank you very much. Young people, trusted with real responsibility, had risen to the occasion.

Well into the night they worked the wall with both hoses, the front edge cracking and crumbling, dagger shards tumbling dangerously close. They managed to hold it at bay, but the expanding skin along the near side kept splitting wide to spill its guts like overripe fruit left to bake in the scorching heat, steadfastly refusing to follow the course mere mortals had dared assign.

Eventually the great beast grew weary and fell into fitful sleep. After an hour with no obvious change, Rochelle agreed to let Mika and Wipu try to penetrate the crust that concealed the ancient secret entrance. They took turns with the jack-hammer and a 16-pound sledge, relentlessly battering the layers of porous rock. Rochelle barged in with the Bobcat every few minutes, clearing scree from their path, sometimes climbing down to hand-shovel debris. Quarter- and half-sticks of dynamite would have made this a lot easier, but she'd resisted the temptation to keep some handy, outright blasting all the more likely to draw unwanted attention . . .

Not to mention felony charges.

That would certainly sound impressive during an adoption-petition hearing. *And where exactly did you leave the child while you planted bombs in a public park?*

Utterly exhausted, Mika and Wipu finally admitted needing a break from pounding, their accomplishment a gaping tunnel extending some dozen feet into the rock. Rochelle had estimated ten feet max, but now feared the *ʻaʻā* may have oozed part way into the overhang-protected chamber.

As if hose-wrestling constituted a break, Mika and Wipu assumed water duty while Viku positioned the jack-hammer. Pubo tested the sledge with one wide swing—

And broke through!

Rochelle jumped down from the Bobcat and hurried over, shining the light inside. She recognized the jumble of broken rocks leading down into the lower tube and, without meaning to, grabbed Pubo and hugged him.

"We do all d'work!" Wipu shouted over the roar of his hose.

"And Pubo gets all the glory!" Mika finished, exaggerating his pique.

Rochelle stepped back and let Pubo take the last few whacks, the opening now a horizontal gash as big as the original. She played her flashlight over the pimpled face of the ʻaʻā wall, the beast now looking like some massive slug dripping slime as it slept, its relentless Gulliver shower courtesy of blond- and black-haired Liliputians.

Sending Pubo and Viku for Poco's body, Rochelle waved her flashlight to summon Dabu and Mauterre.

Then over Mikalu's objections, she entered the cave alone, climbing down the shadow-shifting rocks, her lantern held high to check for any sign of compromise to the tube's structural integrity. Everybody's efforts had accomplished near miracles this night, but she wouldn't hesitate to veto their final tribute at the first sign of danger.

She inched along, playing light over the walls. The draft was gone, the air stagnant and redolent of sulfur, the ventilation fissures up in the hillside now sealed forever. The tube looked solid enough, if only a mega-ton of pasty scorching lava hadn't parked itself on the roof . . .

She climbed back out just as they laid Poco, still in his body bag, on a flat, foot-high rise in the swirling rock. Dabu's and Mauterre's flashlight beams were carefully working their way down from the spring.

Rochelle had Wipu keep one hose trained on the ʻaʻā while everybody else dragged the other back across the newly crusted lava-river bed, anchoring the nozzle to direct its flow down between the banks. Since Wipu's hose had some extra slack, they dragged it below the tunnel entrance and piled it with rocks, sending its stream across the flats where it eventually poured into a shallow ravine and headed for the sea.

"Ro-zhill!" Dabu screamed.

She whirled in time to see neon rivulets spiderwebbing down from the upper wall's makeshift dam. Farther up, the caldera boiled and churned, eruptions hurling fireworks to the sky, white-hot Sweet Autumn stars raining from tephra clouds.

A widening flow suddenly gushed down its original course, Dabu and Mauterre trapped on the wrong side!

"Run!" Rochelle shouted, everybody sprinting across the deadly terrain.

Hands clasped, Dabu and Mauterre raced for their lives.

They jumped into the bed, lava surging right at them. Mauterre stumbled, nearly went down, but Dabu yanked her up, kept her moving.

He rolled onto the bank and literally dragged her up, collapsing backwards as she fell on him, the lava rushing past.

Rochelle and the Taokes bounded across and leaped, the flow already several yards and widening. They crashed to the other side, pulling the kids away from the blistering heat.

Lava collided with the hose's gushing stream and erupted in great clouds of hissing steam.

Everybody had made it out—

Except Mikalu!

"Mika!" she screamed, her words carried into eddies of ash-choked wind.

And she saw him through the mist, navigating deadly rivulets, trying desperately to come to her, Poco's body over his shoulder.

He'd gone back for his friend.

And now he was trapped, snakes of scalding steam coiling around him.

Still more lava converged on the other hose, the lower plain now a deadly griddle, hissing and popping, the glassy surface cracking and breaking.

The river had widened to twenty feet, twenty-five now, no way to jump, Mika tangled in a lethal web of fire.

"Chopper!" Rochelle shouted, Viku taking off at a dead run, thirty minutes, an hour, no way to get back in time.

She lost sight of Mika until the steam parted for a second, the scene lit in a macabre Halloween orange.

He was hugging Poco, streaks glistening down his cheeks.

"Meeg-loo!" called Dabu, his voice breaking. Mauterre covered her face and wept.

"Hose!" shouted Rochelle.

Wipu and Pubo grabbed it, wrestling it over to Rochelle, the water gushing every which way.

Mikalu was gently laying Poco back on the makeshift bier, his friend's body just inches above groping fingers of lava filling the crisscrossing cracks.

Rochelle grabbed the nozzle and aimed it toward him, the maelstrom shrieking with exploding steam, a curtain of shimmering orange light blocking their view.

"Mika!" she screamed.

There amid the clouds, she caught a glimpse of him watching her, and for an instant she believed what Poco had told her, that Mikalu knew something, some intangible truth that she'd never quite grasped.

The mist swirled around him, and he was gone.

An invisible beast roared to life, his growls echoing from the void.

Up and down they played the water, their desperate hopes of cooling a path proving futile, the scalding steam too lethal for any man, Mika's last chance to escape now gone.

The growling rumble grew louder.

And Mika burst from the steam!—driving the Bobcat, splashing through puddles of fire, his tires trailing thick black smoke.

He barreled toward Rochelle, right into the hose's spray, full-throttle, bouncing wildly—

Straight into the lava stream!

Halfway across—

Stalled, the tires on fire.

Boom! blew the right front. Mika rolled into a ball under the canopy, fiery slag raining around him.

Rochelle dragged her crew back from the onslaught, aiming water right across the dozer.

Boom! Boom!

He was waiting for the last to blow, holding his breath, dozer fuel poised to explode and claim the life Mika had denied Pele's wrath—

Boom!

He scrabbled atop the dozer, a sheet of water directed at his legs.

And he leaped!

He caught the edge of the bank and rolled, coming to his feet, gasping for air, his hair both soaked and singed along one side.

"I'm okay!" he promised Rochelle. She grabbed and held tight, his arms around her. "I'm okay."

"You could've been killed!"

"Hadda try, Rochelle, but I failed. I failed bad 'cause I hadda leave Poco."

"No," she whispered, "you had to save Poco's friend."

They turned and watched, the rivulets converging, lava rising around Poco's makeshift bier. Up the distant rise, Pele's caldera roared with exploding fire, flinging molten shrapnel into the gathering black clouds.

Pele had beaten them, had taken Poco's body on her own terms. Not now, Rochelle wanted to cry, not like this, not after everybody had given so much . . .

And for an instant, she might have seen something eerily familiar, right there hovering amid the flames of eruption.

She rubbed her eyes and looked again.

It was a face, the curious visage of an old woman, bigger than life, watching fiery light transform the land.

Rochelle felt dizzy, her throat choked with sulfur. She tried to focus, still glimpsing fleeting images of that woman, dark eyes shifting in the undulating waves of rising heat, always looking back.

Mika followed her gaze, but shook his head. "Damn lava," he lamented, the vision escaping him.

"Please, wait here," Rochelle said urgently, surprising him.

"Where you go—?"

"Please, just let me," she called back, running toward the crates, stumbling in the darkness.

She found Dabu's duffel bag and carefully removed the sprig of *ohelo*, then ran as fast as she could up the rise.

"Is this what you want?" she gasped, out of breath, scrabbling as fast as she could. She would never believe those silly Hawaiian superstitions; but dammit!—Pocomea did, and he deserved better.

A fiery droplet splatted in front of her, then one behind, smoky spatters now smacking the rocks all around her.

A clap of thunder echoed across the land, ragged bolts of lightning twisting through the air, black clouds crashing into blacker sky.

She flung the *ohelo* up near the lip, heat and stench driving her back. A large plop of molten slag barely missed her, thunder exploding in her ears.

She turned and tried to run, stumbling and tripping over splintered shards.

A flashlight beam appeared below, Mika sprinting toward her.

She felt a splat in her hair, and she screamed, shaking her head madly, but felt no burn, no fire . . .

Only water.

Another drop.

Then another . . . rain spattering the rocks, the sky rent by a ragged web of lightning, Mika still running, booming thunder echoing off Mauna Loa.

She met him above the *'a'ā* wall, folding herself into his arms, her body shaking, rain streaking their clothes.

"Steam—the kids," she breathed, barely able to talk, sudden urgency in protecting Mauterre and Dabu, reason be damned.

They hurried back to join the others, tracer bullets of rain lancing the lava, orange tendrils of steam bleeding into the air. Poco's remains lay unscathed on the riser, streamers running off the waterproof body bag.

Lightning ripped across the sky, and the wind kicked up, stoking the flames of Pele's cauldron to fling sparks against the clouds.

Sheets of downpour rolled in from the east, exploding like popcorn in the lava.

"To the crates!" Rochelle ordered, everybody sliding and splashing across the slick rock.

An apparition appeared to the south, a mercurial silhouette trailing slipstream spray, a man running this way, a Taoke . . . Viku!

Mika and Wipu started wrestling the shippers together, open sides away from the wind.

Viku ran up, gasping, "Can't fly—in d'storm! Let's get d'hose—!" Then he saw Mika, and his face lit up. Grabbing him in a bear hug, he shouted, "How you do that? No *haole ever* beat d'lava like that!"

"Trashed your Bobcat, brah!"

Viku laughed. "You mean *your* Bobcat now, *kāne!*"

The Taoke men piled into one crate, Rochelle and Mika pressing in around the kids in the other, everybody cold and soaking wet. A lone flashlight cast chill shadows and reflected the warm glow in Mika's sapphire eyes. Dabu pulled his duffel close, their jackets appearing like rabbits pulled from a magical hat. They draped them around the group, everybody snuggling close, Dabu cradled in Rochelle's arms, Mika holding Mauterre, legs all entwined, a wadded tangle of life couched against the storm.

A shimmering veil of water cloaked the opening, strobes of lightning detonating thunder bombs in futile attempts to roust lurking invaders. Rochelle's chest pounded, and she could feel Dabu's heartbeat against her arm, Mika holding her hand. Exhausted, she lay her head against the wood. Mauterre closed her eyes, turning her cheek to Mika's shoulder. Cool water dripped through the wooden slats, droplets snaking down Rochelle's face, hazy mist filling the tiny space.

How could she have come to this point?

At thirteen, Rochelle DuFortier had vowed to take charge of her life, a young woman seizing control, calculating her future, maximizing her options, making her own choices . . .

When had she chosen this?

Where in the long-term planner had she scheduled a night for endangering children? For fleeing a deadly electrical storm to cower in a fragile box perched precariously at the edge of an erupting volcano?

She closed her eyes and tried to conjure postcard views from the *Train à Grande Vitesse*, wending along the River Garonne, her face pressed against the glass . . . but she had never traveled to those places, never had the chance to make them real, to claim them as her own.

An icy chill scurried up her back, sharp breath, a shiver.

She tried to picture the warm and dry mansion in Chicago, Grandpa's house even now waiting patiently for her return; and she remembered thunderstorms scaring her as a little girl, and crawling into bed with Mommy to feel safe . . . but that place was halfway around the world now, and her mother would never again come home.

She braced herself for that familiar sinking feeling, that sensation of floating free before plunging toward the rocks . . .

But the crate held fast, the raging storm seething in its impotence against such determined souls.

And Mika held her hand, Dabu's breaths warming her cheek, Mauterre safely cradled by a gentle man who would never leave a child to face her fears alone. She squeezed his fingers, stroked Dabu's longish wet locks, pressed her leg firmly against Mauterre's . . .

"Hoo-eee!" Wipu shouted, invisible in the other box. Everybody laughed, the sleepy children roused.

"Least we tried!" Mika announced to the rain.

"You betcher ass!" Wipu concurred, his brothers echoing similar sentiments.

"For Poco!" Rochelle called out.

"For Poco!" shouted the others, Mauterre joining in, Dabu sensing the rising rhythm.

"For Pogo!" he exclaimed, everybody laughing again before fading to sighs, their tension slowly dripping to the wooden slats.

"Hey," Pubo said as the rain settled into a steady patter, "you 'member that time Poco fall sleep up on d'ridge? One big *mo'o* lizard, it come try take bite of his toe!"

Guffawing like a drunken bar stooge, Wipu added, "*Mo'o* spit him out, too—come say he cook too long in d'sun!"

"No wonder I see *mo'o* wash his mouth in d'stream!" Viku laughed.

They spent more than an hour swapping Poco stories, Mauterre translating for Dabu in the tight confines. Surely no funeral service, no wake had ever packed the mourners into wooden crates clinging to a rain-deluged volcanic expanse, yet somehow it seemed a fitting tribute for the man who loved this corner of the world.

Dabu called out, "Remember first time I see Pogo, you guys try stealing black corals, think he tries to hurt me . . ." His voice trailed off, everybody falling silent, the *tap tap tap* of raindrops falling into rhythm with Rochelle's heartbeat.

"Poco, he never hurt Dabu," Pubo said quietly.

"Poco never hurt no one," Viku added.

"Yah," said Wipu and Mika together.

A warm fog settled over Rochelle, everybody drifting in hazy remembrance.

Pubo quietly added, "Poco, he all d'time first one say *I break you face*, though." He chuckled.

"Wai-Nuikai," said Viku, "—got d'hard heads just like *nā* Taoke."

The air was brightening, a tinge of pre-sunrise blue streaking the sky, the rain crying itself down to sniffles. Clouds yawned and drifted off, poking around the mountaintop for places to rest.

One by one Rochelle's team crept from their crates, stretching and taking deep breaths, that sulfur odor cleansed from the air, the world transformed to a sparkling jewel.

The caldera had calmed, visible as little more than a hint of orange glow beyond the rim, no hot lava escaping the crater, its gently furrowed slopes shining like candle wax.

The first rays of sun shot across the land, glittering the splashes of painted basalt, curious mist drifting here and there to explore Pele's latest masterwork, a decorator's nuanced accents in obsidian and smoked glass.

Rochelle wanted to be first to check Poco's remains—to spare the others—but everybody gathered and moved as one, family and neighbors drawing nigh, Dabu bringing his duffel. The scorched hulk of Bobcat dozer jutted grotesquely from solid rock, frozen for eternity in the tortured throes of fiery death.

Surprised, amazed, they found the body bag lying unscathed, glistening with dew drops in the morning sun, swaddled by the warm breeze wafting from Poco's beloved sea.

"Is time we say good-bye," Mika said quietly.

"I get d'chopper," Viku suggested, Mika nodding. They shook hands, and something important passed between them, some intangible truth understood only by men who'd come together to honor another.

As Viku trotted off toward the south, Rochelle checked inside the tube, no change from before, the shovels and lantern still waiting patiently. The others had gathered near Poco, awaiting her signal.

The pallbearers stepped forward, three Taoke men—one barely thirteen but already as big as any in the ways that count most.

Mika watched solemnly while they gently slid Poco inside, then followed and helped them navigate the tortuous climb down into the tube, Mauterre leading with the lantern, Rochelle at the rear with a flashlight and Dabu's bag. They moved carefully up the dark passageway, the older Taokes surprised and impressed by nearly two centuries' tributes lined along notches cut into the solid rock wall.

Dabu and Mika dug the grave; then Wipu and Pubo lifted Poco into position.

Everybody stood awkwardly for a moment, but Rochelle knew lingering posed too much danger, so she stepped forward and lifted the first shovelful of sand into place. Soon the others began taking turns, passing the shovels around, until Poco was finally covered, resting for eternity near his mother and grandparents.

And the older Taokes began to chant *mele*, joined by Mikalu, a native Hawaiian trio, even if one sported singed blond hair.

Rochelle pulled Dabu and Mauterre close, all three swaying in time with the island rhythms . . .

And Rochelle noticed the empty slot above Poco's grave.

She lifted the lantern and scanned down the wall, discovering that no others had been carved, some ancient ancestor maybe sensing that Pocomea would be the last Wai-Nuikai to come home.

The chamber fell quiet.

Dabu reached into his bag and produced a small bronze octopus, Rochelle's gift from Shedd Aquarium, its mischievous face capturing Poco intimately. When he handed it to Rochelle, she felt her eyes welling with tears. She touched its cheek, then passed it to Mauterre, the young Miss Dixon misting up as she brushed its cheek, too. She held it for a moment, then handed it to Mika, who gazed fondly at the face before closing his eyes and passing it to Pubo. Wipu had to turn away, Pubo wiping his eyes and handing it back.

Mika took a deep breath, then solemnly placed it on the shelf. He stepped back and whispered, "Bye, Pocomea Wai-Nuikai, *kaina hoa.*"

"Bye, Pocomea," all but Dabu whispered.

Rochelle added, "Bye, *kaina hoa*—little brother friend."

Dabu stood with head bowed, his shoulders quivering. Rochelle stroked his hair, and he raised his head, wiping his eyes, then stepped forward and signed farewell to his friend, finishing with the words:

"Bye, Pogo."

And Rochelle felt an odd vibration, an eerie sound rumbling along the walls . . .

"Volcano?" she said—then more urgently, "Volcano!"

They hurried down through the tube and scrabbled up the rocks, bursting into blinding slashes of rising sun. The caldera was churning again, orange gobs splashing into the sky, fingers of molten lava creeping across the rock, barely enough time to jump clear, everybody gathering outside the original river bed to watch rivulets stream down and pool in the cracks.

The *'a'ā* wall had expanded like a massive rotting hulk, giant pimples bursting to ooze cruddy pus. Suddenly the behemoth cracked and split, fiery muck gushing out, smoke faeries dancing off into the rising mist.

And the front edge collapsed, melting into a deep, suppurating morass, hot waxy rock dripping in globs to obscure the cave entrance.

And still the wall inched forward, swelling with infected boils, popping and bleeding in dribbling streaks.

It collapsed again, burying the cave under several yards of slag.

Not satisfied, the wall began expanding for another onslaught.

"She knows," Mika breathed.

And Rochelle felt icy cold liquid soaking her feet, everybody scurrying back to the brush line as sparkling water cascaded down the slope, a torrent gushing from the spring. She squinted and gazed up toward the generator and pump, both now quiet and waiting patiently to be airlifted across the ridges.

A dragonfly appeared from nowhere, hovering in the air, its wary eye scanning intruders on his morning beat.

A lizard crept up onto a rock, turning its face to the sun and closing its eyes.

A *nēnē* goose circled high in the sky, then followed the stream eastward, disappearing in the blinding glare of a new day.

The dragonfly darted to the left, then rose in fits and starts up the slope just as the kids' rock piles broke free and tumbled in the wash, the remains of both hoses slowly sliding downward.

Nature cleans up people's messes—when it can, Rochelle thought. It always moves on with little more than passing interest in its brief guests. No wonder those who spend their lives together carving out the smallest, most fragile space want to rest for eternity close to the heart of the very place that sustained them.

Poco's lifetime had passed too quickly, but as a *kama 'āina* he understood that time is short for all children of the land, and that each must find in his commitment to others the obligation to preserve whatever tiny part of the world he leaves for those who come after.

That Pocomea, he sure was one smart octopus.

Thwap! thwap! thwap! echoed the chopper coming across the ridge, an iridescent-blue whirly-winged dragonfly swooping in to land.

"We go home now," Mikalu said, taking Rochelle by the hand, everybody drawing near.

The official funeral service loomed in the coming hours, soon to be followed by a court hearing to argue Auntie Dix's fate, and standing strong for Mauterre even as it broke Rochelle's heart to watch a mere child find honor in letting go of the one she loves.

The sea's trade winds lifted them to the sky, and horizontal slashes of morning sunlight flooded the cabin to bathe its passengers in a golden nimbus glow.

As Viku circled the scene for one last look, she felt Mika's hand at the small of her back, and she knew he was proud of how Poco's family and friends had come together.

She searched the boiling caldera for one last glimpse of the old woman, but all she could find was the pyroclastic release of geo-physical pressure from deep in the bowels of a living island.

Could that old woman possibly appreciate that Rochelle had made some excellent choices after all?—and that she would never for an instant accept a thousand days alone in the most exquisite palace if it meant giving up one night cowering with loved ones in a rain-drenched box clinging to the slopes of an erupting volcano?

The chopper banked toward the south, and Rochelle caught her own reflection in the glass, those familiar eyes gazing back.

And she noticed something for the first time, the simplest truth, there from the start . . .

She didn't need that old woman to remind her what matters most, or to say that making the right choices can lead to a magnificent—even if unexpected—life.

And she remembered what she'd discovered that night standing between Cambridge and Boston on mist-shrouded Longfellow Bridge, searching the waters for guarantees in the face of an uncertain future:

That old woman never existed.

At least not yet.

Rochelle DuFortier would look for her again someday—maybe in, say, fifty years or so.

And with a little bit of luck, she would find her in the mirror looking back.

And together they would smile, remembering what a blond-haired boy named Mikalu had known all along.

Nā lewa papala

Papala Skies

Night after Pocomea's funeral

An insect chirruped through the screen as a pale curtain of moonlight washed the stone window-sill, intermittent breaths of warm breeze swirling about the room. Rochelle sat near the bed, watching Mauterre breathe softly under the linen sheet. Thirteen still looked so very small, so fragile and vulnerable . . . especially now to a woman determined never to forget.

Rochelle's own thirteenth year had shaped her in ways she might never fully comprehend, the guilt-laden grief wrapped in profound lonesomeness, the paralyzing fear of being snatched from her home after already losing so much . . . She'd had trouble remembering her mother back then, but that had grown easier over time, learning to put aside the pain long enough to recapture those sublime—if fleeting—moments: the sparkles in Mom's eyes as young Rochelle tried on new outfits, those graceful yet deft hands teaching a daughter how to shape and pin her long raven hair, strolling hand-in-hand through the Field Museum's great halls after a morning window-shopping along Michigan Avenue, and sometimes just glancing up to catch her gazing from across the room.

"Rochelle?" Mauterre whispered. "What are you doing?"

Just watching my little girl grow up.

"There's something I want you to see, but instead of waking you, I wound up sitting here thinking how lucky I am that you're part of my life now."

Mauterre eased from under the sheet, her nightgown fluttering in the breeze, and she hugged Rochelle. Sitting back on the edge of the bed, she said, "I think I was having a dream about the, uh—" She stumbled over the pronunciation: "—the omma-kooey. Dabu told me about it."

"*'Aumakua?*—a family's spirit protector?"

"Um, yeah. He says the Taokes have their very own." She appeared deep in thought for a moment, then looked up into Rochelle's eyes, her long tresses shining in the moonlight. "Do you think *we* have one?—an *'aumakua,*

I mean."

Rochelle took a deep breath, carefully considering her words. "Well, you know I'm better at explaining things with physics, so I don't much believe in phantoms floating around keeping an eye out, but I'm not sure that's what *'aumakua* really means. A true family is stronger than simple blood ties, or state-sanctioned marriage licenses, or court-ordered guardianship papers . . . It's people who love each other so much that they discover a kind of *'aumakua* looking out for each other."

"I like that," said Mauterre. She gazed off toward the window-sill for a moment, lost in thought. Finally, in a tiny voice, she said, "We lost some of ours with Auntie Dix and Pocomea."

"But that's not true, Mauterre. They'll always be part of our *'ohana*. Maybe that's why the Hawaiians refer to *'aumakua* as *spirit* protector; even after members of our family are gone, we still find strength in remembering what they left us, and in knowing how much they loved us."

Mauterre turned back, her eyes glistening in the pale glow. "I don't feel as scared as I used to," she whispered.

Rochelle smiled, her own eyes misty. "It's taken me twenty-two years, Mauterre, but for the first time, I don't feel so scared, either."

"I bet I know why," she said, wagging her eyebrows suggestively. "You are *so* lucky."

"Don't get ahead of yourself, smarty-pants."

"Why not? *Some*body has to."

"You just get dressed and meet me outside." Rochelle stood and winked. "We have things to do."

When she tapped at what used to be Pocomea's room, the door swung open, flickering lantern light playing across the carved-*koa* dresser. Mika lay curled up in his trademark blue boxers, Dabu sprawled in frayed Mega-mart undies, the sheet twisted around one leg. Their funeral suits hung neatly from hangers pegged to the wall.

"Wakey, wakey," she said, crossing to Mika and snapping the elastic on his drawers.

"Mmmm," he cooed, reaching out to take her hand, pulling her toward him.

"Control yourself," she teased, glancing toward the sleeping boy.

Mika looked over his shoulder and rolled his eyes. "I keep taking d'sheet back, and this all d'time still happen. That boy sure got one cold leg."

"He'll give his wife fits someday—but she'll think he's worth it," she added, noticing again how small thirteen looked, so fragile, so vulnerable. "See if you can get him up; I have something to show you two." She slipped out and closed the door to avoid embarrassing the young teen.

She found Mauterre outside, soon followed by the guys, Dabu rubbing sleep from his eyes. The valley spread before them, mist rising from shifting shadows. The shimmering panorama floated in open space against a backdrop of velvet sky, a bright disc of full moon rising toward the center of planetar-ium dome.

"You have *lau hala* mats?" Rochelle asked.

Mika led them around to the *lanai*, surprised to find two bundles of *papala* spears. "Where these come from?"

"Special ordered," Rochelle said, suppressing a smile. "The funeral director knows an old taxidermist in Hilo who makes them."

Mika gazed upon Rochelle, clearly moved by her gesture. "Thank you," he whispered.

"Is nothing," she dismissed.

The men hoisted spears while the ladies carried mats, their ragtag cortège wending along the tortuous lagoon-side trail, up to the wide ledge jutting over the mouth of the cove.

Still holding Mauterre's hand, a bundle on his shoulder, Dabu gestured to Rochelle, pointing to the higher spot where Poco used to sit and gaze across the sea. She wanted to sign, *Be careful*, or to go along to keep them safe, but she dared not, instead biting her lip and nodding approval, handing him a lighter and watching as they climbed near the top of the rise to spread their mats.

Rochelle produced another lighter, testing it with a flick, then turned to Mika.

"I not feel right about this," he said, surprising her. "Poco, he not come find us here."

"Why not?"

"I go live Chicago-side now."

"Seduced by skyscrapers and Lake Michigan and Shedd Aquarium, were you?" she asked with mock earnestness.

"I not talk about *d'city*, Rochelle," he said, rolling his eyes. "I mean living close to you, *wherever* you go."

She felt her heart pounding, surf pummeling the rocks below. She refused to make this easy for him. "But what if I set up my haptics center somewhere else?"

"Rochelle, how come your mother never moved back to France?"

"Well . . . she had *me*."

Mika turned and looked up the rise, watching a hazy silhouette of Mauterre, her friend showing her how to hold the *papala* spear. "Your mother, she could have taken you with her."

"By then her home was in Chicago," Rochelle insisted.

"No, her home was to be with you."

"Mika, I don't think you could stand to live away from this island."

My home will always be where people love me, no matter how far I go to find it.

"It sure takes you long time to see d'truth, Rochelle, but I stay close from now on, and I prove it to you."

"But you grew up here, and you have your business, and your friends—"

"I cannot inherit this place, Rochelle. Maybe you not able to keep it, either, not even by selling your big house and spending all d'money on legal."

Tell me, Rochelle, can a place really be so important?

"Besides," he went on, "only chance is if you live here, claim as next-of-kin *'ohana* home, but you got Mauterre now. You never bring her to stay here, never do to her what you were so 'fraid of when you were just thirteen."

A tiny voice from up the ridge called out, "Auntie Dix!" as a *papala* spear soared into the sky, trailing sparkles and dancing on the winds.

"Don't you think the Wai-Nuikais would at least want us to fight for their home—even against the odds?"

"This is *my* home, too, Rochelle, and I do anything to save it—except be away from you."

Dabu's voice rang out: "Pogomea!" Another spear followed, Mauterre clapping her hands as it sailed across the lagoon and twirled itself into cinders sashaying down to the rippling waters.

"My turn," Rochelle said, hefting a spear, pausing while Mika set fire to it. "Pocomea!" she called out, flinging it over the sea, watching until it sailed beyond the horizon.

"Pocomea!" Mika shouted, hurling another right behind hers.

"Pocomea!" echoed Mauterre, her flaming tribute curving straight upward, consumed by the moon.

Rochelle said, "Tell me again why Pocomea and his ancestors never got chicken skin from jumping off this cliff."

"*Nā* Wai-Nuikai, they all d'time believe d'sea knows they belong here."

She took a deep breath and gazed toward the eastern horizon. "You'd follow me anyplace—like Boston or even La Réole?"

"This is true, Rochelle. I never lie to you."

"I do believe you, Mikalu—all d'time, by and by."

"Ha! So we go to France then, Haole-girl?"

"Nah," she said, sighing a long breath into the breeze, "—but I do want us to visit Tulsa someday."

She glanced up to see him smiling, so she hefted another spear, then stepped to the edge of the cliff and studied the crashing waves just long enough for him to light the tip. She flung the *papala* with all her might and called out, "Gina!"

Your mother, she will find you here.

And Mika kissed her.

Just like that, and she knew he meant to.

She felt herself soaring with the trade winds, dancing amid the stars, their hearts syncopating a crescendo backbeat while ocean waves cymbal-crashed along the rocky shore.

"Woo-hoo!" shouted the giggling kids.

And there across the valley, atop the distant ridge, she glimpsed the familiar moon-cast silhouette of a big man. He raised his arms in the diver's *okay* sign before shimmering into the rising mist.

"He knows," Rochelle said.

"All d'time," Mika added. "I tell him."

They turned to face the water again, side by side at the brink, holding hands. The waves seemed to be calling their names.

"The ocean," she said, "—you think she knows that *we* belong here now?"

"We find out—eh, Hawaii-girl?"

"Yah, brah, but you already know d'truth, all d'time."

He smiled, then looked down at the water and squeezed her hand. "I hold tight," he promised.

She squeezed back. "I won't *ever* let go."

And together they stepped out, their very own *'aumakua* promising to guide them safely home.

More Books by Stephen Geez

General Fiction
Dance of the Lights
What Sara Saw
Papala Skies
How It Turns Out

Media Thriller
Fantasy Patch

Mystical Adventure Series
Rich Mr. Fixx: *Crystal Clear* #1
Rich Mr. Fixx *Spider-Boxed* #2
Rich Mr. Fixx: *Hot Doggies* #3
Rich Mr. Fixx Graphic Flashback #1: *Shell Game*

Science Fiction
Invigilator
Zhasou Pure

Essay Collection
Been There, Noted That

GeezWriter How-to
How-to series for writers

The Fresh Ink Group

Publishing
Memberships
Share & Read Free Stories, Essays, Articles
Free-Story Newsletter
Writing Contests

Books
E-books
Amazon Bookstore

Authors
Editors
Artists
Professionals
Publishing Services
Publisher Resources

Members' Websites
Members' Blogs
Social Media

www.FreshInkGroup.com

Email: info@FreshInkGroup.com

Twitter: @FreshInkGroup

Google+: Fresh Ink Group

Facebook.com/FreshInkGroup

LinkedIn: Fresh Ink Group

About.me/FreshInkGroup